TRUTH TO TELL

TRUTH TO TELL

Claire Lorrimer

This first world edition published 2008
in Great Britain and the USA by
SEVERN HOUSE PUBLISHERS LTD of
9–15 High Street, Sutton, Surrey, England, SM1 1DF.

British Library Cataloguing in Publication Data

Lorrimer, Claire
  Truth to tell
  I. Title
  823.9'14[F]

    ISBN-13: 978-0-7278-6660-8   (cased)
    ISBN-13: 978-1-84751-075-4   (trade paper)

All Severn House titles are printed on acid-free paper.

Typeset by Palimpsest Book Production Ltd.,
Grangemouth, Stirlingshire, Scotland.
Printed and bound in Great Britain by
MPG Books Ltd., Bodmin, Cornwall.

For Tilly and Max with love

Acknowledgements

I would like to thank Alice Sluckin, Chair of the Selective Mutism Information and Research Association, for her expert advice on mutism; John Scott for historical information regarding blood categories; Graeme Clark for invaluable computer assistance; Edenbridge and East Grinstead libraries who were unfailingly helpful when Google wasn't; and lastly, Cynthia Turner who kept the domestic wheels turning and Pennie Scott for research, support, encouragement and for being an ever willing sounding board.

One

Aubrey Beauford put down his newspaper and looked across the room to where his wife was sitting on the sofa opposite him, her tapestry work untouched beside her. His spouse of the last thirteen years was, at last, soon to produce another child. She had fallen pregnant with George, their eldest son, on their honeymoon, and, following two miscarriages, had subsequently produced two more boys, Vaughan, aged six and Robert, now four.

With only a few weeks before the birth of their fourth baby, Frances was singularly unattractive with her pasty complexion, downcast mouth and her expression even more irritable than usual. After the last boy's birth, she had declared she would never have another child no matter how much Aubrey wanted a daughter. If he would agree to forgo his marital rights, she would be a lot happier and more agreeable to live with. It was not that she objected to sex. Whilst she didn't enjoy it, she accepted what she called her 'married obligations', but she abhorred the consequences. When she discovered she was carrying their son Robert, she told him she was no longer prepared to risk another pregnancy.

'Frances, my dear, I'm afraid I am going to have to insist you go down to the country tomorrow or the next day,' he said now. 'I could be wrong but it is my considered opinion that we may find ourselves at war, and I cannot allow you and the children to remain in London.'

He waited for the objections which he knew would be forthcoming. Although the boys loved the holidays spent at Farlington Hall, their large country house, Frances hated their Sussex estate. Born and brought up in London, she disliked everything about country life, more especially the winter shooting parties which were Aubrey's greatest pleasure. It was a sport she disapproved of whilst welcoming the regular supply of game which resulted. This year, he had ignored her objections and promised their eldest son a shotgun, young Robert a puppy, and all three boys ponies.

Had she not been pregnant, Frances had stormed at him, she would have divorced him. Having her own private income, Aubrey had little doubt that she could afford an independent life, but he knew she would never willingly face the social scandal of a divorce. Nor would she readily forgo the advantages marriage to him had brought her. As the eldest surviving son, he had inherited the title when his father, a baronet, had died; his position in society was assured and this was one of the main reasons Frances had agreed to marry him.

She had been quite pretty as a debutante, with several suitors from the same nouveau-riche background as herself. She had refused to commit to any one of them, determined to elevate herself socially if the opportunity arose. Aubrey, who she had met quite by chance in the tea room at Fortnum and Mason, had fitted her plan despite the fact that he was ten years older than herself, already a little thin on top and portly round the waist. His father, Sir George Beauford, had expired some five years previously; his mother, Lady Mary, was still alive and would become her mother-in-law.

Aubrey was far from ignorant of these facts, which Frances had openly admitted in an unguarded moment. Since he had long ago fallen out of love with her, the admission had not bothered him. Whatever was missing in their marriage in the way of affection was made up by the advent of the three sons Frances had given him, albeit unwillingly. The boys were everything a father could wish for – handsome, intelligent and engaging. However, he did still crave the possession of a daughter. His beloved sister, Victoria, had died of diphtheria at the age of fifteen, and he had never quite stopped grieving for her. A daughter would, he firmly believed, partially fill the gap his little sister had left.

Frances' refusal to have any more children after Robert's birth had seriously concerned him. Three long years passed before she would allow him into her bed again and he had been too much of a gentleman to force her. A few too many glasses of champagne at their neighbouring hunt ball had softened Frances' stance and when he promised her an American Packard motor car, she was too thrilled to close her door that night. He had bought the car as he'd promised but Frances' pregnancy, which resulted from their brief sexual rapport, prevented her driving the car herself as she grew larger. Aubrey forbade her to do so as he considered it risky in her condition, besides which his former head groom, Joseph, was well able to act as her chauffeur whenever she wished; and he allowed her first call upon the man's time.

Their doctor had attempted to cheer her, telling her that babies carried much to the fore of the abdomen were frequently girls, but Frances had simply burst into tears and reiterated that she had never been so nauseous with the boys and would readily change this baby's sex if it were possible. She looked now at her husband's impassive face and said tearfully: 'You should be having this baby, not me, Aubrey. It's not fair! Moreover, I will not go down to Farlington Hall. At least here in London, my friends can come and visit me. I'll be even more bored in the country than I am now with this baby restricting my activities. Besides, why should it matter if there is a war? You said yourself the present trouble was all in outlandish places like Serbia and Bosnia and names I can't even pronounce. I won't go, Aubrey! Since I have got to have this wretched baby I'm going to have it here.'

Aubrey quelled his impatience in deference to her condition.

'I spoke to Doctor Matthews this morning. He assured me it would be at least another three weeks before the birth. My mind is made up, Frances. You may wish to take risks but I have no intention of allowing you – or indeed the boys – to do so. You may not be aware that there are such things as Zeppelins – airships that can fly over the Channel and drop unknown horrors on our city. If in a week or two the possibility of war seems less likely, you may come back to London.'

Frances regarded her husband furiously, knowing full well that he, not she, had the power to decide her actions. Joseph would not drive her even to the Albert Hall or to Fortnum's without his master's authority. Her husband could order Nanny, Mrs Mount, the cook, her maid Ellen, even Edie, the parlour-maid, to depart at a moment's notice to Sussex and they would obey him. She would be left here in London with no servants to look after her, a virtual prisoner in her present condition.

Seeing the look of resignation now replacing the defiance on his wife's face, Aubrey's voice softened.

'Perhaps the country would seem less onerous, my dear, if you took a companion with you – your sister, perhaps? You so rarely see her and she is the only surviving member of your family, after all.'

'I don't wish to see her!' Frances snapped. 'You know very well Angela and I have nothing whatever in common. She can only think about two things – the theatre . . . and men, of course. Not a day goes by that I don't thank the Lord for taking my poor parents into His tender care where, it is to be hoped, they know nothing of the life Angela leads!'

Aubrey, too, thanked the Lord for cutting short the lives of Frances' snobbish mother and father, who, the latter having made a phenomenal amount of money in steel, had been as determined as Frances herself to marry his two daughters into the upper classes. Frances, of course, managed to fulfil their dreams but Angela, petite, blonde, with a pretty singing voice, had had other ideas for her future. From the age of twelve, when she was taken to her first theatre, she had determined upon a future for herself as an actress – preferably a famous one acclaimed the world over.

Three years younger than her sister, Angela was engagingly pretty and flirtatious, and as ambitious as ever. The nearest she had ever come to a star part in a theatrical performance was to become, briefly, an understudy. Nevertheless, with the money her parents had left her and the small salaries she earned from minor parts on the stage, she led a completely independent life. Never short of admirers, she spent her non-working hours enjoying herself – something Frances seemed incapable of doing. On the few occasions when Angela came to stay, it was as if a bright shaft of sunlight lit up the rooms. Her charming tinkling laugh could be heard all over the house, interlaced with light-hearted chatter. Aubrey found her an attractive little thing and turned a blind eye to the faint hint of vulgarity about her clothes and speech.

The boys adored her; and George, the eldest, had announced he was going to marry her when he was old enough. Frances was furious and despite Angela's intervention, sent him up to his room for being impertinent. Aubrey quickly recognized that his wife was jealous of her younger sister's charm and popularity; and not least, of her freedom. Once, when Frances had admitted to yet another infant on the way, Angela had tried to commiserate, stating ill-advisedly: 'Poor old thing! Just imagine, Fran, counting this baby, you will have been pregnant altogether three years! Never mind,' she added hastily when she saw Frances' expression, 'maybe this time you'll have a girl.'

Two days later, as Joseph negotiated the Packard carefully out of the suburbs and onto the moderately traffic-free London to Brighton road, Frances ignored the excited chatter of her three young sons and, indeed, the ineffectual quietenings of Nanny.

She would have to employ someone more qualified to manage the boys, she thought irritably; a tutor, perhaps, who would exert some discipline over them. Their behaviour was Aubrey's fault – he spoiled them. Heaven alone knew what would happen if they did have a girl this time. At least he would have to pay attention to the discipline required by the maternity nurse she had engaged to take care of the new baby. Nanny, who looked after the boys, had been Aubrey's nurse-maid when he was a little boy and doted on him to the extent that he could do no wrong in her eyes.

As the car passed through the village of Crawley, Frances reminded herself that in September, George would be going to Eton, Aubrey's old school. Hopefully, Vaughan and Robert would be much more manageable without their elder brother egging them on to misbehave.

Such thoughts concerning her young sons disappeared abruptly as she felt a twinge of pain in her lower abdomen. She recognized its similarity to an early labour pain and for a moment, she panicked. She couldn't possibly have the baby in the country! Farlington Hall was miles from anywhere and for all she knew, the nearest village, Elmsfield, might not have a midwife, let alone a competent one. The woman who had delivered all her other babies in London was highly efficient and booked to attend her with this birth. Aubrey must have been mad to even think of sending her thirty miles out of London when she was so near her delivery date.

But the pain quickly subsided and did not return. Relieved that she had probably suffered little worse than wind, Frances reminded herself that she had another three tedious weeks to wait before she could be relieved of the uncomfortable bulk which was making every movement, even sitting, so uncomfortable.

The boys had started squabbling. They knew that their parents were getting another baby and that their father was praying for a girl. George, who worshipped his father, felt threatened that his place as favourite was in jeopardy. Vaughan, the quiet, artistic one of the three, had announced that he had chosen a name for the girl baby. To her intense irritation and refusal, he had chosen Angela, after the aunt they all loved.

'Who wants a stupid girl? I don't!' George was saying, his cheeks pink with irritation. 'Anyway, Papa said we can't be sure what it'll be.'

'I don't care what it is!' four-year-old Robert announced. 'I'm bored of always being the youngest. I just want it to arrive!'

And so do I, Frances thought as Nanny made further fruitless attempts to quieten the boys. I, too, want this wretched baby to be born, and then I'll be free to do what I want – like Angela. Things are going to change in future. I'll run Aubrey's house for him and entertain his friends, but that's all I'll do. Never, ever, ever again will I let him give me another child. Never, never . . .

She was still muttering the word as Joseph turned the car into the drive and the big mansion house that was Farlington Hall came into view.

Two

Harold Varney looked anxiously at his wife as she lowered herself on to the sofa beside him. 'Are you very uncomfortable, my love?' he enquired solicitously.

Copper swept back the tendrils of red hair that had come loose from her blue velvet snood and were clinging to her damp forehead. Harold maintained her hair was one of the many beautiful things about her, but as a child, she had been endlessly teased by her brother, Bertie, who was fair-haired. She must be a foundling, he told her, left by the gypsies; she would never find a husband when she grew up, not with flame-red hair like hers. No matter how often their father insisted it wasn't flame-red but a burnished coppery colour like chestnuts when they first emerged from their shells, Bertie continued teasing her and by the time she was five, he had stopped calling her by her proper name, Caroline, and called her Copper-head. Although her parents tried to insist on the use of her real name, much to her distress the nickname had stuck. She didn't mind it now because Harold loved her hair and the name!

'I'm fine, darling,' she replied untruthfully. Her beloved husband worried quite enough about her without her complaining to him every time her back ached or the baby kicked. As the doctor had told her on her last visit, at her age a little discomfort in these last weeks before the birth was only to be expected. Thirty-four was, after all, old for a first baby.

It was not as if they hadn't wanted a child years ago when they were first married, Copper had told the doctor when they had moved into Foxhole Cottage in the village of Elmsfield. She and Harold had agreed she should ask the doctor's advice as to what could be wrong with her. After a careful examination, he'd been unable to give her an explanation for her

failure to conceive. He had called Harold in for an examination and even questioned him as to their method of love-making,
but could still not explain why there was no pregnancy. When,
many years later at the age of thirty-four, Copper had visited
the doctor because of several weeks of continuous nausea, he
had told her with a broad grin that she was not ill, as she
supposed, but pregnant. She and Harold were ecstatic. Boy or
girl, they didn't mind – only that the baby should be born
healthy. To that end, Dr Campbell said, he would feel happier
if, in the light of her age, she went into their cottage hospital
for the birth. Then, if there were any last-minute complica-
tions, he and the nurses would be there to safeguard both her
and her longed-for baby.

Harold was the headmaster of the small local school where
there was only one other teacher – an unqualified middle-
aged lady who taught the very young pupils. Harold had been
educated at a grammar school, where he'd achieved such excellent results in his exams he'd been deemed well qualified to
train for the profession of teacher. He loved his work and took
great pride in the school upon which he had lavished all his
time and attention until he'd met and fallen passionately in
love with one of the newly arrived young nurses at the local
cottage hospital.

His courtship of the pretty twenty-year-old girl was
approved by both sets of parents and within an unusually short
space of time, a year after their first meeting, the couple were
married. Harold's takeover from the retiring headmaster of
Elmsfield village school had enabled them to move into the
schoolhouse, Foxhole Cottage.

'Would you like me to read to you for a little while?' Harold
asked.

Copper declined her husband's offer although she loved to
hear his voice relaying stories by the popular author Rudyard
Kipling or plays by the notorious playwright Oscar Wilde
whilst she busied herself with her sewing. In the early months
of her pregnancy, she had stitched an enchanting layette for
the coming child.

'It's far too pretty for a boy!' Harold had teased her when
she had shown him the soft flannel nightdresses with their
delicately embroidered yokes. Copper was convinced the baby
would be a girl even though Harold's family had produced

only boys – Harold, and his two brothers, both of whom had died, one in infancy and the other, a missionary in Africa, of malaria.

'Let's just talk, dearest,' Copper said as she tried to ease herself into a more comfortable position. 'With the baby due so soon, we really ought to decide upon a name.'

'I know, I know!' Harold said sighing. 'But no sooner do we decide upon a name than we discard it.' He drew another sigh and then added: 'We haven't yet considered Georgina for a girl – in honour of our king.'

Copper shook her head.

'I think it's too masculine, as it would surely be shortened to Georgie.'

'I agree,' Harold said. 'I suppose we could consider Victoria, for the old queen?'

At the age of forty, Harold still had thick dark brown hair which, being naturally curly, tended to fall across his forehead no matter how short it was cut. But for his trim moustache and small pointed beard, he wouldn't look in the least like a schoolmaster, Copper teased him. She looked at him lovingly as she replied now to his suggestion.

'Victoria sounds too elderly for a baby girl, don't you think?'

'Well then, my dear, what do you think of Leila? Byron used it in one of his poems – *The Giaour*, I think it was.'

'I quite like it,' Copper said with a smile. 'I tell you what, Harold, I will settle for Leila if you agree to Harry should we have a boy.' She gave a deep sigh as she looked at her husband. 'If it is, I do so hope he will be just like you!' she said.

Harold was about to tell her he hoped fervently that a girl would be just like her, but Copper suddenly hunched forward, clutching her stomach as she gasped. He saw at once that she was in pain.

'Is it the baby?' he asked.

'I think so!' Copper gasped again and then, to Harold's relief, she let out her breath and straightened her back. 'Doctor Campbell said first babies were usually late.' But her instinct told her their baby was almost certainly on its way.

She struggled to her feet with Harold's arm protectively round her. He looked deeply worried so she smiled reassuringly at him.

'Don't look as if the world is coming to an end!' she said. 'There's nothing to worry about. Thousands of babies are born every day – every minute probably if you include the whole world—' She broke off as a second pain engulfed her. 'Maybe you *should* take me to the hospital now!' she conceded. 'I think our baby is in quite a hurry to be born. You'll see my suitcase in the cupboard in the baby's room if you will be kind enough to fetch it. There's everything I need in there.'

Copper was quite calm as Harold helped her into the tiny Ford car they had purchased second-hand the year before. Not only was she prepared for the birth, but the little room adjoining their bedroom was ready too, the bassinet prettily covered with white muslin, the walls freshly wallpapered with a pattern of roses and violets. Crisp cretonne curtains hung either side of the latticed window. She felt almost breathless with excitement and would have been without a worry but for the knowledge that Harold was a bundle of anxiety beside her. She was pleased when they drove up to the hospital, where he helped her inside.

Neither expected the confusion that seemed to reign in the reception hall. There were porters with stretchers and nurses with bundles of fresh sheets hurrying by. Both doctors, including her own Dr Campbell, were by the desk, one of them on the telephone.

'Oh dear, Mrs Varney!' Dr Campbell exclaimed as he put down the receiver and caught sight of Copper. 'This really is unfortunate.' He regarded her anxiously. 'Maybe you won't birth the child until later tomorrow. How often are your pains?'

'They were every ten minutes or so, Doctor! But they have eased a little now.'

'Possibly it's just a warning, my dear,' he said hopefully. 'Anyway, you had better stay now you are here. We'll try to find a room for you and I'll see you as soon as I can.' He turned to the receptionist who was about to take yet another telephone call. 'Can you get one of the nurses to find Mrs Varney a room, please?' Turning back once more to Copper, he said apologetically: 'I'm afraid I'll have to leave you. I have to scrub up before the first casualties arrive.'

To both the receptionists' and Harold's consternation, all the nurses seemed frantically busy. Meanwhile, Copper had doubled over once more with pain. The look of excitement had gone and her face was white and tense with the effort not to cry out. Dr Campbell did not reappear, and growing ever more anxious, Harold managed to catch hold of the arm of one of the nurses hurrying past.

'Somebody's got to help us!' he said, his voice as authoritative as when he was administering discipline at school. 'My wife's been in pain for the past hour. She's going to have a baby!'

The nurse paused and unexpectedly smiled as she recognized him. She had been one of Harold's first pupils and thanks to his excellent teaching, had, like him, won a place at grammar school.

'I'm awfully sorry, Mr Varney!' she said. 'I'll attend to your wife the moment I can. There's an emergency, you see – a dreadful train crash at Burgess Halt and an awful lot of people have been injured – too many for Burgess General to take. So we're getting the overflow as soon as they've managed to get the injured out of the wreckage. We're moving some of the convalescent patients into the day room and getting their ward ready for the casualties.'

She looked at Copper's white face and said gently: 'Just sit down over there in that chair. You'll be quite all right. Babies can take hours to come, you know. Yours may not come until tomorrow morning!' Seeing Copper gasp as yet another pain took hold of her, she added: 'I'll try and find a porter to take this load of sheets up to the ward and I'll come back and help you to a room where you will have some privacy. The labour ward is being used for additional casualties. So you'll have a nice double room all to yourself . . . at least, unless, heaven forbid, we get even more mothers deciding to have their babies tonight!' She turned back to Harold. 'You'll look after your wife until I get back, Mr Varney, won't you? I'll be as quick as I can.' With which she disappeared.

Copper tried to smile as she removed Harold's hand where he was gripping her arm. 'I'll be perfectly all right now I'm here, dearest. You heard what the nurse said – I'm to have a room all to myself. So you go home now.' As he started to protest she said gently: 'Really, Harry, you can't do anything to help me, and,' she added with an attempted smile, 'I won't have to worry about you worrying about me!'

Harold still looked concerned. 'I can't possibly leave you here on your own. Suppose . . .'

He got no further before his former pupil returned and helped Copper out of her chair. 'You can kiss her goodbye, Mr Varney!' she said smiling. 'I promise to telephone you as soon as you become a proud parent. Your wife will be in Room 12.'

No sooner had a reluctant Harold left the building than the nurse said: 'They are nearly all the same – fathers-to-be. By the look on their faces, you'd think they were the ones having the baby! By the way, my name's Hope, which reminds me, are you hoping for a boy or a girl, Mrs Varney?'

With her cheerful chatter, Copper was able to forget a little of her growing apprehension whilst the nurse undressed her. The pains were now coming at regular intervals and were much stronger. She was not the least surprised when the nurse told her she was already in the second stage of labour and would quite likely have her baby within the next hour or two.

'We have waited ten years for this baby!' Copper confided between the painful waves of pain. 'So we don't mind whether we have a son or a daughter.'

But the nurse was not listening. 'I'm going to see if I can get hold of the midwife,' she said, but with little hope of success she thought. When she had last seen her, she was in attendance upon another woman about to give birth – a Lady Beauford, who was a lot more demanding than Mr Varney's wife. Admittedly she was having a bad time – the baby was in the breech position and Sister Joan, the midwife, was so far unable to turn it into the correct birth position. If she did not succeed, the doctor would almost certainly have to perform a Caesarean and that was the last thing they needed with so many of the train casualties to be seen to.

Looking extremely tired and not a little exasperated by her patient's constant demands, Sister Joan had left the room for a brief respite during which she informed Copper's nurse that she had 'a real pain in the neck' in Room 13! Lady Beauford was to have had her baby in London she related but her husband had thought she would be safer in the country if there was a war, and now the doctor at Burgess General who had seen her at her home, Farlington Hall, had told her she could not undertake the drive back to town as her waters had broken and of course that meant she had started labour. Burgess General had been too busy to admit her and had sent her on to Elmsfield Cottage Hospital, where it had fallen to the midwife to look after her.

'You'd think she was the Queen!' Sister Joan confided to her younger colleague. 'The bed's too hard; the sheets are cotton, not linen as her ladyship is accustomed to; she has not been given anything to ease the pain and she will never, ever have another baby. It wasn't even as if she had wanted this one!'

'My patient is just the opposite!' Nurse Hope said. 'It's her first baby and she's quite old, which is why Dr Campbell wanted her in hospital where he can keep an eye on her. I know her husband, Mr Varney – he was my headmaster years ago. His wife is called Copper – she's red-headed, you see. What's your patient called?'

'Lady Beauford, Frances Beauford,' the older woman told her, adding with a sigh: 'I suppose I shouldn't stand here telling tales about her, but she really is a pain in the neck. She refuses to believe I finally managed to turn the baby right way up for her. Swears she's dying!'

They both laughed and the midwife was still smiling as she disappeared down the corridor towards the small hospital operating theatre.

In Room 13, Frances had been alternately moaning and screaming as her labour pains came with increasing frequency. She was frightened and furious in equal measure. The midwife had been unable to reach Aubrey on the telephone and she badly wanted him here – not to sit by the bed and hold her hand, but to see she had the proper care and attention befitting her status.

Since for the moment there was no one to hear her screams, Frances now kept them and her thoughts to herself. Silently, she raged against the fact that she was being treated here in this potty little hospital as if she was of no more importance than one of the villagers they usually catered for. The baby's birth was not due for another three weeks – or so her London doctor had told her. This afternoon the doctor at Burgess Hospital had blatantly disagreed. One had only to look at her size quite apart from the regularity of her pains to be certain she was now in labour. Moreover he thought it unlikely that the infant was premature. Two casualties from the train crash had just been brought in and were near death, so he had no time to examine her more thoroughly before announcing she was to be taken straight to Elmsfield Cottage Hospital for the delivery.

Frances' protests had fallen on deaf ears. They had become even more voluble when at Elmsfield the doctor told her the baby was in what he called a breech position and she must wait a while in the hope that it would right itself ready for delivery head first. She was to undress and get into bed and he would give her something to slow things up.

Frances didn't want anything slowed up. She wanted to get the whole ghastly business over with, go home and forget she now had a fourth child. If Aubrey wanted, he could gloat over it if it was a girl. If not, it would serve him right. George's school fees and expenses were not to be ignored, the lists of his requisites seemingly endless – uniform, sports equipment, books, clubs, tuck, shoes and boots, pocket money – bills Aubrey ignored until payment was required and he told Frances she must make more economies when three sons' expenses had to be met!

Frances hoped the baby would be a boy – as a punishment. But somehow she doubted it. The births of her three sons had been painful, of course, but relatively uncomplicated. On each occasion, she had given birth in the comfort of their London home with a maternity nurse on duty twenty-four hours a day to see to her needs. Aubrey had been on hand to fill her room with flowers and her arms with expensive presents.

She was reminded now that once this wretched baby was delivered and she was out and about again after the lying-in period, she would be able to drive his last present to her, her lovely new yellow Packard. Maybe she could persuade him to take a holiday. The two of them could drive down to the South of France and enjoy the sunshine in Cannes. She had never been to a casino but one of her sister's wealthy admirers had taken her to Monte Carlo for a weekend and Angela related that a casino was one of the most exciting places in the whole world.

The reappearance of the midwife brought Frances' reverie to an end and her thoughts turned unhappily back to the reason for her being here in this poky little hospital room. She would have space for three such rooms in her lovely bedroom in London.

'Did you find a doctor?' she demanded.

The midwife nodded as she approached the bed.

'Indeed I did, but some of the casualties who have been brought in are terribly injured and need his attention. Now that your baby is lying correctly, I shall be delivering it for you. I am a qualified midwife, Lady Beauford, so I can assure you I am more than competent.'

Had it not been for the fact that her pains were now so frequent and so severe that she needed the morphine the nurse was offering her, she might have continued to complain, but by now she had resigned herself to the problem of getting rid of the unwanted child in her womb. She saw little point in trying to 'be brave' as the midwife was urging her, and permitted herself to scream as loudly as she felt inclined. The noise, loud though it was, did not distract Copper Varney, who, with gritted teeth, was also about to give birth in the adjoining room.

Three

Frances looked across the breakfast table at her husband who was, as usual, enjoying an Arbroath smokie, busy – or pretending to be busy – picking out the fish bones. Her mouth tightened.

'I am sorry that you cannot agree with me but in this instance, Aubrey, I will not be overruled. Victoria can go to the village school until she is eight. Then she can go as a boarder to the Convent of the Holy Virgin in France where I went. They don't take girls until they are eight so Elmsfield will do very well for the next three years.'

Suitably shocked, Aubrey looked up from his plate into his wife's determined face.

'I simply do not understand you, Frances!' he said in quiet, measured tones that belied his inner irritation. 'You are forever trying to improve the boys' speech and manners as befits their class, yet you intend to allow Victoria who, I might point out, is at a most vulnerable age, to mix with the village children. Personally, I have no objection to the school per se, but I do question your objection to my wish to hire a tutor for Victoria. Now all the boys are away at school, surely we can allow Nanny to retire?'

Frances' mouth tightened still further. 'I don't doubt that you can hire and fire your staff with the maximum ability, Aubrey, but you have no understanding of domestic management. Nanny may not be well enough educated to give Victoria scholastic instruction, but she is an excellent housekeeper. You may not be aware that I have not yet replaced Beddington since she left us to become an office worker. Regrettably a great many domestic staff have decided since the war that there are more interesting jobs to be had for women than being in service. Fortunately, Nanny has been acting as housekeeper very satisfactorily. Moreover, she is a very good seamstress and, I might remind you, sees to the boys' uniforms and packing. Lastly, Aubrey, it is not my intention to relieve Nanny of the task of supervising Victoria when she is not at school.'

It was a moment or two before Aubrey spoke. Then he said: 'Had you thought how useful a tutor would be to take the boys off your hands in the holidays? You yourself told me last holidays that they were getting out of hand; that Nanny couldn't cope?'

'We are not discussing the holidays!' Frances said pointedly. 'By all means let us employ a tutor for the holidays if that is what you wish. I dare say there will be plenty of unemployed soldiers – officers who have had a good education, can play cricket and that sort of thing, who are looking for just such employment. But I don't want a person like that living with the family all year round. Nanny will still be perfectly capable of looking after Victoria here at Farlington Hall on her own when I am in London with you, more especially if the child is at school during the day.'

'The "child" does happen to have a name,' Aubrey muttered as he returned to his kipper, now cold on the plate in front of him. He knew the folly of trying to argue with Frances over such matters. He knew, also, that any inconvenience caused by the arrival of a daughter five years ago would bring the customary accusations down upon his head. Frances had not wanted a fourth child; she had not wanted a daughter, particularly a captivating little creature like Victoria. Even after five long years, his wife was still furious with him because of the pain, discomfort and inconvenience of the birth. However, he had doted on the infant from the moment the nurse had put the baby in his arms, and subsequently was so happy to have the daughter he'd always wanted, he was prepared to put up with Frances' bad temper. Unbeknownst to her, he gave a large cheque every year to the hospital which had been responsible for the little girl's safe delivery.

What Aubrey could not fully understand was Frances' total lack of interest in their daughter, which had continued even when a few years after the birth the baby had metamorphosed into an enchanting toddler with a crop of unruly dark brown curls and a pair of sparkling hazel eyes. Adored by her three older brothers, her nanny and all the domestic staff, not to mention himself, Victoria was always laughing and, as far as he could ascertain, she was no trouble at all. Neither was she spoiled. Nanny would happily have spoiled her had Frances not laid down a list of rules, which had to be strictly obeyed by her and her charge. He, too, would have spoiled the little girl, who would coming running into the room when Nanny brought the children down to spend time with their parents after tea, and fling herself in a most unladylike way into his arms – an action not even Frances had been able to curb.

Aubrey put down his knife and fork and pushed his plate away. Going to the sideboard where a silver dish of scrambled eggs was keeping hot under its cover, he gave himself a generous helping, his mind elsewhere. He was recalling the time when Frances' sister, Angela, had remarked upon the tiny girl's adoration of him and his of the child. Laughing, she had asked Frances if she was not jealous. Frances had not been pleased.

'Jealous of a *child*?' she had said scornfully. 'Don't be ridiculous, Angie!'

It was indeed ridiculous, Aubrey told himself now as, forking scrambled egg into his mouth, he recalled the incident. He knew very well that Frances was no more in love with him than she had ever been, and a rival for his affections would not concern her. As far as Frances was concerned, her unwanted daughter meant little more to her than the pleasure she got when a member of her coterie of London friends admired one of her possessions. When Nanny dressed Victoria in one of her pretty Liberty frocks and brought her down to the drawing room, the visitors were enchanted.

'She's so pretty! So sweet! So amusing!' they cooed. 'Not very like you to look at, Fran, but a bit like your sister, perhaps.'

'You're so lucky to have such a dainty little girl! My Evelyn is so clumsy . . .'

'My Loveday is far too plump!'

'Joan does nothing but sulk when I try to introduce her to my friends.'

Returning home unexpectedly one afternoon, Aubrey had overheard such comments and was shocked by the women's disloyalty to their children. Frances seemed to think nothing of it.

'We share all our problems,' she told him. 'I tell them how irritating Victoria can be, forever asking questions; why this? Why that? How does this work? Why is the moon white? It's enough to drive you crazy. The sooner that child goes to school and we get some peace the better.'

Aubrey finished his breakfast and picking up his folded copy of the *Times*, informed his wife that he was going into his study for half an hour before meeting a friend for a game of golf. They would lunch at the golf club, he told her, so he would not be home until teatime.

His absence was of little interest to Frances who, in half an hour, was due to go to London to her hairdresser. The boys had gone down to the lake to fish for trout which was in abundance there – George was soon to start his last year at Eton in a few weeks' time, Vaughan about to join him there and Robert would be returning to prep school; only Victoria was home, being looked after by Nanny. Aubrey had suggested the child should have another little girl come to the Hall for companionship but, as Frances had pointed out acidly, they did not know anyone suitable here in the country who had a girl the same age.

'I saw a little blonde girl when I was in the tobacconist's,' he had pointed out. 'She was with her mother buying sweets. She looked about the same height as Victoria, and the mother looked perfectly respectable.'

'Then I suggest you find out who they were,' Frances had replied tersely. She was off to London and the next day she would be out playing bridge with three friends, and didn't have time to bother about something so unimportant.

Aubrey, however, did take time to find out about the little girl in the post office, which also served as a tobacconist and a sweet shop. According to the postmistress she was the schoolmaster's daughter – an only child doted on by her parents.

'They had to wait a long time for her, you see,' Mrs Quick had added, pleased to be able to impart this extra piece of knowledge to the customer known to the villagers as 'the Squire'. Sir Aubrey was not at all snobbish and no one had anything but good to say of him. His wife was another matter, acting the lady of the manor with never a smile for anyone in the village. They all knew the Beaufords had a large house in London, and that if they were staying in Farlington Hall for more than a weekend they brought their London servants with them. In addition to those already in service at the Hall, the extras were needed if the family was having a weekend house party.

There had been far fewer of these during the war when all the men were away fighting for their country; but when last year the whole ghastly conflict had finally come to an end, the Beaufords had started entertaining again – mostly those of Sir Aubrey's shooting and golfing friends who had survived the conflict. On such occasions, volunteers from the village, glad to make an extra shilling, acted as beaters for the guns or as caddies on the golf course, and if her ladyship was in London extra staff were engaged to help at the Hall.

Aubrey was informed that the headmaster of Elmsfield village school, Harold Varney, frequented the local public house, the Fox and Vixen, around midday on a Sunday after church, so he went there the next weekend with the express purpose of meeting him. The two men got on very well. Finding the man both erudite and cultured, Aubrey confided his wife's plan to send Victoria to his school the following term. He was hugely relieved by his companion's enthusiastic response.

The school, the headmaster told him, was above average scholastically, so the educational needs of Aubrey's little girl would be more than satisfactorily met. As for the social side, it did a child no harm to learn that not everyone lived and spoke and behaved as their families did. Things were changing very rapidly in this post-war world and Aubrey might find that his daughter wanted a career when she grew up. Women who had participated in war work had discovered that there was more to life than keeping house and having babies! To have an understanding of how the working classes coped with their lives would be very advantageous to Victoria when she grew up, Harold Varney maintained.

'I have a little girl about the same age as your daughter,' Harold told Aubrey. 'She, too, will be starting school next term. Her name is Leila. I will ask her to watch out for your daughter, who may feel a little strange at first not knowing any of the other children.'

It was on a bright sunny August morning that Aubrey decided as soon as his golf game was over he would tell

Victoria about the little friend awaiting her at school. His daughter should spend the afternoon with him instead of walking with Nanny who, Victoria declared, could never answer any of her questions.

'She only knows the oak tree because it has acorns!' Victoria complained to him. 'I want to recognize all the others, too. Which one is "the whispering tree"? I asked Joseph and he said he thought it was a poplar, but I don't know what a poplar looks like!'

Looking at his five-year-old daughter's scowling face, Aubrey laughed. She was riding Snowball, Robert's outgrown pony, and he was walking beside her as they made their way through the spinney to the open fields beneath the South Downs. His own horse, along with all but the elderly carriage pair, had been requisitioned during the war, and he had not had the heart to replace her. Instead, much to his head groom's dismay, he had bought a car, a Bentley, instead, and poor Joseph had had to exchange his favourite riding breeches more often for a chauffeur's uniform.

It always amused Aubrey to see how cross and exasperated Victoria became when the knowledge she sought was not forthcoming. The boys teased her, talking about trigonometry and decimal points and Julius Caesar and then refusing to tell her about them. Not that they didn't adore her but their interests were entirely masculine; their rugby, cricket, fishing and bicycle riding always excluding her. Victoria was desperate to follow Robert to prep school although she knew perfectly well that girls never went to boys' boarding schools.

His daughter's concerns about her lack of knowledge of their country's trees gave Aubrey the ideal entrée to the subject of her initiation into the village school – something Frances for some obscure reason of her own had left him to do. It was as if she felt guilty that her daughter should have such unconventional schooling, more especially as it conflicted so markedly with her usual snobbish observance of the social conventions of her class.

Victoria's small face glowed with curiosity when Aubrey informed her she would be going to the village school in September. He hastened to add that there was already one other little girl who would be starting school at the same time with whom she could make friends.

'She is the headmaster's daughter and her name is Leila,' he told her.

Victoria nearly fell off her pony as she bounced up and down with excitement.

'I have met her already, Papa!' she said. 'Nanny and I were throwing bread to the ducks on the pond in the village and she came down with her mama to do the same as us. So we took turns and she told me her name and I told her mine and then her mama, who is a very nice lady, told me I would see Leila at school as she knew I would be going there, and she said it would be nice for us to be friends just like you said!'

Aubrey looked up at his daughter in astonishment. 'You mean, you already knew you were to go to Elmsfield School after the summer holiday? Why ever didn't you tell me?'

Victoria frowned. 'I thought you'd know already!' she said truthfully. 'Didn't Mother tell you?'

Aubrey decided this was a question best left unanswered since he had no intention of letting his small daughter know he and her mother were often at loggerheads.

'So tell me about this friend you are going to have. I believe she is the same age as you.'

Victoria was smiling once more. 'We're *exactly* the same age!' she said happily. 'Do you know, Papa, Leila's mama and mine both went to the hospital and were given their babies on the same day? So you see, Leila and me are sort of twins.'

Aubrey smiled. 'Of course, I had quite forgotten. I first met Leila's father at the hospital when we were both—' He broke off, remembering suddenly that children knew nothing of childbirth. Victoria thought a stork brought babies and usually laid them under gooseberry bushes.

As if following his train of thought, Victoria asked, frowning: 'Papa, why did the stork take me and Leila to the hospital and not to our homes?'

Whilst her father was still trying to think of an adequate reply, she added: 'Perhaps both of us had measles and the stork knew there would be a doctor at the hospital to give us the right medicine!'

It was not an unreasonable assumption as young Robert had only just recovered from a nasty bout of measles, which was obviously on Victoria's mind. Hiding a smile, Aubrey evaded an answer to his daughter's question and posed one of his own.

'Has your new friend any brothers like yours? They could meet Vaughan and Robert if their ages are similar.'

As he turned her pony's head towards home, she looked quite sad as she said: 'No, Papa, Leila's all on her lonesome. Her mama said that was why it would be so nice for her to have me for a friend. Papa, must I wait till school starts to see her again? Couldn't she come to tea with me? I could show her my tree house and she could have a ride on Snowball if she wanted.' Without waiting for his reply, she continued: 'I'll ask Mother when we get home.' She drew a deep sigh. 'I s'pose she will say no. She told Nanny I'm not to mix with the village children and Leila lives in the village in the school-house because of Leila's papa being the headmaster. Their house is called Foxhole Cottage. Isn't that a lovely name, Papa? I wish we didn't live in something called a Hall. It sounds like a passage, doesn't it?'

She was still chattering as they returned to the house where her two younger brothers were now riding their bikes up and down the gravel drive. They waved to Victoria and their father as they disappeared round a bend on their way to the Lodge, where Fred, the head gardener, and his wife lived.

Victoria was smiling.

'I expect Mrs Brompton has made some scones especially for the boys!' she confided in her father. 'She usually does in the holidays. George said we mustn't tell Mother or Cook 'cos they wouldn't like it. It's a secret!'

Aubrey wasn't quite sure if it was ethical for him to remain silent over a ruling Frances must have made, thereby contradicting it; but a few extra scones for growing boys hardly seemed worth the repercussions which would undoubtedly ensue. Since the terrible losses of able-bodied men during the last war – some said close on a million – it was no longer easy to find servants, gardeners as well as indoor staff. Brompton was elderly now and needed a young lad to help him with the heavier tasks, but he was an honest, decent, hardworking fellow who had been with them for over thirty years.

It was quite possible, knowing Frances as he did, that she had objected to the gardener's wife feeding her precious sons! Were she in one of her moods, she might well berate the well-intentioned Mrs Brompton and then Fred might give notice. Fortunately, the fact that the couple had the use of the Lodge was an incentive for them to remain as long as their health permitted. There was, too, the fact that Brompton loved the garden, which he had tended so meticulously over the years.

It was just as well he did so, Aubrey thought as he walked with Victoria and her pony round to the stables, since seldom a week went by without Frances making one complaint or another; Brompton had picked yellow roses instead of the pink ones she had wanted; the grapes he had harvested from their greenhouse were not as ripe as they should be; the grass on the croquet lawn had not been cut low enough. There was always something wrong and only very rarely did she praise poor old Fred.

Come to that, Aubrey thought wryly as he lifted Victoria off her pony and together they put Snowball in her stable and gave her a pail of water, there was always something he himself had done wrong, according to Frances. As for praise, that was never forthcoming. Any love she possessed went to her eldest, George. George had been blessed with exactly the right temperament to cope with his mother. He could always diffuse her anger or her criticisms with an arm round her shoulders and an affectionate laugh as he told her: 'Please don't be cross with me, darling Mama. Honestly, I didn't mean to upset you. You know how it hurts me to displease you!'

Both Aubrey and the boys knew perfectly well that George, whilst doing exactly as he wished, was very well aware that if his mother learned of a misdeed she would be angry, but with his fair hair, large heavily lashed blue eyes and cherubic expression, he could quite literally get away with murder – and not just with Frances. Cook, Nanny and the maids all adored him and Frances positively doted on him. Throughout the latter half of the war she had lived in fear that the conflict might continue long enough for her darling George to be involved.

Now she lived in fear that he would pursue his dream when he left Eton next year, and accept his godfather's invitation to spend a year or two on his tea plantation in Ceylon instead of going up to university. Infuriating Frances, Aubrey had encouraged the idea, saying it would be good training for the day when as eldest son George would eventually inherit the estate.

With a sigh Aubrey put such thoughts from his mind as he took his daughter back into the house and sent her upstairs to change out of her riding clothes. Going into his study, his eyes thoughtful, he sat down behind his desk and allowed his thoughts to return to the carnage of the recent war. He knew the idealists believed that despite the terrible bloodshed, winning the war would bring about a better world for everyone, but now, a year later, they were beginning to realize that this was the reverse of the truth. Not only was the country close to bankruptcy due to the cost of the war but also the short post-war boom in industry had not lasted. The ensuing slump had as a consequence brought unemployment for those who had survived. Life was difficult too for the vast numbers of widows and women with no men to be husbands. Young women went to the towns to find work as typists, secretaries, nurses and shop assistants, and many widows had become the family breadwinner. The pre-war social order had given way to unrest, depression and sometimes extreme poverty.

It was by no means a better world his sons and daughter were inheriting, Aubrey thought as he got up from behind his desk and walked across the room to settle down in his favourite armchair, from which he could look through the open windows across the lawns to the lake. The cost of maintaining Farlington Hall and the estate was escalating and Frances was becoming more and more resentful of the economies they were now obliged to make. She had never really liked Farlington Hall, his deeply loved family home, for whose survival he had knowingly married without real affection.

The smell of jasmine wafting in through the casements from the south wall turned his thoughts to a happier theme. The war had ended before his sons could be killed, as were those of so many of his friends. He had the boys to be proud of; he had his beautiful home and above all, he had his enchanting little daughter. What more could he justifiably want?

Four

1920

Frances paid the taxi driver and, clutching her new embroidered handbag, pulled her silver fox stole more securely around her shoulders then rang the front door bell of her mother-in-law's London house in Park Lane. That morning she had been summoned to tea (rather than invited) that chilly March afternoon, the autocratic old lady paying no regard to what other arrangements Frances might have for that afternoon.

'I want to see you on a matter of urgency!' she had declared. 'When Aubrey came to see me yesterday, he informed me you were here in town. Please be prompt, Frances, as I shall be going to the opera this evening and my hairdresser is coming to do my hair at five o'clock, so I shall expect you here at half past three at the latest.'

Frances knew better than to be even a few minutes late. Punctuality was but one of her mother-in-law's rigid dictates. To be suitably attired was another and Lady Mary was never sparing in her criticisms of Frances' taste.

'Really, my dear, with your complexion you should never wear green, and if you must wear that three-quarter-length coat, camel is quite wrong over a silk dress and it should certainly not have a belt – belted coats went out of fashion last year!'

Such remarks both mortified and angered Frances but she was far too submissive to do anything but nod her agreement. Coming from her background she was respectful of her mother-in-law's lineage. She was not only the widow of a well-respected soldier and baronet, but the daughter of a long dead Scottish earl, and Frances never even considered disputing her opinion on such matters of taste. She thanked her mother-in-law for her helpful advice, whilst secretly she simmered and took her bad temper out if not on her personal maid then on Aubrey, or, if she were to be found, Victoria. It was never on one of the boys.

Johnson, Lady Mary's butler, opened the door and preceding Frances through the hall into the large ground-floor drawing room, announced her arrival just as the grandfather clock in the hall struck the half hour.

I couldn't be more punctual than that! Frances thought silently as with a bright smile on her face she walked towards the tall imposing figure of her mother-in-law. The seventy-year-old dowager looked a statuesque figure, straight-backed, ample-bosomed in a fashionable dove-grey tea gown. Her white hair was immaculately arranged. It hardly needed the attentions of the hairdresser, Frances thought whilst admiring the magnificent rope of Beauford pearls which adorned her mother-in-law's chest. She now extended a be-ringed hand towards Frances.

'Come and sit down, Frances!' she said, her manners as perfect as her appearance. 'I trust you are keeping well.' Not waiting for an answer, she lifted a pair of silver-mounted tortoiseshell lorgnettes to her eyes and added: 'I have to say you are looking a trifle pasty, Frances. Perhaps you are overdue some bracing country air.' She frowned, her lips pursing as she continued: 'Aubrey tells me you have not been home for three weeks.'

She had not needed to add further comment to her implied disapproval, her words more than adequate to cause Frances' mouth to tighten.

'I doubt my husband is missing me, Lady Mary,' she said. 'Ever since Aubrey decided to turn the croquet lawn into a lawn-tennis court, he spends all his time there supervising the labourers. He says the court is for the boys, tennis being a much more sociable game than cricket or rugger, and that I should appreciate the fact that tennis is quite the fashion these days. So you see, Lady Mary, as I couldn't contribute in any way to Aubrey's project if I were at the Hall, I thought it an opportune time to come to town for some shopping.'

Her mother-in-law was about to speak when the parlour-maid came in with the tea things. At home in the country, unless they had guests, Frances could not be bothered with the tiny cucumber sandwiches and cakes that were customarily provided with afternoon tea. Both she and Aubrey were perfectly well satisfied with a slice of Mrs Mount's fruit or seed cakes. When the boys were home from school they still enjoyed nursery tea upstairs with Victoria, with bread and honey, scones and home-made ginger or shortcake biscuits. Mrs Mount frequently complained that their appetites were insatiable – and Victoria no better than her brothers – but Frances was well aware the cook enjoyed their enthusiasm for her baking.

Frances' attention was brought smartly back to the present when her mother-in-law, as if reading her wayward thoughts, referred to her only granddaughter.

'I want to discuss Victoria with you, Frances!' she said. 'Aubrey tells me the child is achieving very good results academically which, as I pointed out to him, is hardly very important for a girl. In fact I have always maintained a girl has a better chance of making a good wife if she is not too clever. Men don't like clever women. However, be that as it may, I am far more concerned about my son's comments regarding Victoria's friendships with the village children, especially as she is hand-in-glove with one particular child. I am surprised you have not stood up to Aubrey in this instance, Frances.' Her frown deepened. 'I cannot think how you permitted Victoria to go to the village school in the first place. I don't have to tell you that it is not the custom for children of our class to hobnob with the labourers' children.'

Frances' cheeks reddened and she was momentarily silenced, it having been her decision rather than Aubrey's to send the child to Elmsfield village school. It seemed that Aubrey had been decent enough in this instance not to bring his mother's wrath down upon her head – something that would surely have happened had her mother-in-law known the truth. She was certainly not going to inform her that Aubrey had at first been opposed to the idea.

'We don't think the experience is doing Victoria any harm, Lady Mary,' Frances said. Neither she nor her mother-in-law had been able to bring themselves to a more intimate way of addressing one another. To call this stately, autocratic woman 'mother' was beyond her. 'Victoria's particular little friend is the headmaster's daughter,' she added calmly. 'The child has been well brought up. Her speech may be a trifle common but

I have yet to hear Victoria copying her. I'd say the reverse is the case and Leila copies Victoria. As for manners, if anything, Leila's behaviour when she comes to tea with Victoria is a lot better mannered than your granddaughter's. Victoria can be very impatient as well as controversial. I do my best to discipline her but Aubrey dotes on the child and spoils her quite dreadfully.'

Pouring Frances and herself a second cup of China tea, Lady Mary decided not to object in this instance to Frances' criticism of her son. For one thing, she knew it was true. When Aubrey came to visit her, which he did punctiliously twice a month, he talked of little else but his daughter's charming personality, her attractive looks, her intelligence, which he deemed to be way above the average for her age. He did not try to hide the fact that he adored her whereas his affection for his three sons was perfunctory. Unlike Aubrey, she thought her eldest grandson's clever way of disarming his mother when she was criticizing him amusing. She could see that young Vaughan, being so quiet and dreamy, was growing up more like his father. Robert was a mixture of sunshine and showers; his brother's shadow.

Victoria, on the other hand, was a live wire, openly affec-tionate, mischievous, with an ingrained sense of humour, which Lady Mary knew frequently infuriated her daughter-in-law, who made no secret of the fact that she intended to pack the child off to board at her old convent in France as soon as she was old enough.

Lady Mary did not altogether share her son's adoration of her granddaughter. For one thing, Victoria bore no resem-blance whatever to any of the Beaufords, and since she had none of the family traits – fair hair, Grecian nose – it had to be assumed that the child took after her mother's side – an unwelcome supposition. She had never approved of – still less cared for – her daughter-in-law, although she had understood perfectly well that Aubrey, still a bachelor at thirty-four, had been attracted to the buxom Frances, not only because of her looks but by her considerable wealth. Frances' father, a commoner by the name of Len Snelling, had made the enor-mous sum of close on a million pounds in 1898 providing equipment for the army fighting the war against the Boers, not that he had ever admitted to this fact but Aubrey had found it out when his father-in-law died.

Frances' father had been only too willing to settle a large amount of money on her when he knew his elder daughter was hoping to marry into the aristocracy. As a wedding present he had offered to restore the Beauford ancestral home, Farlington Hall, which was in a bad state of repair owing to the huge debts incurred by Lady Mary's husband, the late Sir George. Despite the fact that she neither liked nor approved of Frances' background, she had raised no objections to the marriage, which she could see was entirely to Aubrey's advantage. Although not wealthy enough to support her son's not inconsiderably costly lifestyle, she herself was able to continue to live in the manner to which she had been accustomed all her life owing to her inheritance from her own wealthy parents.

Lady Mary's silent acceptance of her son's wife did not, however, oblige her to like Frances and she endured her company more or less on sufferance. Quite correctly, she had summed Frances up as a spoilt, overbearing, self-centred snob whose manners and dress sense often left much to be desired. However, it was some consolation that Frances had given Aubrey three fine healthy sons, as well as the daughter to whom he was devoted.

When the parlourmaid had removed the tea things, Lady Mary glanced at the bracket clock on the mantelpiece and turned back to her daughter-in-law.

'I particularly wanted to see you today, Frances, as I am hoping I can enlist your support – verbal support – regarding Victoria's schooling. I have tried to accustom myself to the present arrangements for her. Indeed, I have given the matter a great deal of thought but find myself still utterly opposed to it. A village school is no place for my granddaughter who, provided I live long enough, I shall present at court. What kind of background is she being given for her ultimate place in our society?'

Once again she lifted her lorgnettes and regarded Frances, whose expression was a mask of evasion.

'It is well known that the first seven years of a child's life are when the foundations are laid,' she continued. 'I think it was the Jesuits who said, "Give me a child until it is seven and it will be mine for the rest of its life!" I may be misquoting but the fact remains Victoria *is in a totally wrong environment*. You *must* make Aubrey see this for himself. He evades any discussion of the matter with me but perhaps he will listen to you. I have no doubt you agree with my views.'

Frantically, Frances tried to think how she could extricate herself from this unhappy dilemma. Not for anything was she prepared to admit that the idea of Victoria attending the village school was hers, that she was the one who had conceived the idea, because for one thing it suited her not to have to exchange the compliant Nanny for a bluestocking governess who might despise her for her ignorance, and for another, because her small daughter invariably got on her nerves. As Victoria was still too young to go to boarding school, she was pleased to have the child out of the house, however unsuitable the school.

'Of course I will talk to Aubrey, Lady Mary,' she said in as normal a voice as she could contrive. 'However, he seems very satisfied with the way things have progressed this first year.' With a flash of inspiration, she recalled Aubrey's comments regarding the headmaster. 'He has a high regard for Mr Varney, the headmaster,' she added. 'I understand he is a graduate from one of the prestigious Oxford colleges . . . I don't recall which one.'

Lady Mary looked at her sharply. 'Then what is the man doing in an insignificant village school?' she commented drily. 'If he obtained a good degree, why is he not in a better situation?'

Frantically, Frances searched her mind for further attributes made by her husband but to which she had barely bothered to listen. 'I think Mr Varney won a scholarship from a grammar school as a boy – something like that – and being an idealist, he wanted other poor children to have the educational advantage he enjoyed.'

Lady Mary sniffed. 'Trust Aubrey to put a man like that on a pedestal. Always the Good Samaritan,' she added vaguely. 'Well, see what you can do, Frances. The child has only been at the school for a term and a half so not too much harm can have been done yet. I trust both you and Nanny are watching Victoria's diction? There's nothing less attractive than vulgar speech. It's one of the sure ways to tell a person's background, as I am sure you are aware.'

Indeed she was only too well aware, Frances thought, having endured hours of boring tuition from the elocution teacher her parents had employed to rid her of her northern vowels.

Fortunately Victoria's diction was faultless, her school friend's almost so. Victoria had been pressing her to invite Mrs Varney to tea, which she had steadfastly refused to do, but now she thought it might be a sensible move. She could establish the woman's background, and if it was not satisfactory, she would insist an end was put to the children's friendship.

She looked up into her mother-in-law's immaculately powdered and rouged face. Despite Lady Mary's professed appointment with a coiffeur, her white hair was faultlessly dressed, coiled in a smooth bun high on her head. Her piercing blue eyes were the same colour as Aubrey's but lacked his softness. Frances was aware however that her husband's looks belied his character. When she had agreed to marry him, she had come close to loving him. Certainly she believed he could be manipulated because he appeared so easy-going.

It was less than a year before she saw an unexpectedly stubborn side to her husband's character. In small insignificant details, he allowed her to do as she wished; but when it came to wider issues with which he disagreed, he would brook no argument. Once, when he had decided, against her wishes, to give employment to a one-armed war casualty, she had accused him of disregard for her happiness. She had gone even further and accused him of marrying her for her money. It had come as a very nasty shock when he admitted that was partly true; that the monetary benefits she had brought with her were one of the reasons he put up with her petulance, her hardness of heart, her lack of interest in the sexual side of their marriage.

Despite their ensuing emotional separateness, by unspoken mutual consent, their marriage remained steadfast, each having come to accept a mode of living that suited them both – namely that they led their own lives with little interference from one another. Frances now spent a great deal of time in their London house, meeting friends for shopping expeditions, having dress fittings, enjoying bridge afternoons or attending matinees. In these post-war years, there was always a good play or musical to see, such as *The Beggar's Opera* or an Ivor Novello revue, or a new Somerset Maugham or Bernard Shaw play. Then there were the cinemas when together with one or more of her friends, they would sit on plush velvet seats in the balcony secretly falling in love with the Italian actor Rudolf

Valentino or admiring Gloria Swanson, and afterwards, taking tea at Fortnum's or the Ritz.

The fact that she did not have her husband as escort meant very little to Frances. There were very few women after the war who, even if their husbands did survive the carnage, had not subsequently lost them either to lethal wounds or gas poisoning. Frances often wondered how Aubrey had survived four long years of trench warfare with nothing worse than trench foot and the loss of two toes. He told his children he had a Guardian Angel and they innocently believed him. Despite her convent upbringing, Frances had no such religious leanings.

Aware that her thoughts had been wandering again and that Lady Mary was expecting her to make some comment, she produced one of the sentences she had prepared before the visit to fill just such a lapse in her attention.

'I had a letter from George last Wednesday. He asked me to give you his fond love when next I saw you and tell you that he had got into his house rowing eight.'

Lady Mary sniffed.

'I am well aware of that. George does occasionally write to me, Frances, or has it slipped your mind I am his grandmother?'

Frances blushed, two angry red circles staining her sallow cheeks.

'I'm delighted George has remembered the instructions I gave him when he went back to school,' she said keeping her tone of voice neutral. 'Boys these days are so lacking in consideration for their elders and betters, are they not? One has constantly to remind them that elderly relations take great pleasure in being remembered.'

Despite her annoyance, Lady Mary was unable to think of a remark which would put Frances firmly back in her place. Frowning, she turned and looked once more at the clock.

'I'm afraid I must put an end to your visit, Frances. As you can see it is nearly time for my coiffeur to arrive. However, I hope to see you again before too long, and meanwhile, do please see if you can persuade Aubrey to remove Victoria from that dreadful school.'

She tugged sharply on the bell rope hanging by the fireside and almost immediately the door opened and the butler stood ready to show Frances out.

'Shall I summon a taxi, m'lady?' he asked, aware that a taxi cab would be waiting at the end of the road for such a purpose.

Having said her farewells to her mother-in-law, Frances was more than pleased five minutes later to be seated in the back of the taxi cab, which was now winding its way through the traffic to Harrods. With a refreshing sense of freedom, she drew a deep breath and, deliberately forgetting the past hour and a half, she turned her thoughts to her coming purchases. She needed a new powder compact, the enamelled one in her handbag having become somewhat scratched. She also needed a set of new table mats and napkins for every day use, and she might, if something special caught her eye, buy herself a pair of leather gauntlet gloves – everyone was wearing them and her less well-off friends would really admire and envy her.

If there were time – and only if there were time before she met Angela, who had obtained seats for the musical *Chu Chin Chow* – she might go to the children's department and buy Victoria a party dress – velvet, with a cream lace collar, would suit her. With Easter not so far off and the children likely to receive a lot of invitations to Easter parties, she had no wish for Victoria to appear in last year's taffeta. Nanny, who was a surprisingly good seamstress, had offered to let the dress down because the child had outgrown it; but although Frances would otherwise have been happy with this economy, as she had no wish to waste money on beautifying her daughter, there was the possibility – indeed, likelihood – that one or two of the parents of the other children would recognize last year's dress and suppose her to be either too poor or too mean to buy something new.

The happiness Frances had felt on leaving her mother-in-law's house now gave way to a wave of depression. Keeping up with the Beaufords' aristocratic friends required much thought and care for small details that could expose her own lower-middle-class background. She had long since mastered the diction of the aristocracy. It was the unsuspected minor differences which could so easily trip her up. Good taste, for example, was one of those indefinable things one couldn't really learn except by watching and copying those who had it. She knew better than to buy herself a frock or gown, still less a hat, without one of her friends accompanying her. Then she would hum and hah over something she personally liked not admitting to wanting it until the friend made approving remarks.

Now, after nearly nineteen years of marriage, Frances was readily accepted by the wives of Aubrey's friends and colleagues as a member of their society. Only once, when at a rather boring function she had had a little too much to drink, she had transgressed good etiquette by boasting to a fellow guest about her late father's ability to make money, at the same time allowing her speech to revert. As a consequence, the woman declared Frances must have come from some- where in the industrial north, and Frances had not been invited to her house again despite the fact that her husband was a close colleague of Aubrey's.

As the taxi drew to a halt in front of Harrods' imposing main entrance, a green-and-gold-uniformed doorman hurried forward to open the door for her. Stepping out on to the pave- ment, supposing the concierge was watching her, she gave the grateful cab driver an overlarge tip, and feeling suddenly happier, she sailed into the shop. Glancing at her watch she realized there might not be time after all to buy Victoria's dress as well as her own requirements and as she went up in the lift, she decided the dress could wait until another day. The fact that the little girl might be eagerly waiting to see what her mother had chosen for her and might therefore be bitterly disappointed if she came home empty-handed simply did not occur to Frances, whose concerns as always were first and foremost for herself.

Five

Copper was making honey sandwiches for Leila's tea when her daughter came running into the kitchen, her cheeks pink with excitement. Her school socks were halfway down her legs, her red jersey was on back to front and her blue velour hat hung on her chest suspended by its elastic. Disregarding her mother's flour-dusted apron and the honeyed spoon in her hand, Leila flung her arms round Copper's waist declaring quite unnecessarily: 'I'm home, Mummy, and,' she added breathlessly, 'I've something really exciting to tell you!'

She paused to draw breath and waited until Copper had cut the sandwiches into neat triangles and put them on the bread and butter plate before she continued. 'You know it's my birthday next week and it's Vicky's birthday, too, and she's having a party and she asked her daddy if I could be invited so we could have our birthdays together, and he said yes, and can I go, Mummy, please? Vicky says they'll have balloons and different coloured jellies in their own little paper cups and they'll play games and usually there is a surprise like last year, there was a Punch and Judy show and Vicky says she thinks this year there might be a real conjuror because that's what she told her daddy she wanted and he always does what she asks and . . .'

'Just wait a minute, darling, until I can sit down and take this all in,' Copper said as she retied the bow on one of her little daughter's golden plaits. Leila had brought such joy into her life and Harold's. Of course, after Leila's unexpected conception they had hoped that there would be more children, or at least a boy baby. But it hadn't happened and now, almost six years after Leila's birth, they never thought about their infertility. Leila filled their lives with her ever-ready chatter, her bright smiles, her loving hugs and kisses.

Harold had to admit that their daughter was not by any means top of the form: many of her peers were quicker and academically far brighter. But she did have a lively imagination and was such an enthusiastic pupil that, schoolmaster though he was, he was not dismayed by his child's limited scholastic development. It did not compare with that of her little friend, Victoria, from the Hall, who showed signs even at this early age of exceptional ability.

'I suppose that's because of her background,' Copper had suggested. 'Victoria will have learned much from her brothers and their nanny. The few times I have spoken to the woman when she brought the child here to play with our Leila, she struck me as being very caring. She was Sir Aubrey's nursemaid, you know.' Copper had linked her arm lovingly through her husband's, adding with a smile: 'Our Leila should be the clever one, with an Oxford scholar for a father!'

Leila was now tugging gently at her sleeve.

'Please, Mummy, you're sitting down now. Please say I can go. I'll be really, really good and remember pleases and thank-yous and not to interrupt when a grown-up is speaking and I won't talk with my mouth full. I can go, can't I? Vicky says she doesn't care if any of her other friends don't go so long as I'm there, and it *is* my birthday too!'

Having given an ecstatic Leila the answer she craved, it was nevertheless the child's last remark which troubled Copper when later she told Harold of their daughter's excitement.

'I know they are both still only very little girls so it doesn't matter too much that they come from such different backgrounds. But if this devotion continues, Harold, what will happen when Victoria goes away to boarding school? Her parents won't want her mixing with children in our circumstances when she comes back for the holidays. In fact, I'm not very sure if Lady Beauford is very happy about it now.'

She drew a deep sigh before continuing: 'There have been several occasions when Leila has invited Victoria back to tea after school and the child has not been able to come. There are always excuses, of course, but they do sound a bit false, judging by Victoria's responses. According to Leila, Victoria told her it was always best to ask her father who would be bound to say yes – and you're not to laugh, Harold! How can I ask Sir Aubrey if his daughter can come to tea? Besides, although you run into him sometimes in the Fox and Vixen, I never see the gentleman.'

Although Harold sympathized with her worries about Leila's future happiness, as he pointed out, the future was a good many years away. By the time they were older, the girls might have quarrelled and ceased to be friends – something which happened frequently with young children. Meanwhile, there was clearly nothing for Copper to worry her pretty head about seeing that their daughter was to be guest of honour at little Victoria Beauford's birthday party – and quite right, too, seeing it was also Leila's birthday. Now Copper need not go to the trouble of baking a birthday cake!

A week later, breathless with excitement, Leila stood with her father outside the big oak front doors guarding the entrance to Farlington Hall. She felt like a princess in the beautiful new pink taffeta party dress her mother had made for her. Her white socks were also new as were the silver pumps with their black elastic fastenings. Her fair hair had been washed the night before and was now loose and tied prettily off her forehead with a pink silk bow. Over the top of her party frock was a black velvet cape.

Because of heavy threatening rain clouds it was almost dark, and as the butler opened the front door bright light flooded the driveway. Indoors, colourful balloons were hanging from each of the big oil paintings adorning the walls of the hall, and to Leila's delight, they were dancing to and fro in the sudden draught. A parlourmaid appeared offering to take Leila upstairs to one of the guest rooms to leave her cape.

'I'll go now, dear child!' Harold said bending to kiss his small daughter. 'I'll be back to collect you at six!'

It was very far from the first time that Leila had been to Victoria's home so she was not intimidated by the wide curving staircase leading up to the galleried landing above nor by the huge horned stag's head which hung from one wall, or even by the menacing knight-in-armour standing in the shadows holding his pike. He was rumoured to be one of the Beauford ancestors and according to George, Victoria's eldest brother, his skeleton was still inside the armour; but the girls only half believed him.

Unexpectedly, it was George who awaited Leila when she came back downstairs. Looking surprisingly grown up in a dark suit and tie and stiff collar, he grinned at her in his usual friendly way.

'Vicky said I was to come and find you. Happy Birthday, by the way!'

He shoved a small parcel into her hands. 'It's from me and Vaughan and Robert!' he said with a shrug. 'Not much, I'm afraid, but Vicky said you hadn't got one!'

Speechless as much with excitement as with astonishment at this strangely affable George, who usually considered himself far too grown up even to notice her and his sister, Leila tore off the wrapping to find a slim, beribboned box holding a fountain pen. She did not have one and, as Victoria knew, she had longed to own one. Impulsively, she reached up and kissed George's cheek. At the advanced age of eighteen, the eldest of the Beauford boys was now nudging five foot ten, and Leila was obliged to stand on tiptoe. Victoria, coming out of the drawing room into the hall, saw the embrace and clapping her hands, chanted the nursery rhyme: *'Georgie Porgie, pudding and pie, kissed the girls and made them cry!'*

Although his little sister could be cheeky at times, George was well aware that she adored him and knew she was going to miss him when he departed to Ceylon in a week or two's time.

'I'll make you cry if you don't shut up, Titch!' he said, but he was smiling as he strode off in the direction of the dining room.

Vicky flung her arms round Leila and they hugged each other as they exchanged birthday greetings. Vicky then linked her arm in Leila's.

'You look so pretty, Leila,' she said. 'I love your dress. I expect your mother made it, didn't she? I don't much like mine! Mother bought it in London but I hate, hate, *hate* green and I so much wanted a blue one.'

'Doesn't she know what your favourite colour is?' Leila asked in a surprised tone as Victoria led her past her father's study and into the huge panelled room known as the ballroom. Not that they ever had balls there any more, Victoria had told Leila, although they were regular occurrences before the war. 'It's because so many of Mother's and Papa's friends got killed,' she had explained. 'Papa always says how lucky he was only to lose his toes.'

Living as the children did in the country, neither Victoria nor Leila saw much of the aftermath of the four years of fighting.

They were not privy to newspapers, which only the grown-ups read, and they saw nothing of the disabled, out of work, bitter men on the streets of London, trying to earn a pittance selling matches and the like, nor those desperate for work, standing in queues for the dole. Leila's first-hand sight of the war casualties had happened only once, shortly after the war had ended. Her father had taken her with him to visit an army officer in a Brighton nursing home. It had had a profound effect upon her; young though she had been, she never forgot the sight of the pale, good-looking young man lying in a high hospital bed. Balanced on top of the white sheet covering him was a little wooden gadget holding a small tube reaching to his mouth, on the end of which was a cigarette. He was thus able to smoke the cigarette without using his hands. Only his eyes had moved because, her father had told her, the poor fellow had been paralysed by a piece of shrapnel from a German shell. He was a former pupil of her father's and was a keen sportsman before he had joined the army in France at the age of seventeen to fight the invading Germans.

The patient, who her father addressed as 'young James', didn't return Leila's pitying smile, but his eyes – a deep tortured brown – followed her wherever she moved. She had not known the word 'wistful' or she would have described him so to her mother when she returned home. 'You mustn't cry, my darling,' her mother had said as she tucked Leila into bed and heard her prayers. 'Your soldier's life was saved; and Daddy says he is being well cared for in a really good nursing home.'

But she had been too young to be able to explain that she had actually felt his despair because he would never walk again, or, indeed, have a little girl like her to kiss him goodnight.

Such memories were far from Leila's mind now as she surveyed the big brightly lit ballroom. A dozen or so children in party frocks, only one of whom Leila recognized, were playing Blind Man's Buff in the centre of the room. On seats around the wall, in sombre greys, browns and navy blues, sat a number of women busy chatting amongst themselves who, seeing Leila's gaze, Victoria explained were governesses or nannies.

'Mother doesn't want them in the drawing room and Mrs Mount wouldn't want them in the kitchen and Mother says they must come in here to make sure all of us children are behaving properly!' She pointed to a rounded figure in grey bombazine. 'There's Nanny!' she giggled. 'She's wearing her Sunday dress!'

There was no chance of further conversation as the two birthday girls were pulled into the centre of the group to play Pass the Parcel. Tea followed the games, with the promised multicoloured jellies, fancy biscuits and a huge chocolate iced birthday cake with both Victoria's and Leila's names on it. Victoria's brothers joined the younger children in order to have a share in the feast and remained to see the visiting conjuror. It was not until then that Victoria's parents put in an appearance. Their presence immediately dampened the somewhat overexcited chatter of the children and it was soon time for the party to come to an end, the invitations having stated that guests should be collected by six o'clock. Parents, and family chauffeurs, arrived on time.

Harold Varney was waiting for Leila to appear from amongst the children descending the wide staircase. Most were wearing their hooded capes and were struggling to free themselves from their governesses' restraining hands. As he stood in the draughty hall he shivered, thinking ruefully that he should have heeded Copper's request for him to wear an overcoat. The heavy downpour earlier had brought a chill to the July evening and he'd felt quite cold as he'd driven up the hill from the village in the old Ford. He turned when he felt a light touch on his elbow.

'I do hope I'm not late, Sir Aubrey,' the young woman said regarding him apologetically. 'The invitation said six o'clock but . . .' She laughed prettily. 'I'm afraid I forgot the time. I'm Lavinia Holborn, by the way and my daughter, DeeDee, is at school with your Victoria.' Seeing the look of bewilderment on Harold's face, she laughed again and added: 'We haven't met yet, Sir Aubrey. We only moved to Elmsfield last month. I've met your wife, of course, and I believe your mother knows mine – Agnes Fortescue? The old dears are both widows of baronets so they have lots in common . . .'

She would have continued in her breathless outspoken manner had Harold not interrupted. 'I'm afraid you are mistaken, Mrs Holborn. My name is Harold Varney and my daughter is Leila. Sir Aubrey Beauford is Victoria's father.'

Far from being embarrassed by her faux pas, Lavinia Holborn laughed.

'Trust me!' she said brightly. 'My husband says I'm absolutely hopeless jumping into things without thinking what I'm doing. Do please forgive me! It's just that when I arrived and saw you standing here, I thought you must be Sir Aubrey because Victoria is so like you . . . I mean you both have that odd little way of lifting your eyebrows!' She drew a deep sigh. 'Oh, dear, there I go again, making personal remarks when I should know better. Whatever would my nanny have said?'

Harold hastened to reassure the charming young woman standing beside him. He was now aware who she was. The daughter, Dorothy, who she referred to as DeeDee, he had met when she'd come to the school with her father, who was considering enrolling her next term. He'd found him to be a delightful, extremely well-educated man who had been just old enough to serve in the Royal Flying Corps. He had stayed in Harold's study, where they discovered they had much in common. He had emerged from his wartime experiences a far more enlightened individual than many of his class, who would not have considered crossing the social boundaries. His wife, Lavinia, he had told Harold, was longing to follow in the footsteps of her favourite novelist, Rebecca West. She, too, had a wider outlook on life than that of her society friends.

It was not surprising, Harold had thought, that Lady Beauford had soon introduced herself to the new arrivals in the neighbourhood and that little Dorothy had been invited to Victoria's party.

Knowing how much Copper would like the Holborns, especially the authoress, because she herself was such an avid reader and also loved Rebecca West's novels, Harold was about to invite her to tea when a small figure came flying down the stairs and Leila threw herself into his arms. After a quick hug, he put her back on her feet and was about to introduce her to his companion when her own small daughter, DeeDee, also arrived.

'By the look of you, you've both had a wonderful time!' he said, retying the neck cords of Leila's velvet cape, which had somehow managed to come loose. As he was performing this task, Aubrey Beauford stepped forward and put a hand on his shoulder.

'Can I offer you a quick one, Varney?' he asked hospitably. He liked the headmaster very much – found him an intelligent conversationalist and would have made a closer friend of him had Frances not deplored the very idea of inviting someone of a schoolmaster's social standing to the house.

'Chatting to him – if you must – when he fetches or collects the child when she comes to play with Victoria is one thing, Aubrey, but asking him to drinks . . . well, really!' had been her comment.

Although Aubrey had long since decided his life was a lot easier when he let his domineering wife have her own way, occasionally he would stand his ground, as he did in this instance. If Frances complained, he would point out that she herself had permitted the schoolmaster's daughter to be guest of honour at their daughter's birthday party. Not, Aubrey thought wryly, that Victoria would have given her a single moment's peace had she refused to do so.

Harold declined his offer. He knew Copper was on tenter-hooks at home, waiting to hear how Leila had enjoyed the event. As it was, she had set aside her longing to arrange a birthday party herself for Leila – something she had been planning for weeks before Leila, innocent of such plans, produced the invitation to Victoria's party. It was typical of his wife's unselfishness that she put their daughter's pref-erences before her own and made no mention of her own disappointment.

He was not surprised therefore to see Copper waiting at the front door as he parked the Ford outside Foxhole Cottage. Leila ran up the path and flung herself into her mother's arms, nearly dropping the basket of birthday presents she had received, amongst them George's fountain pen.

'I shall treasure it always, for ever and ever until I die!' she declared, as her mother led her into the sitting room, her father following close behind. She continued to chatter, announcing that George, who she'd once thought a horrible tease, had changed – perhaps because he had just left Eton and was no longer a schoolboy. Maybe one day she would marry him if he went on getting nicer, she declared. Then she and Vicky would be real sisters – well, sisters-in-law.

Vicky had told her a secret about George – that he was going to go and live with his godfather in a place called Ceylon and was going to plant tea. Vicky hadn't known how you could possibly plant tea but her mother wouldn't talk about it because she didn't want him to go; and her daddy had said it would be a good adventure for him. Relating this now to her parents, she added with a small frown of perplexity:

'Vicky's father said it would untie his mother's apron strings. But Lady Beauford doesn't wear aprons,' she added innocently whilst her parents doubled over laughing.

Harold and his wife were still smiling as Copper went into the kitchen to make Leila a cup of cocoa. They were unconcerned about their six-year-old's statement that she was going to marry George one day so she and Vicky could be 'sisters'. They were both aware that juvenile friendships seldom lasted twenty years, beside which, the girls' lives would inevitably take them in different directions. When Victoria left her boarding school she would almost certainly be presented at court and would eventually marry a rich young man. If Leila followed the career Harold believed could be her choice, she might take a shorthand and typewriting course when she left school and find work as a secretary to the local Elmsfield solicitor or doctor and maybe marry a young legal or medical partner. On the other hand, Copper thought Leila might like to train as a nurse like herself as she had a very caring nature. But whatever she chose to do, she would not be moving in the same circles as Victoria Beauford.

Leila's future was not however, the subject of conversation between her parents after Copper had cleared away their supper dishes and Leila was in bed. They employed a charlady to clean the house and who took home the laundry to wash and iron, but Harold's salary could not run to the employment of a cook-general. Copper made no complaint, as she loved cooking, baking in particular, and was good at what she produced.

'Something very odd happened at the Hall this evening, my dear!' he said, laying his newspaper down on his lap. Copper was knitting a warm jersey for Leila to wear in the garden next winter, and she let her needles rest whilst she gave Harold her full attention. She knew by the tone of his voice that whatever he was about to tell her was preying on his mind, and he had only been waiting for a moment when they would not be interrupted before he confided in her.

He proceeded to tell her about the pretty young authoress who had momentarily mistaken him for Sir Aubrey Beauford.

'I would have taken it as a simple mistake seeing the good lady had never met him,' Harold told Copper, his brows drawn

down in a puzzled frown. 'I was standing there in the hall in
my suit so obviously I didn't look like the butler or one of the
servants. But then—' He broke off for a moment, his eyes
thoughtful, and his head on one side as he considered the matter.
For some reason, he found he did not after all really wish to
impart his concerns in detail to Copper. Yet not to do so would
give them more importance than they deserved.

'It's just that she – the authoress – thought I must be Victoria's
father because of the resemblance . . . she said we each have one
eyebrow higher than the other! Of course, I thought she was
just making it up, but . . . to tell you the truth, I am beginning
to think she's right . . .' He hesitated, even more reluctant to give
voice to his fears.

Copper burst out laughing. 'Really, my darling, you should
be the author, not this Mrs Whatever-her-name is. Matching
eyebrows! Sounds like something out of one of Sherlock
Holmes' mystery stories.' She paused before adding on a more
serious note: 'I know one of your eyebrows is a bit higher than
the other but I dare say lots of other people's are too. I read
somewhere that no one's face is identical on both sides. Anyway,
I've certainly never noticed anything odd about Victoria's
eyebrows. For heaven's sake, Harold, whatever next!'

Harold's taut expression did not change. 'I know it must
sound silly to you, dearest, but I looked at little Victoria's face
as she waved us goodbye and –' his voice dropped almost to
a whisper – 'I'm almost certain she does have an eyebrow like
mine. I mean, the light was behind her and she was waving
her arms about but—'

He stopped, wishing he had not after all confided these suspicions to his wife, although he had sounded far more vague
about his observation of Victoria than he'd actually been. He'd
seen for a certainty that the child did have a slightly raised
eyebrow, albeit hers was the right one and his was the left. But
it wasn't just that. Writers were by nature of their work keen
observers. Mrs Holborn must have seen something else – the
shape of his face, his head, his colouring – to mistake him for
Victoria's father.

As he had driven Leila home, only half-listening to her
excited account of the birthday party, he had been trying to
deny the possibility of anything so bizarre as a resemblance
between him and the Beauford child. Yes, she had been born

at the same time as Leila in the same hospital. Not that Copper could possibly have left with the wrong baby. Had he not been there within an hour of Leila's birth? Held her in his arms? Marvelled at the tiny fingers and toes; smiled at the wisps of hair on her otherwise bald head. Then the nurse had taken her away and he'd not seen her again until the following morning when Copper had handed the bundle in her arms to him to hold. He had been enchanted all over again, marvelling at the changes since birth even a few hours could make. 'Even her hair colour has changed from dark to fair,' he'd said, his heart bursting with love and pride.

Now he couldn't get the memory out of his mind. Leila was fair-haired – always had been; Victoria was dark-haired . . . like him. Both babies were born in the same hospital on the same night. Was there a possibility, however, remote, that they could have been accidentally exchanged? His stomach knotted painfully at the mere thought.

Copper, however, clearly had no such terrible suspicions. On the contrary, she was smiling as she picked up her knitting once more and proceeded to work again.

'Honestly, Harold, do you think I wouldn't have noticed if there had been even the slightest resemblance between you and Vicky? Besides, how could there be? I don't know what's got into you! Whatever it is, my darling, put it out of your mind. Hundreds of people have snub noses or cleft chins or widow's peaks or whatever. Even if Victoria does have uneven eyebrows like yours, it doesn't mean anything.' A little smile played at the corners of her mouth as she looked up at her husband. 'It would only mean something if, unbeknownst to me, you had had a secret love affair with Lady Beauford – and somehow I don't think you would have fancied that!'

It was Harold's turn to smile, his heart lifting a little as he allowed himself to believe his wife's insistence that he was being absurd. He even attempted to lighten his own mood still further with a teasing remark.

'Don't you be so sure of yourself, young lady!' he said as he got up and went across the room to kiss her. 'I'll have you know I've secretly fancied that gorgeous woman all my life!'

So his kisses were mingled with their joint laughter and for the present, Harold was able to push his ugly fears firmly to the back of his mind.

Six

It was not Nanny's habit to listen to the servants' gossip but for once she did so as Sally, the parlourmaid, talked excitedly about the authoress, Lavinia Holborn, who had called the previous evening to collect her daughter, one of Miss Victoria's birthday guests. It so happened that Nanny had only a month ago chosen a novel by Lavinia Holborn from Boots' lending library. The girl who'd served her had recommended the romantic novel, which she said was in the style of Ruby M. Ayres.

Since they were not literary works and had little educational value, Nanny always covered the lurid jackets of these romantic novels with brown paper so that Lady Beauford would not happen upon one and think her ridiculous to be reading love stories at her advanced age. In point of fact, she did not care for Sir Aubrey's wife and had continued in service only because of her love for his children.

Sally was still chattering excitedly as she put her eleven o'clock cup of cocoa on the schoolroom table.

'You know Jenny as comes up to the Hall to help when there's a party? Well, me and her was tidying up after the party and guess what she told me, Nanny . . .'

Nanny disapproved of gossip and seldom listened to it, but there was no stopping Sally. Jenny had been upstairs helping the young ladies find their cloaks and such after Miss Victoria's party, she related, and she'd been in the front hall downstairs when the authoress had mistaken the headmaster for Sir Aubrey.

'It was Miss Victoria having the same funny eyebrow as what the headmaster's got!' Sally ended breathlessly. 'And Jenny says as how that's quite right, and Nanny . . .' She paused once more for breath. 'Jenny thinks her, Miss Victoria and Miss Leila got mixed when they was born and she said as how I mustn't tell no one as I might get her into trouble for telling me and—'

'No more you should be, Sally!' Nanny broke in sharply. 'You should know better than to listen to such nonsense. Now off you go before my cocoa gets cold.'

Leaving Nanny to her cocoa, Sally went back downstairs disappointed that Nanny had not shared her interest in the astonishing possibility of the little girls' parentage. She nearly collided with her mistress, who gave her a reproving stare.

'You may now be a parlourmaid, Sally, for which eleva-tion, I might say, you have Crawford, not me, to thank, but that does *not* entitle you to use the front staircase. Now go back up and use the back staircase, and don't let me see you coming down this way again – unless your duties demand it!'

Sally muttered an apology which, once she had pushed her way through the green-baize door to the basement, quickly changed to calling her mistress 'a stuck-up ballyrag'. She informed Mrs Mount that if the mistress didn't speak to her more civilly she might well give in her notice and apply for the job that was going at the greengrocer's. Their former employee, a young lad from the orphanage, had joined the army towards the end of the war when manpower was getting so short, and had suffered from gas poisoning ever since. A month ago he'd died and Mr Jenkins, the greengrocer, had decided to replace him with a strong girl who would not be expecting the same wage.

'Carting vegetables about's dirty work!' said Mrs Mount as she drizzled olive oil into the mayonnaise she was making. 'No fancy uniform like you're wearing, what you're so proud of!'

Sally grinned. 'I know that, Mrs Mount, but there's things to be said for a job like that. Eight in the morning to six at night – now that would be a right treat.' She hesitated, her cheeks colouring as she added self-consciously: 'It wouldn't half please my boyfriend, Sid. He gets right fed up when I'm on duty here and he can't take me into Haywards Heath to the flicks. It was Charlie Chaplin last week and he said he'd take that Mavis from next door if I couldn't go!'

The cook paused in her beating to look at the pretty young girl standing in the doorway. Sally had been with the family for several years and Mrs Mount really liked the cheerful, good-tempered little Irish maid. She'd be sorry to see her leave although she couldn't blame her for wanting to do so. The mistress was a right tyrant – always complaining and never so much as a friendly smile when she came down in the mornings to plan the day's menu.

The master was a different kettle of fish – ever ready with praise for the dishes she baked; said her soufflés were the best he'd ever tasted, and no cook ever made a better steak and kidney pudding than the ones she made him. She stayed in service mostly for the master but also for the children who she'd watched grow up since birth. There was Master George, almost a man now and a fine young gentleman – just beginning to take note of the girls! She'd seen him watching young Sally's skirt blowing in the wind when she was hanging up the washing! Master Vaughan was the quiet one – used to like to sit on her knee and have a cuddle when he was younger – something the poor child never got from his mother for all Lady Beauford was fond of all three boys. Not so keen on Miss Victoria, though – jealous of the way the master doted on her, she supposed. Just as well he did or Miss Victoria might not have been such a happy little girl – mischievous, of course, but bright as a button!

By now it was nearly half past eleven. The vegetables were ready prepared for boiling; the steak and kidney pie was in the oven along with the rice pudding and the master's favourite, a nice apple Charlotte, so she could sit down at the scrubbed wooden table and enjoy a cup of tea with Sally. Mr Crawford was in his pantry cleaning silver ready for the weekend visitors – fishing friends of the master's; so for the next five minutes she and Sally could gossip to their hearts' content. As she said to her now, down here in the kitchen, she didn't get to know as much of what went on upstairs as did Mr Crawford and the maids. She poured out two steaming cups of tea and when she and Sally were both seated she asked the girl to bring her up to date.

Sally needed no second bidding. She had not yet recovered from yesterday's excitement of seeing a real, live lady novelist. Mrs Mount preferred the weekly magazines to books, which took up too much of her time and concentration. She liked the love stories, some of which were serialized by writers like that new young lady author, Denise Chesterton, in the weekly

Christian Novels Library, but couldn't be bothered with a whole book.

She was not, however, thinking of books or love stories when Sally came to the point where the novelist had mistaken Miss Leila's father for the master.

'Jenny heard Mrs Holborn remark that Miss Victoria and her father had the same eyebrows which is why she'd mistaken him for Miss Victoria's father!' Seeing the look of disbelief on the cook's face, Sally added earnestly: 'Honest, Mrs Mount, Jenny said she heard her plain as I hear you now. My mum, who was in service like me afore she got married, she said it's rude to remark on what people look like, but Jenny said the schoolmaster didn't seem to mind none.'

'A load of nonsense if you ask me,' Mrs Mount said putting down her teacup and resting her elbow on the tabletop, chin in hand. She was not nearly so interested in the behaviour of the authoress as in the remark she'd made. She had never met the schoolmaster so she had no idea what he looked like, but this reference to the likeness to Miss Victoria had suddenly brought to mind the day six years ago just before the outbreak of war was announced. The mistress, newly arrived from London, had to be rushed into Elmsfield Cottage Hospital when she went into labour. Of course, they'd all said at the time the master should never have insisted on her travelling in her condition, but the baby wasn't due for several weeks and he'd been concerned about the dangers there could be in the city if war broke out. Be that as it was, the mistress had had her baby in the local hospital the night there'd been that awful train accident and Elmsfield Cottage Hospital had had to take the overflow from Burgess General.

As her memories returned they became more vivid. The housekeeper had stayed in town to look after the house in Eaton Terrace for the master so it was Ellen, the mistress' personal maid, who was sent for to take nightclothes and toiletries and the like down to the hospital. Next thing, it had been sheets and pillowcases wanted as being so busy, the hospital had run short and the mistress wasn't having any cotton or twill sheets to lie on when she was accustomed to linen! It was bedlam down there, Ellen had related in one of her rare moments of relaxation with the servants – nurses and doctors and porters all running round like scalded cats and the mistress ringing her bell all the time and no one with the time to mollycoddle her or the other patients what with some of the train casualties dying in the tiny operating theatre.

Mrs Mount now recalled quite clearly the maid's white, shocked face when she related that such was the shortage of nurses, Matron had actually asked her if she would go into the room next to the mistress' and get whatever the patient was wanting. Not that Ellen had been able to help because the lady in there, who she was told later was the headmaster's wife, was asking for her baby. One of the nurses had taken it away to be washed and weighed but hadn't brought it back. The poor soul feared it might have died! Ellen had managed to find out that it was perfectly all right; that both this lady's baby and the mistress' little girl had been put in cots in the room they called the nursery and someone would take the babies to them when there was time.

It was this part of Ellen's account which had remained foremost in Mrs Mount's memory and was now dancing in circles in her brain. Suppose – just suppose, she thought, that those two babies had got muddled up and been given to the wrong mothers? Would a mother know if the baby handed to her was hers; was not in fact the one she had given birth to? It was twenty-six years since she herself had given birth to her only daughter. She had had the child at home and could still recall the pain and the kindly midwife giving her twenty drops of laudanum to ease the birth. Where the woman had obtained it, neither Mrs Mount nor her husband had known but they had rewarded her the best they could for the relief it had given. After the baby was born, she'd been only half-conscious whilst the midwife had washed the infant and returned it to her. Would she, she now asked herself, have known if that small red wrinkled infant had not been the one she had birthed? *Would the mistress and the headmaster's wife have known they had the wrong babies?*

The more Mrs Mount considered the matter, the more anxious she became. Was she the only person who suspected the dreadful mistake which could have occurred? Clearly Sally had not made any such connection and was only interested in the gaffe her favourite authoress had made. Was she herself getting soft in the head even imagining such a possibility? If by some extraordinary chance she was right, the consequences could be appalling. It would be a shocking scandal, and in any event, what could be done about it?

Mindful that her heart was palpitating and that she had allowed her thoughts to run into the realms of a nightmare, she decided there and then that she was being unreasonably fanciful. People were always imagining likenesses that did not exist. Even the elderly Mr Crawford let his hair down one Christmas and had remarked that Sally looked a bit like the film star Theda Bara, which was absolute nonsense. There was nothing 'vampish' about young Sally.

Aware that her mind was wandering, Mrs Mount drew a deep breath and straightened her back as if it might stiffen her decision to keep her suspicions entirely to herself. They were, after all, only suspicions, and if they were wrong, she could be in a very great deal of trouble were they to get to the ears of her employers. Like as not she would lose her job, which she could ill afford to do, her wage being quite a bit higher than the five pounds a month that was customary, having been in the Beaufords' employment for all of twenty-six years now. Half the money she earned went each month to her unmarried sister who looked after their eighty-year-old mother in their tiny flat. Now in her dotage and suffering from dementia, she had to be cared for day and night, so there was no chance her sister could go out to work. Thus Mrs Mount was the sole provider as there was no income other than the pittance of a war pension handed out by the army after their father was killed in the Boer War.

No, she told herself now, there was no reason for her to put her job and her family in jeopardy. It certainly wouldn't earn her any thanks and could only cause a great deal of anguish if what she now suspected turned out to be the truth. Those two poor little girls' lives would be turned upside down, and as for their parents – well, the master for one would be devastated. He adored Miss Victoria and there was no way she was going to allow it to be her fault if his heart was broken. If for that reason alone, her lips were sealed.

When Sally went into the kitchen at four o'clock, she found Cook fast asleep with her apron over her head. She woke her gently with the reminder that the mistress would be ringing for her afternoon tea at any minute, and that she was just about to take a tray up to the schoolroom for Nanny. Joseph was to drive her down to the village to fetch Miss Victoria at five o'clock from the Varneys' house, where she had gone to play with her friend after school.

'Thought you might want to be woke, Mrs Mount,' she said apologetically, 'seeing as how the master said there'd be unexpected visitors for lunch tomorrow and could they have Cook's jugged hare, please!'

Mrs Mount rose stiffly from her chair. Although much was already prepared for tonight's dinner, she still had the devils-on-horseback to prepare for the savoury, and the garden peas to shell for the master's favourite soup. Now she must find time to fetch the hares from the cold store where they were hanging, skin and joint them, so she could get the big cast-iron casserole on first thing in the morning.

As Sally went upstairs to draw the curtains and turn down the beds, Mrs Mount set about her work, the possible hospital mix-up tucked far to the back of her mind. The butler, who had been upstairs seeing that the decanters were properly filled and the drawing room was tidy, kept her thoughts from straying as he regaled her with a list of the master's guests who were coming for the fishing weekend. Two of the gentlemen would have their wives, he informed her, so there would be fourteen extra on the Saturday. Three of the gentlemen would be driving themselves but four were bringing their chauffeurs so Joseph would have to put up camp beds for them in his quarters over the stables. One of the titled ladies coming was bringing her own maid – he'd warned Ellen – so there would be a great deal of extra work for all the staff.

He looked at Mrs Mount's anxious face but before she could say anything, he added: 'The master said he realized this would all be a bit much for you, Mrs Mount, and he's telling the mistress she must get extra help in from the village. Sally will know of some girls who can help in the kitchen. Her young man lives in Elmsfield, doesn't he? And then there are those two women you had up last time and that girl, Jenny. He said to tell you he was sorry it was such last-minute notice.'

It wasn't the first time such a thing had happened and wouldn't be the last, Mrs Mount said. The master was always very generous with tips after a busy weekend and of course the guests left tips, too; so such a weekend did benefit their finances. Joe, the under-gardener, would come indoors and act as boot boy and like as not, sort out the gentlemen's fishing tackle for them. Young Doreen, the kitchen maid, was coming back from her annual holiday next day and Mr Crawford now told her that two of the Eaton Terrace staff would be coming down from London on the train to lend a hand.

Tiring as such weekends were here at Farlington Hall, Mrs Mount secretly enjoyed them. Sometimes, one or two of the gentlemen would come down to the kitchen after they'd had a few brandies, and sit themselves at the table with their glasses half full and shower her with compliments about her food. She was a good cook and when she wanted she was more than just good. A guest had once told her he'd not eaten better at Buckingham Palace when he'd dined at the King's table. They'd raise their glasses to her and being somewhat merry, would joke a bit freely, saying they were going to divorce their wives and marry her so they could eat as well every day.

No, she didn't really mind the fact that she would be up to her eyes over the weekend. When dinner was over tonight, she'd sit down and start making a list of the provisions she would need. No meat other than two fine hares the game-keeper had brought in last Wednesday now hanging in the game safe, and a fine twenty-pound salmon on the cold marble slab in her larder which had been put there two days ago after the master's return from a three-day fishing trip on a friend's estate on the River Spey.

Mrs Mount nodded thinking happily to herself that the two days hanging the hares had had would be just right this warm weather – a bit smelly, perhaps, but that was the way the master liked them, well marinated in his second-best port! With a contented smile, she went to get the tall basket of garden peas Joe had brought up to the house that morning to pod, cook and push through the sieve for the master's soup. Her concerns about the two little girls' likeness to each other's parents were now very far from her mind.

Seven

It was a bitterly cold January day and Leila had been immensely pleased when her father decided to leave school early and she was therefore able to come home in the car with him in preference to her daily walk to and from school. She was sitting now in her father's armchair by the fire being taught by her mother how to knit. The wool Copper had given her was a bright cheerful red and not too many stitches were dropped as the scarf Leila was attempting to knit for her favourite doll, to her delight, measured several inches long.

In the middle of the room, Harold Varney sat at the table marking exercise books. This was a task he normally did at school after the pupils had left, but the extreme cold and dark, rain-threatening sky had prompted him to break his routine and drive his small daughter home. Every now and again, he looked up from the books, a frown creasing his forehead as he stared at Leila's blonde hair shining in the lamplight as she bent over her task. Occasionally, he would glance at his wife's head, wishing she had not followed fashion and cut short her beautiful waist-length hair. But that was not now the cause of his present concern.

Six whole months had passed since the afternoon when the author had assumed he was Victoria Beauford's father, a day he now wished fervently he could forget. He would also like to be able to forget that day at Elmsfield Hospital when, all too easily now, he could recall looking at the baby on his second visit and saying to Copper how remarkable it was that newborn infants could change so quickly in a matter of hours. The remark had had no great significance at the time and Copper had thought nothing of it; but ever since Lavinia

Holborn's mistake he couldn't forget it. All autumn it had haunted his day and night thoughts as well as his appetite.

Throughout the festivities, he'd tried to put his fears out of his mind. Apart from Christmas Day itself, which they had spent quietly at home together with Copper's widowed mother who was visiting them from Scotland, he'd managed to keep his anxiety at bay. But once his mother-in-law had left and the fancy-dress ball up at Farlington Hall was over, his nightmare thoughts returned and actually made him impotent. It was then Copper decided to prise the truth from him. Once again, she refused adamantly to take such suspicions seriously.

Whoever had heard of such a thing as two babies switched at birth so the parents were given the wrong child! Yes, it was true, she said, that Leila did not take after either himself or her but one had only to look at the wedding photograph he'd had especially coloured for her thirtieth birthday to see that Leila with her fair hair and blue eyes took after Copper's second cousin – the one who lived in Australia. As for Victoria Beauford, she looked a twin to her middle brother, Vaughan. Their noses were identical even though the boy's hair was not as dark a brown as Victoria's or 'brassy blonde' like his mother's. But in spite of all these comments, his fears would not go away. Leila's voice now brought his attention back to the present.

'Daddy, why do you keep staring at me? You're always doing it and it makes me feel I'm doing something wrong.'

Before Harold could think of a reply to Leila's accusation, Copper said quickly: 'It's because you're growing so pretty, darling. We can't take our eyes off you!'

Leila's doubts changed to smiles. 'Vicky says you keep telling me I'm pretty and nice because you haven't got any other children to spoil. She has to share her mother with George and Vaughan and Robert so that's why Vicky doesn't get a lot of hugs and kisses and compliments from her. But she does get lots from her father. Vicky says it's because she's his favourite.'

'Parents don't have favourites!' Copper said, echoing her own mother when she had complained as a child her parents thought more of her brother, Bertie, than they did of her. Poor Bertie had joined the Royal Navy at the start of the war and had lost his life when his ship was torpedoed by the Germans.

Relieved to have his true reasons for speculating about his daughter's parentage diverted, Harold was more than a little grateful to his wife for her tactful intervention. He now joined in the friendly debate as to whether mothers and fathers should kiss and cuddle their sons who, Leila maintained, probably wouldn't like it once they'd stopped being babies.

'Robert said boys are different. They aren't soppy like girls and they don't cry when they fall over like Vicky and me do.'

'Like Vicky and *I* do!' Harold corrected automatically. ' "Me" can't fall over!'

'Me can! Me fell over in the playground this morning. Look!' She lifted her skirt and pointed to a small graze, her blue eyes twinkling.

'Teatime in five minutes!' Copper intervened, hiding her smiles as she told her small daughter not to be cheeky.

'You're a minx, young lady!' Harold said, pushing back his chair so that Leila could curl up on his lap. 'Now tell me about your homework. Has Miss Robinson given you any sums to do?'

The number of children now attending Elmsfield Village School had increased in the last two years, and he had been permitted to engage an elderly spinster to look after the five- and six-year-olds. Miss Robinson, though now in her late sixties, was a remarkably fine teacher and the children loved her.

Whilst Leila was rattling off a list of spelling words to learn and sums she had to do, he was not really listening. All he could think of was the one certain fact – he could never, ever agree to be parted from this child. He would as soon be parted from his beloved wife. What puzzled him was his wife's ability to adopt a mental state of denial. Somehow, he supposed, she had managed to convince herself that the children's likenesses were simply figures of his imagination. When he tried to make her understand the seriousness of the situation, she regarded him pityingly as if he was overworked and not thinking straight. Perhaps after all he should try to delude himself, or at least put the awful notion to the back of his mind until – God forbid – there came a time when he would be forced to face the truth.

Copper's announcement that tea was ready sent Leila flying off his lap and on to her chair at the table. There was always something especially nice at teatime when she came home after school – drop scones or hot buttered toast or muffins with chocolate or cherry cake for afters. Her mother was a wonderful cook, which fact she had related to Vicky's Mrs Mount who got paid for her hard work, which, Leila thought, was a bit unfair on her mother who didn't get paid!

'I get paid with love!' her mother had told her when she'd voiced her feelings, which remark Leila found quite satisfying since poor Mrs Mount didn't have a husband to love her. Unfortunately George, who used to tell the cook he adored her when she baked him nice things for his tuck box when he was away at school, was now a long way away in a strange country, so neither she nor Mrs Mount ever saw him at the Hall. But Leila's affections remained steadfast and she still thought she might marry him one day.

Last week, when she and Vicky were exchanging secrets, which was always the first thing they did whenever they were on their own, Vicky said she had decided not to get married or have babies. She had stolen Sally's *Daily Mirror* and read all about a young woman who had got drowned in a river but that was not the important part. The exciting part was that before she died, she went to a real college in Oxford like the one her daddy had been to, only for girls.

Vicky said her mother had insisted girls weren't allowed to go to colleges, so she was telling fibs. She really, really wanted to go to university because Miss Robinson had told her you had to have something called a degree before you could become a vet – and that's what she wanted to be when she was old enough. If she could have whatever she wanted, she had told Leila, she would have six horses, twenty dogs and ten cats but they only had their ponies and her father's gun dog because her mother said it was bad enough moving children and staff to and from London without a lot of animals too. Victoria had further told her that Robert wanted to go to university because he wanted to become the Prime Minister instead of Lloyd George and rule the country, and if her brothers went, Vicky stated, she would, too, even if she was a girl.

Having related all this to her father, Harold replied that he fully believed Victoria showed enough promise for her age to be certain of getting into one of the four Oxford colleges that were for women.

'What about me, Daddy? Can I go with Vicky?' Leila now asked her father.

Harold caught his breath. His darling girl did not show the same ability to absorb and store knowledge as her little friend; but he hated the thought of undermining her present self-confidence.

'We'll have to see how you both get on at big school!' he prevaricated. 'Some people are good at some things and others at different things. Now look at you, sweetheart – you're becoming a really splendid knitter. Is that a scarf you are making for your doll?'

Easily diverted, Leila gave the future no further thought; but that night, all Harold's thoughts returned in force to torment him. If heredity was anything to go by, Victoria should indeed have inherited his ability to learn and to retain knowledge whereas Aubrey Beauford, decent enough chap though he was, could not be considered a very erudite fellow. A rowing blue, he had got into university on the strength of his sporting abilities, not his academic achievements, as he had laughingly informed Harold while they were enjoying a beer together down at the Fox and Vixen. The more Harold lay there in the darkness thinking about it, the more similar in character did his gentle, good-humoured, caring little daughter seem to be to the baronet. Even were he to give Leila private coaching, he could not imagine her as a future academic.

Copper lay beside her husband feigning sleep. She was in no doubt as to what fears were tormenting him – fears she pretended not to share lest they increased his own. Although she tried very hard not to do so, when Victoria came to tea, and reached out to take a biscuit off the plate, she'd been shocked to notice that the child's hands were replicas of Harold's. Unlike most people, his ring finger was as long as his middle finger – and so was Victoria's. She had noticed, too, that the aquiline shape of their noses was similar despite Victoria's being so much smaller.

Now, whenever she saw the little girl she tried hard not to look too closely at her. If her own and Harold's fears were verified, what would be the outcome? Would the Beaufords want to claim Leila as their own? One thing was certain – no way would she allow Lady Beauford to take Leila away from her. If such a thing were ever to become likely, she would run away – take Leila to some far-distant country where they could never be found. Harold adored his daughter and would surely never agree to losing her. Nor, hopefully, would Lady Beauford be willing to part with her child. She did have three other children but they were boys; Victoria was her only girl ...

Unable to find the comfort of sleep, Copper's thoughts continued to torment her until the early hours of the morning when sheer exhaustion brought an end to her torment. She longed to share her fears with Harold but knew that doing so would somehow make them even more real. For the same reason, she had not asked Harold what was wrong when he tried but failed to make love to her. Their close relationship had been a physical as well as a mental one and if the regularity of their sex life had been unadventurous, it had suited them both for their love-making to be routine. Now, although Harold took her in his arms as always and began kissing her with all his usual passion, he would suddenly draw away from her and with an exaggerated sigh, announce that he was really too tired to make love and needed sleep.

The fact that Copper knew he was not asleep, despite his exaggeratedly deep breathing, endorsed her fears that he had something so disturbing on his mind – so unsettling – that it affected him physically and he was simply unable to sustain his erection because of it. It was not as if he had any worries at school, where his job was secure. Nor had he any money worries, since their income, though small, was more than sufficient for their needs. She even found herself wishing that he did have something to worry about – other than the horribly disturbing discovery concerning the two little girls. She wanted desperately to be able to tell him of her own anxiety; to have him tell her she was being ridiculously imaginative and must put her suspicions aside once and for all. But this was something she dared not do.

For the present, she decided, she must take one day at a time. If she busied herself with her household activities she might manage to convince herself that she was indeed being ridiculously imaginative and that her night-time fears were nothing less than absurd.

Eight

1922

Frances Beauford sat in the taxi taking her from Victoria Station to Park Lane wishing that she had worn her new apricot crêpe-de-Chine dress and stole in preference to the beige and white coat and skirt. The August afternoon was far hotter than she had anticipated after the rainy week preceding this visit to her mother-in-law. The taxi window was opened but only slightly lest it disturbed the osprey feathers adorning the side of her smart cloche hat, and such air as filtered in brought no relief.

She ceased looking at the passing traffic and sat back whilst she removed her white kid gloves inside which her hands had been perspiring. It was on days like this, she thought, that she actually preferred living at Farlington Hall rather than in their London house, which was closed for the summer holidays. It would be pleasantly cool on the lawn in the shade of the old beech tree, and quiet, too, as the boys' tutor, Godfrey Gregson, together with Nanny, had taken all the children to Brighton for the day.

Mr Gregson, Frances thought now, was by no means for the first time proving quite an asset, although when he applied for the part-time job as summer holiday tutor to the two boys, she had serious doubts as to his ability to control them. Despite being still in his teens the young man had joined the army on leaving school and survived the war which had claimed, among a million others, the life of his father. Six months later, he had been accepted at his father's old university. His widowed mother still had four younger children to support and had difficulty raising the money to pay all her eldest son's university fees. Thus Godfrey, still a student himself, applied for the task of tutoring the Beaufords' two sons during the summer holidays and was both surprised and relieved to be given the job.

Frances thought twenty-four years of age far too young to control two growing boys but Aubrey maintained that if the young man had been thought old enough to discipline his soldiers during the war and to survive with an excellent record, he could perfectly well manage Robert and Vaughan. Aubrey was proved right and the tutor was occupying her sons throughout the summer holidays, coaching them with cricket, teaching them tennis and, as he was a capable driver, taking them on outings such as to Hastings where there was a historic castle and thus the trips were of an educational value. Very occasionally, Frances permitted Victoria to accompany them with Nanny there to supervise her.

An overturned coal cart brought the taxi to a halt in Grosvenor Gardens. Although Frances was almost in sight of Hyde Park Corner, she was not going to walk the short distance to Park Lane in the extreme heat, and she instructed the driver to turn round and take her a different route. Lady Mary was always punctual to a minute, and would be certain to remark upon it if she was late. Frances' apprehension at the coming hour or two with her mother-in-law increased. She herself was only summoned to the house in Park Lane when Lady Mary had a complaint or criticism to make, and Frances knew only too well why she was to be cross-questioned this afternoon. Aubrey had taken it upon himself to tell his mother of his concerns about Victoria and the other child.

Victoria was now eight years old and almost as tall as Robert. He was small for his age, but Victoria's height was alarming. Neither Aubrey nor any of his relatives were tall – reaching five foot ten at the most. Nor were her own family tall; yet here was Victoria head and shoulders above her contemporaries and able to wear Robert's last year's outgrown plimsolls. This in itself would not have been so disturbing but Aubrey had become quite friendly this past year with the schoolmaster, even inviting him to a shoot, and the man towered above her husband, standing at least six inches taller.

Frances was gratified when at last Aubrey, who had until recently chosen to bury his head in the sand like an ostrich, could no longer ignore her suspicions; but she had certainly not wanted him to involve his mother, which, inevitably, he did. Within a week of his last visit to his parent, Lady Mary summoned her to London.

Frances was in little doubt that Lady Mary was no fonder of her than she was of her mother-in-law, but tolerated her, knowing that she would never do anything to taint the family name. Nevertheless, a scandal of sorts could well be pending and Lady Mary would certainly wish to discuss the situation now Aubrey had told her that the girls might have been swapped at birth and their natural child was not Victoria but Leila Varney. If there was any truth in such suspicions, her mother-in-law would be horrified – not so much at the knowledge Victoria was not after all a Beauford, but that the rightful child was being brought up by a working-class couple.

The taxi drew to a halt outside Lady Mary's house and with a deepening feeling of unease, Frances paid the driver and then followed Johnson, the waiting butler, into the drawing room. Her mother-in-law stood up to greet her. She was dressed in a fashionable ankle-length black silk day dress, which had a round, high neck and a buckled belt draped at the hip. A necklace of jet-black beads reached to her waist. Her white hair was, as always, immaculately curled, and a black velvet snood held the carefully rolled coils of hair in place. The large diamond and sapphire ring on one hand was obviously a family piece as was the diamond bird-shaped brooch on her bosom.

'Frances!' She bent forward as if to kiss her daughter-in-law's cheek but her lips remained a fraction of distance away. 'I trust your journey was not too uncomfortable with this heat?' Without waiting for an answer, she indicated where she expected Frances to be seated opposite her. As the bracket clock on the mantelpiece chimed four o'clock, Isobel, the elderly Scottish parlourmaid, brought in the tea.

Accustomed as Frances was to Lady Mary's preferred routine for these compulsory visits, only pleasantries were exchanged whilst they drank their tea, the weekly Tuesday night wireless broadcasts, which had started in February, being the subject most interesting to her ladyship. It was only after the parlourmaid had cleared away the cake stand and removed the silver tray with its pretty Georgian tea set that Lady Mary broached the subject which had necessitated Frances' visit.

'Aubrey tells me a matter of considerable concern has arisen concerning my granddaughter. I do hope, Frances, that you are able to tell me his fears are unfounded?' She stood up and walked across to the grand piano on which stood a large silver framed photograph of Aubrey as a boy.

'He was always such an imaginative child!' she said sighing. 'Not very clever, I have to say, but a charming little boy. As you know, Frances, we lost our other children to diphtheria, so Aubrey has always meant a great deal to me being the only one left. I cannot bear to think of him unhappy.'

It was so unusual for Lady Mary to reveal to her daughter-in-law any sentiment other than one of disapproval, Frances could think of nothing appropriate to say. A reply, however, was not expected. Still standing by the piano holding the photo frame, her mother-in-law said: 'My son seems to have this extraordinary misapprehension that Victoria is not his daughter; that she and another child were accidentally exchanged as infants and given to the wrong parents.'

Momentarily Frances was speechless, unsure whether she was expected to have been aware of this, which indeed she was, but had opted not to inform her mother-in-law. Fortunately she was given no time to formulate a response. Turning from the photograph to look intently into Frances' anxious face, the older woman continued: 'Aubrey gave me to understand that you, too, have serious misgivings, Frances. Perhaps you would enlighten me as to your reasons for giving such a ludicrous suggestion even a moment's consideration? Aubrey says there is no family likeness to himself or to you but I have always supposed Victoria takes after me. I too had dark curly hair when I was a young girl and was thought to be unusually intelligent for my age. I can't imagine what Aubrey is thinking of. Of course the child is a Beauford!'

It had never crossed Frances' mind that Victoria bore even the slightest resemblance to her grandmother, and the thought remained very firmly unvoiced as she said uneasily: 'The fact is, Lady Mary, we are concerned because of Victoria's increasing resemblance to the headmaster, Mr Varney, and, indeed, of their child's likeness to Aubrey. It was not noticeable when the girls were younger but recently – well, there have been one or two cases where people have presumed Victoria to be the headmaster's child; and one of my friends remarked that Leila Varney bore what she called "a curious likeness to Aubrey".'

'Poppycock!' Lady Mary's voice was sharp enough for Frances to catch her breath. 'If my memory serves me right, you gave birth to Victoria in hospital and, Aubrey tells me, so was the other child. I accept that it was only a third-rate village hospital,' she added disparagingly, 'but even if an incompetent nurse gave you the wrong infant, you would certainly have known it was not the one you had birthed.'

Frances was momentarily silenced as she recalled the pain-filled hours preceding her daughter's arrival, the pandemonium in the hospital, and her own total lack of interest in the baby they brought back to her after its birth and it had been cleaned up and weighed. She could recall only relief that the labour was all over, and irritation because Aubrey had been so absurdly ecstatic now that she had finally given him a daughter. The fact of the matter was, she had been far too exhausted even to look at the infant the nurse wanted to put in her arms, and had told her to remove it.

Such memories were clearly not to be recounted to her mother-in-law, who was now saying sharply: 'Have you discussed this with the . . . Varneys, did you say? Aubrey informed me he had not and told me quite sharply that he would not entertain the idea. Moreover, Frances – and this is why I have asked you to come here today to see me – he told me quite forcibly that even had the babies been exchanged in error, under no circumstances would he do anything to put matters right. Victoria, he said, was his dearly loved daughter and would remain so, no matter what!'

Aubrey had said no such thing to *her*, Frances thought, although she did not doubt Lady Mary's words. As far as she was concerned, she just wished the whole unfortunate business would disappear. Since she had been obliged to have a fourth child, she might as well be satisfied with Victoria, who was brighter, though perhaps not as pretty, as the Varney child. With a sudden stab of misgiving, she found herself wondering whether Leila Varney could be her own flesh and blood. She felt no emotion of kinship when the child came up to the Hall to play with Victoria. The boys seemed to like her – treated her much as they did their sister, but more kindly as she didn't tease them or try to join in their games as Victoria did.

Frances drew in her breath as her ponderings took her deeper into this unwelcome problem. Just supposing the girls were now swapped and Victoria went to live with the Varneys, would she mind? Aubrey certainly would. As for her own feelings, involved as Victoria was with her school friends, sports and her pony, she rarely saw her from day to day. Nanny had the care of the child and Frances only saw Victoria when she was brought down from the schoolroom to the drawing room for an hour before her bedtime; and not at all when she was staying in town. Aubrey saw a great deal more of her because he went out of his way to seek her company, taking her riding or for long walks through the woods where, he maintained, he instructed her on wildlife and forestry and such subjects quite unsuitable for a small girl. He for one, would not be parted from her.

'Are you listening to what I have been saying, Frances?' Lady Mary's voice brought her sharply back to the present. 'This stupid supposition cannot be allowed to continue. Rumours such as this may begin as insignificant; but they grow, especially in villages. Ideally, it would be best for the schoolmaster to be relocated some distance away, but Aubrey tells me that he is thought to be an excellent teacher and there would be no possible excuse for having him transferred elsewhere.'

Frances nodded. 'It is a fact, Lady Mary, Mr Varney is most competent. The boys' new tutor has told us that he is far better educated – and if one may say so, better bred – than the average village headmaster. It seems a surprising number of his old pupils have got into the grammar school as a result of his teaching, and it is generally accepted that he could not be improved upon.'

She did not add that the novelist who she secretly admired, though not sufficiently to include her in her social circle, sent her child to the village school just because she thought so well of the headmaster.

For a few moments, Lady Mary was silent. Her thoughts were milling round in her head as she took in not only what Frances had been saying, but also its implications. She was far more deeply shocked than she cared to show by the idea that Victoria was not related to the Beaufords. Aubrey had declined to investigate the matter further and had made his feelings clear enough on his last visit. The uncertainty was preying uneasily on her mind. It was abhorrent to her that rumours were circulating – especially amongst the local villagers – that her granddaughter might not legitimately be so. The sooner this unfortunate suspicion could be disproved the better, she now declared to Frances.

'It cannot be allowed to continue!' she added. 'These rumours gather momentum if nothing is done to quash them. They also cast doubt upon the Beauford lineage. Just suppose Victoria were to marry, as is possible, into an aristocratic family and it was discovered after she had had children that their origins were working class! And there is the question of legitimacy – would her offspring be illegitimate? It does not bear thinking about, Frances, and we must prevent such eventualities at all costs. I will not have our family name disgraced!'

Frances had never seen her mother-in-law so emotional, or heard her raise her voice except on a memorable occasion to berate a maid for dropping a hot coal on her Aubusson carpet.

'I do agree the rumours must be stopped, Lady Mary,' she said. 'But I'm sure we must remember that they *are* only rumours.' She paused only for a minute before adding: 'Would you like me to go down to the hospital and make some enquiries? Discreetly, of course. I don't imagine they would want any adverse publicity any more than we would.'

It was an unfortunate choice of words.

'Publicity! *Absolutely not!*' Lady Mary exclaimed. 'If the newspapers were to get hold of such a story . . . it's unthinkable!' Her normally pale face had coloured a deep pink. 'Really, Frances, I have to say all this is causing me sleepless nights. It cannot go on. Let us hope you are right and that these dreadful rumours are as lacking in substance as you say. I shall leave it to you to talk some sense into my son. If there is genuine cause for concern then he must tackle the problem without further delay. Only ostriches bury their heads in the sand as he is doing – and I told him so. You must make him see reason,' she repeated, standing up.

This Frances took correctly to be her signal for leaving. Lady Mary crossed the room once more to pull the bell rope and instructed Johnson to call a taxi to take Frances to Victoria Station. Frances picked up her gloves and beige suede handbag and held out her hand.

'Thank you for the tea, Lady Mary,' she said politely. 'Now I am aware of your feelings, I will do what I can to alleviate

your concerns which, I assure you, I share.' With a sudden
flash of inspiration, she added: 'I will find a pretext to go to
the hospital and ascertain their procedures for dealing with
newborn babies. I will say that I have to report to a committee
currently dealing with maternity care in the country.' Seeing
the look of disparagement on her mother-in-law's face, she
improvised quickly: 'At least I would be able to judge whether
or not conditions were such that a mistake *could or could not
have* happened.'

Lady Mary sighed. 'I suppose it could do no harm, Frances,
but I fear more dire steps will be needed if these rumours
continue. Please keep me informed.'

The return of Johnson, announcing the arrival of the taxi,
put an end to their conversation, much to Frances' relief.
Although her mother-in-law had not exactly implied that it
was her fault all these rumours had started, she nevertheless
believed she would be blamed if, heaven forbid, it was ever
proved that Leila Varney and not Victoria was her child.

For the first time, Frances felt a deep sense of foreboding.
As she settled herself down in the ladies' only carriage of her
train, she tried to envisage the future if the girls had indeed
been swapped. Was there a way such a thing could be proved?
And if there were, would Aubrey agree to have his beloved
daughter's legitimacy put to the test?

For the rest of the journey Frances did her best to discount
her anxiety by reminding herself that her mother-in-law had
acknowledged that the rumours could be unfounded. She
herself was far from convinced Victoria was the Varneys'
daughter, although there were occasions when she had had
doubts. But even in the unlikely event that it could be proved
Victoria was not theirs, one fact was irrefutable, Aubrey would
not be parted from the child he'd always believed was his.
His love for his daughter was patently greater than his affection for his sons; and far, far greater than his love had ever
been for her.

As the stopping train wound its way slowly through the
suburbs and into the Surrey countryside, a thought came into
Frances' mind which caused the dejected droop of her back
to straighten. Suppose all these rumours and suspicions could
be proved to be unsustainable? Suppose the times of the births
were so far apart that either she or Mrs Varney would have

seen they had been given the wrong child? Now that she thought of it, she could recall with complete clarity how appalled, indeed shocked, she had been when the midwife had held up her first-born, George – a repulsive blood-spattered squalling object that looked like one of Mrs Mount's skinned rabbits! But two hours later, after she had had time for a restful sleep, the midwife had returned and held George out to her looking quite human, pink-cheeked, blue-eyed, wisps of golden hair on his head. He'd borne no resemblance to the infant she had seen earlier.

Momentarily, Frances' thoughts returned to Victoria's birth; how resentful she had felt at having this fourth child and how exceedingly painful the birth had been. Afterwards, when the nurse had brought the baby to her to hold, she had been unable to bring herself to take it and had turned her head away, instructing the nurse to remove the baby from her room.

So she would not have known if she'd been offered someone else's baby, she realized, but Mrs Varney – from all accounts Leila was her first child – would have paid it far more attention.

As the train now puffed from Surrey into Sussex, Frances knew that she could not, under any circumstances, discuss such a possibility with the headmaster's wife. She could not write to the hospital and ask for details of times of births, as curiosity would be aroused with the possibility of even more rumours circulating in Elmsfield, but she could write to Somerset House and get copies of both children's birth certificates.

It did not occur to Frances that birth certificates would not provide this information, only a date, not a time of birth. Moreover Aubrey kept such documents in a safe and she did not wish him to know of her plan to delve deeper into the rumours he preferred to ignore.

In a far happier frame of mind than when she had left for London that morning, Frances now alighted at Haywards Heath station. As the train drew away from the station in a noisy cloud of steam, she walked down the platform, her steps almost jaunty as she caught sight of Joseph waiting to take her home.

Nine

Halfway through his two-month term of employment, Godfrey Gregson had been allowed a weekend in which to visit his family. He had given to his mother half of the fifteen shillings, his salary – the first money he'd earned since he had left the army – and used the rest to buy tickets for the cinema showing of *The Three Musketeers* with Douglas Fairbanks, which they were longing to see, and take them all out to tea afterwards.

There had been no lack of conversation, his family eager to hear every detail of his life with the Beauford family at Farlington Hall. His brothers were particularly interested in Vaughan and Robert's life at the famous Eton College; his young sister in Victoria, who was only a year older, and her friend, Leila Varney. Ann had demanded descriptions of both little girls, which he had freely given, but which left him with a strange feeling of uncertainty. Had he told his family Victoria was dark-eyed and dark-haired, Leila fair with bright blue eyes like her father? It was only on the train taking him back to Elmsfield that he recalled his mistake. The headmaster wasn't fair-haired.

He gave it no further thought until his return to Farlington Hall. He'd been entrusted with a key to the big front door as, contrary to her ladyship's orders, Sir Aubrey had maintained he was not to be obliged to use the servants' entrance since despite his poverty he was the son of a gentleman and should be treated accordingly. This, to his amusement, was relayed to him by Sally who, he'd quickly realized, had little liking for Lady Beauford but doted on Sir Aubrey.

As he went into the hall, which was pleasantly cool after the August heat that had plagued him on his return train journey, he could hear Lady Beauford's voice through the open door of the library. She was talking on the telephone in her usual dictatorial tones sufficiently loudly for him to distinguish what she was saying. She was clearly berating the local doctor.

'Of course you can be of assistance, Doctor Campbell. I'm sure you must have access to current medical procedures. There has to be a way of distinguishing one human being from another other than by appearance.' There was a slight pause before she added even more forcibly: 'If you are not aware of any, then I suggest you make enquiries from your more enlightened colleagues.'

Godfrey remained where he was, curiosity overcoming his awareness that it was ill-mannered, to say the least, to eavesdrop. There was a further pause before Lady Beauford said in even sharper tones: 'No, I don't know anything about blood groups and I am really not interested in what the Americans did in the war, Doctor Campbell, or their introduction of blood transfusions, whatever they may be. Now please do as I ask and find out the name of the best man in Harley Street who specializes in hereditary factors. I want such information before the start of the autumn term. Is that clear?'

Godfrey was now agog with curiosity. As he turned to go upstairs he heard a masculine voice which he recognized at once was Sir Aubrey's. The tone sounded almost beseeching.

'I do seriously beg you not to pursue this any further, Frances. What good can it possibly do? On the contrary, you may turn two innocent little girls' lives upside down, not to mention our own. Even if there was a mistake all those years ago, does it really matter?'

'It most certainly does!' was his wife's sharp rejoinder. 'As your mother said yesterday, the Beauford lineage has been unsullied for hundreds of years and if Victoria is not a Beauford, in due course any children she has will be illegitimate. Your mother is insistent we discover the truth, Aubrey, and I am entirely in agreement with her.'

Only then did Godfrey turn away. He made his way upstairs as silently as he could, shocked to have heard that his suspicions about the girls' identities were endorsed by his employers. By all accounts they were no longer willing to turn a deaf ear to the rumours which had been circulating. Maybe, like himself, Lady Beauford had become aware of the servants' gossip which Sally had relayed to him.

As he hurried along the landing to his bedroom he was further shocked to realize that it must be Lady Beauford's intention to prove whether or not the two little girls were growing up in the wrong homes. Surely, he asked himself, she couldn't intend to part with her daughter, which must happen if both were returned to their rightful parents?

He went across to the bedroom window and stared at the fountain splashing in the centre rose garden at the far end of the lawn. It could not possibly be her ladyship's intention to do such a thing, he told himself. Only a week ago, she had informed him that she was expediting Victoria's entry to her convent boarding school, the reason being that the child was too far advanced academically to continue at the village school. There'd been no mention of the Varney child.

It was true that Victoria was far ahead of her age group, whereas her quiet, self-effacing little friend took some time to master new concepts before she could embrace them. Young Leila Varney resembled Sir Aubrey not only physically but also characteristically. In the same way that the gentle, good-natured man, looking always for a quiet, simple life, allowed his strong-willed wife to dominate him, so Leila was happy to let the volatile Victoria take the lead.

As Godfrey unpacked his overnight case and changed from his rather hot tweed suit and waistcoat into cooler lightweight grey flannels and a clean shirt, he felt a surprising surge of concern for Sir Aubrey. If uncovering the truth about the children's identities was what Lady Beauford wanted, she would in all probability succeed in the same way she always seemed to achieve her wishes. *But would it be possible to discover the truth from blood groups?*

Godfrey frowned as he tried to recall the little he had learned about the subject in his sixth-form biology lessons. He recalled the class's astonishment on learning that there were four different types of blood, which could differ from one sibling to another but would in part match one or other of their parents. Beyond those facts, he could remember nothing, although in a discussion with friends at university the subject of blood transfusions, introduced by the Americans during the recent war, had caught all their imaginations. He'd told them about his severely wounded sergeant who had been given life-saving blood from another soldier and how the wounded man had survived.

But none of these snippets of remembered knowledge answered the question now foremost in Godfrey's mind. *Could a blood test prove that little Victoria Beauford was in fact Mr Varney's daughter; that Leila Varney was actually a Beauford?* If it were so proved, he told himself with an unwelcome feeling of impending anxiety, he could only envisage it heralding a period of intense emotional pain for all concerned.

Harold Varney, too, was no less shocked and apprehensive when he learned of her ladyship's intentions. When Sir Aubrey invited him to a meeting in the garden of the Fox and Vixen for a discussion 'of singular importance concerning the children', he'd had little doubt his fears were about to be realized. For month after month he had gone on hoping that the rumours about the two children had been forgotten. Copper had ceased talking about the subject. Eighteen months had passed since the rumours had first surfaced and stupidly he'd started to believe they had died down; that they would eventually disappear altogether. It was the only way he had been able to bear the thought that his beloved daughter was not after all his natural child.

For so many years he and Copper had both longed for a child and all but given up hope until Leila arrived. From that moment on, neither of them had hungered for a second child, perfectly content as they were with the one God had sent them. Now, it seemed, Sir Aubrey was as reluctant as he was to pursue the matter. He admitted as much to Harold as soon as they were seated at one of the oak tables in the pub .

'It's like this, Varney,' Sir Aubrey said awkwardly, 'both my wife and my mother feel we have a duty to ensure we . . . er . . . we . . . well, that we have the right children. You've heard the silly rumours, of course.' He cleared his throat. 'Don't believe a word of it, m'self. Dare say you know what I'm talking about?'

'Indeed yes, I do!' Harold said uneasily. 'Personally, I think it best if we leave things as they are.'

'Quite right! Quite right!' Sir Aubrey grunted. 'I'm in total agreement with you. However, my wife and . . . well, my mother . . . very determined women. They think it's my duty to find out what's what. Frances was a part-time hospital visitor in the war, you know; saw a bit of medicine, stuff they doled out to the poor chaps who'd been shelled, that sort of

thing. Seems some of the poor devils had to have this
newfangled whatsit – thing the Yanks brought over – blood
transfusions. Saved a lot of lives, of course.'

Realizing he had been rambling, Sir Aubrey forced himself
to get down to the nitty-gritty, knowing full well that he would
never have a moment's peace from his mother's and wife's
nagging if he delayed any longer.

'It's like this, Varney. They think if both our daughters and
we ourselves have our blood tested, it will determine once
and for all that we've got the right girls, eh? At least, my wife
says it will though I can't see how m'self. However, I do
see her point about stopping any more gossip.'

As if he heartily disliked what he'd had to say, he got up
suddenly and disappeared indoors to get them both a second
drink. Harold felt a moment of pity for the man, who clearly
was not strong enough a character to stand up to his wife or
his mother. If he were to disapprove of any of Copper's
demands, that would be the end of the matter. However, there
was just a chance he could halt Lady Beauford's scheme before
it went any further.

When Sir Aubrey returned he said: 'I happen to have a little
bit of knowledge about blood. There are four types, of which
only one is compatible with the others. Members of a family
do not necessarily all have the same blood type. You and your
children may differ one from another. For example, your son,
George and I may have the same blood type but that in no
way indicates we are related.'

Seeing that Sir Aubrey was having a little difficulty in
absorbing the facts or in understanding their relationship to
his present dilemma, Harold said simply: 'We cannot prove
by blood types if a person is related to another, only that one
person is *not* related to the other.'

Sir Aubrey had been listening with a look of bewilderment
on his face. He gave Harold an apologetic smile. 'Can't quite
seem to take it in,' he said gruffly. 'Medical stuff – not really
my scene, y'know! Anyway, Varney, seems to me the matter is
out of our hands. Only thing I want to say is let's keep all this
palaver under our hats, eh? Frances has arranged for us and
Victoria to be tested up in town. So if you and your wife and
daughter get done here in Elmsfield, maybe Doctor Campbell
won't jump to any conclusions. What say, Varney? D'you agree?'

Harold nodded. In one way, he agreed with Lady Beauford that the quicker the rumours were quashed once and for all, the better. He'd been relieved to hear that she had decided to remove Victoria from the school a year early and send her off, young though she was, to board at her old convent. Leila would miss her friend terribly, of course.

He now decided that the least explanation he gave Leila for the coming tests, the better it would be. He would tell her simply that knowing which type of blood you had could save your life if ever you needed to be given someone else's.

At teatime that evening, as he expected, Leila accepted without query his little lecture about blood groups and the need for her to be tested. Copper, however, was horrified and after Leila had gone to bed, she begged him to refuse Sir Aubrey's request.

'Just suppose,' she said tearfully, 'just suppose it was discovered that we *have* been given the wrong babies and the Beaufords wanted to take Leila from us . . .'

Harold silenced her with the promise that no one on earth would make him agree to part with their child. His promise undoubtedly reassured Copper but left him feeling distinctly uneasy. Would the law allow him to keep such a promise? He put the thought quickly to one side.

A date was made with Dr Campbell for the following week, and as Leila made no further mention of the tests, he presumed she had lost interest.

This might well have been a correct assumption had not Victoria been told by her mother that her test in London was a secret. She promptly decided to share it – as she always shared secrets – with Leila. Unfettered by any promises, Leila told her friend delightedly that she, too, was to be tested. Totally unaware of the drastic implications incipient in their chatter, the two children exchanged excited comments in the schoolroom of Farlington Hall, indifferent to the fact that Nanny was sitting by the window with two pairs of Robert's socks, some grey wool and her darning mushroom and could hear every word they were saying.

It did cross the old woman's mind that she should tell the children to keep such accounts of their tests a secret lest the older boys or even the servants heard of them and started speculating as to the reason. Seeing as much as she did of the little girls, she had no doubt whatever that they had been exchanged at birth. Leila was the very spit of Sir Aubrey in all kinds of little ways; she was like Vaughan, too, quiet and dreamy; whereas Victoria was like quicksilver, picking up the rules for a new game even quicker than her brothers, racing through books intended for girls twice her age. And, not least, she had the dark good looks of the headmaster.

Threading a length of wool into her darning needle, she picked up the worst of Robert's socks and pushed the mushroom into the heel. As she did so, she heard Victoria say in a near whisper: 'Let's not tell the boys, Leila. Let's keep it a secret. We haven't had a good secret all this holidays.' Her voice now became dramatically deep as she intoned: 'I swear by Almighty God and the Holy Ghost and King George that I will keep this secret. Now your turn, Leila. Don't forget King George. You forgot him last time.'

Unable to dispel her innermost anxieties about the future, Nanny tried not to wonder for how long would the children's secret be safe.

Ten

L ord Hanbury looked over the top of his horn-rimmed spec-
tacles at the two women seated opposite him. The elder,
Lady Mary Beauford, he had met on a previous occasion, but
the younger of the two, her daughter-in-law, was a stranger.
Accustomed as he was from years of observing members of
the public in court, his first impression of her was of a cold
strong-willed woman who would not take kindly to having her
wishes thwarted.

His clerk came into the room carrying a large silver tray laden
with sherry glasses, a decanter and a delicate Meissen china
plate with finger biscuits arranged tastefully on it. He welcomed
the delay it afforded him before he must impart news he assumed
would be extremely unwelcome.

Lady Mary, however, with no regard for her daughter-in-law's
wishes, waved the clerk aside, announcing that she never took
alcohol before the evening.

'I've no wish to waste your time or mine, Lord Hanbury!'
she said turning to the white-haired barrister sitting behind his
large, leather-topped desk. 'As you arranged today's meeting, I
presume you have looked into our problem and found no legal
drawback to the plan of action I explained in my letter?'

Lord Hanbury did not reply immediately. He was well aware
of the Beaufords' predicament – one he had never yet encountered during his long and highly successful years at the Bar. By
no means a sentimental man, he had not been entirely unmoved
by the plight of the two little girls reared by each other's parents.
He would have been happy to find a legal precedent that would
have ensured their future happiness. But such was not the case,
as he now told his clients.

'The 1891 Custody of Children Act does deal with parental
rights to their legitimate offspring,' he said, tapping his fountain pen on the pristine blotter in front of him. 'However,

Professor Landsteiner's studies make it quite clear that whilst blood types can prove in certain cases that a child is *not* that of a supposed parent, even had that child the same blood type, it does not constitute proof that he or she *is* their biological offspring. These facts are recognized by the courts, ladies, and constitute the present problem.'

'Are you saying a parent has no right to claim their own child?' Lady Mary asked sharply.

'Indeed not!' Lord Hanbury said. 'I am saying that it is impossible through the testing of blood for a parent to prove a child is theirs – merely that it is not so.'

It was the daughter-in-law who now spoke. Frances had been listening carefully to the barrister's comments having discovered to her intense irritation that the two birth certificates sent to her by Somerset House contained the dates but *not* the times of the births. Now it seemed her doctor's findings were correct and one fact had been firmly established – Victoria was not their child.

She looked across the wide mahogany desk to the imposing, white-haired figure of the barrister, and said: 'As the blood tests have proved that Victoria is not our child, then presumably she is the Varneys', and their child is ours . . .'

At this point the old lady spoke. 'What we are hoping to hear from you, Lord Hanbury, is that my son can legitimize the Varney child and include her in our family.'

The barrister looked down at the papers on his desk and clearing his throat before he met his clients' penetrating stares, said: 'I must repeat the point I just made. There is no way of proving that the young Miss Varney is indeed your daughter. I do appreciate the fact that this blood-test result –' he sifted the papers and drew one out which had been sent to him by Lady Mary's family doctor – 'indicates that the child could be yours, but it is not a legal certainty. All that can be proven in a court of law, should it ever come to that, is that the child you believe to be yours cannot, alas, be so. The tests do show that she can be the Varneys' offspring. It would appear that in all probability, the children were exchanged at birth. I'm afraid I can find no legal precedent for a case such as this and I could not promise that a judge would find in your favour should you decide to take this further.'

He looked at his clients' unyielding expressions and withheld a sigh.

'I should warn you, ladies, that such a controversial case would result in a great deal of publicity if for no other reason than that it would create a precedent in law; and, if I may so, the public are always especially interested in the affairs of the aristocracy. It could not be kept out of the newspapers – all of which notoriety would be very unpleasant for both families and not least for the two children. Moreover I must advise you that you would incur a very great deal of expense with no guarantee or even likelihood of a verdict in your favour.'

Lady Mary's response was immediate. 'I am not concerned with cost, Lord Hanbury. I am concerned with the Beauford lineage. If the Varneys' child – I should say our child – does not come under my son and daughter-in-law's jurisdiction, there is no knowing what may become of her in the future. As to that I can but hope the medical profession will pull up their socks and discover a way of identifying one human being from another.'

She reached into her brocade handbag and withdrew a sheet of paper containing a chart entitled 'Blood Type Calculator' – a copy of which her doctor had reluctantly given her. She knocked the page with the back of her hand before passing it to the barrister. He had already seen a copy sent to him by Sir Andrew but he made as if to study it once more before saying: 'It may seem a little complicated for you to understand but I do assure you the facts are indisputable. However, your wish to adopt the Varneys' child could be arranged legally although the child's birth certificate would remain unchanged. You would, of course, need the present father's agreement.'

Lady Mary met the barrister's questioning look with a shrug, which indicated to him that she considered his last remark super-fluous.

'I have every reason to believe he will agree,' she said firmly. 'His social position as a mere schoolteacher is considerably lower than that of our family; the child would have the opportunity to make an infinitely better marriage if she has been properly educated and presented at Court. If the man is fond of his supposed daughter, he will naturally want what is best for her.'

'And your child, Lady Beauford?' Lord Hanbury asked Frances. 'Is she to be given to the headmaster and his wife?'

'Certainly not!' Lady Mary replied. 'I'm very fond of Victoria. Frances will raise both girls.'

Lord Hanbury decided to keep his misgivings to himself. For one thing, he could not bring himself to believe the schoolmaster and his wife would give up so easily the child they thought was theirs. Although his own daughter was now a married woman in her thirties, he could not conceive of giving her to the care of another family when she'd been a child. However, it was not his duty to project his own views. The only thing he must do before the two women departed was to warn them yet again that there was no legal proof of parentage to support their intentions.

Lady Mary shrugged off the warning as she and Frances drove back to Park Lane.

'It is unfortunate to say the least, but as I said to Lord Hanbury, I don't expect there to be any necessity to employ legal assistance. I know Aubrey keeps saying the Varneys are devoted to their child, but all the more reason why they should want the best for her.' Her mouth set in an even more determined line as the cab drew up outside the house. 'One thing we must avoid at all costs, Frances, is any publicity. The utmost secrecy will be necessary – totally necessary,' she reiterated. 'If we have any trouble with the Varneys, I will simply have to pay whatever is necessary to ensure their silence.'

It was as well her mother-in-law could afford to carry out such a threat, Frances thought as she followed Lady Mary into the house. She and Aubrey most certainly could not. Although her father had left her a rich woman when he died, nearly all her wealth was in stocks and shares from which she had received regular dividends. During last year's worldwide economic depression her investments were so depleted as to render her virtually penniless. Aubrey was quite hopeless where finance was concerned and it was she who dealt with the crotchety old accountant when he came to Farlington Hall to remonstrate about their inability to stay in the black. She was sick and tired of hearing him tell her they simply must make more economies; that the estate was no longer producing the income it did before the war; that were it not for Lady Mary's generous cheques there was a serious threat that the bank would call in the overstretched overdraft and they would be obliged to sell Farlington Hall.

Such threats seriously worried Frances, not so much because she would mind the loss of the estate, which in her opinion ate money that might have been spent far more interestingly on their London house, but because of the scandal that would ensue.

The only redeeming thought was that Lady Mary would never allow such a thing to happen, and despite her threats to Aubrey never to bale him out of debt again, it was more or less completely certain she would do so for so long as she was able – for she, too, had been hit by the economic depression.

Now, it seemed, she was willing to put her hand in her pocket if required, to buy both the Varneys' silence and, presumably, their complicity. Well, her mother-in-law had a great deal of influence with a large number of people – people who over the years had received favours which she had no hesitation in calling in. On their way to see the barrister, Lady Mary had told Frances that she was well acquainted with the Education Secretary and should it be necessary, she could probably engineer an important promotion for Harold Varney – a housemaster appointment at one of the better known public schools, perhaps. With Lady Mary's endorsement, such an appointment could well be possible as Varney was well spoken and, according to Aubrey, exceptionally well educated.

'It would have an added advantage, don't you see, Frances,' her mother-in-law said as she gave her hat and coat to her maid. 'Leila's parents would have to remove from Elmsfield to another part of the country, and with both girls boarding at your convent school in France, there would be nothing more to gossip about.'

Even so, Frances thought uneasily as she bade her mother-in-law goodbye and caught a taxi to take her to Victoria Station, Aubrey was proving far more of a stumbling block than either she or Lady Mary had anticipated. Although he had in the first instance agreed to go to London to have his blood tested by Sir Andrew, he had flatly refused to accept the specialist's findings, nor would he carry out his mother's wishes to pursue enquiries as to the legal position with her barrister. Despite Lady Mary's fury, he had unaccustomedly dug in his toes and refused to be involved. In the privacy of their bedroom, he had told Frances with unusual lucidity: 'I love my daughter and that's what she will always be to me – my daughter. As for the other child, I won't raise any objections, Frances, if you wish to adopt her, but I will not be a party to forcibly taking her away from her family. Those two parents are every bit as proud of and devoted to young Leila as I am of Victoria, so you and Mama should think twice before you ruin everyone's lives!'

Although Aubrey's final remark was not worth considering,

Frances was nevertheless astonished and not a little perturbed by the unusual vehemence, not to say clarity, with which Aubrey had expressed himself. It was rare indeed for him to use more than half a dozen words in any sentence – if, indeed, he spoke at all. At least, not to her! She had heard him expounding at great length to his gamekeeper about a fox picking off the young pheasants and whether it was kinder to shoot it or trap it first and then shoot it. If the conversation was about animals, he could be quite voluble. It was one of the reasons he got on so well with Victoria – they always had horses to talk about.

As the train slowed down on its approach to Haywards Heath, Frances found herself wondering not for the first time how it was that Aubrey seemed quite indifferent to the fact that Victoria was not actually his child; was not the daughter he had craved for so long. Was he wilfully refusing to believe the results of the blood tests or was he just choosing to ignore them? He had made no comment at all when she had shown him Sir Andrew's report, leaving the room and only reappearing briefly for luncheon before disappearing again. When she had tried to reopen the subject after the children had gone to bed, he had told her that it would be best for all of them if she and his mother let the matter drop. All he would say – and it was the last thing he would say – was that in his opinion it was much too late to change the girls' identities. When they were infants perhaps it could have been done without too much heartbreak. But not now.

'It's far, far too late, Frances!' he had told her.

As with a burst of escaping steam the train drew alongside the platform, Frances stepped out of the carriage and made her way down the stairs to the taxi rank outside. The sun had gone in now and grey clouds were scurrying across the darkening sky. She retied her batik silk scarf more closely round her throat and hurried towards the waiting taxi, unhappily aware that for once she lacked the self-assurance of her mother-in-law. She had become used these past twenty-one years to Aubrey falling in with her dictates, and only very rarely disputing her wishes and decisions. This, she realized as she climbed into the comparative warmth of the cab, was going to be different. No matter what she or his mother said, he was going to support Varney in his refusal to let them adopt his child.

Eleven

Immediately following Frances' announcement that she would 'deal with' the Varneys, Aubrey realized he could no longer remain uninvolved in his wife's determination to prove the two girls' parentage. He'd known instinctively that to meddle in the matter could only end in trouble. To his wife's surprise, he continued to assume his most unusual mantle of authority and quite literally forbade her to so much as pass the time of day with either of the Varneys until he had had time to talk to them.

A week later, he had still not done so and he determined to see if he could persuade Frances to reconsider the stand she and his mother were taking. Hearing her voice in the hall, he plucked up the courage to summon her to the morning room, where he had retired to read his newspaper.

Frances regarded him now from her chair facing him as he tapped his unlit pipe against the marble surround of the fireplace.

He was, she decided, refusing to meet her eyes; a sign of nervousness which she now considered encouraging. Whatever it was he was about to suggest, he obviously knew she would object, and unless there was a good reason not to do so, she imagined she could gainsay him.

The authoritative tone of his voice came as a surprise as he said, 'I will not have you walking into the Varneys' house and announcing that we have decided to adopt Leila. And don't think I am unaware of the legal position, Frances. Lord Hanbury has had the courtesy to write to me and tell me of your and Mama's meeting with him. As things stand, he tells me, you have no legal right to take that child away from her parents.'

Recovering quickly from her astonishment at Aubrey's masterful tone of voice, Frances bit back her angry retort and said quietly: 'I have no objection if you rather than I visit the Varneys, Aubrey. You made your feelings clear that you disapproved of your mother and me seeking a legal opinion after we had received the results of the tests . . .' She looked up at him, her pale blue eyes cold and challenging. 'But as your mother said, in this instance you cannot behave like an ostrich and bury your head in the sand. The truth will not go away – Victoria is *not* our child.'

Seeing the look on her husband's face, her voice softened slightly. 'I know how much this fact will have upset you – you always doted on her, to an unreasonable degree in my opinion. However, be that as it may, if Victoria is not our daughter then Leila Varney is, whether we like it or not. I may remind you, Aubrey – and not for the first time – that the hospital almoner was adamant, there were *no other babies born* that night. Leila Varney is our child, Aubrey – a Beauford.'

Aubrey stood up, his face impassive as he walked to the door. Glancing once more at his wife's rigid countenance, he said quietly: 'We have three sons, Frances, as well as Victoria. The Varneys only have the one child. Somehow, contrary to your belief, I do not think they will agree to part with her.'

It was on the tip of Frances' tongue to say that since it had been proved the girl was not theirs, the Varneys would be obliged to part with her whatever their objections, but for once, she held her tongue. Aubrey seemed to have made a friend of the schoolmaster – even drank with him in that insignificant little village public house! He seemed at times to pay no regard to the fact that he came from a titled, aristocratic family and that people such as schoolmasters, though not servants, were certainly not suitable friends.

Frances sighed as she left the room and walked towards the green-baize door leading to the Hall's extensive kitchens. They only kept four kitchen staff since the war, those of the family retainers who had not been killed in France having chosen other occupations, factory work, chauffeuring, even shop work. Many of the female staff had left for employment allowing them more congenial hours and, it had to be said, better pay. As Aubrey had remarked when she was complaining at the lack of trained housemaids, the world was changing; the war had somehow blurred the rigid divisions between those who were served and those who did the serving. He had even suggested he might one day invite Harold Varney and his wife to tea. She, of course, had refused to be present if he did so and he'd not repeated the suggestion. One thing she could usually count on with her husband was that he would always avoid controversy and only on the rarest occasion interfere with her wishes or plans. For him to speak so forcibly about her proposed visit to the Varneys had come as a shock.

Despite the authoritative way he had spoken to Frances, Aubrey was dreading the meeting he had arranged with Harold Varney and his wife for the following weekend. He had not invited them to the Hall fearing Frances' interference, but suggested he called in at Foxhole Cottage. As he walked up the brick pathway the following Saturday morning, he noticed the pretty, colourful borders on either side of him and realized that one or other of the Varneys was a keen gardener. Undoubtedly, they had worked hard to turn a rough piece of ground dotted with a few vegetables into so charming a place.

His unease increasing, Aubrey knocked on the front door, which was opened almost immediately by the Varneys' daily woman, who showed him into the sitting room. The child, Leila, was curled up in a chair by the window reading a book, which on seeing him she immediately put down. Jumping up, she went to greet him, holding out her hand.

'Mummy and Daddy will be here in a minute,' she said with a shy smile.

Aubrey felt his heart lurch. The small face regarding him was so like Robert's that it took his breath away. He'd not realized before quite how obvious it was that this little girl was a Beauford – his daughter; his child. She was a pretty little thing with large blue eyes and bright golden hair tied back in two pigtails. Her voice was soft, charmingly modulated, her gestures graceful. She was far more feminine than his beloved Victoria, who, were she dressed in boys' clothes, might well pass as one of her brothers! There were times when she surpassed them in courage and endeavour and other times when she plied him with questions he was unable to answer and which made him realize his own limitations.

Aubrey's reflections ceased as the door opened and the headmaster and his wife came in, his arm round her shoulders. She looked pale and anxious but managed a tentative smile as she invited him to be seated.

'Will you have a cup of tea, Sir Aubrey, or would you prefer a glass of sherry?' Harold enquired, but his guest shook his head. Harold turned and smiled at his daughter. 'Go into the kitchen, sweetheart, and ask Mrs Clark to give you some of your mother's lemonade. Then she can help you ice those fairy cakes you baked yesterday.'

Leila disappeared without protest and Harold turned to face his guest. It was the first time Sir Aubrey had been inside the cottage and Harold was aware that this proposed visit was not a mere social call. Sir Aubrey had muttered over the telephone that he wished to discuss the blood tests they'd all had recently. He looked across the room at his wife's white face and knew that she feared the worst. Neither of them had slept much the previous night. Now, looking at Sir Aubrey, he realized that the man looked every bit as anxious as Copper. He was clearing his throat nervously as he settled himself on the edge of an armchair.

'I've come to see you and your . . . er, your wife . . . well, because my mother and . . . er . . . my wife feel something should be done . . . you know?'

When Harold remained silent, Aubrey continued even more incoherently: 'That London fellow . . . supposed to be one of the best . . . legal fellows and that sort of thing.' He cleared his throat once more. 'Seems he has looked into this . . . er, mix-up . . . and he's written me a letter. Hadn't asked for it but . . . well, thought I ought to know, I suppose . . .'

He broke off, took a white silk handkerchief out of his breast pocket and wiped his forehead. Looking once more at Harold, he blurted out: 'Probably all stuff and nonsense. Good little hospital . . . don't make stupid mistakes despite what our specialist thinks. Tell you the truth, Varney, Mrs Varney, I wish to goodness my wife had never got the wind up . . . my mother's fault, probably . . . always was a bit fanatical about blood lines. You'd think we were the only family that predated the Magna Carta . . .'

He broke off once more, aware that he had deviated from his plan to come out with the facts. Fearing he might never find the courage to do so, he blurted out the truth in a rush of words.

'Victoria, my daughter. That's to say, the legal chap says she *isn't* my daughter. Positive, he says. I'm afraid it looks as if there has been a mix-up – terrible mistake. We've got the wrong girls, eh, Varney?'

Copper gave a small cry of dismay. It was not unexpected but for months now she had been refusing to admit to herself that not only could the mistake have happened, but that by appearance alone it looked very much as if the babies had been wrongly identified.

She and Harold had discussed the situation one night when neither of them could sleep. They had agreed that to all intents and purposes, if not by birth then in every possible other way, Leila was their daughter and would remain so. She had nothing against Victoria Beauford; she was Leila's best friend and a bright, cheerful child for whom Harold had great academic hopes. He believed he could get her eventually into one of the women's colleges if she continued to do so well with her studies. Not even the knowledge that Victoria might be the very same baby she had carried lovingly for nine months before her birth could arouse any maternal feelings towards her. Harold had agreed that it was best for all concerned to leave matters as they were. Now she was ice-cold with fear as Sir Aubrey told them his wife and his mother wanted to take Leila from them because she was *their* child.

As if to compound her fears, Harold was now asking Sir Aubrey what he had in mind. 'My wife and I are utterly devoted to our daughter, to Leila,' he added. 'As I'm sure you are to your little girl!'

Aubrey looked suddenly more relaxed. 'Absolutely spot on, Varney! Wouldn't part with Victoria for the world. I told my wife, it would have been different if the child was a boy – eldest son and all that; but can't see that it matters one iota the two of them being girls; they'll get married and then . . .' He gave a sudden boyish laugh feeling much as he might have done if he had beaten his wife and mother in a game of rummy. 'Then as married women, the girls won't be Beaufords or Varneys! Storm in a teacup, if you ask me. Best leave things as they are, I say.'

His face clearing, Harold stood up and with a rare gesture of intimacy patted his guest on the shoulder. 'I'm so very pleased to hear you say that, Sir Aubrey. My wife and I have had one or two unpleasant worries that if the girls were indeed mistakenly swapped, you might feel it our duty to hand Leila over to you. Frankly, I doubt if we could bring ourselves to do so, even if the law demanded it. I take it that's not the case?'

Glad to be able to say so, Aubrey now told the couple that there had been no mention whatever in Lord Hanbury's letter of the possibility of a law case. On the contrary, he'd written that there was no legal precedent for such an unfortunate situation.

Suddenly, for a single moment as he stood up to leave, he recalled the young, fair-haired child who had greeted him on his arrival and his awareness of her remarkable likeness to Robert. Then Varney opened the front door for him and walked with him down the brick path and he thought enviously how much happier Varney and his wife seemed in their unpretentious cottage than he and Frances were in all the grandeur of Farlington Hall.

It was only as he climbed into the Bentley, in which he had chosen this afternoon to drive himself, that it occurred to him that if Frances and his mother persisted in taking legal steps to adopt the Varneys' child, the Varneys would have equal claim to Victoria.

As the engine sprang to life and he headed back up the road towards his ancestral home, Aubrey's mind was momentarily diverted by the sheer pleasure of handling the motor car. Like all their other cars, it had been handed down to them by his mother, who chose to buy a new model every year. Of course, he was grateful to her and for the fact that her allowance just about kept their financial heads above water. But if the truth be told – and Aubrey never even allowed himself to think about it – he did not really love his mother; nor indeed particularly like her. She was a cold, reserved woman.

As a young child brought up by a nanny, he had not only been in awe of his parents but had actually dreaded the times when his nanny had been instructed to take him downstairs to the drawing room when his mother wished to see him. There had been no hugs or kisses, or even encouraging remarks. More often there were criticisms because fear made him tongue-tied; or his hair was ruffled or he was too shy to converse with the visitors. His father had been even more intimidating – a tall upright mustachioed man, quite often in uniform, who barked out orders rather than spoke them, his steely grey eyes staring critically at his small son. No, he had not had a happy childhood, and although Aubrey did not like to admit it even to himself, he still feared his mother. Now, driving home, he could not subdue the terrible feeling of anxiety that despite his reassurance to the Varneys, neither Frances nor his indomitable mother would allow matters to remain as they were.

Twelve

Godfrey looked at the flushed face of the small girl who had asked to speak to him alone after breakfast before he started work on her father's library. Her brothers were back at school and this Saturday morning there would be nobody around in the schoolroom. Nanny, now acting partially as the housekeeper, had announced that she was putting the week's laundry away in the linen cupboard; a job which took all of half an hour.

'It's a secret, Mr Gregson,' Victoria said importantly. 'And you've got to promise not to tell my mother what we talk about.'

Not altogether sure whether he should agree to converse secretly with Lady Beauford's daughter, he decided she could have nothing of any significance to discuss with him, and when she demanded for a second time that he should guarantee his silence, curiosity got the better of him and he agreed. The two of them were by now in the empty schoolroom seated on opposite sides of the big wooden table.

'Well, what's this all about, Victoria?' he prompted her. 'Were you and the boys up to mischief and they've gone back to school leaving you to take the blame?'

Victoria swept the question aside. 'No, it's nothing to do with *them*,' she declared forcibly. She hesitated only briefly before she blurted out in a low dramatic voice, 'It's about adoption. I looked it up in the big red King George's English dictionary and it said, *receiving a child and treating it as your own.*'

So intense was Victoria's expression that it was with difficulty Godfrey restrained a smile. 'That's quite right, so what's the problem?'

Victoria drew a deep breath. 'It isn't a *problem*, it's a puzzle – and it's dreadfully important.' She drew a deep breath and, looking straight into Godfrey's eyes, continued: 'You know Annie, don't you – the maid who brings our meals up to the nursery. Well, she was drawing the curtains in the drawing room and Mother was on the telephone in the library.' She drew another deep breath before saying wide-eyed: 'And she heard Mother say she was intending to *adopt* Leila!'

Godfrey was totally unprepared for such a confidence. Playing for time, he said: 'You should know by now, Victoria, that eavesdropping is wrong and if Annie did hear what she told you she'd heard, then she had no right to gossip to you.'

Victoria sighed. 'I know that, Mr Gregson, but you mustn't be cross with her. She only told me because she knows how much Leila and I love each other, and if Mother *is* going to adopt Leila, then she'll be my real sister, but I don't know if she would want to be adopted because her parents love her very much and she loves them and she mightn't want to leave them and even if she did, they mightn't want her to come and live with us and that's why I didn't think adoption meant what it said in the dictionary and that's why I wanted to ask you because I couldn't ask Mother or Papa, could I, because then I'd get Annie into trouble, but you promised . . .'

Finally Victoria ran out of breath and an uneasy silence filled the schoolroom whilst Godfrey frantically searched for the right thing to say. He had a distinctly uneasy feeling that the maid had heard exactly what she'd reported to the child, but as Victoria had just said, after having put the matter to her quick, intelligent mind, what if neither the Varneys nor their daughter wished the Beaufords to adopt her? Could they insist upon it? He could not recall ever having heard of a similar situation. It seemed pretty certain that all the rumours about the disparity of the children's physical attributes to their existing parents had proved to be well founded, but was there any proof? He simply didn't know.

Next week, the long vacation would come to an end and he would return to Oxford. Thankfully, he would not be here to become involved in what he could only foresee would be a disaster. He had become quite attached to the two boys who'd been in his care these past two months and it crossed his mind that they, too, would become involved – not only by young Leila's inclusion in the family, as they all seemed quite fond of their sister's sweet-natured friend; but suppose the Varneys were to claim Victoria? How would the boys react to the loss of the girl they had always presumed was their sister? According to the conversation he'd overheard, he'd gathered that Sir Aubrey was opposed to any change. It had not failed to imprint on his own mind, Godfrey thought, how the man doted on his only daughter, quite often to the exclusion of his sons, with whom he had no more than an affectionate if somewhat distant relationship.

Victoria had been watching the changing expressions on the tutor's face but now her patience was exhausted.

'I want to know if you think it's really going to happen, Mr Gregson. Mother wouldn't have said that if it wasn't true, would she? Do you think she means to tell me? Or Papa will tell me? And should I tell Leila? Maybe she knows already . . .'

Her voice trailed away uncertainly and Godfrey knew he must find some kind of answer for her.

'I think you should do and say absolutely nothing to anyone,' he told her gently. 'As you yourself warned me, Annie might even lose her job here if your mother found out she had not only been eavesdropping but had passed information to you that Lady Beauford clearly did not intend you to know. I'm sure if there is any truth in all this, Victoria, you will be told in due course. Hard as it may be for you, you must remain ignorant for the time being.'

Seeing the look of denial on Victoria's face, he said quickly: 'Annie may have heard only a part of your mother's conversation. For all you know, your mother was telling a friend how fond she was of Leila and that she would like to adopt her – which doubtless she would. She knows what close friends you two girls are. So you see, you can only cause trouble if you raise the subject with anyone else. I have promised not to say anything so you, too, must keep Annie's gossip to yourself, difficult though you may find it to do so!'

Victoria looked downcast. 'I suppose so. Mr Gregson, it wouldn't be fair to Annie if she was dismissed, but I did want to tell Leila. We *always* tell each other everything. It's what best friends do.'

'No, not even Leila!' Godfrey cautioned. 'She might wish to tell her parents, who would talk to your parents, so you see you must remain silent for the time being. It's my turn now to extract a promise. Do I have your word, Victoria, that you will keep this to yourself?'

'I suppose so!' she murmured dejectedly. 'Thank you for listening to me, Mr Gregson.' She gave him a sudden, sweet smile. 'I wish you weren't leaving us. It's been fun having you here. The boys were dreading you coming, you know, and now they want you to come back next holidays.'

'Thank you, Victoria, for those kind words!' Godfrey said smiling. 'I hope all three of you will write to me from time to time so I shall not lose touch with you. It is my hope that your parents will employ me again next summer. We will drive down to Hastings and see the smugglers' caves again, shall we?'

This promise of Victoria's favourite outing cheered her at once and, successfully distracted, she extracted a promise from Godfrey to play a game of badminton with her on the new tennis court and she ran off quite cheerfully downstairs, the problem of her secret knowledge momentarily forgotten.

It was some time, however, before Godfrey could put it from his mind. If Leila really was the Beaufords' child, it was more than likely they would want her to become part of their own family. But that could spell tragedy for the Varneys even while it would give the child they loved many advantages. Apart from a private schooling, Leila would eventually 'come out', be presented at Court and introduced to a bevy of eligible young men, one of whom she would doubtless choose to marry. She was not an academic child and her future with her present family would be a mundane one – serving in a draper's shop, perhaps, or as governess to a titled family's children; perhaps a typist or even a secretary. Were it not for the fact that he was making some very wealthy friends at his college, to whom he would eventually introduce his sisters, they, too, would have working rather than privileged lives.

Be that as it may, he told himself as he changed into white tennis trousers and an Aertex shirt and made his way to the recently laid out tennis lawn, it was easy to see the advantages for Leila, but what prospects were there for Victoria if the Varneys insisted on having her, *their* child, to live with them? Granted, Victoria would have an extremely erudite and educated father able to channel her remarkable abilities in the right direction. Ultimately, she might even get to university, an opportunity now enjoyed by many more women since their inclusion in university life, and even be awarded a degree, which would not have been possible two years previously. She could become a doctor, even a politician, although that was unlikely since only women over thirty had had the vote these past four years.

Her future would be promising, but what of the present? The separation from her brothers? Her pony? Her bicycle? The motor car rides to the seaside? Her music and dancing lessons? She would have to leave her beautiful home here at Farlington Hall, and not least, she would no longer enjoy the devotion of her father, Sir Aubrey.

Maybe, he thought, he could make himself believe in the hope he had given Victoria – that the maid had got the wrong end of the stick and reported as a fact what had been no more than a passing whim of Lady Beauford's. He decided to think no more about it and as it happened, circumstances determined that he entirely forgot Victoria's confession. Aware that he had only a week left to enjoy the beautiful countryside surrounding Farlington Hall, after his game of badminton with Victoria he decided to use his free lunchtime hour to tour the locality on his bicycle – George's bicycle which had been stored in one of the old stables when he went abroad.

They were enjoying a mild Indian summer and the autumn air was soft and inviting when, wearing no more than grey flannels and his Aertex tennis shirt, he wheeled the cycle round to the front drive. Still on foot, he barely had time to step on to the grass verge before a smart little Morris two-seater swept round the corner of the shrubbery. Missing him by no more than nine inches, it was pulled up with a screech of brakes outside the front door.

Tiresome little show-off! Godfrey thought as he picked up his fallen machine and stared across the gravelled drive at the diminutive helmeted figure climbing out of the open-topped Morris Cowley. The driver, he now saw when she removed her goggles, was a woman, not the wealthy young blade he had supposed.

Longing for a car of his own, he'd envied his wealthier fellow students at university who owned them, but needing every penny for his family, he'd known he would not be able to afford a car for many years to come, not even the Tin Lizzie as the little Ford car was known. The Morris Cowley that had nearly run into him was in a league far above that, and he stared somewhat wistfully at it, wishing he were in the driver's seat.

The driver now came across to the verge where he was standing, and as she removed her helmet, he saw that she was remarkably pretty.

'I say, I'm most dreadfully sorry!' she said, her aquamarine blue eyes smiling disarmingly as she looked up at him. 'I've only had that dashing little number for a week and I'm still learning where the controls are.' She gave him another dazzling smile and without a trace of shyness added: 'Do say you'll forgive me! Who are you, by they way? You're not George grown up beyond belief, are you?'

Godfrey found his voice. 'I'm Vaughan and Robert's tutor, Godfrey Gregson!' he said. 'What a top hole little car!'

She gave a contented sigh. 'I know! I absolutely adore her. I think it is a she, don't you? I'm Angela – Angela Bartofski, by the way. I know that's a bit of a mouthful. My late husband was a Russian, you see. Just call me Angel, and I'll call you Godfrey.' She gave a sudden laugh which crinkled her astonishingly brilliant blue eyes and curled the corners of her mouth. 'Can't very well shorten that to God, can we?' Seeing the slightly bewildered look on Godfrey's face, she took a deep breath. 'I can see you haven't got the vaguest idea who I am – I'm Frances' sister. You know, Lady Beauford's younger sibling – only surviving, actually. I dare say you've heard of me – black sheep of the family.'

She stopped to draw breath as the sound of a gong filtered through an open window.

'That sounds like the gong for lunch,' Godfrey said. 'Don't let me detain you, Mrs Bartofski.'

'Angela! Angel!' she reminded him, adding, 'Aren't you coming in to lunch?' She smiled up at him. 'It will be so nice to have some *young* company. My late husband, poor dear, was in his seventies and all his friends were old cronies, which did make life just a bit . . . well, tedious.'

'I have already had my lunch in the schoolroom,' Godfrey told her. Much as he would have liked to further his acquaintance with this intriguing young woman, he knew his employer would abhor the idea. 'I was about to go for a bike ride when . . .'

'When I ran into you!' she said laughing. 'Never mind, I'm sure we shall run into each other again.' And with a cheery wave, she disappeared into the house, her helmet and goggles swinging in her hand.

As he rode away, Godfrey decided that there had been a definite invitation in the young woman's eyes, and although he was alone, his cheeks coloured. Surely Lady Beauford's sister could not actually be flirting with him? For heaven's sake, she must be in her thirties at least and what possible interest could she have in a young man ten years or more her junior?

Ten minutes later, as he cycled through Farlington Hall's beautiful beech woods, Godfrey dismounted and found a fallen log to sit on whilst he tried to rationalize his thoughts. Angela – Victoria's much talked of Aunt Angela, no less – was by her own account a widow. Her husband had been in his seventies! It was inconceivable. Surely a beautiful young woman could not have fallen in love with an old man like that – a Russian? He seemed to recall one breakfast time Sir Aubrey handing a letter to his wife saying it was from America, from her sister? If she had been living in the United States, that might account for her complete lack of formality. Within minutes of meeting him, she had treated him like a friend despite knowing he was an employee.

Suddenly Godfrey smiled. Sitting in the warm September sunshine filtering through the leaves of the trees, he was imagining Lady Beauford's face if she could have overheard his encounter with her sister. What had she said was her surname – Baroofski? Bartofski? Something like that. No wonder she had been bored if the poor old chap she married had been at death's door and the only company she'd had was that of his elderly friends.

Really, it was none of his business, Godfrey reflected as he mounted George's cycle once more and took the path through the trees to the gorse-covered common land on the perimeter of the estate. The fact that he had found the slim, pretty, laughing young widow singularly attractive – more so than any girl he had so far met at university – was best quickly forgotten. Women like her, who were widows, could no doubt be as flirtatious as they wished just for the fun of it, but it was not something he, a mere student of twenty-four, should take in the least seriously. In another week, he would have left the Hall and with a busy day tomorrow cataloguing the books in Sir Aubrey's library, in all likelihood he would not even see the good lady again.

Godfrey had no way of knowing how wrong that supposition was.

Thirteen

'I've put you in the Hogarth room, Angela!' Frances said as she led her younger sister into the dining room for lunch. 'I gave Victoria your old bedroom. I don't suppose you mind!'

In point of fact, Angela did mind, although 'only the teeniest bit', she would have said to anyone else but Frances. She had been looking forward to returning to the pretty bedroom her sister had allotted her when, not long after her marriage to Aubrey, their father had died and the Snellings' family home had been sold.

Although Angela had loved the pretty flowered wallpaper, the dainty chintz curtains and the magnificent view over the tops of Farlington Hall's beech trees to the South Downs beyond, she had not enjoyed her older sister's dominant, restrictive management. She loved the old Elizabethan house and the surrounding countryside, but had no wish to live down in the country where she knew her hopes of a theatrical career would never materialize. Such was her ambition that as soon as she was old enough she had gone to live in London, despite Frances' warnings of poverty, of flea-ridden grubby digs, of inevitable social banishment. A lone female of Angela's age and prettiness, Frances had forecast, could even invite rape since Angela would have no chaperon or protector.

Steeling herself against her sister's arguments, Angela had braved the unknown and moved up to the big city, only returning to Farlington Hall occassionally. She was never there at Christmas as she had always been able to get a part in a pantomime even if at other times she was unemployed.

To be fair to Frances, Angela reflected, despite her sister's disapproval of her chosen theatrical career, she had continued to act as a surrogate mother to her, giving advice Angela did not want or take, attempting on each of her visits to persuade her to return home, settle down and get married 'before she was too old to attract a husband'. But whilst Frances made her welcome at Farlington Hall, Angela was never invited to stay at Eaton Terrace, lest Frances' society acquaintances discovered she had a younger sister on the stage!

She had not begrudged Frances the generous dowry settled on her by their father although she herself had been obliged to manage on a legacy of one hundred pounds a year. It was not money she had wanted from her late parent but freedom, and her father's death had set her free to pursue her search for fame. She took any job offered to her; be it in the chorus of a variety show or a minor part in a theatrical play or a pantomime, no matter how insignificant the venue. The digs she lived in were of little consequence to her. She used her allowance to pay for singing and dancing lessons and it was the consequent improvement which gave her the chance of a minor role in the chorus of a musical show. It was there that Nikolai Bartofski had noticed her and fallen passionately in love with her. He was, he'd told her, living in New York, where he had a great deal of influence with the new wireless broadcasters in the United States.

Whilst the ability to transmit wireless signals over the air was in its comparative infancy in Angela's country, her Russian admirer had told her it was far advanced in America, where they already had three hundred broadcasting stations. Without doubt, he'd informed her, if she married him and went back to the States with him, he would be able to progress her career, make her a star.

Angela had believed him whilst Frances demanded to know what on earth possessed her ever to consider marrying an unknown Russian who was not only without a title, but in his seventies. It had been a fearful shock to Frances when she had eloped with Nikolai without informing her sister of her intention. But that was all of three years ago, Angela thought now, and poor Nikolai had been dead for the last one of them. What she had not yet told Frances when she had announced her arrival back in England in a telegram yesterday was that her husband had left her a small fortune!

Her first sight of Aubrey put such memories from her as she and Frances entered the dining room. Smiling happily at

her brother-in-law, she ran into his outstretched arms and
returned his fond embrace.

'You look younger than ever!' she exclaimed as he released
her. 'And gracious me, you're as handsome as ever, Aubrey.
Why, I've only been home ten minutes yet already I've seen
two far more captivating guys than ever I saw in the States.
You and that handsome tutor I ran into in the drive would
have the American girls fighting for a date!'

Only with difficulty did she now refrain from laughing at
Frances' disapproving scowl, which remained in place
throughout the meal.

'You must forgive my Americanisms, Fran,' she said later
as she followed Aubrey into the drawing room and dropped
into one of the comfortable armchairs. She drew out a slim
silver cigarette case. 'The lingo as well as the accent are
terribly catching,' she added with a mischievous smile at
Aubrey.

Frances sat down opposite them, a look of resignation
replacing the scowl on her face.

'I suppose you can't help it, but do try to speak properly
in front of Victoria,' she said tersely, adding tight-lipped: 'And
will you try and remember I do hate being called Fran. It's
so vulgar!'

With an effort, Angela remained silent. She had, she realized, forgotten how pernickety Frances was. She turned her
large blue eyes to Aubrey.

'I do hope you have forgiven me for eloping with Nikolai
the way I did, Aubrey. Fran – Frances wrote and told me you
were all so upset,' she said. 'It just seemed the best thing to
do at the time. I'm really sorry. I suppose I should have told
you before I left the country, but I only made up my mind
to go with Nikolai forty-eight hours before his boat sailed. I
wasn't in love with him, you see, so it didn't seem fair; but
he knew that and still wanted me to go. He was a very generous
man as well as kind. Before we left England he even gave
me the money for my return fare if I wasn't happy living
with him.'

Aubrey was looking at the pretty young woman who, had
she been several years older, he would have much preferred
to court when his mother had first introduced him to the two
unmarried daughters of the steel tycoon. His mother had

insisted he courted the elder sister, Frances. Even then, young as she was, Angela had been the prettier but she was without a dowry and her leanings towards the theatre made her unacceptable to his mother. As the only surviving son, she had insisted that his wife must be a suitable mother for the future Beauford heirs.

Where Frances now looked decidedly matronly, Angela had kept her petite figure. Her short wavy hair was a wonderful silky blonde, her lips outlined in a slightly shocking scarlet lipstick. Had she had lovers before her marriage, he found himself wondering. She must now be in her mid-thirties, but she could hold her own with any female a decade younger.

'Aubrey!' His wife's strident voice broke in on his thoughts. 'For heaven's sake, stop staring at Angela. You'll make her nervous!'

Angela laughed. 'Not me, Fran – Frances. Most of my life on the stage I was praying people would stare at me, notice me. That's what being a performer is all about.'

Sensing a further rebuke from Frances, Aubrey said quickly: 'In your letters to Frances, you said you were disappointed not to have made headway – getting into broadcasting or the theatre, I mean.'

Angela bit her lip. 'Well, no, Nikolai didn't have quite the clout he had led me to believe. I did get a little work but the competition was overpowering. America seems to be bursting at the seams with beautiful girls who have magnificent singing voices, and can dance professionally as well.' She smiled wistfully. 'There was also the matter of my age. To be over thirty in America is to be far too ancient for the chorus, and they said my voice was not strong enough for transmission by air.'

'You should never have gone with that man!' Frances declared. 'If I'd known you were about to commit such a folly, I would never have allowed it.'

Angela's face relaxed into a smile. 'Which was one of the reasons I didn't tell you! May I remind you, dearest sister of mine, that I was thirty-one when I met Nikolai – beyond family intervention, I think you will agree, however well meaning. Besides, things have not turned out so badly. Nikolai has left his entire fortune to me, bar one or two minor bequests.' She turned to Aubrey, her eyes dancing: 'I believe I am now a wealthy widow, Aubrey, so if you need a contribution to restoring a roof or modernizing the Hall, you have only to ask me. Or, indeed, if any of the children have educational needs . . . ?'

'We manage perfectly well without charitable assistance, thank you, Angela.' Frances' sharp rejoinder interrupted Aubrey, who said:

'That's very kind of you, Angela, but as Frances says, we manage as we are. Now, tell me, my dear, did I understand you to say just now that you had run into young Gregson? Very nice fellow, Gregson. Down from Oxford for the long vacation. Been the boys' tutor these past two months. Clever young chap, y'know. Spoke to his college tutor before we took him on; said he was likely to land a double first. Family a bit impoverished – the war, you see. With his father killed in the war, Gregson supports his mother and sisters. Frances likes him, too, don't you, m'dear?'

Frances sighed. 'I've nothing against him, Aubrey, and he has managed the two boys very well. However, there really is no need to bore Angela with Mr Gregson's family history. He's leaving next week and Angela is hardly likely to meet him again.'

Despite her thoughts, Angela managed to keep her face impassive. A week was quite a long time and she expected to be not a little bored down in the country. Flora and fauna were not of more than passing interest to her although she did enjoy tennis and she hoped the grass court would be dry enough for her to play a game or two with Aubrey. She liked the bright lights, dancing, jazz, cocktail bars, the cinema and above all, the theatre. Well, not quite above all – her most favourite occupation was the enjoyment of love – love in all its many manifestations. The first meeting with a new lover; the early flirtation, the 'will I, won't I?' decision-making; the assignations; the surrender, and the big adventure of sex itself.

Marie Stopes having made it possible for women like herself to have affairs with no danger of becoming pregnant, Angela saw no reason for keeping her suitors at arm's length. She had rarely cheated on Nikolai, despite the fact that like his other promises his description of his passionate needs did not materialize. He'd died suddenly of a heart attack and although she'd felt genuinely sad at the time, it was as if a heavy yoke had been lifted and she was free again.

Before anything else, she had decided, she would go back to England, not to the big grey stone Victorian edifice in which her parents had chosen to live, which was long since sold, but to the Beaufords' beautiful Elizabethan mansion. She'd loved Farlington Hall from the first moment she had seen the mellow brick house. Aware as she was that Frances preferred the town house in Eaton Terrace, Angela felt that Farlington Hall was wasted on her sister.

'I'll take you up to London as soon as you have rested,' Frances was saying. 'There's nothing to do down here now. The boys have gone back to school and Aubrey will be having a lot of his boring old shooting chums down to kill a few more birds. Fortunately, he allows me to make myself scarce, don't you, dear? And I don't doubt the men prefer the place to themselves.'

'Don't any of them bring their wives? Their girlfriends?' Angela asked Aubrey mischievously. She herself had once been invited to one such country house weekend by a young man who'd taken a fancy to her and hung about the stage door until finally she had agreed to go away with him. She'd known perfectly well what the invitation included – she was to go as his girlfriend, a part she could carry off quite easily with her background. Although everyone had behaved impeccably during the daytime, there'd been a great deal of movement in the corridors at night, including that of her escort to her room. Everyone had seemed to enjoy themselves hugely, as had Angela herself, her admirer turning out to be a practised as well as an ardent lover. Was it possible, she wondered now, that Aubrey gave similar parties when Frances was in London? Somehow she thought it unlikely.

The memory brought with it a nostalgic longing for the passionate ardour Nikolai had promised but was never able to supply. It was high time, she told herself, that she found another lover – and who better than the good-looking athletic young man who had eyed her so appreciatively when they'd met in the driveway?

With Frances now occupied in if not an argument, a heated discussion with Aubrey about the children, Angela decided she might as well excuse herself and go in search of the handsome tutor, who, she presumed, would be in the schoolroom or the library if he had returned from his bicycle ride. As yet, she had not encountered her young niece, Victoria, so her wish to do so provided her with an excuse to leave the room. As she closed the door behind her, she could hear her sister's strident voice declaring that Aubrey should 'leave matters in the hands of your mother and me because in the circumstances, sentiment simply doesn't come in to it!'

Poor Aubrey, Angela thought as she went slowly up the wide staircase, still allowing himself to be bullied by her domineering sister! The only person she knew who could dominate Frances was her mother-in-law. No wonder Aubrey was so easily cowed, growing up with a mother like Lady Mary.

Hearing voices in the schoolroom, she opened the door and saw Godfrey seated opposite her niece, a backgammon board between them. Both stood up as she went into the room and Victoria ran across to hug her.

'Aunt Angela!' she cried. 'It's so absolutely ripping to see you! Mother said you were coming but she didn't know when. I love your tartan dress. You look absolutely divine!' Her eyes sparkled as she added confidentially: 'That's what all Mother's friends say about each other's clothes.' She mimicked their high-pitched voices, saying again: 'How absolutely *divine*, darling!' before she burst out laughing.

Angela hugged her. 'Well, *you* look absolutely divine, darling!' she said. 'And how you have grown!'

'I should jolly well hope so,' Victoria replied. 'I was only five when you got married and went to America. I missed you dreadfully.'

'I missed you, too, sweetheart!' Angela told her, not altogether truthfully. 'Now, my darling, shall we sit down?'

'Oh, goodness, I'm forgetting my manners!' Again Victoria mimicked Frances' voice. 'Can I introduce you to Mr Gregson. Mr Gregson, this is my Aunt Angela!' She giggled as Godfrey, who had risen to his feet when Angela came into the room, now stepped forward and shook her hand.

'Actually, Victoria, we have already met – when your aunt arrived!' he told the child. His eyes were glinting with laughter as he added: 'We almost had a slight collision, but I have forgiven her!'

Looking into Victoria's questioning face, Angela explained how she had nearly run him over.

'I do hope your bicycle is none the worse for wear, Mr Gregson?'

'Unharmed, I'm pleased to say, as it happens to be George's cycle which I borrowed.'

'For which I am truly thankful,' Angela said, adding: 'It's time I went and unpacked my cases, unless Pauline has done it for me.'

Victoria sighed: 'Oh, Pauline got dismissed ages ago. The maids never stay long, you know. Mother gets cross if they do something wrong and they're frightened of her. I tell them it's silly to be scared. I'm not! George once told me before he went to Ceylon: "Just say you're sorry and don't argue even if you didn't do anything wrong. Ma soon gets over it!" '

Victoria knew her mother would not get over hearing George call her 'Ma', but of course he never did so to their mother's face.

'The maid is called Sally – she's really nice,' she told Angela. 'She does upstairs mostly. Ellen does down, and Annie is our nursery maid. Annie's the prettiest, isn't she, Mr Gregson. I think she is in love with you! She always blushes when you talk to her!'

'And you'll do more than blush if your mother hears you talking like that!' Godfrey said, his voice only half serious as he saw the laughter in Angela's eyes. It struck him again what an attractive woman she was, her face and manner belying what he guessed to be her age. For the second time that day, he found himself questioning whether she was flirting with him. Surely not, he thought, and yet . . . yet there was something in the tone of her voice, in her posture, in the direct expression of her eyes which made the improbability seem possible.

Victoria took hold of her aunt's arm and all but dragged her to the door as she begged her to come to her room so she could show her the Meccano set George had bequeathed her. Angela turned and looked directly at Godfrey's handsome boyish features. His expression told her that she was not mistaken in thinking he found her attractive.

'I hope we'll see each other later. My sister told me what an excellent tutor you are, and old as I am, I'm sure you could teach me something worth knowing!'

Fortunately for Godfrey, Victoria did not notice that now

it was he who was blushing. Still tugging at Angela's arm, the child said innocently: 'Mr Gregson is terribly clever, Aunt Angela. He knows absolutely *everything*!'

'Then I shall look forward to finding that out for myself, won't I, my darling?'

Angela was speaking to Victoria but her eyes were still on Godfrey's face.

Fourteen

For one long day, Copper had been on tenterhooks. At breakfast, Harold had opened a letter which, when she'd handed it to him, she could swear was from a woman. Not only was the envelope scented but the handwriting was unmistakeably feminine. She had waited patiently for him to read it and report the contents to her, even more urgently as she saw his expression change from one of curiosity to anger and then to a look of distress.

'What is it, Harry?' she'd asked as he pushed his uneaten plate of scrambled eggs to one side and put the letter back into its envelope.

'Is it something exciting?' Leila asked.

'Nothing to concern you, Leila,' he said dismissively. Nevertheless his daughter noticed something different in his tone of voice. It was not in her nature to be inquisitive, or indeed, to notice details such as nuances of speech. A loving, contented child, devoted to her parents and adoring of her very best friend, Victoria, she sailed through life with few ups or downs, her face usually brightened by a placid smile.

Avoiding his daughter's enquiring glance, Harold looked across the table at Copper's anxious face and said: 'I am going into school this morning and I have an appointment this afternoon to meet the parents of a child starting next term. I'll be back as soon as I can and we can talk about this –' he held up the letter – 'when I get back.' It crossed Copper's mind that Harold might have sent Leila out of the room in order to reveal the contents of the letter. But he did not do so. It seemed to her as if he was deliberately avoiding her eyes, as if he were trying to avoid her questioning him again.

Despite her efforts to occupy herself with shopping, gardening, cooking, the hours seemed to crawl by until at long last she heard his footsteps outside the front door. Instead of hurrying to meet him as was her habit, she sat down heavily in one of the kitchen chairs. The kettle was simmering on the range and it would take but a minute to make a pot of tea if it was wanted. It was as if she knew by some strange instinct that this had to be bad news and a cup of hot, sweet tea was the only restorative she could think of.

Carrying his briefcase and an armful of books, Harold let himself into the tiny hall. Putting them down on the oak chest, he hung his hat and coat on the coat stand and glanced into the sitting room. Seeing it empty, he realized Copper was in the kitchen. For a moment, he stood facing the closed door, unwilling to impart the facts which he knew he could no longer avoid telling her. Then straightening his back he opened the door and went in. As Copper rose to greet him, he put his arms around her and bent to kiss her tenderly on the forehead. She lingered for a moment in the safety of his arms and then with an effort, she said calmly: 'Let us both sit down, dearest, and you can tell me what has been worrying you . . . it was that letter you received this morning, wasn't it?'

Grateful to have his wife's encouragement, Harold sat down beside her at the kitchen table, and took her hand in his.

'You are right to suppose there was unwelcome news in that letter,' he said quietly. 'Of course, I shall do everything in my power to negate the proposal—' He broke off, realizing that he had not yet informed Copper of the contents of the letter. So intense were his feelings that he feared he would be unable to speak in the calm, controlled voice that would prevent his wife panicking. Feeling as violently opposed as he was to the writer's intentions, he decided to give his wife the letter to read for herself. Taking it from his breast pocket, he handed it to her. Quite suddenly, the scent from the expensive writing paper pervaded the room.

The letter was crested and came from Lady Mary Beauford. Her hands trembling, Copper brushed a stray lock of hair from her forehead and began to read the thin, sprawling but perfectly formed writing.

Dear Mr and Mrs Varney,
    I understand from my son, Sir Aubrey, that you are aware of the results of the blood tests made upon *you*

and your daughter and Victoria and her parents. You will, therefore, have been aware that by some dreadful accident, the two children were handed to each other's parent shortly after birth. In other words, Leila is my granddaughter and Victoria is your child.

You will also have realized from your own and others' observations of the two girls that there can be no doubt whatever about the facts resulting from the tests. Clearly this situation cannot continue. I have given the matter much thought and have in both our interests taken legal advice as to the future for these unfortunate children.

Perhaps we should consider it advantageous that the girls are such good friends and because of this, your daughter would not feel too strange were she to join Victoria at Farlington Hall and become part of her natural family. She is, of course, undeniably a Beauford with the bloodlines of an aristocratic family going back to the time of William the Conqueror. This fact, and the addition of three brothers who she already knows, are but two of the advantages young Leila will receive when she is in my son's care. I shall personally finance her schooling at the Convent of the Holy Virgin where I understand she will receive as comprehensive an education as befits a child of her abilities.

My son has pointed out to me that Leila is your only child and I have agreed that you will be permitted to see her no less than once a week and that you may have her to stay with you for a week during the summer holidays by arrangement with my daughter-in-law. You will doubtless wish to see Victoria from time to time. Although she is not by birth one of my son's family, she has grown up believing herself to be so. I see no need to disillusion her until such time as she is old enough to understand what happened in the hospital that disastrous night. Meanwhile, my daughter-in-law and my son wish to formally adopt Leila so that from now on, she is understood to be a member of our family.

My son is of the opinion that you might raise objections to these decisions but I have, as I said earlier, taken legal advice, and since there is no precedence in law for a case such as this, a legal appeal by yourselves (should

you contemplate it) would undoubtedly fail since the
child you had thought to be yours is indisputably of our
family. I trust, therefore, that you will have no objections to us implementing the above mentioned plan at
the earliest opportunity.

Lady Mary's signature covered the remainder of the page.

For a minute, Copper did not speak. Then in a shocked
voice, the words poured from her trembling lips.

'You will not agree to this, will you, Harry? I shall never,
ever be parted from my baby. Leila *is* my baby, my little girl
and even if it is true that she and Victoria were swapped at
birth, I don't care. Harry . . .' She looked up at him, her voice
anguished. 'You do agree with me, don't you? You love Leila
as much as I do. We won't have to hand her over to the
Beaufords, will we?

Harold drew in a deep breath and exhaled slowly.

'Not if I can possibly help it!' he said quietly. 'But I won't
lie to you, my dear, Lady Mary says in that letter that she has
taken legal advice. We know from the tests that Leila is not
genetically our child. Logically, given the circumstances, she
must be theirs!'

Copper's face had turned a deathly white. 'You sound as
if there is nothing we can do!' she murmured close to tears.
'Surely they can't just take Leila away from us as if . . . as if
she's a family heirloom, or something? Harold, I won't . . . *I
can't let her go*. I know she adores Victoria and loves going
up to the Hall to play, but we're her mummy and daddy. She
loves us—'

'I know! I know!' Harold broke in, his own voice none too
steady as his arm tightened around her. 'I feel exactly as you
do and I've thought of little else all day. I am going to write
to my former tutor, John Scotforth; you remember me telling
you about him, my dear? He started life as a lawyer and
although he retired some time ago, I don't doubt he will have
kept very much up to date with legal changes. He may be
able to advise us of our legal position. You see, my dear, I
fear there is very little hope we can change Lady Mary's mind,
although of course I shall write to her. From all accounts, she
is a very formidable lady and according to the estate manager
who I meet from time to time at the Fox and Vixen, as the

senior member of the family she takes it for granted that Sir Aubrey and Lady Beauford come under her direction.'

Copper stood up, straightening her back. Her cheeks were flushed a deep pink as she declared: 'What do women like her know about children's feelings? Victoria spends most of her time with her nanny, not her mother, and I'll bet Sir Aubrey was brought up by a nanny.' She sat down suddenly as if her moment of aggression had given way once more to despair. 'Harry, tell me this isn't true: it isn't going to happen?' She burst into tears and Harold put his arms protectively around her.

'I can't promise you it won't happen, my dear, but I do promise to do everything in my power to prevent it. I don't want to raise any false hopes, but it has crossed my mind that in the last resort, we might threaten to lay claim to Victoria. That would be a much fairer exchange even though I know it's not what we actually want. In point of fact, I'm very fond of Victoria – she's a bright, intelligent, thoroughly nice little girl. I wouldn't in the least mind adopting her, but *not* if it means us losing Leila.' He glanced at his watch and said quickly: 'Leila will be home any minute, my dear. I strongly suggest we say nothing at all for the time being. I will go up to the Hall after tea and see Sir Aubrey if I can. Despite what his mother says, I have a feeling he is still on our side.'

Seeing a slightly less doleful expression on his wife's countenance, he forbore from adding that he doubted very much indeed if Sir Aubrey would be allowed any say in the decision-making.

Sir Aubrey was out riding with Victoria when Harold drove up in his old black Ford. The maid, whose younger sister went to Harold's school, explained the position and suggested the headmaster might like to wait in the library.

'Mr Gregson's in there, sir. He's cata-something the master's books. He's ever so nice and he'll be someone to talk to whilst you's waiting. You didn't want to see her ladyship, did you, sir? She's in London.'

For which Harold thanked his guardian angel. The very last thing he wanted was a scene with the Sir Aubrey's autocratic wife. As Sally showed him into the library he felt the first faint glimmer of hope since he'd read Lady Mary's letter at breakfast. He knew Sir Aubrey to be particularly devoted to Victoria and was not willing to consider parting with her any more than he and Copper could contemplate parting with Leila. Somehow he could not imagine Sir Aubrey ceasing to idolize Victoria simply because she was not after all a Beauford.

The room was deserted and he walked over to the tall bay window looking down across the formal flower beds to the beautiful copper beeches at the end of the lawn. His thoughts, however, were with his wife. He shared the dreadful fear that was tormenting her and which he must, somehow, manage to allay. Such was his love for her, he would have taken her fears upon his own shoulders were they not there already.

Returning to his stance by the fireplace, Harold pondered once more the possibility of threatening a talion – namely that they would fight to have Victoria if Leila was handed over to the Beaufords. He supposed that in a way, it was a sort of blackmail; but anything was excusable rather than having their beloved daughter whisked away from them – '*have her once a week*,' Lady Mary had said in her letter, and '*for a week in the summer holidays.*'

The library door opened and Godfrey came into the room carrying an armful of ledgers. Dumping them on the nearest table, he went forward to shake Harold's hand. During the summer holidays, he had met the headmaster on several occasions: on the towpath when he and the boys had been fishing in the river, and on Elmsfield village green where the local lads were doing their best to score against a visiting cricket team. They had also met at the summer fête, which traditionally was held in the grounds of Farlington Hall. According to Victoria, Mrs Mount was always in a horrible temper when the village ladies invaded her kitchen to help with the teas!

'Has someone told you Sir Aubrey is out riding with Victoria?' he said when Harold explained his reason for being there. 'I don't suppose they'll be an awful lot longer.' He smiled. 'You'd think that the child would be a pain in the neck . . . spoilt, I mean, the way her father dotes on her. He even went out last week and bought himself a hunter so he could ride with her. The boys said their father had always wanted a girl and had all but given up hope after young Robert was born. Then along came little Miss Mischief! Bright as a button, but I expect you know that. She goes to your school, doesn't she?'

Aware that he had given no praise to the headmaster's daughter, Godfrey added quickly: 'The little fair-haired girl who comes to play with Victoria is your daughter, is she not? She's such a pretty, happy child. Her manners are far better than Victoria's. You must be very proud of her, sir.'

'I must give the credit to my wife. It is she who sets an example for Leila!' Harold replied. He was about to ask Godfrey what he was reading at university but before he could do so, Sir Aubrey came hurrying into the room.

'I do apologize, Varney!' he said, holding out his hand to shake that of his visitor. 'I had no idea you were coming to see me, and I'm afraid young Vicky demands no less than a two-hour ride. Quite exhausting!' He turned to put his bowler hat and riding crop on the table and turned briefly to Godfrey.

'You getting on all right, young fellow?' he asked with a smile. He winked at Harold. 'Got him cataloguing my library – dreadful mess. My fault. Can never remember where books go. Don't read much myself, but people like to borrow them. I understand there are quite a few first editions in that lot, eh, Gregson? You must feel free to borrow anything you fancy reading, Varney.'

Was Sir Aubrey talking so much in order to delay the confrontation which he must surely know was the reason for his visit? Harold asked himself. But one thing he was certain of, this man was not devious.

Godfrey now tactfully made his departure and Sir Aubrey beckoned Harold to one of the two large wing chairs which stood either side of the grey marble fireplace. As Harold sat down, his eye caught two silver-framed photographs on the mantelpiece – one clearly of Sir Aubrey and Lady Beauford on their wedding day; and the other of the four children, the boys in a semicircle standing self-consciously behind their sister. Victoria must have been about five at the time and was wearing a white muslin dress and a white hair band with a bow at the side.

With a shock, Harold realized that he was almost certainly looking at a photograph of his daughter; his own flesh and blood. He was so overcome by a rush of conflicting emotions that it was a moment or two before he could answer Sir Aubrey's polite enquiry as to why he was there.

'Expect you feel much the way I do!' he said gruffly as Harold struggled to speak. 'Damn fool nonsense, if you ask me. Got my mother and my wife all het up about bloodlines or some such nonsense. Children are not thoroughbred horses, in heaven's name! Best let sleeping dogs lie – that's my opinion, but . . .'

Glad to have an opening, Harold said quietly: 'But your wife feels differently!' He finished the sentence for the older man, who could not bring himself do so. 'I received a letter this morning – from Lady Mary saying you wished to adopt Leila. She wrote as if it was a foregone conclusion and pointed out that my wife and I had no chance of a legal appeal should we be contemplating opposing her decision.'

'I'll be damned!' Sir Aubrey exclaimed, reaching in his pocket for his pipe and busying himself filling it. 'Never said a word to me. Knew I'd disapprove, I dare say. Look here, Varney, my own feelings are pretty simple. I'd like us to forget all about those damned blood thingummies.' His expression turned to one of resignation. 'But m'wife – well, she feels the same way my mother does – that a wrong was perpetrated and must now be put right. Says I can't just bury my head in the sand and say we do nothing. What's your way out of all this, Varney? You deal with children . . . headmaster and all that. If it was your decision . . . ?'

Harold leant back in his chair, feeling pity as he regarded the portly figure of the wealthy, titled but utterly miserable man opposite him. He gazed directly into Sir Aubrey's anxious face.

'I'd do nothing, sir! That is to say, I would let the truth emerge quite naturally. We are fortunate in being neighbours – we can see each other's –' he quickly corrected himself – 'our natural daughters every day without having to lose touch with the little girls we have always thought of as ours. With care, tact and above all the will, we can encourage them to spend a lot of time in each other's homes so that eventually they both feel equally at ease in either. When they are a great deal older, maybe then we can tell them the truth if they have not already gauged it for themselves; and it can be their choice as to whether they do or do not wish to change their surnames; live permanently with their biological parents!'

Sir Aubrey was beginning to look almost happy.

'Damn good idea, Varney. Go along with it—' He broke off, his look of anxiety returning. 'Could put it to my wife but . . . well, it might be better if you could suggest it, Varney. She has nothing against you, I know. Thinks you're a cracking good headmaster. Whereas I . . . well, she thinks I'm too weak with young Vicky, spoil her and all that. Dare say I do! Always wanted a pretty little thing to indulge. Lost my younger sister, y'see! Only fifteen years old and I—' He cleared his throat, before concluding, 'Got a bit lost there, Varney. Really just want to say I'll back any proposition you put to my wife as long as Victoria stays with us. Now, how about a snifter? Could do with a whisky and I'd be glad if you'll join me.'

For a moment, Harold hesitated, aware as he was of Copper waiting at home for some good news to relieve her fears. Then he looked at Sir Aubrey, whose expression was uncannily like that of a very small boy desperate for a playmate to relieve his loneliness. Harold's voice barely concealed his pity as he said: 'Just a quick one then. I'll be happy to join you.'

Fifteen

With no real interest in her sister's married life in New York, Frances retired to bed not long after dinner. It had been a tiring evening in which she had found herself very much on the defensive, Angela having most irritatingly decided to take Aubrey's part against her.

Not that it would make any difference to the outcome, she consoled herself as she climbed into the huge double bed which Aubrey no longer shared. For some years now, he had confined himself to the single bed in his dressing room. It was her mother-in-law who, as was so often the case, was now calling the tune, and Frances had no doubt the indomitable Lady Mary would override any objections to her wishes regarding the girls. The Varney child – her child, she now knew but found hard to believe – was to become part of the family.

Frances herself did not much care if such was to be the case. She really had very little to do with the children. Of course, she was devoted to her handsome eldest son, George, now twenty years old. She missed him sorely, his amusing chatter, his light-hearted comments about her friends, which were often very funny but never waspish, his sense of humour. A man in stature and handsome enough to draw admiring remarks from her women friends, he had an easy charm, which he'd used effortlessly whenever the situation demanded it. Now his letters home were the highlight of her otherwise pedestrian life. It had been at very least a bitter disappointment to her when he had opted to go abroad instead of to university. If she'd had her way she would have made him wait to go travelling until he came of age, but for once Aubrey had overruled her.

Frances settled herself more comfortably against the soft duck-feather-filled pillows. Extinguishing her bedside light, she lay back and for one of the rare moments in her life, she allowed herself to consider her feelings with complete honesty. The truth, she now admitted, was that George was the only one of her children she truly loved. Not, of course, that she wasn't fond of the other two boys. Victoria . . . well, she had never seemed to understand the child. According to Victoria's teachers, and, indeed, the servants, she was a pleasure to have around – intelligent, happy, sparkling with the enjoyment of life. As far as she, Frances was concerned, there was a great deal too much sparkle. The girl never seemed able to sit still for more than a moment, was forever asking questions and demanding to be allowed the same advantages as the boys. Even more irritating was Victoria's habit of reminding her of some promise or remark she had once said, which the child pointed out, conflicted with her present opinion. The fact that Victoria was usually right was even more annoying.

'But, Mother –' Victoria had ceased calling her Mama or Mummy when the boys chose the more adult name – 'you told me yesterday I was to wear this blue taffeta when my godmother came to tea!' reminding her that she had no right to complain because Nanny had not dressed her in the new pink silk she'd just bought for her in London.

In many ways, Frances reflected now, it didn't matter what Victoria was wearing, she always managed somehow to look pretty – something she had never managed to do as a child. It was always her young sister, blue-eyed Angela with her golden ringlets and rosebud mouth, who drew the admiring glances.

If she were to be totally honest, brutally so, Frances now told herself as she turned restlessly from one side to the other, she had never felt a maternal love for Victoria from the first moment the nurse in the hospital had put the scarlet-faced infant in her arms. The labour pains birthing her had been far worse than those she'd had when she'd brought the boys into the world, bad enough although they had been! It was hardly surprising she had never really loved Victoria – the blood tests had entirely vindicated her – she should never have had maternal feelings for her. And a final truth, one which had shocked Angela as well as Aubrey when she had pronounced it downstairs, she would not mind in the least if the Varneys demanded a straight exchange.

A half smile curved Frances' thin lips as she recalled the scandalized look on Aubrey's face. For one of the very rare moments in his life, he had been quite out of control when he accused her of being jealous because he loved Victoria so much. She'd argued fiercely that it was an insult even to suggest that she might be jealous of a child. Yet now she had to admit to herself that he was partially right. It had always irritated her beyond measure that Aubrey adored Victoria and indulged her every whim, a pony, a bicycle, a piano, even a train set she'd wanted because the boys each had one. But these indulgences were not the real reason why she resented her small daughter. The real reason was because they manifested her husband's unfailing devotion to the child.

She had always known that Aubrey did not love her – not the way she had wanted to be loved; that he'd married her because his mother had told him to; because she was her father's heiress. Being the man he was, he had always behaved towards her with the utmost civility, decorum, consideration – in other words, impeccably; but that did not constitute love.

Her heart suddenly hardening, Frances determined that his mother's and not his wishes would decide the outcome of the girls' futures. As far as she was concerned – and she intended to say as much to Lady Mary when she went to see her next week – it would be best for everyone if the whole matter was cleared up as soon as possible. The two girls should change places and, if possible, the Varneys would be told to remove themselves to some other part of the country – or better still, to Canada or Australia. Doubtless Lady Mary would finance such an outcome. As for Aubrey, he would just have to do without the one love of his life.

In New York, Angela had seldom retired to bed before midnight. She was still wide awake when Frances retired, Aubrey soon after. She felt thoroughly unsettled – not because of the uncertainty of her own future but because of the heartbreaking news her sister had related that evening. At first she had found it difficult to believe but it was obvious from the letters Frances showed her that the doctors knew what they were talking about – the babies had been swapped.

Poor old Aubrey! had been Angela's first reaction, knowing full well how he adored Victoria; how reluctant he would be to part with his daughter. It was not only Aubrey who was going to suffer but the unfortunate couple who would be losing their only child, for whom she felt even more sorry. She had argued quite vociferously with Frances that there was a really good case to be made for leaving matters as they were; that the children had no need to know the truth until they were adults and it was no one else's business.

Frances had all but shouted her down, going on about the Beauford family line as if the Beaufords were royalty. It wasn't even as if she had latent maternal feelings toward the Varney child, who, it now seemed, *was* her daughter. As far as Angela could gather, Frances only knew the headmaster's child because she came to play with Victoria at the Hall.

Angela wandered through to the kitchen knowing that Mrs Mount would long since have gone to bed and the huge room with its large black iron Eagle range would be deserted. It was her intention to make herself a cup of coffee, but on reflection she decided it might make her even more wakeful. She remembered suddenly that upstairs in her room was a bottle of whisky which she had purchased on board the *Mauretania*, in which luxurious liner she had crossed the Atlantic. It was to be a present for Aubrey but she had forgotten to take it downstairs when she had dressed for dinner.

Deciding to go and find it, she went upstairs to her room, where it was still on the dressing table where she had left it. Annie, the maid who had unpacked for her, had laid her cream silk-crêpe nightdress decoratively on top of the pink floral eiderdown. The room looked welcoming but she was disinclined to drink by herself. Despite the frustrations of her marriage to Nikolai, she had never yet resorted to liquor to assuage her loneliness, and unlike several women she'd met she had never become an alcoholic. Nevertheless, she did enjoy the expensive wines Nikolai could so easily afford to buy, and before he became ill his one enjoyment in life was sitting with her in their penthouse apartment sampling one of his brandies or liqueurs which he managed to acquire from Canada. For the past two years there had been Prohibition not only throughout the United States, but in Russia, too, where it was called 'the dry law'. Well able to afford the inflated price of this illegal liquor, Nikolai saw no reason to deny himself, or her, the harmless pleasure of alcohol.

Although she had never loved her elderly husband, she had grown very fond of him. She missed his companionship. What she had not commented upon to her sister was that she found Nikolai's impotence hugely sexually frustrating. Not inexperienced in sex before she married him, she had freely enjoyed liaisons with fellow artists, albeit brief affairs rather than love affairs. Nikolai never knew that on the few evenings when she went out on her own, she was actually drinking at private parties frequented by thespians and artists, and occasionally ended the night in some man's bed.

Angela did not consider herself to be a nymphomaniac. For the most part her life was devoid of sex, but that did not stop her wishing things were otherwise. Tonight, for instance, she would not by choice be in her bedroom drinking by herself; she would be out at a cocktail bar or the theatre or other such places where she would not be alone. Not that there were such places in Elmsfield! she told herself ruefully. Still restless, she wandered over to the window, the tumbler full of whisky and water in her hand. It was a sparklingly clear night, the three-quarter moon glinting on the dew covering the lawn, the sky almost white with starlight. Suddenly, she glimpsed a figure approaching the house from the stables. It was, she realized, the young tutor, Godfrey Gregson.

Her heart missed a beat. There was no doubt in her mind that brief though their meeting had been, he'd found her attractive – and he was undoubtedly so. Did he know how old she was, she wondered? Quite often she had been given a part in a play as an ingénue because, so the casting director said, she still looked like a girl even if she wasn't one!

Slipping off her bronze glacé kid evening shoes so that her footsteps would make no noise on the stairs, Angela tiptoed down to the hall carrying the bottle of whisky carefully in one hand. Guessing Godfrey would come in by the garden door, she skirted the library and morning room and was in time to see him emerge from the gunroom, where he had been removing his galoshes.

'Great Scott, you gave me a fright!' he exclaimed. 'I thought everyone had gone to bed.' He stopped, seeing the bottle clasped in her right hand. She was leaning against the wall, an amused smile on her face as if she had heard a joke he'd somehow missed. Surprisingly, she had no shoes on and her pink-stockinged feet emerged from beneath the floating skirt of her pale gold evening gown. She looked both mysterious and astonishingly attractive.

'Sorry I scared you!' she said huskily, her voice slightly accented. 'I couldn't sleep, so when I saw you in the garden, I thought you weren't sleepy either and I might persuade you to join me in a whisky. This is good old Scottish Haig!'

Godfrey tried to recover his equilibrium although his thoughts were racing. Had this very attractive woman sought him out simply for company, as she'd implied? It was utterly unconventional. For one thing, he did not know of any woman or girl who drank spirits. Wine, certainly, when served at a meal; but she had been living in the States and perhaps things were different out there.

'You aren't going to refuse my invitation, I hope, Godfrey? You told me your name when we met and needless to say, Victoria told me, too! She's very much a fan of yours. She says you always know the answers to absolutely everything! Is that true?'

Godfrey was no longer in doubt that Lady Beauford's sister was now flirting with him; moreover, that he was beginning to enjoy this night adventure. He wasn't accustomed to drinking whisky but was nothing loath to try. But where was this mutual indulgence to take place?

Almost as if reading his thoughts, Angela said: 'Why don't we go up to my room? It's in the east wing so no one will hear us. My sister, as I am sure you know, is easily shocked by even the slightest deviation from convention. We'll be uninterrupted there.'

There was now no misunderstanding Angela's implications, Godfrey told himself as he followed her upstairs. He knew she was not long widowed but obviously she did not intend to go into mourning! He decided he would follow her lead physically as well as metaphorically.

The house was indeed devoid of human sound or activity as, followed closely by Godfrey, Angela quietly opened her bedroom door and then closed it again behind him. Then she went over to the marble washstand and picked up the empty tooth glass, which she carried to the bedside where a water jug and tumbler had been placed for her night-time use. Then she turned to smile at Godfrey.

'Make yourself comfortable!' she said, sitting on the edge of the bed and patting the space beside her. She gave a sudden low teasing laugh: 'Unless of course you wish to bag the armchair?' Without waiting for his answer, she poured a glass of whisky and handed it to him, before refreshing her own. 'Here's to the future!' she said raising her glass. 'Let's hope it's a good one for both of us.'

Godfrey had still not spoken a single word and now felt it was about time he did so. Instinct told him that this very attractive young woman had invited him for something more than a drink in her bedroom; yet his upbringing had been a conventional one and, like nearly all the other undergraduates at university, he had been extremely strictly brought up – as were his own sisters. They all knew there were girls who 'didn't' and girls who 'did'. Girls from the upper classes and professional working classes came into the first category. Girls who sometimes 'did' usually had jobs such as waitresses or were chorus girls or came simply from loose-living homes; or, of course, were prostitutes. Like all the other chaps, they had been warned about the danger of having sex with whores and none of his friends had dared do so. With few exceptions, he and his friends were virgins. Now, if this relationship developed as he suspected it might, he had only the very vaguest idea as to how he should behave. How did a chap go about making love to a woman, moreover, an experienced older woman, as he deemed Angela to be?

Correctly gauging the young tutor's growing nervousness, Angela suggested they made quicker inroads into her bottle of whisky.

'It helps to release tension!' she said, reaching out to take one of his hands in hers. 'See, your fingers are as taut as if I were about to put them in a bowl of boiling water.' She lifted her own glass and held it to him to drink. Then she took the tumbler from him and taking his hand once more, placed it over her breast. Looking into his eyes, she said softly: 'I know we're almost strangers, Godfrey, but I'm hoping we can now get to know one another a bit better!'

It was as close as she could have got without actually telling him that she wished him to make love to her; and Godfrey was by now only too willing to do so. He was wondering whether he dared remove her dress when she did so herself.

Then she removed his jacket and tie, and slipping his braces off his shoulders she removed his shirt and leaning forward, kissed him directly on the lips – a long, lingering kiss, which was to Godfrey unbearably provocative. Forgetting everything else, he pushed her back against the pillows and was attempting to cover her body with his own when she whispered: 'Let's take it slowly, lover. Has no one ever told you how special it can be to explore each other first? How much greater then is the conquest afterwards?' Instinct told her that this was a first time for Godfrey and she kissed him gently. 'I'll teach you,' she whispered. 'I'll show you how to love a woman!'

Such was Godfrey's hunger for the strange, beautiful woman in his arms, he was unable to delay what she called 'the conquest', but she was not angry with him as he lay breathing deeply beside her. Instead, she kissed him tenderly saying it would be better for both of them presently, the second time. Godfrey, still steeped in wonder at his first sexual experience, did not believe there could be 'a second time presently' but as the big grandfather clock in the hall downstairs struck midnight, a laughing Angela happily proved him wrong.

'I was going to beetle off to town tomorrow,' she said as they lay in each other's arms completely satiated. 'But I don't think I will leave yet – not if you're staying, Godfrey!'

He turned his head so that he could kiss the tip of her nose as he said smiling:

'I'm here for another week. I'm due back at Oxford but I had planned to spend the last few days with Mother and my brothers and sisters as I see so little of them now I'm up at university.' He gave a deep sigh. 'I wish we could go off somewhere together but I can't disappoint them. I'm really sorry.'

Angela sighed. 'Their gain, my loss, but I do understand. Besides, dear boy, I am thirty-four years old – far too ancient for you.'

'Oh, but I don't care about your age. You're young to me. I need you ... I mean, I ... oh, hell, Angela, I can't just say goodbye to you after ... after the most wonderful night of my whole life. I've *got* to see you again. I think I've fallen in love with you!'

'Well, don't think anything so silly!' Angela replied gently. 'I'm flattered, naturally, but sooner or later you'll fall for a girl your own age and then you'll really discover what love is all about. What we have shared is plain, honest sex . . . and affection,' she added seeing the hurt look in his eyes. 'We'll have other nights like this if you want them, Godfrey. I'll come up and stay in a hotel near your college every once in a while. You may not be free to do as you please but I . . . well, I am the proverbial merry widow, am I not?'

'I do love you!' Godfrey declared, meaning it. 'I love the way you laugh and make fun of yourself and your honesty and . . . everything about you . . .'

He would have kissed her again but Angela told him it was time for him to go back to his own bedroom.

'We would probably fall asleep if you stayed and next thing it would be morning and Sally would be bringing in my tea. You have only to imagine my sister's reaction if the maid went shrieking off to tell her that her sons' tutor was in her sister's bed!'

Reluctant although he was to leave her, Godfrey was smiling as he quickly donned a few clothes and, carrying the remainder and his shoes, crept quietly along the corridor and up the stairs to his room. He barely had time to consider what the following day would bring before he was asleep. Angela, however, remained awake long enough to realize with a tinge of anxiety that this unexpected but charming young lover was not going to be quite as easy as she had supposed to dismiss from her thoughts.

Sixteen

Vaughan and Robert were playing cricket on the wide sandy beach. Vaughan, being the elder, had chosen to bat first having roped in Victoria and Leila as fielders until a second family containing eight children arrived and settled themselves on the sand nearby. Having first unpacked the picnic basket, fishing nets, cricket bats and all the paraphernalia needed for an uninterrupted day at the seaside, it was not long before the newcomers were invited to join in the game. Since the family party comprised mostly boys with two older girls, Victoria and Leila were able to drop out. Their chief enjoyment during this wonderful summer holiday in Cornwall was fishing for crabs and the tiny silver fish in the rock pools which stretched out to sea on either side of the bay.

So far, during the first two weeks of August, the sun had shone every single day. Nanny had ensured the maids drew the curtains across the windows so that their bedrooms in the big cliff-top house which had been rented for the month were not too hot at night for sleeping. She was not an enthusiast for beaches, and every morning Vaughan and Robert had to carry a deckchair and cushions down to the beach for her to sit on, her lined old face shaded by the parasol Victoria was obliged to carry. Despite the moderate comfort thus achieved, she still wished she was with her sister in Bexhill, with whom she was going to live when she retired.

'It's so silly of Mother to insist Nanny came with us!' Victoria said as she and Leila gathered up their buckets and fishing nets and hurried across the sand towards the rocks. They were now carrying their sandshoes, which Nanny had insisted they wear since they might get stung by jellyfish or pricked by sea urchins if they went barefoot. They had also removed their panama hats with their hot, uncomfortable elastic chinstraps, and contrary to Nanny's orders, had tucked their frocks into their knickers.

'You would have thought Aunt Angela could manage to look after us two girls without Nan's help, wouldn't you?' Victoria went on. 'Mr Gregson manages the boys so I don't see why we need poor old Nanny.'

Leila smiled. She didn't mind the old woman's fussiness half as much as Victoria did, but then she was having such a wonderful time she wasn't able to find fault with anything at all. It was as long ago as last Christmas that Victoria had confided in her the secret news that her Aunt Angela had offered to take all the family including Leila to Cornwall in the summer and would rent one of the big houses overlooking a beach at a small seaside resort called Newquay. Their nanny had looked it up in the *Universal Reference Book*, which was never far from her elbow, and announced that although Newquay did have a harbour, there were fewer than five thousand inhabitants – not a fraction of the civilized community which inhabited her home town of Bexhill.

Victoria had imparted this piece of information to Leila with increased excitement. Although she and the boys had enjoyed many seaside summer holidays in the past, they were as often as not at south-coast resorts such as Brighton or Rottingdean where there was almost no sand and certainly no rocks or caves, which, Aunt Angela informed them, they would find in abundance in Cornwall, where she, alone of the six of them, had visited in the past with a friend.

Newquay not only came up to Leila's expectations but surpassed them a hundred times. For weeks she had lived in fear that her parents would not permit her to accept the invitation. A month was too long, her mother had said. It was not just that she and her father would miss her but that she might become homesick, having never spent even one night away from them before; and Cornwall was a very long way away. Suppose she were to become ill. It would take her father a very long time to drive them down to the West Country to take care of her! Beside which . . .

Quite often, her mother would fail to find a better reason and would simply turn away as if she were about to cry. Sweet-natured as Leila was, she had immediately offered not to go

if doing so would make her mother unhappy. Was a compromise possible and she be put on a train after one or two weeks
and sent home in the care of a Universal Aunt? Victoria's
brothers, she'd informed her mother, had quite often been taken
back to school by one of the paid travelling chaperones if Sir
Aubrey's chauffeur was busy elsewhere. Victoria, on one of
her visits to tea with the Varneys, broke her promise to Leila
and added her pleas for Leila to be allowed to accompany the
family to the seaside.

Finally, both Leila's parents had agreed she should go but
on the understanding she would write home no less than once
a week and if she was at all homesick, Victoria's Aunt Angela
should go to the nearest telephone and send her parents a
telegram.

As both girls now tucked their sun frocks more firmly into
their knickers and bent down over a likely looking rock pool,
Victoria said suddenly: 'I would have been utterly, utterly,
utterly miserable if you'd not been allowed to come. It's strange
when you come to think of it, Leila, that it was *my* mother
who kept on about it. She never usually bothers what I do,
and all that talk about us getting to know one another better
– as if we weren't already the best friends we ever could be!'

Conversation stopped briefly whilst Leila netted a small crab
and tipped it into her bucket. Her eyes were thoughtful.

'My mummy was strange, too. All she usually wants is just
for me to be happy and Daddy kept reminding her of that; I
just know she wanted me to stay with her. It's like she was
frightened, or something. I even heard her saying to Daddy:
"Suppose they never bring her back!" Well, your aunt is hardly
likely to leave me behind on the beach like a bucket or spade!'

They both laughed, but after successfully netting a few of
the tiny silver fish darting about in the crystal-clear seawater,
Victoria was once more retrospective. Twanging the elastic of
her panama hat, which was lying on the rock beside her, she
frowned as she stared at the surf-topped waves rolling in
towards the shore.

'There is something funny going on, Leila – and I'm pretty
sure it has to do with you. I think Nanny knows what it is but
she won't tell me. She just says there's no point getting fussed
over something which might never happen. I asked Aunt
Angela, too, but she said the same and we were just to have

a lovely holiday which was why she had arranged it so we could all be here in Cornwall together.'

'Daddy said your aunt was a very generous lady and even if she was as rich as you said, she didn't have to spend her inheritance on us children.'

The conversation now took a different direction as Victoria leant closer to Leila so she could whisper a confidence. Whispering was scarcely necessary seeing there was no one in sight for miles around them and that they would be sharing their secret with nothing more than a few seagulls.

'I know it's wrong to eavesdrop and honestly, Leila, I give you my solemn promise I didn't mean to, but this morning when I was in the WC the window was open and Vaughan and Robert were down below on the terrace and I could hear every single word. They were talking about Aunt Angela – saying what an utterly spiffing person she is and no wonder Mr Gregson is in love with her!'

Leila's blue eyes widened and she frowned in disbelief.

'But she's so old, Vicky, and Mr Gregson – Daddy said he wasn't much older than your brother George!' she exclaimed. 'You said your aunt was only a few years younger than your mother!'

Victoria nodded. 'I know, but you have to admit, Aunt Angela is very pretty. Annie said she's the spitting image of Mary Pickford. Anyway, Mr Gregson was kissing Aunt Angela on the mouth! Can you believe it?'

Leila was suitably rendered speechless so Victoria continued: 'You know they go off together every night after we've gone to bed? Well, Vaughan was saying Mr Gregson leaves first – says he's going down to the Ship Inn for a drink and a chat with the fishermen. But Aunt Angela told Nanny she likes walking and as it's too hot in the daytime, she prefers to go at night. But Vaughan said . . .' She paused momentarily for breath. 'Vaughan said although they go off at different times, they come back together holding hands and then they spend absolutely ages kissing each other before they come indoors.'

Leila frowned. 'I don't think that means they love each other even if they do kiss. They don't even talk to each other very much whenever I see them.'

Victoria looked pleased with herself as she said: 'But that's exactly it, Leila. In the Scarlet Pimpernel book I'm reading, the two men who turn out to be the thieves pretend they don't know each other so no one suspects at first that they're partners. I wonder what it's like – being kissed by a man, I mean.'

'Daddy often kisses Mummy and she seems to like it.' Leila contributed the little she could to the conversation, wishing she had not done so a moment later when Victoria confessed she had never ever seen her parents kissing – except once, at Christmas.

'I don't think my mother likes it much!' she said. 'She isn't a kissing sort of person like my father. I think you're jolly lucky, Leila, having a mother like yours who reads you stories and plays games with you and teaches you to knit and cook and things.'

Wanting, as she always did, Victoria to be as happy as she was, Leila said quickly: 'Well, I think you're jolly lucky to have a father who spoils you the way he does! Daddy said once that your father might not be very brainy but that he had a heart of gold.' She gave a sigh. 'I don't suppose that means real gold.'

'No, I shouldn't think so any more than blue blood is really blue. My grandmother says all the Beaufords have blue blood and I know for a fact I haven't and the boys don't bleed blue blood when they cut themselves, so it's just one of those silly sayings people use to muddle us. Anyway, Grandmother is wrong about me having it and I suppose it's because she's pretty old these days, I even heard her saying to Father that *you* had blue blood.' She giggled as she stood up. 'Who cares, anyway? I'm really, really, *really* loving this holiday – and all because you're here, too, Leila.' She paused to draw breath and picking up her panama hat, fanned herself with it.

'It's so, so hot!' she exclaimed, as was her habit, doubling or trebling her adverbs according to how strongly she felt. 'Let's go back and ask Nanny if we can swim. Bet she says not until after lunch. I know, we'll get the boys to ask her. She never says no to them if they keep on long enough!'

Before rounding the last rock, both children stopped to put on their hats and sandshoes and release their frocks from the confines of their knickers. Victoria fretted against these restrictions but Leila was more than willing to comply with them, so happy was she just to be at the seaside with Victoria and her brothers. She had never been on such a holiday before and only ever spent at most a day by the sea. Tomorrow, Mr Gregson and Aunt Angela, who insisted upon being called that although she wasn't her aunt, were taking them all to Padstow for the day. It was to allow Nanny a day off duty, Aunt Angela said, ignoring Nanny's insistence that she did not need one. They might even – Victoria had told her – go for a boat ride in a fisherman's trawler and if it was calm enough, fish for mackerel which they could take back to the house and cook.

If there really was such a place as Heaven, Leila thought, Newquay with the Beaufords must be it. There was only one tiny fly in the ointment and that was the half-buried certainty that her parents had not really wanted her to come, and that her mother wouldn't be happy again until she got home.

For the third time, Copper read the ecstatic letter from Leila posted from Newquay the previous day. Her eyes were full of tears and Harold sighed.

'It can't go on like this, my dear. First you are in tears because you think Leila will miss us, then when you hear what a wonderful time she is having, you are in tears because she obviously isn't missing us!'

Somehow, Copper managed a half-smile.

'I know it sounds silly when you put it like that, but, Harry, suppose she never wants to come back to us? I knew all along this was Lady Beauford's plan. You should never have said we would only allow them to adopt Leila if you truly believed it was best for her. That woman is obviously going to do every-thing possible to entice our daughter away. I want you to tell her – tell Sir Aubrey, that if they take Leila away from us, we shall take Victoria away from them.'

Harold sat down on the sofa beside his wife and put his arms round her shaking shoulders. Taking a large white hand-kerchief from his pocket, he wiped away her tears.

'My dear, I do understand how you feel, but you are not being entirely rational, are you? Suppose the Beaufords let us have Victoria without argument – and they might; would it compensate you for the loss of our girl? No, it wouldn't! As a matter of fact, I'd really enjoy having Victoria under my roof. Last term, she and I got into an extraordinary debate about whether it was right to permit a lady to become a lawyer.' He broke off, sighing. Aware that his wife found the topic irrelevant, he concluded: 'I do hope that the convent Lady Beauford keeps mentioning is able to give Victoria a really good educa-tion – she could do so well if . . .'

Once again he pulled himself up short, realizing that his wife was not capable of thinking right now about anything other than their daughter. Of course he missed Leila too, espe-cially as it was the summer holidays when he had no school activities to engross him. But unlike Copper, he was always able to keep his mind active, mostly reading, but he was also writing a history of the education provided by the state for children whose parents could not afford to pay for a private school. The subject interested him enormously and he fought tirelessly for better facilities for his own little school. It was a drop in the ocean, he knew, but every now and then, a child with Victoria Beauford's intelligence came into his orbit and made all his efforts worthwhile.

Harold was painfully aware that for the first time in his married life he had not been entirely honest with his wife. He had not lied to her but neither had he revealed the extent of his excitement at the thought that Victoria, with her bright, forward-looking, enthusiastic mind was actually of his beget-ting. It was not that he loved Leila any the less just because by all accounts she was Sir Aubrey's child. Nor could he ever feel less than a paternal love for her, whatever her origins. It was simply that he could not stop his brain from enacting imaginary scenarios where he and Victoria shared debates, ideas, plans; and as she matured, he could watch her mind develop under his guidance.

He had not been able to bring himself to discuss with Copper the possibility that the Beaufords would permit Victoria to join them on the walking holiday in the Lake District, which he hoped to arrange before the girls started at their new school in September. Tit for tat. Of course, Victoria might not want to leave her brothers, her pony and her luxurious home. There was so much the Beaufords could provide to tempt Leila to live with them, and so little he and Copper had to offer Victoria in exchange.

He and Sir Aubrey had had yet another very long discus-sion, man to man. Each had fully appreciated the other's point of view. Both knew that it was Frances Beauford and Sir Aubrey's mother who were determined to force the issue of a direct exchange of the children. It had taken all Harold's intelligence to devise a delaying tactic that was acceptable to the two women. He had pointed out that simply ordering the two children to exchange homes could only have a disastrous effect upon them, as would the knowledge that they were not truly members of their supposed families. Let them come to the idea gradually over the next year, he had suggested; spend more time in each other's homes. He would raise no objections to Leila going in September with Victoria to Lady Beauford's convent, or even, if Lady Beauford insisted, that Leila should attend the school as a distant cousin of Victoria's with Beauford as a surname. But he and Copper must be allowed access to their daughter – to Leila, and to choose the moment when the girls should be told about their birthrights. If Lady Beauford would agree to such conditions, he would not take any legal action to try to thwart her wishes to raise Leila in the manner in which a Beauford daughter would be brought up in ordinary circumstances.

Aubrey had had little hope of Frances' compliance but surprisingly, his mother had done so. At all costs, she said, publicity must be avoided or it could ultimately affect the girls' marriages. No matter what the medical tests might show, people would always question which set of parents the girls came from and it was Lady Mary's intention that Leila should marry at least into the aristocracy as she had no wish to have great-grandchildren who were commoners. Hopefully Victoria, of whom she was fond, would also marry well. Carefully managed, they could be presented at Court together and be known as cousins.

Having so far successfully delayed any immediate action by the Beaufords to remove Leila from them, Harold felt it would be unwise to refuse to permit Leila to go to Newquay. He sensed, as did Copper, that Lady Beauford was going to put every temptation in Leila's way so that the child herself would eventually want to go and live with Victoria at the Hall. At the moment, there was a deep, loving bond between the little girl and her mother in whose company she had spent nine-tenths of her life. In fact they had been parted only for the few hours in the days when Leila was at school or on one of the occasions when she had gone to the Hall to a party or to spend the day with her friend.

Harold's reflections came to an abrupt halt as he realized the 'friend' he'd been thinking about was actually his daughter, his flesh and blood. Victoria even looked like him! Secretly, he admitted that he did feel a kinship with the little girl; moreover, retrospectively, he could see that he had felt it even when she had first come to his school and he had given her her first mathematics lesson. She'd been the only child in a class of thirty who had picked up the concept of numbers; the logic. If four times five made twenty, then five times four must do so also. Whilst the other children were counting strokes on their slates in order to see the fact for themselves, Victoria was busy working out that the same idea applied when you were adding up but not when you were subtracting.

With an effort, Harold stopped such reminiscences and turned his attention back to his unhappy wife. He kissed the top of her head and said cheerfully: 'I have planned a little surprise for you, my dear! I have made some enquiries and *The Four Horsemen of the Apocalypse* is showing at the cinema in Brighton. I know you are a great admirer of Rudolph Valentino, so tomorrow we shall drive down to the coast, find somewhere nice to have a meal and then go to the matinee. We haven't had an occasion like this since before Leila was born, and I shall very much enjoy having you all to myself!'

Copper's eyes shone through her tears, and she turned and kissed him gently on the lips.

'I'd absolutely love it, dearest!' she said. 'You're so good to me, Harry. I'm so lucky to be married to you.'

Harold smiled. 'And as I have so often said to you, my love, how lucky I am to have you for a wife when I might be in poor Sir Aubrey's shoes and be married to her ladyship!'

When she had stopped laughing, Copper's expression became thoughtful. 'I do feel sorry for him,' she said. 'He must be as upset as we are by . . . well, by what's happened. He loves little Victoria the way we love our Leila, doesn't he?'

Harold nodded, unwilling to voice his thought lest he reduce his wife once more to tears. Sir Aubrey, he would have replied, might wish Victoria was his natural daughter, being as she was the greatest joy in his life, but at least he wasn't, like Copper and himself, in immediate danger of losing his much-loved child.

Seventeen

Leila could hear Victoria crying in the cubicle next to hers. It was one of the very rare occasions she had known her friend to dissolve into tears, whereas she herself could cry quite easily if she hurt herself or someone upset her. Her father used to tease her about it, saying she turned her tears on like April showers – no sooner did they appear than the sun came out again and she was smiling! But this was different. Victoria who never cried was sobbing, the noise slightly muffled by the eiderdown she had pulled over her head.

Despite Leila's fear of the punishment which might result from her daring, she slipped out of bed and crept in the darkness to the adjoining cubicle, hoping that none of the other eighteen girls in the *dortoir* would waken. They were for the most part French and had done little to make the two new English girls welcome. The nuns at the Convent of the Holy Virgin were very strict and she and Victoria were often punished for not complying with an order they had failed to translate. The French girls thought it amusing and did nothing to help them interpret the orders.

They had been at the convent for four weeks. It seemed to Leila as if it was five years. She was desperately homesick and now, as she slipped under the bedclothes next to Victoria, she assumed her unhappy friend felt the same. When Victoria's sobs had subsided a little, she whispered to Leila in a choked voice.

'I don't miss home so much as I miss Papa!' she confessed. 'He promised to write to me twice a week and tell me how Snowball is and if the Jessups' rabbits have had their babies yet and . . .' The tears began to flow anew. 'Leila, why aren't we getting any letters? They can't have *forgotten* us!'

Close to tears, Leila could think of nothing to comfort Victoria or herself. She was as concerned at Victoria at this total lack of communication from home. Ever since Lady Beauford had left them at the convent there had been total silence.

'Even the boys promised to write although I know they hate writing letters!' Victoria said shakily. 'And Nanny said she would send a postcard from Bexhill to say how she is enjoying her holiday with her sister. I think if she likes it there, she might want to retire but Mother said she was to stay on as housekeeper as she is so good at it.'

She broke off when she heard the dormitory door open and both girls held their breath as the nun's habit rustled when she glided quietly down the length of the room. Fortunately, she did not pause to look inside each cubicle and before long the door closed behind her.

Victoria had stopped crying now and her whispered voice was almost back to normal as she said: 'I just can't understand how Mother could possibly have liked being in this horrible place when she was our age! I'd have died if you hadn't been here too! I wonder why the other girls won't be friends. It wouldn't be quite so bad here if they weren't so nasty.'

Leila, who had been given some French conversation lessons by her father once he had known she was coming here, had overheard two of the French girls talking.

'They think we consider ourselves superior to them!' she said. 'Just because we belong to the British Empire and they are only a country, even if they do have colonies,' she added.

Victoria drew a deep sigh. 'Anyway I absolutely *hate* it here!' she said. 'I've made up my mind to write to Papa tomorrow and tell him I want to go home. He said if I wasn't happy, he'd come and fetch me whatever Mother said; but that I must try it out first; that boarding school wasn't easy if you weren't accustomed to it but the boys had settled down and I would probably do so too. But I haven't . . . and you don't like it either. Papa's just got to come and rescue us both!'

Dramatic although this statement sounded, Leila entirely agreed with the sentiment. She was painfully homesick and missed both her parents even more than she could explain to Victoria. After their wonderful shared holidays, in Cornwall and then their climbing holiday in the Lake District in

September, she had even looked forward to going to school in France with Victoria. They always managed to have such magical times together. But this was very far from magical. The nuns were not actually unkind but there was no gentleness, no affection and very little tolerance if by accident they did something wrong and broke one of the many strict rules. She was in trouble even more often than Victoria, mainly because she did not always answer immediately when she was spoken to. The fact that she was often called Leila Beauford was something she and Victoria quite liked because it made them seem like sisters, but nevertheless it was often the cause of her failure to answer when she was addressed. She would have replied instantly had they asked for Leila Varney!

It was her turn now to sigh.

'I suppose I'd better go back to my cubicle,' she said reluctantly. 'I hope it won't be long before your father comes to get us. Will you ask him in your letter to tell Daddy and Mummy why we want to come home? I know they won't make me stay here on my own if you go back.'

In the darkness, Victoria nodded.

'I'll write as soon as I wake up before the bell rings!' she said. 'Then I can give the letter to Sister Mary Joseph after breakfast so it goes in tomorrow's post.'

Victoria's letter, not very tidily written as her letter pad was on her knees, blotched here and there with tears, was nevertheless entirely explicit. Filled with her customary adverbs, she explained how utterly, utterly, *utterly* miserable she and Leila were and how absolutely *nobody* was willing to be friends with them and they were both really, really, *really* homesick and please, please, *please* come quickly and take them home.

As she had told Leila, she gave the letter to Sister Mary Joseph before breakfast, managing to request that it went *très rapidement par ce quelle êtez très, très, très importante!'*

The letter never even reached the postbox, let alone Sir Aubrey. Like all the other communications between the two girls and their families, Mother Superior withheld them. She was acting on the instructions of Lady Beauford, a former pupil who was now a generous benefactor. It was possible, Frances had informed the Mother Superior, that the girls might appeal to their fathers to take them back to England, but under no circumstances did she wish them to leave the convent before the end of term. She had insisted they must settle down to boarding-school life and accept considerably more discipline than they had been accustomed to at home. It was best, therefore, that they were not distracted in Leila's case by her mother's letters and in Victoria's case by her father's; by letters saying they missed the girls. Nor was there anything to be gained by forwarding correspondence from the girls to their parents expressing any unhappiness they might feel.

These strictures were in the girls' best interests, Frances had insisted, and she would like Mother Superior's word that she would enforce this embargo for the time being. Once they had settled down, she implied, an exchange of letters could begin.

Having read the correspondence passing from the Varneys to Leila and from Sir Aubrey and on one occasion, the nanny, to Victoria, the nun saw at once that Lady Beauford had good reason to curtail contact in such a manner, albeit it was somewhat unethical, to say the least.

Back at Foxhole Cottage, Copper had written at least every other day, doing her best to hide how much she missed Leila and longed for the school term to be over. Sir Aubrey, too, had reiterated his promise to Victoria that he would come at once to take her home if she was genuinely miserable. He'd had no wish whatever to see his only daughter despatched to a convent boarding school in France and could not understand Frances' reasoning that this was the first step towards their adoption of Leila.

'It will accustom the girl to separation from the father and mother who have given her their undivided attention all her life. It will also accustom the parents to being without her,' Frances had reiterated, adding that Victoria and Leila would become even closer friends in such an environment, and both girls would be eager for Leila's transfer from her own home to theirs.

'The Varneys can hardly continue objecting to my plan to adopt Leila if the girl herself wishes to be part of our family – a rightful part, I would remind you, Aubrey,' she had concluded with a final reminder that Aubrey had been the one who insisted they did not simply remove Leila the previous year when they discovered the truth about the girls' parentage.

Wondering if she could possibly be right to send the girls

abroad, Aubrey held his tongue. But after two weeks' total silence from Victoria, he went down to the village to see Harold Varney. He, too, it seemed, had had no communication from his daughter.

'I suppose it is just possible they are enjoying themselves too much to be bothered about us!' Aubrey suggested, as the two men walked down the main street to the Fox and Vixen. 'Or perhaps they are being kept too busy?'

Harold looked doubtful. 'Leila knows how desperate her mother is to hear from her – and it's certainly not like her to break a promise to write at least twice a week. It did cross my mind that the school had a policy of banning communication for a week or two until the new girls had settled down. I suppose Lady Beauford hasn't suggested such a possibility?'

Sir Aubrey shook his head. 'I'm afraid my wife thinks I make too much fuss of Victoria.' He coughed uneasily. 'You know, Varney, I'm very much against this whole business of . . . well, m'wife and my mother seem to think your girl will . . . well, eventually want to be part of the family – our family, I mean; but . . . all seems a bit unfair on you, eh? I mean, suppose Frances and the Mater are right and young Leila did want to come and live with us? Well, would you and the wife think about having another child, d'you think?'

He gave another cough. 'Told the wife it's probably too late for all that, and anyway, you'd have every right to have Victoria come and live with you but . . . well, dashed if I could bear that . . . really fond of the girl . . .'

Sir Aubrey's voice trailed away unhappily and Harold felt a great pity for the man, who was clearly out of his depth – as indeed he was himself, he thought. His meeting with Lady Mary on one of her rare visits to Farlington Hall had not been an easy one. The old lady had been too clever simply to claim the law was on their side and if they wanted they could simply take Leila away. No, she had put it to him that he and Copper could never give their daughter the huge advantages, social as well as financial, which they could give her; a private education, the chance to travel, learn languages, ride to hounds, be presented at Court and not least ultimately to meet and marry a man who could keep her in carefree luxury.

Would Harold or his wife really wish to deprive their daughter of such benefits simply because they would have to part with her? They would still see her from time to time, much as she might see a fond aunt and uncle. Would he deny his daughter all these advantages? Lady Mary had failed to mention the biggest advantage as Harold saw it – that Leila would have Victoria as a sister if he and Copper did not insist on laying claim to *their* child for Leila's sake.

He turned now to the older man and said: 'If I hear nothing by the end of the week, I shall send the Mother Superior a telegram demanding to know why we have not had any letters. If you were to do so, too, Sir Aubrey, your name would carry more weight. I have made enquiries and there is no direct telephone line to the convent in Compiègne so a telegram will have to suffice.'

Aubrey nodded his agreement, hoping privately that Frances would not get to hear of the headmaster's plan. Whenever he had even begun to raise the subject of Victoria, she had immediately refused to discuss the situation and told him to complain to his mother, knowing, of course, that it would be the last thing he would want to do.

By the end of the week, there had still been no communication from either child so Harold went down to the post office and sent his telegram not just requesting but demanding news. The Mother Superior received the telegram from the post boy and having read the contents, told him there was no reply, and put the piece of paper in the nearest waste-paper basket.

'We need money!' Leila protested when she realized that Victoria fully intended to carry out her threat to leave the convent and go home. The two girls were huddled together in the deserted cloakroom, it being the only warm place in the convent on this cold November day. Warm air was circulating through a pipe below the lockers where the pupils' outdoor and games clothes could dry, if only partially, after the rain. 'We need to buy train tickets and tickets for the boat and—'

'I've got some money – French money,' Victoria broke in, her eyes shining with excitement. 'Aunt Angela sent it to me at the end of the holidays when she knew I was going to school in France. She said it was tuck money like the boys get from Papa to take back to school each term for sweets and buns and things . . .' Her mouth was now set in an even more determined line.

'I'd already thought about buying clothes, Leila. As soon as the nuns realize we're missing, they'll start a search for us and we'd easily be caught in our uniforms, and I've thought of something else we can do. You know my gold chain and cross Mother gave me? Well, she said not to dare lose it because it was real gold and cost a lot of money. So we'll sell it.'

Leila's eyes widened. 'But where? Who to?'

'At the market in Compiègne tomorrow!' Victoria replied. 'I heard the *femme de chambre* talking to Sister Mary Joseph about buying some more *cirer* – that's furniture polish, I looked it up – when she went to the market on Tuesdays. We'll sell my chain and use the money to buy some old clothes – French-looking things; and then we'll go to the station and buy train tickets to Dieppe. You remember, Leila, in the train coming here Mother showed us the trenches where Papa fought in the war.'

Impressed though not surprised by Victoria's mastery of the art of running away, Leila contributed what little she could.

'Maybe we should first try getting the French post office to telephone Mrs Quick to get a message to your Papa or mine saying we want them to come and collect us.'

Victoria at once rejected the suggestion. 'Even if we said we were dangerously ill or something, Mother wouldn't believe it. She'd send a telegram to Mother Superior, who'd tell her we weren't. Anyway Mother is bound to know that someone at the convent would have informed our parents if anything was seriously wrong.'

Appreciating the logic of this, Leila did not speak for a moment. Then she said tentatively: 'Daddy said it cost an awful lot of money to go on the boat train and cross the Channel and then get here to Compiègne so he and Mummy wouldn't be able to come to see me. Do you think we'll have enough money to get home? I don't have anything I can sell, Vicky, except my Brownie Box camera. Maybe we would get a few more francs for that.'

Victoria looked momentarily uncertain. Then her face brightened.

'I know what we'll do. We won't even try to get back to

England. We'll get a train to the South of France; to Nice.'
Seeing Leila's bewilderment, she laughed excitedly. 'I should
have thought of it before. Aunt Angela is living there – she
rented a house for the winter. I know where it is because
she sent me a postcard with a picture on it last holidays
and she put a cross where her house is.'

Leila looked even more bewildered. 'But why would we
want to go there?'

'Because it's in France, silly, so it has to be nearer than
England so it has to cost less money to get there. Now listen,
Leila – we can't waste money buying food so tonight at supper,
see if you can hide your *petit pain* and some fruit if there is
any. I don't much like figs but they'll do. Then we'll leave
just before it gets light. No one checks the cubicles until after
breakfast and by that time we should be in Compiègne. If it's
market day, there'll be lots and lots of people there so we can
easily disappear in the crowd.' She caught hold of Leila's
hands and swung her round in an excited circle.

'Just think, Leila, by tomorrow night we could be at Aunt
Angela's house and she's got masses of money so she'll give
us our fares home, I know she will. This time next week, we
could be back with our parents. I know Mother will be
absolutely furious but Papa will be really, really, *really* happy
to see me.' She paused only long enough to look deep into
Leila's eyes and added in a low voice: 'You will come with
me, Leila, won't you? I wouldn't want to go without you.'

Leila smiled. 'Of course I'm going if you are, Victoria!'

She said it bravely but inside, she was trembling with fear.

Eighteen

As the two girls crept on stockinged feet down the back stone staircase to the kitchens, Victoria was buoyed with excitement whilst Leila was shivering not only with cold but with nervous apprehension. Such little food as they had been able to save from the previous evening's meal was now stuffed into the pockets of their Harris tweed overcoats, which they each carried over one arm, their shoes dangling by their laces over the other. Victoria also carried in her pocket a black velvet box containing the precious gold necklace she intended to sell and Aunt Angela's two two-franc notes. They had decided to wear their domestic-science headscarves over their heads in preference to their school-uniform blue-felt brimmed hats, which they thought might too easily identify them as convent pupils.

The huge kitchens were deserted and a tantalizing smell came from the two large ovens where bread was being baked for breakfast. Victoria paused, sniffing the air. Grinning at Leila, she said in a whisper: 'If it wasn't going to be too hot to eat, I'd steal some of that!'

But Leila was too fearful of discovery to manage more than a parody of a smile.

The heavy oak door leading into the kitchen gardens was locked, but from the inside, and Victoria was able after several anxious attempts to turn the big key in the lock. The noise as it did so caused them both to stop and listen, their hearts beating furiously, but there was no rustle of nuns' habits which usually presaged their arrival. Exhaling with relief, they let themselves out into the half-light of near dawn and started to run. As soon as the convent was lost to sight behind them, they stopped to put on their coats and shoes.

'My stockings are soaking wet!' Victoria said. 'Let's take them off, Leila – no one will notice.'

Her fate now reposing entirely in Victoria's hands, Leila removed her stockings and squeezed her cold feet into her shoes. Having slept only fitfully the night before, she had finally admitted to herself that had Victoria not insisted adamantly that she accompany her, she would never have dared to attempt this 'escape', as Victoria termed it. Much as she disliked life at the convent and was every bit as desperate as Victoria for news of her parents, she was frankly terrified of the adventure which lay ahead. Now, suddenly, it was actually happening and she was running after Victoria's shadowy figure in the direction of Compiègne.

The nuns had taken them for exercise on walks through the vast forest of oak trees bordering the convent grounds, and one of the pathways on the perimeter of the woods emerged on the far side in sight of the town. At least she need have no fear they would get lost before they even reached their first destination, Leila told herself.

By the time they left the last of the huge oak trees behind them the sky had lightened and they could see one or two farm carts, loaded with milk churns, cheeses and vegetables for the market, making their way into the town. Leila was a bit upset by the sight of a squealing piglet bumping about on the back of a cart with its legs tied.

'Let's scuff our shoes a bit – put some mud on them,' Victoria suggested when Leila pointed them out to her. 'And unbutton our coats. We'd better buy a valise to put them in once I've bought cloaks for us because we can't look too scruffy if we're going to Nice so we'll need them later.'

Looking at Leila's anxious expression, she added cheerfully: 'Let's have our *petit déjeuner* now – I'm starving. I'm thirsty too but I expect we can buy some milk in the market.'

Leila wished fervently that she had even a small part of Victoria's self-confidence. She had been only partly reassured by her friend's insistence that she knew exactly what you had to do when you were running away. Her brother George, she'd explained, had once told her how he had run away from his prep school when he was only eight years old – and no one had discovered him until he got home. All you had to do, according to George, was pretend that your mother or father were 'just over there' and point vaguely in the direction of a group of people. If necessary, he'd informed his sister, you ask if the questioner would like you to go and fetch your parent; but they never bothered. This was to be the backbone of Victoria's escape plan in which now, as she chewed on a very stale *petit pain*, Leila was to depend.

Surprisingly, George's method worked. Only twice were they asked to identify themselves, once when Victoria approached the man with the trinket stall and told him she wished to sell her necklace; and again when she asked a woman selling capes and cheap cotton dresses to lower the price she was asking for them. It hadn't crossed Victoria's mind, so limited was her knowledge, that even with the reduction, the transaction was so much in the market seller's favour that the woman was highly suspicious of her good fortune. Victoria commented that her mother was waiting in the car in one of the streets behind the square where the market was held. She had further elaborated that her mother had said she might purchase what she wished so long as the capes were of good quality. Doubting the verity of the child's story, the stall holder had decided not to argue the point further since the transaction was so much in her favour.

The sale of the gold cross and chain had been less easily accomplished as the man had recognized the youthfulness of the two young English girls and did not believe Victoria's story that her mother had told her to sell them. Moreover, the price he offered Victoria was a fraction of their value and Victoria, unfamiliar though she was of the exchange differences, strongly suspected that there were far from enough franc notes and coins offered to her to pay for the train tickets they would need. They had not only to travel from Compiègne to Paris but from there to the coast at Nice where Aunt Angela now lived.

However, there was nowhere else Victoria could think of where she might sell the necklace and when the stall holder saw her hesitate and raised his offer a few more francs, she accepted. Her brief moment of concern was forgotten when Leila followed her to a stall some distance away and she was able to buy a cheap cardboard suitcase for a few centimes less than she had expected.

'Probably he thought I was a French girl now I'm wearing this old cape!' Victoria said, her confidence restored. 'Now all we want are some ordinary frocks. We can put our uniforms in the suitcase and we'll look like real travellers.'

Although from time to time the children attracted stares, as the morning wore on there were so many people in the market square that they were barely noticed. They found a woman with four nanny goats, one of which she was milking, and she happily sold the girls a beaker of milk to drink. Thus fortified, they asked for directions to the station and made their way there.

There was a slow stopping train to Paris leaving in ten minutes, they were told. A faster train with far fewer halts would leave after midday. Unhesitatingly, Victoria bought tickets for the early train.

'The sooner we get out of Compiègne the better!' she said to Leila. 'I don't think the nuns will realize we are missing before lunch, but it is possible.' She had left a note on the end of her bed saying that she and Leila had gone to the convent sanatorium to report sick because they had both come out in a rash. There was no need therefore for the nun who supervised at breakfast in the refectory or the sister who took them for lessons to question their whereabouts. Victoria now maintained that the most probable discovery time would be when their lunch was taken up to the sanatorium.

'It's eleven o'clock and if we leave now, they won't even start looking for us until lunchtime,' she said reassuringly to Leila. 'Then they will search the convent and the chapel and then the grounds, and then, most likely, the forest. It could be two o'clock or even later before they realize we've run away and start looking here in the town. We should be in Paris by then, Leila. The man said it wasn't much over sixty kilometres away. Even a slow train should get there in three hours at the very most.'

Only too happy to leave the arrangements to Victoria, Leila asked no questions until they were on the train. They were alone in the carriage apart from a tramp-like old man with a cockerel in a sack on the seat beside him, which, they presumed, he had been unable to sell at the market. From time to time, he gave them a broad friendly smile from a mouth totally devoid of teeth. They were pleased when he left the train at the first stop, his cockerel tucked firmly under one arm, and Leila felt able to speak. Until then, she had been attempting to hold her breath to exclude the smell of garlic and unwashed farmyard clothes.

'Why are we going to Paris?' she asked. 'I thought you said Aunt Angela lived in a town called Nice?'

Victoria stood up and lifted the leather strap securing the window, opening it a fraction to allow fresh air into the carriage.

'Because the man said we couldn't get from Compiègne to Nice and it would be simpler to go from Paris.' She smiled at Leila reassuringly. 'And I do know you can get from Paris to Nice because Aunt Angela told me in a letter about the wonderful journey she'd had travelling on *le Train Bleu* – the blue train. She travelled at night and had a lovely little carriage room all to herself with a comfortable bed and sheets and she slept all night and when she woke up, a train attendant brought her coffee and *croissants* and next thing they were in Nice on the edge of the Mediterranean.'

'So is that what we are going to do?' Leila asked, suitably impressed.

'Well, I'm not exactly sure!' Victoria replied honestly. 'We haven't got that many francs left, and I don't know what the train will cost. I didn't like to ask the ticket man in Compiègne because then he'd know exactly where we were going and could tell anyone who asked him if he'd seen us.'

'Suppose we haven't got enough money?' Leila asked.

The same thought had passed Victoria's mind on several occasions but she decided Leila was nervous enough as it was, so she ignored the question and drew her friend's attention to the crowd waiting on the platform they were now approaching.

'Looks like we won't have the carriage to ourselves much longer!' she said.

Five minutes later, after a brief halt, Victoria's predictions materialized. They now shared their compartment with a jolly, red-faced, plump farmer's wife with two small children and a baby, and a formally dressed middle-aged man carrying a briefcase, a newspaper and a gold-handled umbrella. Although the fat woman did address Leila, neither she nor Victoria could make head or tail of her rough dialect. Looking up from his newspaper, the gentleman spoke rapidly to the woman, who nodded and busied herself with her baby. The man turned to the two girls with a pleasant smile and addressed them in moderately good English.

'I have made the explanation to this woman that you come from another country and do not understand her language!' he said. 'Perhaps you will permit me to introduce myself? My name is Philippe Lélange and I am by profession a solicitor. You are English mademoiselles, are you not?'

Leila was too shy to reply but Victoria immediately held out her hand politely.

'Yes, we are. My name is Kitty and my sister is Sylvia. We are on our way to Paris!'

The man smiled. 'I imagined this might be your destination as, indeed, it is mine.'

Victoria turned to Leila, who was looking at her open-mouthed.

'Don't be shy, Sylvia!' she said. 'Shake hands with Monsieur Lélange.'

Blushing furiously, Leila did so.

'Are you not very young to be travelling to the city on your own?' he enquired. 'Perhaps someone is meeting you at the station?'

Once again, it was Victoria who spoke up. Looking directly into the man's eyes, she said: 'I am a lot older than you suppose, Monsieur Lélange. I am thirteen but small for my age. My sister is only nine. I am going with her to stay with our aunt as our mother is very ill and sadly, our poor papa is dead. Our aunt will meet us in Paris at the station where she will arrive from the south of France so we shall be quite safe.'

'You will be going to the Gare de Lyon!' he said. 'You must allow me to see the two of you into a taxi.' He now understood why these two children were so curiously attired. He had noted the cheap cotton dresses, the thin cardboard suitcase on the luggage rack above their heads, their scuffed shoes and strange capes. Clearly their poor mother had not been well enough to see they were properly dressed. At first he had wondered if they were gypsies' children, especially the dark-haired child; but then she had spoken in a Parisian-accented French and he'd realized they were in fact daughters of educated parents. Poor little things! he thought now. The mother must be very ill indeed to permit these two young girls to travel alone.

Worried lest Leila might suddenly address her by her real name, Victoria said now: 'I am going along the corridor to wash my hands, Sylvie. Do you wish to come with me?'

When they were safely outside and beyond the hearing of M. Lélange, Victoria caught hold of Leila's hand, a mischievous smile in her eyes as she noted her worried frown.

'Don't you see, I had to tell those lies so we can't be traced. If the nuns don't find us in Compiègne and ask at the station, they will know we are on the train to Paris. Now, if they have reported it to the police in Paris, they could be watching for us at the station, and now we can walk down the platform with Monsieur Lélange who, if he is asked, will say our names are Kitty and Sylvia and he is escorting us to meet our aunt because our mother is ill.'

Leila looked at Victoria's laughing face and her unease was now mixed with admiration. How did she think of such things, she enquired. Telling lies was a serious misdemeanour and God might well punish them even if no one else did.

Victoria shrugged. 'George said lies like the one I told are white lies which don't count,' she declared, at the same time not entirely sure George had really meant the outright whoppers she had told their travelling companion. But it was too late now to retract anything and with a caution to Leila to behave like a younger sister and let her do all the talking, they returned to the carriage.

Genuinely interested in his two new protégées, Philippe Lélange continued to question them. Victoria chose her replies carefully saying only that they had lived in London before their father had died, after which they had been too poor to remain there and their mother had taken them to Compiègne, where she had been born. Unfortunately her parents, their grandparents, had not survived the war and so the three of them lived alone with only a kind but elderly village woman to look after them.

Once again, Philippe was lulled into a certain belief in the truth of the child's story. The good-quality tweed coats Victoria now unpacked to replace the thin faded cloaks, he assumed had been purchased in better times before the unfortunate father had died. He was more curious about the contrast in the two sisters' looks but assumed they must each take after a different parent. He had business to attend to in Paris but not until later in the day, and feeling some concern for the two young girls, he now asked if he might be allowed to accompany them in a taxi to see them safely into their aunt's care.

After only a moment's hesitation, Victoria said she hoped she had not misled him; their aunt was unsure of her arrival time and they were to meet her at the Gare de Lyon where her train came in. They were not to worry if she was delayed but were to wait for her in the station buffet.

'So you see, Monsieur Lélange,' she said confidently, 'we would very much appreciate your taking us to the Gare de Lyon, where we shall be quite safe whilst we await our aunt.'

With no reason to doubt the girl, the solicitor felt he had behaved as charitably and responsibly as could be expected of him, and turned his attention to his newspaper for the remaining half-hour of the journey.

Arriving at the busy Gare du Nord railway terminal with its mass of people milling around, trains letting off steam, whistles blowing and frantic activity, Victoria was hugely relieved to be taken with Leila under M. Lélange's wing. He took their tickets from them to hand in with his own to the collector, conducted them outside where he quickly hailed a waiting taxi and ushered them inside. During the journey across Paris, he was kind enough to point out famous landmarks, the Eiffel Tower, Notre-Dame cathedral and the newly constructed tomb for the unknown warrior beneath the Arc de Triomphe. When they arrived at the Gare de Lyon, he not only escorted them to the station buffet to await their aunt, but also refused Victoria's offer of payment for the taxi.

Both girls were quite sorry when he bade them goodbye, leaving his visiting card with Victoria saying how happy he would be if she would send him a postcard upon her arrival to say she and her sister were safely installed in their aunt's house.

'I shall send him a postcard from Nice!' Victoria announced as they waited for the waitress to bring them each a *croissant* and a *café au lait*. 'It won't matter then if he finds out who we really are because by the time he gets it, Papa will have come and fetched us from Aunt Angela. After we have eaten, we'll go to the ticket office and ask about *Le Train Bleu*.' She smiled happily at Leila. 'I just love that name,' she said. 'It'll be fun, won't it, if we can get a sleeper train like Aunt Angela's. I'd much rather sleep on a long journey than sit up. Did you hear Monsieur say he had been to the south of France last summer and that it had taken him all night to get there?'

For once, Leila was in complete agreement with Victoria about the next phase of their escape. Now that a considerable number of hours had gone by without any sign of them being apprehended, she felt a lot less anxious. She was even looking forward to the sleeper train, as Victoria described it.

The 'sleeper train' did indeed have beds – expensive ones for one or two people; but at a huge cost. The train also had *couchettes*, compartments comprising six bunk beds, which were far less expensive but still beyond their remaining meagre number of francs and centimes. Victoria counted them for the third time.

'We've just got enough for one bunk if we don't buy anything else to eat or drink!' she said. 'We'll just have to share, Leila. We can go head to toe if the bunks are too narrow to sleep side by side. Never mind, I expect we'll be so tired by the time the train leaves, we won't be able to stay awake. It'll be fun!'

Shamed by her friend's unfailing optimism, Leila did her best to smile. More realistic than Victoria, she suspected that they might not be allowed to travel on one ticket, not even if they did share a bed. But she said nothing, not even 'I could have told you so' when later that evening, the *chef* of the *wagons-lits* informed them quite forcibly that only one of them could go.

Nineteen

The skies were already darkening when late that November afternoon the post boy arrived on his bicycle at the servants' entrance to Farlington Hall. It was the second time that day he had had to push his bike up the hill to the big ancestral home but it earned him another threepenny piece, given grudgingly by Cook, who maintained he should not get extra pay for doing his job. Sir Aubrey had once instructed her to give the boys a sixpence, which, he considered, they had more than earned, on blistering hot summer days or on bitterly cold or rainy wintry ones. Despite Mrs Mount's belief that threepence was overpaying the boy, it being his second visit today, she was willing to give him an extra penny.

The telegram was addressed to Lady Beauford but as she was in London for the week the butler took it to Sir Aubrey, who was ensconced in his big library wing chair in front of a glowing log fire, a writing table by his side.

'Come in, Crawford, quick as you can,' he said rising stiffly to his feet and holding out his hand for the yellow envelope. The first telegram had arrived whilst he was eating lunch and so concerned him that he had refused his favourite bread-and-butter pudding, much to Cook's displeasure. She had taken a lot of trouble with it, she told Crawford. Her ladyship disliked it and so it could never be served when she was at home, more was the pity. However, when Mr Crawford had relayed the shocking news he'd learned from the master, that Miss Victoria and her young friend were missing from their French convent school, she had been nearly as shocked as Sir Aubrey.

Mother Superior's telegram had not minced words.

The *gendarmes* are widening their search and are now making enquiries in Compiègne itself Stop Meanwhile the Sisters are praying for their safety Stop However I am of the opinion this is a childish prank and the girls are hiding in order to escape Catechism study which instruction your daughter does not enjoy Stop I will telegraph you immediately we have news of them Stop

Whilst Sir Aubrey did believe Victoria quite capable of such naughtiness, for she was a spirited little thing, he had nevertheless been on tenterhooks all afternoon. He could not make up his mind whether to pass the news on to Varney but had decided there was little point in worrying the poor chap since the Mother Superior's second telegram might say the girls were safe and sound.

Now, his hand shaking slightly, he reached for his pen and a sheet of writing paper and wrote a brief reply for Crawford to give the waiting boy.

'News isn't so good, Crawford,' he said as he blotted the paper. 'Seems one of the shopkeepers in Compiègne saw two little girls in the market this morning; said they looked strangely dressed. Most significant was that one had long fair hair like Miss Leila.'

The older man, who had been in service to the family most of his life, was well aware of his master's devotion to Miss Victoria. Over the past few months, there had been endless gossip downstairs – which he had done his best to curb – but as he saw the situation, there seemed little doubt that the two girls had been mistakenly exchanged at birth. He did not entirely understand why they had both been sent away to a boarding school in France, although he knew this had been her ladyship's idea which, according to her maid, Ellen, she had called a compromise, because for the time being, Sir Aubrey did not want Miss Victoria to know she was not his daughter. He looked now at his employer's anxious face.

'Miss Victoria is a very resourceful little girl, sir, and if it was her with Miss Leila in the market, I'm sure that is where she intended to be.'

Sir Aubrey now looked slightly less worried. 'Of course, you're right, Crawford. Up to some mischief, I dare say. Remember that time young George ran away from his prep school? Had the place in an uproar!' He gave a brief laugh at the memory but then his face clouded again as he handed his reply to the butler.

'Best not keep the boy waiting – filthy afternoon. Tell Cook she's to give him sixpence.' He smiled briefly. 'I know she thinks it's far too much – told me her brother only got a penny when he was post boy!'

Crawford hurried back downstairs to the kitchen and returned immediately to the library with a tray containing Sir Aubrey's cut-glass decanter of whisky and a soda-water syphon.

'I know it's a bit early, sir, but in the circumstances . . .'

Sir Aubrey smiled appreciatively at his oldest servant who, over the years, he had come to think of almost as a friend.

'Quite right . . . splendid idea.'

He waited whilst Crawford poured his drink and then said: 'I've a good mind to write a real snorter to that Mother Superior. Should be keeping a better eye on the girls. Come to think of it, Crawford, I've more than one bone to pick with the woman. Not a single word from Victoria in four weeks . . . four weeks, for heaven's sake! When I was at school, we had to write home every Sunday. Mr Varney hasn't had word from his daughter, either.' He gave a worried sigh. 'M'wife says I worry far too much; thinks the girls are enjoying themselves with all the new friends they've made to be bothered about what's going on at home.' He paused, shaking his head. 'It isn't good enough, Crawford, that's what I say – and Varney agrees with me.'

There was a moment of silence whilst the butler made up his mind whether or not to express his views.

'Maybe they haven't written because they have found it difficult to settle down. After all, sir, not everyone gets on well with the Frenchies, do they? Maybe Miss Victoria doesn't want you to be worried about her and that's why she doesn't write.'

Momentarily, Sir Aubrey looked a little more cheerful but almost immediately his face darkened again. Unable to conceal his growing concern, he said: 'Not good enough! I've a good mind to bring them home – once they've found the little scamps. Where the devil can they be, Crawford? Half a mind to go and look for them m'self!'

Crawford shook his head, his voice gentle as he said: 'Of course you're worried, sir; anybody would be, but I'm sure they'll be found soon.' He went across the room to draw the heavy brocade curtains across the windows, adding: 'Children don't much like being out in the dark, do they, so it's more than likely they are making their way back to their school.'

Aubrey's expression became less anxious. 'Yes, you're probably right, Crawford,' he said as he gulped down his whisky, 'but just in case, tell Joseph I want the car ready to drive to France at a moment's notice – plenty of petrol and all that. Now I must try and be a bit less impatient whilst I wait for the next telegram. "Patience conquers the world", according to my old nanny. Can't say it's ever done me much good!'

Crawford crossed the room to pour Sir Aubrey a second whisky. There was the glint of a smile in his eyes as he added a splash of soda water. 'I do seem to recall, sir, that you once told me all you need to stalk a deer is a steady hand, a good eye and ... eh, patience?'

Sir Aubrey laughed. 'Quite right! Let's hope you're right about the girls, too.' He took the glass from Crawford and his look of concern returned.

'Don't think I'll say anything to her ladyship – no point worrying her. Just as well she's in town, eh? Think I'll pop down to the village – have a word with Varney. Good idea, don't you think, eh?'

Crawford nodded. 'A trouble shared is a trouble halved – that's what my old granny used to say, sir!'

They both chuckled but might have found it a lot more difficult to do so had either Aubrey or his sympathetic butler imagined for a single moment that it would be another twenty-four hours before they finally heard that the girls were safe.

Angela went across the terrace and out to the road to pay the taxi driver the large amount of money he was demanding, muttering through his moustache that he'd had only the vaguest idea where she lived from the very brief instructions one of the two bedraggled children had given him. He pointed at the villa into which the girls had disappeared.

'The one with the dark hair ... she tells to me Bartofski – Madame Angelique Bartofski. I know no such a person. She live next to the Église Russe, the other young mademoiselle is saying. *Mon Dieu*, there are two Russian churches. So I must go to each one although *les jeunes filles* have no money – not a single *sou*! I take pity and tell them if the Tante Angelique is not found, I shall drive them to the Bureau de

Commissaire de Police, and if they have not the money for the drive in my taxi, they will surely be put in prison, no?'

It was perhaps most sensible to leave that pronouncement unanswered, Angela thought, and she counted out some notes and a handful of coins and gave them to the taxi driver, whose somewhat belligerent mood now changed. The poor little English children were without chaperones, he declared; he had taken pity on them. No matter how many kilometres he must drive seeking for Madame, he would have done so even into the night. Warming to his story, he altered the context, insisting that had they not found Angela's villa, he would have taken them home to his wife to dry their clothes and feed them.

Only too well aware that the children were indeed very wet, tired, cold and hungry and not very far from tears, Angela bade their supposed guardian angel farewell and went back indoors. Having first found them some of her own clothes to wear, albeit they were far too big, she took them to the bathroom to wash and change and went down to her kitchen to raid the larder for food. Once the girls were clean and fed she would receive a more coherent account of their travels and the reason for them than the garbled story Victoria had started to tell her on their arrival.

As she prepared a cheese omelette and toasted some rather stale bread to freshen it, she realized that she was not entirely surprised by their bizarre behaviour. Frances had told her long before she left England about the girls' fateful births, of Aubrey's insistence that he would not part with Victoria, and her own and Lady Mary's determination that the Varney child should be raised as the offspring of the Beauford family. Although Frances played down the fact that the Varneys were as devoted to their daughter as Aubrey was to Victoria, Frances could not deny to Angela that they were certainly not surrendering their child willingly.

At the time, Angela had thought very little of her sister's idea that isolated as the girls would be in a foreign boarding school, they would become even more devoted to one another and Leila would decide she wanted to live with Victoria in preference to remaining with her supposed parents. The Varneys were quite poor, Frances had explained. They had little to offer the child other than a good education, which was of no importance since she was not particularly intelligent.

'Takes after poor old Aubrey!' Frances had commented unkindly, shocking Angela, who was really fond of her brother-in-law. When Angela questioned what Frances would do if, after all, Leila chose to remain with her supposed parents, her sister had refused to discuss the matter further other than to say, if it did become necessary, the law would be called upon to pronounce in their favour; that Lady Mary had made enquiries at the top legal level and the outcome was incontestable by the Varneys whatever their sentiments.

England, Angela had decided that September, when the lovely holiday in Cornwall was over and the autumn winds were blowing, had lost its appeal for her. She had no wish to return to the United States but she longed to escape the cold winter climate. On one of her visits to London, she had called in at Thomas Cook, the travel agent, who suggested that she might enjoy the climate in the south of France. Nice was a delightful town on the edge of the Mediterranean. Many English people chose to live as well as holiday there, as did other nationalities. There was, moreover, a casino frequented by the wealthy who could be seen gambling huge sums of money on the turn of a card.

Fascinated, Angela went for a week, fell in love with the place, and bought a small villa tastefully furnished by its outgoing French owner so that she had only to pack her belongings and move in. Her bank manager had informed her that her late husband's legacy had left her so rich she had little or no need to worry about the cost of practically anything she wanted; and that included the villa, which barely touched her capital.

Although she was fond of her young nephews and niece, and indeed of Aubrey, there was little Angela minded leaving when she had boarded the boat at Southampton. One sad parting took place when Godfrey turned up unexpectedly to see her off. He had been hoping, poor boy, that he could visit her in London during the Christmas holidays and now confessed he had fallen hopelessly in love with her, and begged her not to leave England.

Angela felt not a little guilty that she had quite blatantly taken him as a lover both at Farlington Hall and on the Cornish holiday that summer. Young, inexperienced as Godfrey was, she should have realized it was fairly inevitable he would think himself in love. But she knew he would get over it when a young girl his own age came into his orbit and this would be far more likely to happen if she was not available. Not least, he had pledged himself to take care of his mother and sisters and he would only have felt guilty for time spent with her.

To be truthful to herself, she had missed him. For all his inexperience, his enthusiasm and youth had made up for it and it had been a happy few weeks before he'd returned to his studies. Now, she seldom thought about him and a fortnight prior to the girls' arrival had been to the Casino where an extremely good-looking, middle-aged Frenchman by the name of Pierre Castel had come up to the baccarat table where she was playing, and sat down next to her. A week later they had become lovers. They had met every day, dined out every evening and made love either in his rented villa or at her home. This evening, he was due to arrive at any moment to escort her to a dinner dance and she had no way of warning him that she was now *in loco parentis* of two nine-year-old girls.

She was a little wary of the intense feelings Pierre aroused in her. He was as ardent as she was in bed, his love-making intuitive, imaginative and adoring. Forty-two years old, he had been widowed ten years previously but, he'd told her, had felt no inclination to share his life again. He owned acres and acres of vineyards in the countryside around Bordeaux, and without exactly saying as much, he had implied he was a very wealthy man. Judging by the expensive cut of his clothes, his gold cufflinks, tie pin and signet ring, and not least the beautiful French Voisin he drove expertly around the locality, she had no reason to disbelieve him. He had shown her photographs of his stunningly beautiful chateau, situated between the towns of Bordeaux and Libourne.

As the two children tucked hungrily into the food she had cooked for them, Angela glanced anxiously at the clock. It was half past six. Pierre would be arriving in an hour. She had not yet chosen which of her evening dresses she would wear, but now there was no need to do so since she would not be going out tonight. She could but hope Pierre would understand that the girls must come first, and that for the time being, their intimacies must come to an end. She had no idea how long it would be before someone – Frances, Aubrey, Leila's parents – came to collect them. First of course, they would have to be notified the girls were with her. The poor souls must be desperate with worry. She would persuade Pierre to send a telegram to Aubrey, who must be extremely worried.

Now it was time she learned why the girls were here. On their arrival Victoria, close to tears, had stated simply that they'd run away from the convent, but she had as yet given no explanation as to why, or indeed why the two of them had not gone back to their families in England but come to her here in Nice.

It was a very tired, quiet and subdued Victoria who, having finished her meal and her glass of hot milk, related their 'escape', as she termed it. They were homesick. There had been no letters – not even a postcard – from home; the other pupils were unfriendly and the nuns strict, making no allowance for the fact that their knowledge of the French language was very limited so they did not always understand the rules or instructions given to them. They were obliged to spend too long in chapel, saying prayers or receiving religious instruction. Possibly, she elaborated, because they belonged to the Church of England and were not Roman Catholics like all the other girls, they were treated with suspicion and unnecessary strictness.

'So you decided to leave?' Angela prompted. 'Why didn't you write to your parents saying how unhappy you were?'

Leila had started to weep quietly whilst Victoria again fought back the tears which were threatening to engulf her. Once more she told Angela that when they had received no letters from home for the fourth week running they decided to run away. It had seemed fun, even exciting, at first, but by the time the sleeper train was due to leave Paris, they had both been tired, hungry and very frightened by the knowledge that they did not have enough money to pay for two fares. Leila had been obliged to hide in the lavatory until the *chef de couchettes* had looked at Victoria's ticket, and only then had they been able to smuggle Leila into the compartment. This had been accomplished by Victoria giving Leila her outer clothing and telling her to get straight into her top bunk without removing the scarf covering her blonde pigtails. Leila had somehow to leave room in the narrow bunk for

Victoria to join her when their fellow travellers had gone to the *première service* dinner in the restaurant carriage.

Mercifully, the girls had been so tired they had quickly fallen asleep despite their hunger, but not for long. There had been a second visit from *chef de couchettes* and when he discovered they had only one ticket between them, he informed them they would both be arrested when he handed them over to the *gendarmes* at the next station.

Too tearful now to be very coherent, Victoria sobbed that it was all her fault; it had been her idea; they had thought it would be easier to get to the south of France than back to England; that she had never guessed it would cost so much money to go on trains and in taxis, let alone to buy food.

'I was just as much to blame!' Leila broke in in a choked voice. 'We really didn't mean anyone to worry about us – well, except the convent, because like Victoria said, the nuns really weren't very nice to us. We weren't really worried we'd get lost or anything – at least, not until we were in Paris and couldn't afford two tickets. By then, we couldn't go back, could we? We just had to go on trying to get to you.'

Angela patted Victoria's hand and stroked a stray wisp of hair from Leila's forehead. She was in no doubt that it was her niece who had been the ringleader in this enterprise, but her little friend had supported rather than discouraged her. Realizing suddenly that it was Leila, not Victoria, who was actually her niece, she put the thought quickly from her. This was not the time to think of that particular dilemma.

'So did the sleeping-car attendant hand you over to the police?' she asked gently.

Leila shook her head. 'A kind lady in our compartment took pity on us and said she would pay my fare. At first the attendant said he would still report us to the police for trying to defraud the French railway company, but the lady gave him some money and told him not to be so silly; that it was perfectly plain we just didn't have enough money to do what we had been instructed to do. You see, Victoria had told him the story about our father having died and our mother being ill and so we were being sent to live with you.'

It was with some difficulty that Angela concealed her amusement at this outrageous but extremely inventive lie. Victoria had stopped crying and now said they had written down the kind lady's name and address: she was French and lived in Lyon, so she would ask her father to send the money to their benefactor.

'Do you think you can spend pounds in France?' she asked Angela. 'I don't think Papa would have any francs.'

'Don't worry about that,' Angela told her. 'I have plenty of francs and we will write to your saviour tomorrow. Now we must go and make up two beds for you. My *femme de chambre* does not return until the morning, so you shall both help me. By then, a friend of mine will be arriving. His name is Monsieur Castel – Pierre Castel. He is French but he speaks very good English so I hope you will converse very politely with him. I shall ask him to drive back into town and send telegrams to your parents. They must be half out of their minds with worry!'

'Oh, dear!' Victoria muttered, close to tears once more. Beside her, tears were already dripping down Leila's cheeks. 'I never really thought about them!'

Leila was too choked to agree. Perhaps fortunately, the distress of the moment was curtailed by the sound of a motor car drawing up outside. A car door slammed and then there was a loud peal from a bell at the front door.

Colour rushed into Angela's cheeks. There was no time now to go and powder her nose, tidy her hair, put a little rouge into her cheeks. Pierre was nothing if not impatient. Even as she thought this, the bell rang a second time. Suddenly very afraid the next half-hour might bring an end to a friendship she now realized had become extremely important to her, Angela handed Victoria a handkerchief.

'Wipe your eyes, darling, blow your nose and then be very kind and open the front door for me. I think it might be Pierre ... Monsieur Castel. He ... he does not like to be kept waiting.'

As if on cue, the front door bell rang for the third time.

Twenty

Copper was close to tears as she hurriedly packed a suit-case for her husband. When Sir Aubrey had arrived at the door the night before with the news that the girls were safe and sound with his sister-in-law in France, she had burst into tears of relief. For the past twenty-four hours she had been sick with worry as to what could have happened to them; wondering how the nuns in the convent could have been irresponsible enough to 'lose' them. She had not even known whether her beloved daughter was alive or dead. Of course Harold had told her not to be so silly as even to contemplate such a possibility; but she knew him well enough to gauge that he was every bit as apprehensive as she was. He'd repeated over and over again that the girls could not be far from the convent since they had no money to go elsewhere, and that the French *gendarmes* who were searching the forest where they could so easily be lost would find them long before they could have starved to death. As far as he was aware, there were no dangerous wild animals in the forest.

But he was unable to answer Copper's querulous question as to why they had chosen to run away in the first place. Somehow, he told her, he thought this was all connected with the fact that neither they nor the Beaufords had had word from the children for the four weeks they had been in France. Sir Aubrey had suggested it was not beyond the realms of possibility that Victoria would not consider writing home of prime importance if she was busy enjoying herself! But Harold could not claim the same indifference to home and family for Leila. She was an intensely loving little girl, he'd told Sir Aubrey; very thoughtful and caring. She had promised her mother she would write at the very least twice a week, perhaps more often if she had time.

When later the next day Sir Aubrey drove up in his Bentley,

announcing that the girls were safe and sound with his sister-in-law and he was going to drive down to the south of France to collect them, Harold immediately asked if he could accompany him. Sir Aubrey looked delighted.

'I was going to take Joseph . . . share the driving . . . put things right if we had a breakdown, puncture . . . that sort of thing, but I seem to remember you telling me you enjoyed tinkering with your car? We could share the driving.' He gave Harold a boyish grin. 'Can't stand it when my chauffeur is sitting next to me – never stops telling me how to drive the blinking thing – "Corner coming up, sir!" "Steep hill, sir, one in three!" Thinks I can't read. No, I'd be delighted to have you aboard, Varney. Get away from that school of yours, can you?'

As it was term time, Harold said, he would announce a half-term holiday during which the pupils must write a story, do ten of the sums in the back of their arithmetic books and learn no less than three of the four verses of the poem *Tim, an Irish Terrier* by W. M. Letts. In such time as they had left when these tasks were done they could do as they pleased. He hurriedly wrote down these instructions for Copper to take to school in the morning.

Copper protested that she must go with them, not to enjoy the journey, as for one thing she was very seasick the only time she had been on a pleasure steamer as a child, but because she knew instinctively that Leila would be wanting her mother there. However, she withdrew her pleas when Harold explained he could not simply abandon his responsibilities as headmaster; that the elderly Miss Robinson who took the little ones would almost certainly turn to her for support should she meet a problem in his absence.

Drying her eyes, Copper closed the suitcase and when Mrs Clark had carried it downstairs they followed Harold out to the car where Sir Aubrey was waiting.

'If we get a move on, Varney, we might just catch the ferry,' he said as he touched his driving helmet to Copper. 'We might even be able to make Paris by nightfall. With an early start tomorrow morning, we could get as far as Lyon. Looked it up on the map whilst you were getting packed. Be a long drive, of course. I reckon around four hundred miles. Leave us another three hundred or so to do next day and with a bit of luck, we should be in Nice by six or seven o'clock the day after tomorrow.'

He turned to look at Copper's tear-streaked face and said gruffly: 'Should be back Wednesday at the latest, m'dear; have your Leila back safe and sound, eh?'

It did not seem to occur to him as it did to Harold that he had not started thinking of Leila as being his child.

Somewhat to Harold's surprise, as they made their way to Newhaven, Sir Aubrey turned out to be an excellent driver. When he remarked upon it, his companion chuckled.

'The wife don't think so!' he said. 'Always insists Joseph drives us.' He gave a short laugh. 'If she's around when we're leaving the house I let Joseph take the wheel, but as soon as we're out of sight, I take over. Like driving. Always wanted to be a racing driver when I was a young man. Wanted to take part in the Brighton speed trials. Best I could do was have a drive round the Brooklands circuit when nothing important was going on. Of course, the Pater just laughed when I tried to tell him what my ambition was; thought I must be joking. Damn nuisance, titles, Varney, don't you know? Envy chaps like you who can do as you please; marry the girl you want – that sort of thing. Duty! That's what m'father used to drum into me even before I knew what the word meant.'

Feeling intensely sorry for his companion, who was clearly not a very happy man, Harold changed the subject and encouraged him to talk about the sports he loved, shooting, deer-stalking, fishing, and, of course, the two black Labradors he had bought to retrieve the game. Everyone in Elmsfield knew his two black Labradors, Nimbus and Frisby. Sir Aubrey would not allow them to be kennelled and they were forever roaming beyond the estate and upsetting the farmers and villagers who had bitches, siring half-breeds, some with short black shiny coats which betrayed their parentage! Whenever he heard about it, Sir Aubrey would send his estate manager to the owner with a generous offer of compensation, thus keeping the complaints to a minimum.

He and Harold stopped for the night at a hotel just south of Paris and it was not until after an excellent meal and two bottles of the local wine that Sir Aubrey started to talk about the predicament they were in with the girls – not this escapade, he hastened to say, but the fact of their parentage. Not wishing to be disloyal to his wife, but feeling it to be his duty to let Harold know the truth, he told him he thought they must both expect Frances, backed by Lady Mary, to insist upon laying claim to young Leila. His normal reticence loosened by the large cognac which had followed the wine, Aubrey admitted that he couldn't see himself handing Victoria over to Harold.

'It's not that I don't have the greatest respect for you – and your wife!' he said in a rare moment of articulation. 'Moreover, I admire the way you've brought up young Leila; and Victoria has told me how . . .' He paused, cleared his throat and continued awkwardly, 'How she wishes her mother were a bit more like your wife . . . reads her stories, cuddles her . . . that sort of thing. Frances . . . well, she admits she prefers boys to girls. Dotes on our George the way she's never . . . well, we like different things, y'see. She likes London life – shopping, soirées, cocktail parties – that sort of thing. I'm a dull sort of chap – quite happy in the country.' He gave a short laugh. 'Rather be having a pint with you in the Fox and Vixen than listen to a lot of chatter over the cocktails at one of Frances' "do's".'

He looked across at Harold with a smile which Harold later described to Copper as 'wistful' as he added: 'Sometimes wish I hadn't inherited a title – life's not your own, don't y'know? It's why I stood up to Frances when young George left school and said he wanted to go abroad. Frances nearly had a fit and said no; but I knew the poor chap would have to take my place when I kick the bucket! Be responsible for the estate and marry someone suitable so he produces a satisfactory heir – that sort of thing. Give the boy a chance to have a bit of fun before he has to knuckle down, I told her!'

He gave a sudden boyish grin.

'M'wife didn't half put up a fuss. George was always her pet – liked to show him off to her friends – good-looking chap, d'you see? But of course, you met him once or twice, didn't you.'

Clearly he did not expect an answer but glancing at his gold hunter watch and yawning, suggested they make for their beds.

'Like to get off early tomorrow,' he said as they walked towards the stairs. 'Breakfast sevenish, eh? And away by eight.'

Harold was more than ready to retire early because Sir Aubrey had permitted him to do a fair bit of the driving and they had covered a good many miles; moreover, they had lost an hour, once to change a wheel following a puncture and again because the engine was overheating due to a slack fan belt. After a long day on the road, they were both tired.

When Harold took the wheel of the big car next morning, the sun was shining brilliantly and the November day was warm enough to allow the roof to be folded back. Both men donned their helmets and goggles, and with rugs wrapped round their knees set off in good heart.

Sir Aubrey seemed inclined to chat when Harold was at the wheel.

'Could have asked my sister-in-law to bring the girls home, I dare say,' he remarked as Harold steered the car along a more or less traffic-free highway. 'Could have brought them home by train, I suppose, but I rather fancied the drive, eh?' He smiled. 'You've met my sister-in-law, haven't you, Varney?'

Harold nodded. 'Only once, but Mrs Bartofski seemed a very friendly, pleasant lady. May I ask a somewhat personal question? I know Mrs Bartofski is a widow and lived in New York for the past few years. When we met briefly at your house, she told me she was thinking of settling down in France. One would have thought that so recently widowed she might have felt her bereavement less if she continued to live with her sister and you in England. Farlington Hall is such a lovely place, and then there is your London home, too.'

Sir Aubrey grinned. 'Never know what the young women these days are going to do next, eh?' He now took over the driving and steered the car carefully past a large, slow-moving horse-drawn wagon laden with charcoal, on its way into the beautiful old city of Chartres. To Harold's amusement, his companion gave the driver a friendly wave as he drove carefully past. They had not yet covered sixty miles so it was too soon to stop for lunch although Harold would have dearly loved to see the city's Notre-Dame cathedral, renowned for its beauty. They did, however, stop at a garage for petrol and a welcome cup of coffee from the thermos the hotel had filled for them. The manager had offered to put up a picnic basket, too, but Sir Aubrey felt they should stop for a quick break and a snack at lunchtime as it was going to be a very long day's drive.

For a short while, they remained silent whilst Sir Aubrey negotiated his way through the busy city streets, their large white Bentley attracting more than a few admiring stares. But as they left the town behind them and Harold once more took over the driver's seat, Sir Aubrey brought up the subject of the forthcoming meeting with their daughters.

'Think we ought to punish them some way or other?' he asked Harold. 'Caused no end of trouble. Haven't told m'wife yet – doesn't even know they went A.W.O.L!' He chuckled. 'Got a nerve, hadn't they? Nine years old and can't even speak the lingo properly and away they go into unknown territory.'

Harold shook his head. 'I think it was a matter of "ignorance is bliss". I'm sure they hadn't the slightest idea what they were getting into. After all, it only took a day to get them across the Channel to Compiègne when your wife accompanied them to the school. They probably thought they would get home just as quickly. I think my advice is not to come down too hard on them. Doubtless their "adventure", penniless and in all probability frightening, was very far from being enjoyable.'

Sir Aubrey nodded. 'Been punished enough already, eh?' he said with a sigh of relief. All he wanted to do when they reached Angela's villa was to give Victoria a huge hug and make her promise never, ever to run away again.

The telegram Aubrey had sent from England before he left arrived at the Villa des Cyprès whilst Angela and the two children were having breakfast – delicious bowls of hot milky coffee and *croissants* fresh from the bakery across the street. It stated that Aubrey and Leila's father were on their way by car to collect the girls. When Angela announced the news Leila nearly spilt her coffee as she jumped up and clapped her hands, radiant at the thought of seeing her father so soon. Victoria looked less happy.

'Do you think Papa's going to be terribly, terribly, *terribly* angry?' she asked Angela tentatively.

Angela put a comforting arm round her niece's shoulder.

'Perhaps not when he hears how unhappy you both were at the convent. If the truth be told, I cannot believe that every single one of the letters you both wrote were lost. Even had they been waylaid, they should have turned up within the last five weeks. I think it is possible the nuns read those letters and decided not to post them.'

'But that's horrible,' Victoria cried. 'They had no right to even read them.'

Regretting she had spoken such thoughts aloud, Angela said, 'I understand how you feel, but maybe the nuns were trying to save your parents' feelings. Think how worried they would have been if they had known how unhappy you both were!'

'I suppose so!' Victoria said grudgingly. 'But what about the letters our parents wrote to us? I'm sure as sure as *sure* Papa would have written to me. He promised! And Leila says she just knows her mother would have written because she was going to be so lonely without her. Her mummy hasn't got any other children, you see!' she explained to Angela, the significance of the child's remark not going unnoticed by her. Victoria's father was devoted but there was no mention of her mother missing her.

By no means for the first time Angela thought how opposite she and her sister were. Granted she had never had children, so perhaps she was in no position to judge what was normal, but Frances' seeming indifference to people's feelings and in particular for the child she had always supposed was her daughter was difficult for her to understand. When discussing the future of the two children, Frances had even remarked that if the worst came to the worst and the Varneys refused to hand over their daughter, she might have to hand over Victoria to them. She had never once referred to the distress this would cause her; only how Aubrey would react, and, of course, the three boys who all loved their little sister, George in particular. He, Frances had told her, was thoroughly enjoying life in Ceylon with his godfather and knew nothing about the blood tests taken by the two families or the disastrous results. Was it possible, she wondered, that somehow Frances had felt instinctively that Victoria was not genetically her child? But her sister was the least sensitive person she knew so it seemed unlikely.

As Angela watched the two girls tucking into the fresh peaches that Pierre had bought for her the previous day, she reflected how nice a person he was turning out to be. When he had arrived the previous evening, he had been charming to the little girls, kissing their hands as if they were adults and promising to take them next day in his car down to the harbour to see the big liners and yachts docked there . . . after they had had a good night's sleep, he'd added. Once they had been tucked up in bed, he'd sat down in her small salon and, impressed by the children's bravery, clearly enjoyed the story of their adventure.

They had shared a bottle of wine, Angela having no brandy in the house. Pierre had not tried to embrace her, sensitively aware as he was that she would have been afraid one of the girls would wake and come downstairs. In a day or two's time, when the girls went home, he would have her all to himself again, he told her smiling. Meanwhile, they could surely risk a kiss! The kiss was prolonged and passionate and ended with Pierre telling her that he feared he might be falling in love. He'd been determined to remain unattached, free to make love to as many women as might take his fancy, he told her. Now, after only two weeks, he couldn't imagine wanting to share his life with any other woman but her.

He made the following day a delightful one for the children. They had woken feeling hugely refreshed and reassured by Angela's belief that their parents would probably be so relieved they were safe, they would not be too angry with them for causing them so much worry. Both girls took to Pierre after a brief hour or two of shyness which quickly wore off beneath his jolly, easy-going manner. In his excellent but accented English, he told them endless jokes which kept them as well as Angela in gales of laughter.

Although both children had been longing to be reunited with their fathers, they so much enjoyed their unexpected day out in Nice that they were not too concerned when, on their arrival back at the villa, Angela received another telegram saying that the Bentley had had a second puncture. With the spare wheel already useless, the two men had just managed to urge the car into the nearest town where to their dismay the only garage did not sell tyres. The garage owner would have to drive to the neighbouring town the following morning to obtain a new one. Thus Aubrey and Harold were obliged to stay another night at a local inn and would not be able to leave until at least midday. The telegram informed Angela that they now expected to arrive in Nice late the following afternoon.

The girls' initial disappointment quickly wore off when the ever-cheerful Pierre said he would take them to the magnificent Natural History Museum and afterwards to see the ruins of the old castle before giving them a slap-up lunch at Nice's grandest seafront hotel.

By now, Angela was not only enormously grateful to Pierre for keeping them all so entertained and happy, she was more than halfway to falling in love with him. He had professed himself quite indifferent to her past life. Coming from a wealthy upper-class family himself, he might so easily have disparaged her life on the stage and considered her socially beneath him. Instead, he behaved towards her not only respectfully, but as if she were a queen. Indeed, he had even called her 'the queen of his heart' during an evening playing cards with the girls. 'I have great need of the queen of hearts,' he had declared, his dark brown eyes searching hers. 'Where is she? I need her to make me the winner. Angelique, it is you who has my heart, I believe!'

Granted it was said teasingly but he had been looking into her eyes at the time and unbelievingly, he had caused her to blush, whilst the little girls grinned and giggled.

Although the following day was not warm enough for the usual intrepid swimmers to bathe, it was nevertheless bright and sunny and the four of them were in high spirits as Pierre drove them to the museum. Afterwards, they walked in the sunshine round the castle ruins – to give them an appetite for lunch, Pierre said. He expected them to eat all five courses, the fifth being a superb iced pudding which was the chef's speciality concocted for a visiting king or queen – he couldn't remember which!

Luncheon at the hotel of Pierre's choice was indeed a feast, and although they had been seated at one o'clock, it was nearly half past three when the concierge brought the Voisin round to the front of the hotel. When the girls were settled in the back, Pierre helped Angela into the seat beside him and in a matter of minutes he had started the engine, saying: *'En avant, mes anges!'* which made both girls look at each other and start giggling again. They had been told by him the day before that Aunt Angela had been named after an '*ange*' – an angel. 'Let's go, my darlings!' Pierre added. 'Or, if you prefer, I shall say: "Let us go, my beloveds!" ' which caused them to giggle even more, and Angela and Pierre to laugh with them.

They were less than a mile from the Villa des Cyprès when their car was obliged to halt, brought to a standstill by a large crowd of people milling about in the centre of the narrow road.

'Looks like there has been an accident,' Angela said. 'Is there any way we can get through, Pierre? I don't want to be late back in case my brother-in-law and Leila's father have arrived earlier than expected.'

Pierre pressed the hooter on the side of his car and slowly, almost grudgingly, the people began to move to one side of the road. As he inched forward, the reason for the crowd of onlookers became clear. A *char-à-bancs* was at a standstill in the centre of the road having presumably taken the corner too fast or on the wrong side of the road, forcing a private car over the edge. The crowd staring down were the *char-à-bancs* passengers, the vehicle now empty. The car had obviously spun off the road and was lying upside down amongst the rocks and scrub, its wheels pointing to the sky, one tyre in shreds. The passenger door had somehow been wrenched off and lay a few yards down the slope in the bushes.

Pierre drew to a halt and asked a bystander if help was needed. He could, if necessary, transport the occupants to hospital, he offered; his own passengers would understand the delay.

It was not necessary, a man in the crowd informed him. A passing motorist had seen the accident and notified the police. Ten minutes ago an ambulance had arrived and taken the two occupants to the Hôpital St Roch in the centre of town. He did not know how seriously they were hurt but he had heard someone nearer to the scene say they were still alive.

'How awful!' Angela muttered. 'Why people should want to stare at such a scene, I really can't imagine. Can we move on, Pierre? Don't look as we go by, girls. It's too horrible.'

But it was too late. Victoria who had been sitting on the left-hand side of the car, had already seen the wreckage. As Pierre prepared to move on, her face white as a sheet, she whispered, 'That's Papa's car . . . the Bentley. My father's car—'

Shocked and not a little frightened, Angela broke in: 'You

must be mistaken, Victoria. Other people than your father have Bentleys, you know. Don't they, Pierre?'

Before he could reply, in a barely audible voice, Victoria said: 'It's white, like Papa's. I saw the door . . . in the hedge . . . it had a dent near the running board. George did it when he was learning to drive and Papa wouldn't have it mended. He said every time George saw it, it would remind him to be more careful. Please, Monsieur Castel, can we turn round and go to the hospital now?'

Beside her, Leila was sobbing quietly, terrified as she was to think that if Victoria was right, her father had probably been taken to the hospital, too.

Twenty-One

Frances took the letter off the silver tray her parlourmaid was handing to her, and seeing the French stamps on the envelope drew a sigh of relief that Aubrey was not here in London with her. He was completely unaware of the private arrangements she had made with the Mother Superior and would have vetoed them had he known. Despite her insistence that there was no need for the children's letters to be forwarded to her at the end of the month, the woman had obviously decided to do so for the envelope was large and quite bulky.

Before she had come up to London, Aubrey had irritated her profoundly, talking of little else but his increasing concern that they'd had no word from Victoria for the past four weeks; in fact, he had been down to the village to consult the schoolmaster to enquire if he'd had news. Had Aubrey been here in London this morning, Edie the parlourmaid would have taken the letter from France directly to him rather than to her as it was addressed to them both.

Frances was well aware that were it not for her mother-in-law's connivance, she would not have dared to act on her own initiative and stopped all correspondence. As it was, Lady Mary had not only approved of her suggestion to throw the two girls together, where they would be dependent upon one another for a considerable period of time, but had endorsed Frances' suggestion that they should be deprived of parental contact for the first two weeks of the school term. What Lady Mary did not know, still less did Aubrey, was that she had added a further fortnight's silence. This she had felt to be necessary as Aubrey had been so much in disagreement with her plan that she was in no doubt he would insist Victoria came home at the first mention of homesickness or unhappiness.

Somewhat to Frances' surprise, the Mother Superior had

agreed to this very unorthodox request. Frances had hinted at disciplinary troubles at home and the need to teach the children that they must grow up a bit, become less dependent upon their parents and siblings and accept a stricter discipline than that to which they were accustomed. In a roundabout way she had highlighted the fact that the girls came from a titled family, and she would be happy to recommend the convent to those of the prospective French bourgeoisie who were debating whether or not they could afford the high fees. Clearly, the Mother Superior had pushed such moral scruples as she might have to the back of her mind, and agreed to Frances' embargo. However, she'd stated, she could not retain the forfeited letters indefinitely since this would amount to theft – a sin she was not prepared to commit – and they would be returned to her ladyship.

Now, as Frances sat down at her bureau and opened the envelope, she assumed it would contain yet more tearful pleas to her parents from the Varney child saying how unhappy she was and would they please try and arrange for her to go home. The expected missives from Victoria were, Frances thought irritably, typical of the girl's passionate, demanding nature. Like the last ones, it appealed not to her, Frances, but to her doting father.

> You must come at once to rescue me, Papa. Leila and I cannot stand living here a minute longer. I shall quite probably KILL MYSELF if you don't come soon . . . We are both so, so, so unhappy . . .

Determined to ignore such nonsense, Frances took out the letter from the Mother Superior that had been enclosed with the children's tear-stained pages. What Frances had not expected was the content. So great was her shock on reading the nun's thin, faultless calligraphy, that her hands started to tremble quite violently and she was obliged to lay the sheets of paper face up on her desk. First and foremost, she was deeply shocked to discover that during the past few days, telegrams had been sent by the Mother Superior to Aubrey despite the strict instructions Frances had given that any communications were to be sent to her at Eaton Terrace. She was even more deeply shocked to gather from the letter that not only had the two children run away, but that the police were involved and had traced them to Paris where the trail had ended. Of course, the Mother Superior had concluded, she would telegraph Sir Aubrey again the very moment the girls were found . . .

Had those telegrams reached Aubrey? Frances asked herself, as she tried to quieten the furious beating of her heart. She was only too well aware that her husband would lay the blame for any harm that came to Victoria at her door. He had not wanted his daughter to go to any convent, still less to one in France. He had ridiculed her belief that the Varney child – their child, Frances now reminded herself with difficulty – would become so devoted to Victoria that she would beg to be allowed to become a member of the family. He had been even more adamant in his rejection of the suggestion the two girls would be exchanged, and made his feelings perfectly clear; under no circumstances was he prepared to be parted from Victoria, who he loved as a daughter; and as far as he knew, Varney and his wife were similarly unprepared to part with their child. In short, Aubrey had wanted to brush the whole unfortunate business very firmly under the carpet, and it was only because of his mother's insistence that Frances had been allowed to carry out her experiment, despite Aubrey withholding his compliance.

Her heart still beating furiously, Frances' next thought was that she must immediately take a taxi round to Lady Mary's house and, if possible, hand over the responsibility for what must happen next to her mother-in-law. She was seriously frightened of Aubrey's anger should any harm have come to Victoria. Normally, it was she who controlled the children's lives and she could overrule all his objections to her decisions with little or no difficulty – with the one exception when he had endorsed George's wish to go to Ceylon. It was with increased uneasiness – even fear – that Frances now recalled that her docile husband could become incandescent with rage – albeit only very rarely. On one such occasion one of his dogs had somehow got into the kitchen at Farlington Hall and eaten the Sunday joint. Aubrey was in London, and in his absence, she had instructed the head gardener to shoot the animal. It had been a spur-of-the-moment reaction which she had instantly recognized as unjustifiable.

She had expected Aubrey to be very angry – and very

distressed – as, in her opinion, he was stupidly sentimental about his animals. But she had not anticipated the violence of his fury, for such was his wrath. For one second, which she preferred not to remember, she had thought he was going to hit her. Now, if he held her responsible if his beloved child came to harm, she dared not think what he might do to her.

It did not cross Frances' mind as she paid the taxi driver and rang the door bell of Lady Mary's house that not once since she had opened the fateful letter had she concerned herself with the danger the two little girls might be in. She was concerned only for herself and what her mother-in-law's reaction might be when she read the Mother Superior's last paragraphs:

> In the circumstances, I very much regret that I cannot permit your daughter and her cousin to continue their education here. Although their disappearance is reprehensible to say the least, I prefer not to expel them. I suggest, therefore, that as soon as they are found, they are returned to your care. I will, of course, forward to you such of their possessions as remain here.
>
> With regard to the fees you have paid for the whole term, I trust you will allow me to retain the balance to compensate for the costs we are currently incurring in the employment of the *gendarmerie* to carry out their search . . .

The letter ended with further promises to telegraph Sir Aubrey yet again at Farlington Hall the moment they had further news of the missing children.

Lady Mary read the letter and then reread the first page. She looked across the room at Frances' pale face. Her voice was cold as she said: 'Clearly you have not read the date of this letter, Frances. It was written *two days ago*. It is more than possible that the girls have been found and Aubrey knows of it. We must go down to Farlington Hall immediately. Aubrey is devoted to Victoria as you well know and I don't care to think what he will do if harm has come to her.' She gave Frances a sharp look and added: 'I'll tell James to drive you back to Eaton Terrace and wait whilst you pack what is necessary. You can then return here to collect me. I shall go down to Farlington with you.' Unexpectedly, her voice softened. 'I have always been quite fond of that child,' she said, 'and I would not want any harm to have come to her. Now off you go. The sooner we are at Farlington Hall with Aubrey the better.'

Although relieved in one way to have her mother-in-law take charge of the situation, Frances was very far from relieved at the thought of facing her husband when Victoria was found. From then it would be only a matter of time before her orders to the Mother Superior to withhold all the correspondence for two extra weeks would be discovered. She dared not allow herself to think so, but she could not entirely dismiss the fear that Aubrey might threaten divorce. Unlike her – and indeed his mother – he did not share society's deep disapproval of divorced couples and their inevitable banishment from social events. He had even one year invited a divorced friend of his to his box at Ascot, telling him he did not give 'two tuppenny damns' for what their other guests might think.

Whilst Ellen packed Frances' valise with such items as she might need in the country, her thoughts were in turmoil which a cup of strong coffee laced with brandy did little to dispel. For the first time she wondered how it was possible for the girls to run away from the convent undetected. Recalling suddenly George's unnoticed departure from his prep school all those years ago, she wondered if Victoria knew of it and had employed the same tactics. So they had been traced to Compiègne and from there she supposed they would make for the coast in order to get a Channel ferry home. But how could they achieve that with no money?

Frances felt a sudden sharp pang of anxiety. They were very young – only nine years old. Suppose some unscrupulous man had taken advantage of their situation and abducted them – kidnapped them, perhaps in the hope of receiving a huge reward for their return? Suppose they had lost their way in that vast forest outside Compiègne, and had died of cold or starvation?

As she sat silently beside Lady Mary in the back of the Daimler her fears were compounded by the old lady's comments. Since all the arrangements for the children to be boarders at the French convent had been undertaken by her, the situation was very serious now that the Mother Superior clearly intended to shift responsibility for the present situation on to her shoulders. To have telegraphed Aubrey as well as herself was implying that he had been cognizant of the arrangement to withhold all correspondence and she could therefore assume as head of the family he had approved of it.

During the drive down to Sussex, Lady Mary glanced through some of the letters the Mother Superior had returned to Frances, and as they approached Elmsfield, remarked in a cold tone of voice: 'It would appear from these, Frances, that your idea of throwing the two girls together whilst denying them contact with their families has proved a disaster. One has only to read a few lines to realize that both of them were terribly homesick and could not understand why their families had seemingly abandoned them. I really don't care to think how Aubrey will take this!'

There was a brief pause whilst she further scrutinized the letters.

'This one is dated, Frances!' she said sharply. 'The Varney child says she has still not heard from her parents but her letter was written only ten days ago. Surely she would have received news from her home at least a week sooner than this?'

Frances caught her breath which seemed momentarily to have left her. After a brief pause, she said: 'I expect the French postal service is not as reliable or prompt as ours,' she muttered. To her relief, Lady Mary had something else on her mind and was not really listening to her reply. However her anxiety was compounded when Lady Mary addressed her once again as James turned the car into the long drive up to the beautiful old house.

'I have been very concerned about the way Aubrey has always doted on Victoria,' she said, her expression stern. 'I know she is his only daughter and arrived late after three sons. His devotion to his last child might be more understandable had he finally had a son after three daughters! It has made the whole business of the mix-up of identities so much more complicated than it need have been. It should have been possible simply to have swapped the girls over to their rightful parents. I dare say they would have been somewhat distressed for a while but given time they would have got used to it. Aubrey's opposition to parting with Victoria has made things very difficult.'

Frances had no wish to deflect criticism from her husband

but nevertheless felt obliged to point out to her mother-in-law that Mr and Mrs Varney were every bit as much opposed to an exchange as Aubrey.

As the car drew to a halt in front of the stone steps leading up to the big brass-studded oak doors, Lady Mary adjusted her skirts and prepared to get out. Her expression was sardonic as she said coldly: 'My dear Frances, a mere schoolmaster is hardly in a position to dictate to my family how we should determine what is best for everyone. I'm sure he is aware that I have sufficient influence with his superiors to get him dismissed should I choose to do so. No, we shall have to make Aubrey take his responsibilities to the Beauford family a little more seriously. I am determined there is to be no scandal, no gossip, and that the Varney child is handed over to us before the year is out. I shall tell him so as soon as we are indoors.'

Her threat, however, was to remain no more than that. As Crawford opened the door into the drawing room, Lady Mary questioned him as to the location of her son.

'The master left yesterday morning, m'lady. He received a telegram from France and he drove down to the village to see Mr Varney. He returned almost at once, telling me he and the headmaster would be driving down to the south of France to collect their daughters and would probably be away for the remainder of the week.'

'The south of France?' both women echoed simultaneously.

'I was not aware we have relatives or friends there,' Lady Mary persisted.

'My sister, Angela!' Frances broke in. 'She has bought a villa down on the coast in a resort called Nice.'

Crawford, who had no love for either woman, spoke up.

'Begging your pardon, your ladyship. The master has indeed gone to Mrs Bartofski's house to fetch Miss Victoria and Miss Leila. Madam sent a telegram to Sir Aubrey informing him that they are there with her. The master told me he and Mr Varney were driving down there in the Bentley. He asked me to get Cook to pack a picnic basket and fill a thermos for him, and Joseph was to put extra rugs and a torch in the Bentley. The gentlemen left about eleven o'clock . . . hoping to catch a ferry round lunchtime. I'm afraid that's all I can tell you, your ladyship.'

'Merciful God!' Frances whispered. Wasn't the news

Crawford had just related more than enough? And she sat down heavily on one of the hard chairs by the door, fanning her face with her gloves.

Lady Mary looked at the trembling woman with barely concealed scorn.

'For heaven's sake, Frances, this is not the end of the world!'

No, Frances thought, but when Aubrey found out she had prolonged the stopping of the children's letters, it would not be the end of the world but might well be the end of her marriage.

'Tell Mrs Mount we shall be here for luncheon, Crawford,' Lady Mary said, removing her car coat, hat and veil. 'And Frances, do stop looking as if the world has come to an end. The children are safe and will be brought home in due course by Aubrey, so we have nothing to worry about. I shall stay here at Farlington until they return.' She looked irritably at the vacant expression on her daughter-in-law's face and said in an exasperated tone: 'Do pull yourself together, Frances, and go and tell Nanny we shall want rooms prepared for us for tonight.'

Feeling much as if she was one of the servants rather than the mistress of the house, Frances went wordlessly out of the room and up the stairs to carry out her mother-in-law's bidding.

Twenty-Two

'I will wait here with the children,' Pierre said as the four of them went into the large hospital reception room. 'If you need me, *chérie*, I shall be here. I think you will find most doctors and nurses speak very good English.'

As Angela started to walk towards the reception desk, Victoria ran forward and caught hold of her arm.

'I want to come with you, Aunt Angela. I want to see Papa . . . Please . . .'

Angela looked at the girl's white face and said gently: 'You shall see him presently when we know where he and Mr Varney are. Now be a good girl, Victoria, and wait there with Monsieur Castel.' Seeing that Victoria was about to protest, she added, 'We don't even know yet if the Bentley was indeed your father's or that he and Leila's father are here in this hospital. As soon as I can find out some more facts, I will come and tell you, I promise.'

With a long tremulous sigh, Victoria went to sit down next to Leila. She was being reassured by Pierre, who was saying that even if the two papas had been in the car accident, neither might be suffering anything worse than a few cuts and bruises. Privately he did not think that likely. What he had seen of the wrecked car, the occupants would have been lucky to escape alive.

'Tante Angelique may be some time,' he told Victoria. 'You can see with all these people coming and going that everyone is very busy. While we wait, let us play a game. Tell me, in England do you play the memory game I Packed My Valise With – and players take it in turn to choose a new item as well as listing the previous ones? My sisters and I played it whenever we were on a long journey. We lived during the winter in Paris, and every summer my parents would take us all to our home in the country near Bordeaux.

It is lovely there. We used to go down through the fields to the river and swim.'

Seeing that he had gained the girls' attention, he started the game, pleased to see them giggling because he often used French rather than English words.

A full quarter of an hour passed with no sign of Angela returning. An elderly man hobbled into the waiting room supported by a well-dressed but portly gentleman who placed him in a chair next to Leila. To Pierre he said: 'This gentleman is a stranger to me. He has just fallen on the pavement outside the hospital and has hurt his leg. He is in some pain and needs to see a doctor. The nurse I spoke to said he must wait his turn.' He glanced once more round the large room, adding: 'I have never known this reception area so full of patients but devoid of staff!'

He hurried over to the reception desk as quickly as his rotund figure allowed. Watching his progress, Pierre saw the man in charge hold out his arms shrugging as if to say there was nothing he could do unless the patient was actually dying! Returning to the old man's side, the Samaritan took his watch from his waistcoat pocket and looking anxiously at the time he turned once more to Pierre.

'I'm afraid I shall have to leave. I am already very late for an important business meeting. A doctor or nurse must surely come soon. Will you be so kind as to keep an eye on him? I am so sorry to leave but . . .'

Without waiting for an answer, he hurried off leaving Pierre with responsibility for the injured old man whose moans were becoming louder. It was clear he was in considerable pain. Both girls were finding it distressing and Pierre suggested they go outside and wait in his car. Victoria flatly refused to budge. Pierre hesitated then he stood up and informed the two children he was going in search of medical help.

'You must try to be patient, *mes enfants*,' he said. 'You must stay here so that both Tante Angelique and I will know where to find you.'

He had barely disappeared through the door into the left-hand corridor when a porter came through the opposite door wheeling a trolley. He was closely followed by a nurse carrying a clipboard and a carton of clean white bandages. Victoria jumped up and hurried across to her. She began in halting

French to explain about the injured man sitting next to Leila. Glancing briefly at the old gentleman, the nurse replied in fluent English: 'I understand you are telling me the old man is in pain but I am afraid we are very busy, and I cannot stop now. I will try and find a doctor for him but it may be a little time before one is free.' Seeing the look on Victoria's face, she added: 'It is not normal in this hospital for this to happen. We are dealing with three quite serious accidents, *vous comprenez*? You understand? All are requiring attention at once. I will try to find an orderly to bring him some pain relief.'

'He has been waiting nearly half an hour,' Victoria protested. 'Can't you help him?'

'Unfortunately, no. You do not understand, Mademoiselle, we have six people very badly burnt in a fire on their yacht in the harbour; and also two Englishmen most badly hurt in the accident when their car overturned. In fact one I am attending now. The other has not survived.'

She hurried away, unaware of the look of horror on Victoria's face. There were many English people now living or holidaying in Nice who made use of the hospital's excellent facilities, and it did not occur to the nurse to connect Victoria with the dead Englishman.

As Victoria stared after the nurse's departing figure, her mind was racing furiously. The nurse had described an overturned car, two Englishmen hurt. Almost certainly she had been referring to Mr Varney and her father. But she had said *one of them had died*. But which one . . . ?

Feeling sick with a dreadful certainty, Victoria started to run, pushing her way unceremoniously past other people, afraid she might lose sight of the nurse, whose uniformed figure she could now glimpse disappearing through two double doors, which swung back together hiding her. Her heart beating furiously, Victoria elbowed her way past an orderly wheeling a trolley loaded with two huge laundry baskets, and pushed her way through the double doors.

There was no sign of the nurse but she could see a long row of open doors on either side of the new corridor where she was standing. Her heart racing, she took a step forward and glanced into the first room where she saw a woman patient in a high hospital bed, her head swathed in a bandage. There were flowers on the window seat and a basket of fruit on the bed table, which endorsed Victoria's guess that these were private rooms. She had only been in a hospital once before, when she had to have her appendix out, but then she had been in the children's ward with many other beds. They would not have put her father or Mr Varney in a ward with lots of other people, she told herself. They must surely be in one of these single rooms.

At that moment, she caught sight of the nurse she had been following. She came out of a room four doors further along the corridor. Recalling that she had said she was attending one of the two men who had been in the car accident, Victoria waited until she had disappeared into the adjoining room, and with her heart beating even faster now, she walked slowly forward, glancing briefly through the three open doors before coming to a halt before the fourth. This door was shut.

She barely had time to wonder why before she had opened it and looked across the room to the bed facing the window. The curtains had been drawn and the room was in semi-darkness. For a split-second she thought the bed was empty but for a pile of folded bedclothes covered by a white sheet. Then she realized by its shape that it was a body in the bed beneath the sheet. She stood for a moment unable to move, part of her wanting to run as far away as she could go, the other part of her brain demanding that she drew back the sheet and identified the dead person. Inside her head, a voice was hammering the nurse's words – 'two Englishmen . . . accident . . . The other has not survived . . .'

'Please God,' she whispered, 'don't let it be Papa. Please! I'll never do anything bad again. Please, God! I'll do anything You want. I'll be a missionary; I'll give all my money to the poor; I'll . . . I'll even nurse lepers but please, please don't let this be my Papa.'

Somehow, fortified by her prayer and her promise to do, uncomplainingly, whatever horrible task the Almighty might select for her in exchange for His granting her wish, she managed to approach the bed. Her heart in her mouth, her stomach a hard knot, she fought against the rising panic and stood praying silently for the courage to turn back the sheet.

Leila, meanwhile, was still in the reception area trying to explain to Angela that Victoria had run off so suddenly she had not stopped to tell her where she was going. A nurse had been talking to her, Leila said to Angela tearfully, and then the nurse had gone off and Victoria had run after her – through the doors to which she now pointed.

Pierre returned whilst Leila was crying quietly with Angela's arms around her. Across the top of Leila's gold pigtails, his eyes met Angela's and he raised both hands, his thumbs turned down. She nodded. as if she already knew the dreadful news that poor darling Aubrey was dead. She had finally managed to see the doctor who had attended her brother-in-law when he was first brought into the hospital. He was alive, unconscious but still breathing. He and another doctor had done their utmost to save him, he'd told Angela, but Aubrey had never regained consciousness. At least he had not suffered, the doctor had concluded comfortingly, informing Angela that she would find the other Englishman, Monsieur Varney, in the adjoining room, before he hurried away.

'I want Mummy!' Leila's tearful voice brought Angela's thoughts back to the present. At least, thank God, this child's father had survived, albeit severely injured.

'Stop crying, darling, and listen to me,' she said, holding Leila at arm's length now and looking into her tear-streaked face. 'Your daddy is alive and by tomorrow I think you will be allowed to see him. He will need you to be very brave when you see him because his head is all bandaged and he has several stitches in cuts on his face. Now don't start crying again, because the doctor told me he will get better given a little time. So you see, you have nothing to worry about.'

This was not the time, she had resolved, to tell Leila that poor Mr Varney was almost certainly going to have his left leg amputated. It was so badly crushed in the accident, the doctor had told her, that it was beyond repair. But before amputating, they wished to stabilize him. If Angela returned next day, he could tell her how things were progressing. It would, of course, be many weeks before the patient would be fit enough to undertake the journey home. Was Angela Mrs Varney?

Having explained her relationship to Aubrey, she said she would immediately contact both men's wives. Now, telling Leila to dry her eyes and go and wait in the car whilst she went to find Victoria, Angela turned to Pierre who thought that in the circumstances she had greater need of his support than Leila.

'Please try not to worry too much, *ma petite*,' he said as Leila disappeared obediently through the entrance doors. 'I have heard my mother say that young children are very resilient. Even if by some mischance, the *petite* Victoria has learned of her father's death, she should recover quite quickly from the shock.' Suddenly, his handsome face broke into a smile. 'See, here she is coming with a nurse and she is not even crying.'

Angela hurried forward to take her niece's hand from that of the sympathetic nurse who said in French, 'The little girl has had quite a shock. We believe she went into the room hoping to see and talk to her papa and . . . well, I think you are aware the gentleman has died. We are very sorry.' She turned to address Pierre, who she had presumed was Angela's husband. 'The doctor has given the child a strong sedative and she should go home now and be put to bed.'

She drew Pierre to one side before adding quietly: 'There are formalities to be undertaken, the funeral and medical expenses and so on, but Matron has said in the circumstances everything can wait until tomorrow.'

As if to alleviate what she presumed was a look of shock on Pierre's face, she continued to chatter, smiling at him in a friendly way as she said: 'We have many foreigners come to our hospital and it has been known for a patient to depart after treatment without paying his account, but never the English; they are always to be trusted, is that not so, Monsieur?'

Somehow Pierre managed to end the conversation, and thanking the nurse, to whom he had given his card, he led Angela out of the hospital where, he now realized, they had spent the last two hours, Victoria walking silently and still tearless by his side.

'Come, *chérie*,' he said to Angela, 'we must take the children home to your house. It is good we all had so large a *déjeuner* as I do not believe any of us will eat very much this evening. If you permit, I will cook for you a soufflé – this I can do most admirably and will, I hope, encourage the appetites.' He smiled at her. 'For you, *mon ange*, I think first I make a strong cocktail to give you strength, *oui*? But before this, I must go to the *Bureau de Poste* . . .' Then added in French, 'To send a telegram to your sister-in-law.'

As Victoria climbed silently into the back of the car beside the tearful Leila, Angela shook her head and thanked Pierre once again for his thoughtfulness. He drove slowly back to the Villa des Cyprès whilst Angela regarded his handsome profile with a feeling of wonder at her good fortune in finding such a man for a lover. She could think of no man she had ever known who would have been kinder, more attentive, more caring than this handsome middle-aged Frenchman. Her thoughts returned to the night they had met when, disregarding convention, he had attached himself to her side and remained there for the rest of that night at the Casino. Could it have been only three weeks ago? He had ordered champagne to toast the fact that they'd both had winning streaks at the baccarat table. Past experience of unconventional assignations had made her cynical and on this occasion she assumed that Pierre, seeing she was unattached and unchaperoned, would be expecting her to go to bed with him.

Despite such misgivings, she was lonely, friendless, still strange to this French town where she had chosen to live, so she had allowed herself to be picked up without even so much as a casual introduction. Yes, they had become lovers. Pierre had not only had sex with her, he had made love to her and she had watched him leave her villa in the early hours of the morning halfway to falling in love with him.

They subsequently saw one another every day and whilst being ardent lovers, they found so much to like and enjoy about each other that they had become friends. From that night on, they dined together most evenings, Pierre like herself being equally unattached.

To Angela's surprise and incredible delight, Pierre confessed that he, too, had fallen in love. His arm around her shoulders as they walked together along the seafront, the moon glittering on the calm surface of the sea, he professed that she made him feel as if he were a youngster again dating his first girl. His life, he told her, had been one of ease, luxury, his wealth and looks making it all too easy for him to attract members of the opposite sex and his affairs had been legion though always brief. Now he realized that the feelings he had for Angela were entirely different; that from the moment he had first set eyes on her, he had wanted to make love to her. Getting to know her had been a revelation, not because she behaved in any particularly winning way but because he found himself for the first time in his life, no longer thinking of what he wanted, needed but how to please her, to win her approval, to take care of her, to see her very beautiful eyes sparkle with happiness – and passion. In bed they were perfectly matched and the boredom Pierre had always experienced following a few days after a seduction never materialized. On the contrary, with Angela he was insatiable.

Still relatively new although their relationship was, not only had he taken the unexpected arrival of the children completely in his stride, but for the last two days, he had happily set out to entertain them and lend Angela the moral support she had needed.

Now, throughout this long dreadful afternoon, he was un-believably supportive – so much so that Angela could not begin to imagine how she would have coped without him. Knowing that Aubrey had not survived the accident, and fond of him as she'd always been, she was deeply saddened not just on poor little Victoria's behalf, but on her own. Victoria had adored her papa – or the man the child had always supposed was her father. As for the schoolmaster, at least he had survived, albeit with major injuries. She dared not contem-plate how long he would have to remain here in the hospital in Nice, far less what arrangements would have to be made for poor Aubrey's funeral. Would Frances come out here to Nice? Or would Aubrey's body have to be taken home for burial in the Beauford vault? George would have to be brought home to shoulder the responsibilities of the eldest son. Would his return compensate Frances for the loss of her husband?

As if guessing her thoughts, Pierre reached out one hand briefly to cover hers.

'Try not to worry, *chérie!*' he said. 'I will take care of all the formalities. I had an aunt who died not a year ago so I am familiar with procedures. You give your attention to *les enfants* while I go back to the *bureau*. I shall be as quick as I can.'

Angela felt close to tears when he dropped the three of them at her villa and drove away. It was as if he had taken her strength with him. But she knew she must not give way to this sudden desolation. As Pierre had said earlier, she must stay strong for the children; for Victoria in particular. It worried her as she led them into the house that although Leila was still wiping the occasional tear from her eyes, Victoria had neither wept nor spoken. She put her arm round the rigid body of the little girl and said gently: 'Monsieur Castel is telegraphing your mama, who I'm sure will come as soon as she can to be with you.'

Victoria's lips opened as if she was about to reply, but no recognizable sound emerged and she seemed to be gulping for breath. Angela's look of concern deepened as it occurred to her that although she had had nothing to eat, the child was choking. There was a look of acute distress on Victoria's face and several times she swallowed convulsively. However, as Angela began to think desperately whether, when Pierre returned, they should take Victoria quickly back to the hospital, the frightened expression left Victoria's face, and although still a little hurried, her breathing returned to normal.

Uncertain whether Victoria was suffering from the shock she had received, Angela decided the best thing she could do now the child was quiet was to pretend nothing unusual had occurred. She turned to Leila, who looked to be on the verge of tears. 'I expect your mama will come here, too, Leila,' she said comfortingly. 'Until then you must be a brave little girl for your father. He wouldn't want to see you in tears, would he?'

'Can I truly see Daddy tomorrow?' Leila asked tremulously. 'He isn't going to die, is he?'

'Certainly not, darling,' Angela replied, unable to look at Victoria's face.

Quickly changing the conversation, she asked the children if they would enjoy the soufflé Monsieur Castel had promised to make for them for their supper. It was a long time since lunch, she added, and they must be hungry.

Leila's face resumed its passive expression.

'Yes, please, Aunt Angela,' she said. 'Shall I lay the table for you? Mummy says I do it very nicely.'

'Then thank you, sweetheart. And you, Victoria? Are you hungry, too?'

Victoria's face was expressionless as she looked up and remembering the nurse had said the doctor had given her a sedative, Angela decided the best place for her was bed. She was clearly still too shocked to want to join in any conversation, far less to eat.

She put an arm round the child's shoulders. 'Come along, darling, bed for you, I think!'

Once again, Victoria's mouth opened as if she was about to answer but although she seemed as if she intended to reply, she made no comment but allowed Angela to take her hand and lead her upstairs to the bedroom she shared with Leila. Angela was unsure whether she should say anything to comfort her, so she waited until the white-faced child was in bed and only then, as she tucked the bedclothes around her, did she say: 'God will be looking after your father now, Victoria, so try not to be too unhappy. One thing he would *not* want is to know you were sad.'

Briefly, Victoria's eyes, tearless, met her own, their expression unfathomable. Later, when Leila, too, had gone to bed, she said to Pierre: 'There was something strange about her behaviour, Pierre. I felt . . . well, inadequate, to start with, but also as if Victoria was trying to tell me that I must be a raving lunatic if I supposed she could be anything other than heartbroken. She's taking her father's death very badly, I fear. I found myself actually wishing she would behave like Leila and burst into tears.'

'She is obviously profoundly shocked. I'm sure you must be, too, *chérie*,' Pierre said, his arms around her. 'She will feel happier once her mama arrives. Did you know, my Angelique, that even grown men injured in battle cry out for their mothers? When your sister arrives, *l'enfant* will soon feel better.'

Not wishing to be disloyal to her only living relative, Angela made no reply as she saw Pierre to the door and he bent to kiss her goodnight. But after his car had disappeared into the darkness, she went back indoors and sat down heavily on one of the kitchen chairs. Try as she might, she could not envisage Frances embracing her daughter, folding her in her arms and perhaps weeping with her for their shared loss.

It was only as she went upstairs to check that the two girls were asleep that she was struck by a frightening thought – Frances was not Victoria's real mother and might well lack any of the maternal instincts so necessary now for the devastated child.

Twenty-Three

Frances was white-faced with shock and surprisingly close to hysteria as she said to her mother-in-law for the second time, 'No, I won't go to France! I don't care what my sister says, she can look after the girls. I won't go!'

Lady Mary regarded the younger woman sitting helplessly in one of the big armchairs, her own expression scornful. Such a display of emotion in front of the servants was not befitting the mistress of the house. Crawford was standing rigidly by the door, the silver salver on which he had carried the telegraph confirming his master's untimely death clasped between his gloved hands. He was, as both Frances and Lady Mary were well aware, waiting to give the post boy a reply.

Downstairs in the kitchens, neither Mrs Mount nor the rest of the staff had yet been told of the shocking news. After forty years in service, twenty of those as butler to the Beauford family, Crawford was far too well trained to show his deep sorrow at the news. Like all the staff, he had always been devoted to Sir Aubrey, their lack of devotion to his ever-complaining wife only rarely expressed.

His eyes turned to the stiff, upright figure of Lady Mary, who had been in residence at the Hall whilst awaiting news of the missing girls – a true aristocrat in his opinion. Standing with the telegram in her hands, she looked remarkably like the Queen in her ankle-length dove-grey silk dress, with the long double rope of pearls hanging around her neck. It was only the slight shaking of the slip of paper that betrayed her emotions.

'I will not have my son buried in a foreign country, Frances,' she said firmly. 'This . . . this French gentleman who has befriended your sister, since he has offered to see to the formalities and make all the necessary arrangements for Aubrey –' her voice shook very slightly as she spoke her son's name – 'to be brought home by train, please be good enough to give your authority for him to do so when you telegraph your reply.'

Momentarily, her voice gained strength as she concluded: 'As far as the child is concerned, since the French doctor seems to think Victoria is in shock and may continue to be so for several days, she will have to remain in your sister's care since you do not consider it appropriate for you to go and bring her home.'

Stung by her mother-in-law's marked tone of reproach, Frances pulled herself together sufficiently to say through all but closed lips: 'Perhaps you have forgotten, Lady Mary, that it is not *my* daughter who is in shock!'

Lady Mary glanced swiftly at Crawford, whose head remained discreetly turned towards the window. Furious with Frances for bringing up the subject of the girls' identities in the possible hearing of the butler, she ignored the comment and virtually ordered Frances to the escritoire to compose the reply the butler was waiting for. Her thoughts, however, remained with the problem of the two young girls, which should in her opinion have been resolved long since. No one doubted now that Victoria was not a Beauford and that the headmaster's daughter must be deemed so. It was a great pity, she thought, that it had not been Leila Varney's father who had been killed in place of her son, when presumably there would have been no authoritative objection to Aubrey adopting the girl Varney had thought of as his daughter. Of course, there was still the wife, who might have objected. But in the meanwhile, since Angela's French friend had seen fit to tele-graph only Frances, Mrs Varney would have to be told the news. If the woman was as devoted a wife and mother as Aubrey had once described, perhaps she would want to go to the South of France to see her husband and child. If so, she could bring the girls back in place of Frances – or indeed her actress sister. She had spoken to Angela only once at Frances' wedding, since when she had not received her, preferring not to acknowledge there was now an actress in the family. She would infinitely prefer Frances' sister not to be amongst the family mourners at Aubrey's funeral. This, she thought, would have to be organized and rather than leave the arrangements to Frances, she herself would contact the undertakers who had managed her husband's funeral so efficiently.

For a single moment, her guard slipped and she was engulfed by sorrow as she allowed herself to accept the fact of her only son's death. Aubrey had always been her favourite just as George was Frances' best-loved child – if, indeed she could be said to truly love any of her offspring. But she must not let herself be too critical of her daughter-in-law, who, if nothing more, had given Aubrey a son and heir, George. George would have to come home now and young though he was – only just of age – he must take his father's place as head of the family. Before Crawford departed with the telegraph Frances was now writing, she must write another to be sent immediately to George, and, she now said to Frances, something must be done about notifying Mr Varney's wife of the situation.

After a moment's hesitation, Crawford stepped forward.

'Begging your pardon, m'lady, if it would be of assistance, Joseph could drive me to the village and I could break the sad news to Mrs Varney . . . if you think it would be fitting, of course. I could take Nanny with me . . . she would be a comfort to Mrs Varney, that is to say, if she is not too overcome by grief herself.'

He had never before made so long a speech, far less one that was tantamount to proffering advice to his superiors. His relationship with Sir Aubrey had been very different – almost that of friends, Sir Aubrey often confiding his hopes, anxieties, uncertainties and equally often, acting on his advice. The least he could do now – even at the risk of incurring a rebuke from either of their ladyships – was to offer such help as Sir Aubrey himself would have done. He had seen the headmaster's wife quite often at the Hall when she was collecting her daughter, and Sir Aubrey had described her as 'a charming little woman, warm hearted and clearly devoted to her husband and child'.

Lady Mary was looking at the butler with unexpected warmth.

'That would be extremely kind of you, Crawford. And whilst you are there, would you please inform Mrs Varney that we consider this tragic accident entirely our family's responsibility; and therefore, if she wishes to travel to France, she is to send a list of all the expenses she incurs to me personally. My travel agent in London, Thomas Cook, will make any necessary arrangements for her, and Lady Beauford can ask Mrs Bartofski to find suitable accommodation for her in Nice. Perhaps you would also make it clear that Lady Beauford and I would appreciate it if Mrs Varney will take it upon herself to look after the two girls until such time as she can bring them home.' She gave a deep sigh, adding: 'I suppose you'd better call in at the school house and inform Miss Robinson of the situation. I dare say the school will have to be closed.'

'Very good, m'lady.' Pleased that he had had the courage to make the suggestion, Crawford took Frances' telegraphic reply and gave it to the post boy waiting in the kitchen. It seemed the lad, having heard from Mrs Quick the postmistress the contents of the telegraph from France, had taken it upon himself to relay the news to Mrs Mount who, in turn, had relayed it to the remainder of the staff – even Nanny, who was rocking herself in the cook's big basket armchair, her apron over her face as she sobbed noisily into it. Mrs Mount, slightly more stoical, offered to make her cure-all for any disaster and brew a fresh pot of tea, but Crawford would not wait for Nanny's recovery. Fetching his overcoat and bowler hat, he summoned Joseph from his rooms over the stables, and set off for Elmsfield.

Like him, Joseph had been deeply attached to Sir Aubrey, whose head groom and chauffeur he had been for the past twenty-five years. During the short ride to the village, his voice rasping with emotion, he kept reiterating:

'He should have let me drive him. I wanted to go but he insisted on taking Mr Varney. *He should have let me drive him.* I knew he wasn't safe for all he thought himself a good driver. It was an accident waiting to happen. He should have let me go with him.'

Crawford patted him on the shoulder as he parked the car at the gateway of Foxhole Cottage, saying consolingly: 'It weren't your decision, Joseph. You can't blame yourself. The master wouldn't want that. If you wait here for me, I doubt I'll be staying long.'

The front door of the cottage opened even before he had reached the end of the brick path. Copper's face was a mask of anxiety as she recognized the butler. She forced herself to withhold her questions until Crawford was inside the house, the door closed behind him. In a voice which trembled, she said: 'You have news from them? From my husband? From Sir Aubrey?'

Crawford steeled himself to speak calmly.

'Yes, madam, but I am afraid it is not good news.' He heard Copper's gasp and hastened to add: 'There was a car accident. Your husband survived but he is in hospital. Her ladyship has been led to understand Mr Varney's injuries are serious but not life-threatening.'

Copper let out a tremulous gasp of dismay. Her hands were clenched tightly on either side of her beige pleated skirt. With an effort, she steadied her voice as she whispered: 'Leila, my daughter? Is she . . . was she . . .'

'No, madam, the little girls were not in the car, but Sir Aubrey . . .' He could hardly bring himself to voice the words. 'Sir Aubrey did not survive.'

Copper burst into tears.

Three hours later, she was sitting in the back of Lady Mary's Daimler trying to control the trembling of her hands as James drove her to London. She was to be met at the Park Lane house by one of the gentlewomen from Universal Aunts who Lady Mary had telephoned with instructions to accompany her to Nice. Copper had never been abroad before, unless her honeymoon on the Isle of Wight counted as overseas. She was, so Lady Mary had told her, to travel on the boat train to Paris and thence on a train with sleeping accommodation. Mrs Bartofski was to meet her in Nice. Copper would have been overcome with excitement were it not for her worry about Harold. No one seemed to know what his injuries were but that seemed of small significance beside the fact that he was alive. As for Leila – Lady Beauford had told her that the nice Mrs Bartofski was caring for her and for Victoria, who, from all accounts, had taken the fact of her father's death very badly indeed, poor child.

Somehow, Copper thought as the countryside gave way to the neat suburban houses on the outskirts of London, she still could not think of Leila's little dark-haired friend as *her* child. She couldn't deny that Victoria not only resembled Harold but had his clever mind, too. She was fond of the little girl, but only with difficulty, and because of Victoria's resemblance to Harold, did she ever feel she could love her.

This was no time to be thinking about *that* particular problem, she told herself as James now steered the car across

Clapham Common in the direction of Battersea. It would be more sensible to do a mental check of the clothes she had flung into a suitcase when the Beaufords' butler had called for a second time and told her of the plans Lady Mary had devised for her. Her heart was momentarily filled with gratitude to the elderly aristocrat who had made it possible for her to go to France to be with Harold. She did not know how she could have survived alone in her house not knowing how he was, whether he was being properly looked after. He would want her there with him without a doubt, as would Leila.

With the dreadful news of the accident, Leila's and Victoria's missing days following their departure from the convent had all but gone out of her mind, as had the reason the children had run away, or why they had chosen to go to Mrs Bartofski's house in the south of France. Why had they not come home? she asked herself. Why had they not written saying how unhappy they were? Why had they ever allowed her precious daughter to be sent to a convent school in a foreign country where they could not reach her if she was ill or unhappy?

These and other questions chased one another through Copper's mind until their arrival at Park Lane put such concerns once more out of her head.

For the third night running, Leila lay awake in the darkness of the bedroom she shared with Victoria. Since Aunt Angela had taken her to see her father in hospital the previous day her tears had dried and now, although she had been horrified by the extent of his injuries, she was reassured by his recognition of her and his assurance that he was going to get better.

Tomorrow, Aunt Angela had told her, Mummy would be arriving and a huge weight would be lifted off her shoulders. There had been so much for her to worry about – not least Victoria. Aunt Angela – and her nice friend M. Castel – had both assured her Victoria was not speaking because she had been so severely shocked. But today they had taken Victoria to see a special doctor at the hospital because they, too, were worried about her continued silence. Aunt Angela agreed with him that Victoria wanted to talk but for some reason could not do so. Such occasions caused her to look so distressed they had all agreed not to ask her questions unless it was really necessary. The doctor had said they must give her time; that naturally at only nine years of age the sight of her dead father had been a big misfortune. She should never have gone to his room – not even with a grown-up accompanying her. It was unfortunate to say the least that the Englishman's body had not been removed. Only five minutes after the child had gone into the room, a porter had arrived with a trolley to collect the deceased and take the body to the mortuary.

He now prescribed another sedative, sleeping pills, and said that if Victoria was not better in a week's time, they must bring her to see him again.

Sharing a bedroom with Victoria, Leila was aware that after Aunt Angela had put them to bed, until the early hours of the morning, Victoria was lost to the world; but as the sleeping draught wore off, she woke and each night got out of bed and, indifferent to the cold, she opened the shutters and sat in a chair by the window staring out into the darkness. No matter how hard Leila tried, she could not evoke a reply from Victoria when she spoke to her although she knew for a certainty she could hear her. But this night, when shortly before dawn Leila begged her to say something – anything at all – Victoria finally spoke in a low husky voice.

'It was my fault! Running away was my idea! Papa wouldn't be dead if he hadn't had to come and find us. It was my fault – and now I'll never see him again.'

Leila jumped out of bed and ran to Victoria's side, putting her arms around her shoulders. Deeply shocked by the anguish underlying her friend's whispered pronouncement, she covered Victoria's face with kisses and said vehemently: 'It was an accident, Vicky. Aunt Angela said a big *char-à-bancs* came round a bend on the wrong side of the road. A passenger saw it happen and told the police your father's car was forced over the edge. They weren't to blame and nor were you. It was just a horrible accident.'

As usual there was no response from Victoria and she continued: 'Vicky, you don't even know if it was your father who was driving. It might have been my daddy. Please, you mustn't blame yourself.'

Victoria's body stayed rigid, only her jaw moving convulsively. In tears now, Leila said desperately: 'Vicky, truly it *wasn't your fault*. Our fathers need not have come to France

to take us home; your aunt said she could have taken us back
on the train. She told me so; only by then your father had set
off with my daddy before her telegram arrived. You mustn't
blame yourself,' she reiterated.

When Angela went to their room the following morning to
tell them it was time to get up; that Pierre would be arriving
soon with hot *croissants* straight from the *boulangerie*, Leila
jumped out of bed and hurried across the room, saying: 'I
think Vicky is getting better, Aunt Angela. She spoke to me
last night.'

Angela looked from Leila's happy face to Victoria's. The
child was sitting on the side of the bed but although she had
looked up when Angela asked her if she really was feeling
better, her eyes were devoid of expression as she stared back
silently. Leila hurried to her.

'Vicky, tell your aunt what you told me. She'll say the same
as me, I know she will. It wasn't your fault.' She turned back
to Angela, tugging at her arm in her haste to relate the few
words Victoria had spoken. 'So you see, Vicky's blaming
herself for . . . for what's happened to her papa, and she
shouldn't, should she, Aunt Angela?'

It was several minutes before Angela could think how best
she could deal with this situation. It was not as if Victoria
was in floods of tears and she could comfort her as she would
any unhappy child. But the little girl was totally withdrawn,
as if by living in her own silent world, she could remove
herself from the pain she was feeling. And dreadful though
it was to consider, in a way it was Victoria's fault that Aubrey
had come hotfoot to France when he'd learned the missing
children were safe with her.

From everything the children had told her since their arrival,
she knew it had been Victoria's idea to run away from the
convent. With Leila's passive if not timid nature, she would
never have devised such a scheme, let alone carried it out. As
Pierre had said, it was quite shocking to think of two nine-
year-old girls from their protected background travelling so
far alone and unprotected. They were not his children yet the
thought of what might have happened to them put shivers
down his spine. Nevertheless, he had added, they must admire
the *petite* Victoria for her ingenuity although he doubted
whether she would have undertaken such an adventure without

young Leila's company.

Realizing that for whatever reason Victoria had once more become speechless, Angela decided to proceed with breakfast as if it was not unusual, and wait for Pierre to arrive. More and more frequently these last few days she had relied on him to take on responsibilities which should have been hers. It was as if they were a married couple, she thought, and Pierre was head of the family! That thought was followed quickly by another – that she wished it were so. No one she could imagine could have been more caring, more supportive, kinder than Pierre and she no longer had any doubts that she loved him. That he continually professed to have fallen deeply in love with her and told her so whenever they were alone, was a warm glow of happiness at the back of her mind whilst she forced herself to look after the girls and do whatever tasks were required of her.

As her *femme de ménage* arrived and went upstairs to make the beds, Angela's thoughts turned to poor Mr Varney. He had had his operation and lost his damaged leg. When she had visited him the previous afternoon to inform him his wife was on her way to see him, he was conscious and referred to the amputation of his leg as if it was of little importance to him. 'A man of great courage!' Matron said as she was leaving his room.

He would need that courage, she told herself now. Pierre had commented that it would be very unlikely he could retain his position as headmaster. Even when an artificial leg was fitted, it would be many months before the poor man could use it freely. Moreover, his doctor had warned them that his ability to hold down such an occupation was even more in doubt as it now transpired he had lost the use of his right arm when the damaged muscles were found to be beyond the skill of the surgeons to repair.

With a sigh, Angela put such fears to the back of her mind and tried to think what she could buy Victoria to take her mind off her father's death whilst she drove Leila to the hospital to visit Mr Varney later that morning. It seemed to cheer both Mr Varney and Leila when his daughter sat quietly at his bedside, her small hand holding his undamaged one.

'Why not *un jeu de patience* for Mademoiselle Victoria?' Pierre suggested, smiling at Victoria over the top of the breakfast table. 'How do you call this in English – a jigsaw puzzle?

This is always a good distraction if you have unhappy thoughts.'

Victoria nodded but once again, said nothing; and once again Angela felt a rush of gratitude to Pierre. Despite having no children, he seemed to have a natural affinity with them.

'I often thought I would like children of my own!' he had once said laughing when she remarked on his seeming interest in the girls. 'I enjoy young people's company because I very much enjoy the chance to be a child myself again. My parents were too busy or too occupied with their own lives to take a small boy to museums or the zoo or to play on the sands at the seaside. Other people's children give me the chance to do these things without appearing too ridiculous.'

His eyes crinkled with amusement as he looked at Angela, adding: 'Would you not wonder to see an old man like me building a sandcastle?'

Both she and Leila laughed, Leila saying thoughtlessly: 'Victoria's daddy came to the seaside in Lancing once and do you know, Monsieur Castel, he rode on a donkey. His legs were so long they reached the sand, and—'

She broke off suddenly as she saw tears welling in Victoria's eyes. Aghast at her tactlessness, she too burst into tears and it was Pierre, yet again, who defused the painfulness of the moment.

'It will be time presently for Leila's *maman* to arrive at the station, so who would like to sit in the front of my car when we go to meet her? We will travel the long way round so we can drive along the Promenade des Anglais and see what all the fashionable ladies and gentlemen are wearing today. It is very windy outside and perhaps we shall see their hats blowing out to sea or their *parapluies* blowing inside out?'

As they left the house ten minutes later, the girls well wrapped up in their newly cleaned school coats, Angela drew Pierre aside.

'I know I have thanked you many times for all you have and are doing for me,' she said looking shyly up into his face. 'What I have not told you, Pierre, is that I am very much in love with you. Frances would tell me – and I know she would be right – that I am being very forward saying such a thing when you . . . we—'

She broke off as he gently covered her mouth with his gloved hand. His eyes were smiling as he said, 'I have not yet met this paragon of virtue which is your sister. However, I would not wish to be responsible for inviting her displeasure, and certainly not with you. I am, therefore, formally proposing marriage to you, *ma chère* Angelique, and after your very charming and welcome remark, I suggest we inform the formidable sister that we are now engaged.'

Still smiling, he gave her a quick kiss on the top of her head and went to join the two children waiting in his car.

Twenty-Four

It was not an easy letter to write, Copper thought as she sat at the desk in Angela's salon, her hand poised over the writing paper. Last night she and Angela had discussed the situation and agreed that the letter to Frances should come from her rather than Angela, although Angela would endorse the plans she was about to propose.

Over in one corner of the window seat, Leila was engrossed in knitting a scarf in thick blue wool, which was to be a present for her father when he came out of hospital. When . . . Copper thought sighing. The doctors refused to give a definite date when he might be well enough for her to take him home. They shrugged their shoulders and said such things as: '*Eh bien! Deux semaines – trois peut-être. Ça depend!*' Two or perhaps three weeks, Angela had translated for Leila. It depended . . . but upon what? It was an uncertainty she could do without, especially with the problem of Victoria. The poor unhappy child, sitting by the window staring into the distance, was steadfastly mute. Both doctors she had seen believed she was perfectly capable of speech. One suggested she chose not to talk and that they might bribe her; another said to punish her or confine her to her room and refuse to let her out until she did speak. But Copper knew instinctively that Victoria was simply unable to talk and that not even a new pony when she went home would break whatever shackles were silencing her.

Such thoughts brought her mind back to her letter. Lady Beauford had so far sent three telegrams requesting – no, demanding – a date when Copper would be bringing Victoria home. 'Her brother George is on his way home from Ceylon and will expect to see her fit and well,' she had written.

Angela, who had told Copper soon after her arrival that she wished to be called by her Christian name, had shrugged her shoulders when she read this particular telegraph and said:

'It will take George a month at the very least to get back from Ceylon. Anyway, I don't believe it is my sister who wants Victoria home. It is far more likely to be Lady Mary, although to give the old dear credit, she has been very generous to you, has she not? Frankly, Copper, I think it would be best for everyone if you left that hotel you are in and came to stay here. You and the girls could have the place to yourselves.'

Seeing the bemused expression on Copper's face, her own had lit up with a smile.

'It was Pierre who suggested it,' she'd commented. 'He welcomes the excuse to have me all to himself in his villa. We are not married but we *are* engaged, as you know, although I don't think either of us mind very much if people will be shocked if I do go there. Pierre has said he will allow me my own suite and that we will behave circumspectly until our wedding.' Angela had gone on to say that they were planning a very quiet wedding, as soon as it could be arranged.

At first Copper had been reluctant to take advantage of the offer for her to move into Angela's villa to be with the girls, but staying by herself in the small hotel where she had a single room had disadvantages. The *directrice* spoke excellent English so her own ignorance of French was not a problem. What had become so was Victoria, who was now her shadow. The first day or two after her arrival, Leila was content simply to know that her mother was nearby; that although she returned to the hotel to sleep, she would be back at Aunt Angela's house in the morning. But Victoria became visibly agitated even if Copper left the room. She never really relaxed unless Copper was holding her close, stroking her hair, cuddling her, even rocking her gently as if she was half her age. She had watched silently whilst Copper had treated Leila in this way when she had first arrived in France, but it was not until Leila voluntarily detached herself from her mother's arms that Victoria had almost unnoticeably taken her place.

Observing this whilst pretending not to, Angela had said later to Copper: 'It is because you are such a natural mother, my dear. You should have had twenty children, not just one! I fear my sister lacks your maternal instincts. I've only ever seen her being overtly affectionate with George on one of my visits to the Hall, but even then not often, and never with Victoria, even when she fell off her pony and broke her arm.'

Copper glanced at her wristwatch and saw that there was still half an hour to go before Angela would arrive with Pierre to take her to the hospital to see Harold. He was getting a little better but unlike her, who worried constantly about his health, he was now worrying about the future. One of the English-speaking doctors had suggested that her husband was far too intelligent not to realize how handicapped he was going to be. Harold had confessed he fretted every waking hour over the consequences the accident would have on his wife and daughter.

They would have to leave Foxhole Cottage, he'd told Copper, as the cottage would be allotted to the next head-master. He had further admitted that like nearly everyone else, his savings were being severely depleted during the current depression. He doubted whether there would be sufficient to pay the rent of another cottage for more than a year or two. The car would certainly have to go.

Copper tried to make light of the situation. She could, she told him, get work as an infants' schoolmistress, or in a haber-dasher's or children's outfitters. Harold had been so perturbed by such suggestions that she quickly promised him she would not try to replace him as the breadwinner, although things had changed since the war, she had pointed out. Married women had taken on many different kinds of work when the nation's men were fighting in the trenches, and many wished to continue working. Now Leila was growing up, it would give her some-thing to do with her time. Harold's reply in a bitter tone was that the way things were turning out, Copper would be busy enough looking after him. He would, she knew only too well, hate his incapacities.

With a sigh, she turned back to the writing paper on the desk, conscious of the fact that she had already wasted a quarter of an hour with useless reflections. What would be, would be – and there was no point in worrying about it now.

I do understand your wish to have Victoria safely home, Lady Beauford. If you insist, I will bring her back at once but I shall have to return here as my husband is not strong enough yet to travel.

Mrs Bartofski has very kindly made me welcome in her home where I am better able to look after the two girls, so would you be so good as to tell Lady Mary that I will not be requiring any more money for the hotel bills.

I wish I could give you happier news about Victoria. She is still finding it impossible to talk and the doctors appear to be unable to put right whatever is wrong. They insist it is due to shock and that time will prove to be the cure. I think you will find her much changed. Where she used to be very self-assured and far stronger in disposition than Leila, it is as if she has temporarily reverted to a much younger age.

She had been about to write that even when they were out walking, Victoria clung to her sleeve as if the outside world was a dangerous place to be, but instinct told her it would not be beyond Lady Beauford, were she to label Victoria's behaviour as abnormal, to have her incarcerated somewhere where she could not be seen! During the many friendly talks she and Angela had shared in the past ten days, Angela had left her in no doubt that Lady Beauford's nature was cold, repressive and dispassionate and that she took after their father, a hard, stubborn man, who had risen to a position of wealth by a ruthless disregard for those he used or bested on his way up the financial and social ladders.

'You may think me disloyal to speak in such a critical way about members of my family,' Angela had said, 'but now your husband has had this awful accident, you will need to be very strong if you are not to be crushed by my sister and her mother-in-law. They will not now have poor darling Aubrey to override their wishes and I am in no doubt they will pursue their intention to take your daughter from you.'

Copper had explained that if Lady Beauford took action to remove Leila, Harold said they would then threaten to take Victoria. To her dismay, Angela had shaken her head.

'Frances would not try to keep her,' she said. 'She told me as much when I was staying with her on my return from America. Lady Mary is fond of her but not to the extent where she would bar the exchange. Her uppermost concern is that Leila is a Beauford and must therefore be incorporated in their family. Believe me, Copper, this would not have been the case had Leila been born out of wedlock, however likeable the

child. I believe the two will be ruthless now Aubrey is dead!'
she warned for the second time.

Returning once more to her letter, Copper now wrote:

> Mrs Bartofski agrees with me that Victoria is not well
> enough yet to return to Farlington Hall. She seems to
> feel safer in the relatively small rooms of your sister's
> villa. We are both hoping that a week or two more in
> this quiet environment will restore her to her normal
> senses and that when I return with my husband she will
> have resumed her normal talkative manner.
>
> Mrs Bartofski will be writing to you shortly and we
> both send our very best wishes for your good health and
> that of Lady Mary.
>
> Yours respectfully,
> Caroline Varney (Mrs)

She was signing her name when she heard Angela letting
herself into the house. Before even removing her smart
kimono-style top coat, Angela burst into the drawing room,
her gloved hands holding what Copper took to be a fur muff.

'Look, children!' she cried, holding up the bundle. 'Look
what Monsieur Castel has brought me!'

Leila ran forward to take possession of the tiny black kitten
and after one delighted exclamation, hurried across the room
with it to Victoria.

'Vicky, look! Isn't it adorable! Have you got a name for it,
Aunt Angela?'

'Not yet!' Angela replied with a smile. 'I thought you and
Victoria might have some suggestions. 'Blackie sounds much
too ordinary.' She looked directly at Victoria's pale face. There
was definitely an expression of interest, of admiration for the
pretty little animal. 'You can have first choice, Victoria,' she
said. 'What name would you choose?'

Leila had been about to speak but a look from her mother
silenced her. She guessed then that Victoria's aunt was trying
to get Victoria to speak. But it was to no avail. Victoria bent
over once to kiss the top of the kitten's tiny head and silently
resumed her place at the window.

With an effort, Angela tried not to sigh. She and Pierre –
it was his idea – had been so sure Victoria would not be able

to resist the temptation to speak when she saw the kitten. Having been told by the paediatrician not to make a drama of it when such an occasion arose, she turned to Leila, who was stroking the kitten's fur.

'Let's call her Tiny, as she's so small!' she suggested.

'Well, she won't always be so little,' Angela said. 'What do you think, Victoria?'

Victoria did not turn round and there was only the slightest shrug of her thin shoulders to betray the fact that she knew an answer had been expected of her but did not intend – or was not able – to reply.

That afternoon, sitting by her husband's hospital bed, holding tight to his uninjured hand, Copper decided Harold had recovered sufficiently for her to tell him the strange story the children had told Angela when, on the day after their arrival, she had questioned them further about their reasons for running away. It was because of the total lack of communication between them and their families, she said.

Harold listened quietly to Copper, before saying gently: 'But we know it was the convent's policy to give all the new girls time to settle in to their surroundings. You will recall that Sir Aubrey told me quite clearly that his wife had said this was both normal and beneficial for the girls, especially for those who were homesick.'

Copper's frown deepened. 'Yes, that's what we were told when you went up to the Hall to ask whether they had had no letters either. But I wasn't happy about it then and nor were you, and anyway, Harry, it was only supposed to be for the two weeks. There were no letters to or from the children for more than a month. No wonder the children were worried and unhappy! So were we. Besides, Harry, even if the nuns confiscated our letters, the children told Angela they wrote to us twice a week. So what happened to their letters? I've thought and thought about it, Harry, and I still can't come up with an answer.'

For a moment, Harold did not reply.

'Perhaps I should have looked into it more deeply,' he said. 'When Sir Aubrey came down to see us, I could see he was as unhappy as we were about the whole idea of stopping communication with the children. Clearly Lady Beauford had overridden his objections.' He gave a deep sigh. 'By then, rightly or wrongly, I felt it was too late to change anything. We had agreed to let Leila go to Lady Beauford's convent, and let's face it, my dear, Leila was very anxious to accompany Victoria, so I felt I . . . we . . . well, we weren't really in a position to question the school's ruling. I only wish I had.'

'You mustn't blame yourself,' Copper said quickly. 'If I had made more of a fuss, you would probably have gone back to Sir Aubrey after the third week. No, whatever the reasons for the absence of letters, it wasn't your fault. It's just that Victoria is blaming herself for running away.'

She now informed him of the problem of Victoria's persistent silence. She had not done this before as she considered the less he had to worry about the better. But now it might help to take his mind off his jobless future, which so concerned him.

'The doctors think it is due to shock that Victoria is now mute,' she told him, 'but our Leila said Victoria had spoken to her since the accident, albeit only once. She had repeated several times that she knew it was her fault her father had died; that if she hadn't persuaded Leila to run away with her, he would not have had to drive out to France to fetch her.'

'I suppose that's true!' Harold said as he shifted uncomfortably in the bed. His amputated leg was the one giving him the most pain, he reflected ruefully. The body's nervous system was a strange thing. He turned his attention back to his wife. 'But Victoria should not feel responsible – it was an accident. Monsieur Castel told me yesterday when he visited that clearly the coach driver could not know his vehicle was about to have a puncture that would force him over to our side of the road. Sir Aubrey did his utmost to avoid the collision. No one was to blame, my dear!'

Copper shook her head. 'I said as much to Victoria but it has made no difference. I'm really worried about her, Harold. She eats practically nothing and has lost a great deal of weight, moreover Leila tells me she is woken several times every night because Victoria has nightmares and sits up sobbing. Leila gets into bed with her and cuddles her and then she settles down, and in the daytime, Victoria clings to me like a three-year-old. It's so strange, Harold, when you think I'm not even her mother . . .'

Her face suddenly suffused with colour as the true fact

struck her – she *was* Victoria's real mother. Realizing what Copper was thinking, Harold said quickly: 'But Victoria does not know that, my dear. Neither child knows the facts, do they?' He regarded her anxious face lovingly. 'The poor child needs maternal comfort and perhaps she knows she won't be getting it from Lady Beauford. Leila once told me her mother never goes to Victoria's bedroom to kiss her goodnight!'

Copper sighed. 'What's going to happen to her when she does go home, Harry? It's so distressing to see her like this. You know what a vivacious child she usually is. It's affecting Leila, too.'

Harold was silent for a moment or two, his brow furrowed in thought.

'I am trying to recall something I read when I was studying child psychology. You remember, Copper, that I thought such learning might prove in my favour when I applied for the headmastership at Elmsfield? There was a young child who was mute. It was by choice. He had had a very bad stutter and his contemporaries made such fun of him, he decided not to speak at all. But I cannot think how this relates to Victoria. No one has made fun of her, have they? Nor told her she was responsible in any way for the car accident.'

Copper gave another deep sigh. 'But she believes it was as a result of her actions. She blames herself. Maybe that and the shock of seeing poor Sir Aubrey dead here in the hospital was enough to affect her brain. I've seen her struggling to talk but it's as if she *cannot* speak.'

They were both silent for a few minutes. A nurse came in with a medicine glass containing three pills, which she gave to Harold with a glass of water.

'You must let me know if the painkillers are not strong enough, Mr Varney!' she said in accented English, and turning to Copper, she added: '*Votre mari*, he is man of great *bravoure*! He never make complain like Frenchmen. My aunt was nurse in the war and she tells to me the English soldiers very brave patients!'

When, having straightened Harold's pillows, she left the room, Copper bent to kiss her husband's forehead and said, smiling, 'I am so proud of you, dearest. Angela – Mrs Bartofski asked me to call her that – she, too, said how much she admired you. I am so lucky to have you for my husband!'

The remark was unfortunate, for Harold's face darkened and he said with a bitterness he could not conceal: 'You may not be so glad when I have recovered and we are back in England. What good will I be as a husband then? I am perfectly well aware, even if you are not, that I shall be unable to continue my career; or indeed any career. Goodness only knows there are enough war veterans, amputees, who have been struggling to find work and are on the dole. We shall lose Foxhole Cottage, of course.' He drew a long, tremulous sigh. 'I try not to think about the future as I lie here, but sooner or later we shall have to face it, my dear.'

Copper's mouth tightened and her back stiffened as she replied: 'Then let it be later. We shall manage, Harry. Nothing matters to me but our being together. As long as I have you and Leila, I can be happy anywhere.'

Seeing the expression on Harold's face, she added anxiously: 'The doctors have not said anything . . . ? You are not going to have to remain in hospital . . . ? You . . . ?'

'No, stop worrying, Copper. I shall be going home in a few weeks' time. No, it is Leila's future that is in doubt. What right have we to keep her with us when she would have everything money could buy and all the privileges of the Beaufords' social standing if we let Lady Beauford have her.' Hearing Copper's little gasp of dismay, his voice softened as he said, 'Do you not agree it would be selfish of us to insist we keep her when in all probability she would be leading a life of genuine poverty with us? I want something better for her than I will be able to provide.'

Copper was close to tears as she gasped: 'You can't mean that, Harry. You know what Leila means to me. We can't . . . just – just give her away as if . . . as if . . .'

'As if it was the best possible thing for her,' Harold said gently. 'You must see that, my dear.'

'No, I don't! I won't . . . I can't let her go, Harry . . . and to that horrible woman! It's not even as if Sir Aubrey will be there any more.'

Harold's expression was determined. 'Leaving Lady Beauford out of the equation, Leila would have two brothers, young Vaughan and Robert, and as he will almost certainly return from abroad, George, as well as that nice old nanny you told me was more a mother to them all than their own parents. And, Copper, although it hurts me very, very deeply to say this, Leila is in fact, their child.'

Copper's face was now deathly pale. 'And Victoria – what is to happen to her?'

Harold's voice was husky with compassion as he said: 'She would stay with the family she believes is hers. When she recovers from this present problem, and I pray she will do so, she will once again be Leila's adored companion. Leila would not only have brothers but a sister, too. Think about it, Copper. I have done little else as I lie here. Believe me, I do know what a terrible decision this would be for you to make but I know equally surely that you are the least selfish person I have ever met. We have to give Leila up for her sake, whatever the cost to ourselves. When you have had time to think about it, I am quite convinced that like me you will realize it would be for the best.'

Copper buried her face in her hands and burst into tears.

Twenty-Five

With the exception of Victoria's continued muteness and her worrying loss of appetite, day-to-day life in the Villa des Cyprès became almost routine. In the mornings, Copper walked across to the shops with the girls and bought whatever food they needed for their meals. After lunch, Angela arrived with Pierre to take charge of the girls whilst she went to visit Harold. November gave way to December and as Angela had warned Copper, Frances wrote again to say this time she was insisting both girls were brought home; that they must not remain in France indefinitely as a date for Harold's recovery was uncertain.

Whilst the two girls sat reading their books in the salon, Angela and Copper were in the warm kitchen. Sitting either side of the pretty white-painted table, they drank coffee and exchanged confidences. They had now become fast friends, so close in fact that Copper confided tearfully that her husband believed they should let the Beaufords have both the girls permanently. Angela was by no means certain that she agreed.

'I do realize they would be financially, as well as socially, better off with Frances,' she admitted. 'But emotionally? Somehow I can't see Frances accepting Victoria's inability – if that's what it is – to communicate. Yes, the child uses hand signals, gestures and nods; but you have to admit, Copper dear, that it *is* frustrating at times.' She patted Copper's shoulder affectionately. 'You are so good with her. So patient. No wonder the child is your shadow.'

Angela had received a taut letter from her sister that morning.

> This situation has gone on quite long enough. I was prepared to accept the present arrangement when I had Aubrey's funeral to cope with, and agreed with you that

it was not the right place for the children to be. But it is now more than three weeks since he was interred and Aubrey's mother is insisting that both girls should be brought home immediately.

She is aware of Victoria's behaviour and says the specialists in London will be far better placed to put things right as they are certain to be a lot better qualified than your local doctors.

Angela had stopped reading at this juncture. She had shown the letter to Pierre that evening; he had burst out laughing.

'Your sister must be one of those English people who think everyone beyond the shores of their country is uncivilized!' he said. 'One day I should enjoy to meet her, *chérie*, and I will wear a tiger skin and carry a spear! Does she not know that the German medical profession is far in advance of the British – the Americans, too, and that here in France we have excellent professors.'

Angela sighed. 'I'm afraid Frances wears blinkers,' she admitted; and then had to explain what this meant to Pierre.

She now read the second page of Frances' letter, which stated quite categorically that she was insisting the girls were brought home in time for Christmas. Lady Mary, too, was adamant that they had been in France quite long enough under the auspices of Mrs Varney. This, itself, she considered, was unacceptable given the still unresolved problem of their identities.

'There may be some truth in that,' Pierre said, putting his arm round Angela, 'although I am in sympathy with poor Madame Varney's wish to remain at her husband's side. When I spoke to him yesterday, I found him very depressed. I can see that it is the first time he has not been in control of his life. As a headmaster, he could manage very efficiently with all eventualities but now . . . now he is no more than a burden to his wife.'

Angela told him then of Harold's growing belief that they ought to surrender their daughter to the Beauford family because of the obvious advantages there would be for her whereas he would have next to nothing to provide for Leila's future. This was not a problem either Pierre or she could solve for the Varneys, she knew, but if Copper were willing for her to do so, she could take over the task of escorting the children back to Farlington Hall for Christmas. She would be able to see George, who, according to Frances, should be arriving home, as well as her two other young nephews, Robert and Vaughan. Pierre would not hear of it.

'It is not my intention to let you out of my sight,' he told her. 'I shall go with you.'

Angela returned his kiss before saying with a half smile on her face: 'You do not know my sister – or Lady Mary!' she said. 'They would be most disapproving if they saw us together. They know we are not married, and probably guess we are lovers.'

Pierre shrugged. 'So! We will be married – perhaps not tomorrow as there will be formalities to complete, but next week, I hope? That is if you have your birth certificate here in France?'

'You are quite crazy!' Angela said laughing. 'In point of fact, I do have the necessary papers, but next week . . . we can't get married like that.'

'Like what? So quick? What is wrong with "so quick"? We are already engaged to marry. You know that I love you and I believe that you love me, *n'est pas*? We shall have an excellent life together. When these family problems are sorted, I shall take you home to my chateau in Bordeaux and you shall occupy yourself refurnishing it to your taste. As I live alone, I have not been concerned with the décor, but when you are my wife, I shall wish to invite all my friends to meet you and you will want your house to be – how do you say it in English? Just . . . *parfait*!'

'Perfect!' Angela said laughing. Then as his arms went round her, she lifted a more serious face to his.

'Pierre, I do love you, very, very much – and not just because you have been so good with the children and so patient when I could not always be with you when you wished. We were having such a happy time together – just the two of us, before the girls arrived and things went so wrong. I would not blame you if you had turned your back and quietly disappeared out of my life. Nor will I ever forget how wonderfully calm and efficient you were arranging for poor Aubrey's body to be sent home.' She reached up her hand to touch his cheek.

'I go cold with horror thinking how on earth I could have

coped if you had not been here,' she continued, 'and yes, I
do love you very, very much, and if we can be married next
week, there is nothing in the whole wide world I would prefer.'

There now followed a frantic few days whilst Pierre saw
to the necessary formalities for the wedding and Angela went
shopping for her dress and her trousseau. Sometimes Copper
and the girls accompanied her but even when she turned to
Victoria for her opinion on a hat or scarf, the child did no
more than nod her approval or shake her head if she did not
like Angela's choice.

It was now arranged that the week before Christmas, Pierre
and Angela would travel with the girls by the Blue Train to
Paris and on to England and after leaving the children with
Frances, they would cross the English Channel once more and
proceed to Paris, where they would start their honeymoon in
the luxurious Hôtel de Crillon. Before leaving England, Angela
wished to introduce Pierre to her former friends. Amongst
these, much to Pierre's amusement when Angela told him
about her boy lover, was Godfrey Gregson. He had written
to say how much he would love to see Angela and her husband
and please, could he bring with him his fiancée, Eleanor, a
fellow student who was hoping to become a doctor.

Angela was delighted to learn that her youthful *amour* had
found a girl of his own age who if she succeeded in quali-
fying would not be a financial burden to Godfrey and his
family. Pierre, meanwhile, teased Angela unmercifully,
addressing her as his favourite seductress and insisting,
unfairly, that it was she who had seduced him that evening
at the Casino when they had met.

Copper and the two girls were the only witnesses at the
wedding in the English church in the rue de France, which
was followed by tea at the grand Hôtel de la Méditerranée.

Leila, once she had recovered from the excitement of the
wedding, was looking forward with great enthusiasm to
spending Christmas at Farlington Hall with Victoria and her
brothers.

'They have a huge big tree with lots of candles and heaps
of presents around it,' she told her father breathlessly on her
next visit to the hospital, 'and stockings at the end of their
beds full of presents, and after church and lunch, they open
all the presents that have been piled up under the tree, and

then Nanny and the servants get their presents and they can stay if they want and watch everyone playing charades.'

She paused only to draw breath before continuing, 'Vicky told me all about it last year – that's when she got her new pony though that wasn't under the tree. Would you believe it, Daddy? Bob – he's the stable boy – brought her new pony *right into the house* and he – the pony, not Bob – had a big silver bow round his neck and Vicky wanted to go and ride him right away but it was raining so she couldn't.'

Once again, she paused, this time to look anxiously at her father. 'You and Mummy won't mind if I'm not here, will you? I mean it's not like we're at home and anyway I don't suppose they'd want us to have Christmas lunch and everything in the hospital. But I'll tell Aunt Angela I won't go if—'

'Of course you'll go, dear child!' Harold broke in. 'Mummy and I will have lots of company with all the nurses and doctors and I dare say some of the patients will be up and about, too.'

Seeing that his daughter was not entirely convinced, he added with an effort: 'In some ways, my precious, it will be easier for Mummy and me if you and Victoria do go home. Mummy won't have you two to look after so she will be able to spend more time with me.'

Knowing how devoted her parents were, Leila no longer felt constrained to remain in Nice with her mother whilst her Aunt Angela and M. Castel took her and Victoria home in time for the festivities.

Victoria did not share her excitement. She wrote on the notepad Angela had given her that Christmas would never, ever be the same without her father. Whereupon she shut herself in her bedroom and Leila, close to tears herself, heard her sobbing.

A week later, however, it was Copper who was weeping as she watched the train carrying Angela, Pierre and the two children puff its way out of the Grand Gare. Other than the unhappy days and nights when Leila had gone to the convent in France, she had never been parted from the child she loved; the child she would always feel was her own despite the medical evidence to the contrary. She realized that Lady Beauford was going to do everything she possibly could to tempt Leila away; that backed by her dictatorial mother-in-law she had no intention of allowing Leila to remain in the family she believed to be hers. In the brief time Copper had been in France and done her utmost to console the inconsolable Victoria, her heart had gone out to the child, and as much instinctively as of necessity, she had mothered her, holding her in her arms and stroking her dark curls as she would have comforted Leila.

How would Lady Beauford react to Victoria's unaccountable silence, she wondered as she made her way back to the hospital. She had discussed this anxiety with Harold who, knowing that Victoria blamed herself for her father's death, believed she would need the treatment of a psychologist rather than that of a surgeon, however worthy his credentials, to operate on her throat. He thought it highly unlikely that the austere Lady Beauford would be sympathetic towards the child.

With an effort, Copper stopped crying and dried her eyes as the taxi drove her from the station to the hospital. Harold would see at once if her eyes were reddened by tears when she greeted him. He had more than enough to worry about without concerning himself with her depression. For a start, the flap of skin covering the stump of his amputated leg had become infected, thus delaying his release from hospital. The doctors had admitted under pressure from Harold that they were worried about gangrene. He was running a high temperature and his head as well as his leg was throbbing despite the somewhat inadequate pain relief they were giving him. He'd had to endure a second operation when they'd removed the stitches and cut away the infected tissue. The wound was now open whilst the nurses treated it with disinfectants. He was in considerable pain, which he was often unable to disguise when she visited him.

It was not only his health which tormented Harold but the disastrous consequences of the accident, not least the expenses his stay in hospital was incurring. He had already received letters from the Education Board saying he was being replaced when the new term started after Christmas and that his salary would cease at the end of the year. His savings were dwindling fast and the money Lady Mary had sent out to France had run out.

At night, when he could not sleep, he considered how much better it would have been had he been killed in the accident. His life was insured and Copper would have been able to

manage on the income from it, albeit small, were she to go
and live with her widowed aunt in Scotland. As for his precious
daughter, Leila would become part of the Beauford family, as
now seemed inevitable in any event. But with a new day and
his dear wife once more sitting so patiently and devotedly by
his bedside, he understood how traumatic his demise would
have been for her, and resolved to put thoughts of death out
of his mind. The doctors still refused to say when he would
be well enough to go home and although he had suggested
to Copper that she should return to England with Leila, she
had refused adamantly to leave him.

He regarded her now as she bent over to kiss his cheek and
saw, as he had expected, her eyes were swollen from the tears
she had shed as the train carrying their daughter away from
her had steamed out of the station. Leila, she told him, had
looked quite happy as she waved excitedly from the carriage
window.

'Before then, as I hugged her goodbye, we were both a
little tearful,' Copper admitted as she settled in the chair beside
Harold's bed. She averted her eyes, as she always did, from
the small mound beneath the bedclothes caused by the basket
arrangement keeping the weight off the stump. It was not so
much that she was appalled by the thought of the amputation
as Harold's own revulsion of his disability. In due course, he
was going to be fitted with a wooden leg which would enable
him to walk again; but he had sustained other injuries in the
car crash, his loss of long-term memory the most serious
consequence. As he had said bitterly to her not a week before:
'How can I ever get back to teaching when I cannot remember
facts and figures which were there in my head for instant
recall whenever I needed them? I have asked my doctors and
they all try to cheer me by saying my memory may recover
in time; but they won't promise it. At very best, I might be
able to do a little coaching.'

Although neither mentioned the thought to each other, both
he and his wife had reached the conclusion that at least Leila
would not have to face the financial hardships which now
seemed inevitable. Copper had silently acknowledged that she
must let her beloved daughter go to the Beaufords. Strangely,
she felt more doubtful about Victoria's future happiness
than she did about Leila's admission to the family. At the

station, Victoria had clung to her sobbing uncontrollably and it had only been M. Castel's gentle handling of the little girl which had persuaded her to board the train.

Until her departure, Victoria had still not spoken and Copper was more than a little uneasy considering Lady Beauford's possible reaction to her daughter's muteness. Both she and Angela were convinced it was involuntary but Lady Beauford, by all accounts a strict disciplinarian, might consider it a stubborn refusal to speak, or possibly Victoria's way of drawing attention to herself. She had discussed this with Angela, who was likewise in no doubt whatever that Victoria was simply too shocked and too unhappy to talk; that she was still blaming herself for her father's death despite them and the doctors telling her this was not so.

It was strange, Copper now said to Harold, how Leila who was once Victoria's shadow had become the dominant one – as if she were the elder. In fact, the events of the past six weeks had matured her almost beyond recognition.

'Perhaps I babied her in the past!' Copper admitted. 'In retrospect, I think I didn't really want her ever to grow up. Before she met Victoria, I suppose you and I were the only real influences in her life. I think somewhere in the back of my mind, I was frightened when she started to quote her new friend: "Victoria says" . . . "Victoria thinks" . . . "Victoria believes". Suddenly it had become Victoria's company she wanted rather than mine.'

With an effort, Harold disguised the pain he was feeling as the last injection of morphine wore off, and said: 'That university friend of mine, Hugh Carter, wrote to me and mentioned that he had met a very interesting Syrian who was on his way back from New York. This man, Khalil Gibran, had written a book of poetic essays and Hugh quoted one in his letter which he thought might interest me as I was involved with children. He'd written that we are only lent our children and that we don't own them. The phrase returned to my mind when I lay here considering the matter of the children's identities. I had to remind myself that we do not "own" Leila any more than the Beaufords "own" Victoria.'

'I don't know that I altogether agree with that sentiment, Harry. Leila has always, ever since I first held her in my arms, felt mine; that she belonged to me, to us . . .'

She stopped when she saw the muscles in Harold's face tighten and his eyes close as pain engulfed him. At that moment, the nurse in her starched white apron and cap arrived to dress his wound. Aware Harold would not want her to see his suffering, Copper told him she would go down to the nearby café and return once she had had something to eat.

Seated in the warm room, the air filled with the smoke of strong Gitanes cigarettes and noisy with the French voices all around her, she was suddenly aware of her loneliness. Since her arrival in France nearly six weeks ago, she'd had the company not only of the two girls but also of Angela, who had proved a wonderful friend. Her new husband had also been a cheerful and optimistic companion, refusing to allow her to become submerged in worry as happened after each visit to the hospital. She could well understand why Angela had fallen in love with him.

He had been of immeasurable help dealing with the French authorities arranging for Sir Aubrey's body to be sent to England; and now he was in touch with a French lawyer as he believed Harold as well as Lady Beauford would get financial compensation from the *char-à-bancs* company. With no knowledge of French, she would have been at a loss trying to deal with such things.

It had been an afternoon of real joy for all of them yesterday when he and Angela were married. Now they had departed to England with the girls and she knew when she returned to Angela's lovely little villa it would be unbearably empty of company. There would only be Victoria's kitten and the morning visits from the *femme de ménage* to keep her from total solitude. In England at Foxhole Cottage, she was accustomed to spending large parts of the day by herself, and she had never minded it, knowing that by late afternoon Harold and Leila would come home to share the warm fire and good food she had been cooking for them.

At a nearby table in the hospital café, a young couple, hands entwined, observed the tears sliding down Copper's cheeks and wondered for whom or for what she might be grieving.

Twenty-Six

Frances was far from happy. Angela had told her in her last letter that the reason the girls had run away was that they were not only unhappy at the convent but desperately worried about there being no letters from home for over four whole weeks. Four weeks! And she had told Aubrey and Mr Varney that the Mother Superior's embargo was only intended for the first two weeks. Knowing Victoria's hold upon her father's affections, she had deliberately lied about the time, telling him it was for a fortnight whilst instructing the Mother Superior that it must continue for four.

Guilt lay very heavily on her shoulders, not least because she found herself glad that Aubrey wasn't here to learn of her deception. It was only small comfort that she could count on the fact that it would be a very long while before Mr Varney would be able to travel to the convent to find out the truth – or even think of it. She had written back to Angela pretending that either the French postal service had been at fault, or that the Mother Superior had misunderstood her orders. Not that there was any similarity between 'two' and 'four' or, indeed, the French '*deux*' and '*quatre*'. And now poor Aubrey had died because his beloved Victoria had run away.

This feeling of guilt was not the only reason for her un-happiness. Whilst some of her friends remained steadfast following Aubrey's untimely death, few of his had issued in-vitations. Life as a widow, she realized as Christmas approached, did not after all consist of the carefree days she had once envisaged. True she was technically in mourning, but unlike her mother-in-law she refused to wear mourning clothes or to retire quietly to the country to grieve in solitude, as Lady Mary seemed to expect.

The fact was, she did miss Aubrey, not so much as a person, a companion, for they had led their own lives to all intents and purposes; but whereas he had dealt with their finances, the management of their estate and the outdoor staff, it seemed all those boring problems were now laid at her door. To add to her depression, Vaughan and Robert were home for the Christmas holidays and had begged to be allowed to spend them at Farlington Hall as they had in the past and not in London as their mother wished. Both boys were far more interested these days in their sporting activities than in visits to museums or art galleries or, indeed, the theatre. They did enjoy the cinema – delighting in Charlie Chaplin in *The Kid* and Douglas Fairbanks in *The Three Musketeers* – but Farlington Hall, they insisted, was 'home'.

Although Frances pretended ignorance, she was well aware that London for her two sons meant smart clothes, genteel behaviour, boring trips round the shops. They had pointed out to her in no uncertain terms that in the country they could wear their rough clothes, tweed jackets, old knickerbockers, thick socks, boots, and go shooting in the woods, riding their bikes or, if it was wet, play endless games of billiards, listen to the gramophone in the schoolroom or fish in the lake. At least at Farlington they did not disturb her bridge games as happened quite often in London.

Although Frances would not admit it, she had been frequently lonely in the Eaton Terrace house, which only seemed to burst into life when the boys were back on exeats. Now down in the country, they were so fully occupied with their own pursuits she only saw them at mealtimes. Trying now to overcome her depression as she went down to the kitchen to give Cook her instructions for meals for the day, she reflected what a pity it was that Godfrey Gregson had been unable to come this Christmas holiday as tutor to the boys. He had been a very pleasant addition to the family and the boys had enjoyed his company. He had written to say that his mother and sisters were arranging an engagement party for him and his fiancée and that he could not be spared.

Somewhat to her surprise, it was Mrs Mount who cured her depression. Her sleeves rolled up and her arms white with flour, she was busy mixing pastry when Frances walked into the big kitchen.

'Morning, m'lady!' she said, pausing to wipe her hands on her apron. 'Been a frost last night, Mr Crawford said. He seems to think we might even get snow for Christmas. Be a nice welcome for Master George and Miss Victoria.'

'Well, yes it would, although I'm still not sure if Master George's boat will arrive in time for Christmas Day. I'm expecting Mrs Bartofski – I should say Mme Castel now, of course – and her husband and the two girls the day after tomorrow provided their train is not delayed. You'll be busy for the next few weeks, I'm afraid.'

Mrs Mount shook her head. 'I'll be that pleased to have something to occupy my mind!' she declared. 'Stops me thinking about the poor master. Keeps me awake at nights, sometimes it does, thinking about that nasty car accident. Shouldn't wonder if them French roads are as second rate as them as made them. Not that the Huns aren't . . .'

Knowing her cook's prejudices regarding foreigners, Frances tried but failed to break in before the woman could get into full sway. Mrs Mount had lost one son and two nephews on the Somme and blamed the French for not doing more to protect them. Memories of the war always depressed Frances but now she was cheered by the cook's references to George – George, her best-loved son, who, on hearing of his father's death, had immediately started the long journey home.

If it had served no other purpose, Frances told herself after she had settled the choice of meals with Mrs Mount, Aubrey's untimely death had had this one wonderful consequence – George would be back and, hopefully, to stay. It was hard to think of him now as Sir George. He would, of course, be taking his father's place and that would put an end to his tea-planting escapades in Ceylon. Before Aubrey's death, he had written to say he might remain there indefinitely as he was so much enjoying the life. Now he would have to accept the responsibilities he had inherited. His grandmother would make him see this was his duty even if she herself was unable to do so.

Frances shivered as she walked through the big draughty hall, which was bitterly cold despite the huge logs burning in the grate. Ignoring the red muffler one of the boys – Robert, probably – had tied round the neck of the mounted deer head, and the woollen gloves on either antler, she made her way into the drawing room and rang the bell for one of the maids to come and make up the fire. The temperature outside had dropped quite considerably in the night and she seemed unable to get warm. When the maid had completed her task and gone, Frances went over to her writing desk and drew out the last letter Angela had written to her. She had read it several times and on each occasion felt more anxious. What did one do with a child who appeared to be mute? She had spoken to the London specialist who had offered to see Victoria when she returned to England but thought time might be the answer, how long he could not begin to say.

The doctor here tells me he doubts there is anything physically wrong with Victoria's throat although he did think it might be sensible to have her tonsils out when she gets home,' Angela had written. 'She seems to need either Leila or Mrs Varney beside her – it's as if she is afraid of being alone, especially at night, when she has nightmares. Mrs Varney is the soul of patience as Victoria seems to need mothering like a much younger child . . .

There was a great deal more, mainly about how wonderful her new husband had been throughout, how he was looking forward to meeting her and finally a paragraph about Leila – what a sweet, good-natured child she was and how at times a turn of her head, a mannerism, reminded her of poor dear Aubrey.

Frances did not want to be reminded of her late husband. She had had to endure at his funeral over a hundred and fifty people telling her what a charming, delightful man he had been and how devastating it was for her to contemplate a life without him. She had thought uneasily, even guiltily, of the many years she had in effect lived her life without him. Certainly she had denied him access to her bed as well as her company. Now, holding her sister's letter in her hands, she found herself wondering if Victoria's strange behaviour was because Aubrey had always adored her and she was resenting the fact that he was no longer alive to spoil her. Reluctantly, she told herself that had Aubrey been alive, he would almost certainly have known how to deal with Victoria now.

Frances straightened her shoulders as she recalled her mother-in-law's words – Victoria was not a Beauford, not her child. She must concentrate on bringing Leila into the family. Lady Mary, devastated though she was by her son's death, had gone so far as to say that Mr Varney's injuries might ease the current deadlock regarding the exchange of the two girls. He would lose his position at the school, and with intermittent memory loss as well as the loss of his leg, he might well prove unemployable. If so, he would doubtless deem it a blessing if the Beaufords adopted Leila. Moreover, Lady Mary had pointed out, he would be equally happy for them to keep Victoria, of whom, as Frances knew, she was quite fond.

It did not occur to Frances, as she put Angela's letter back in the drawer, to feel any pity for the Varneys, who were about to lose everything it seemed but their lives.

'Vicky, come and look! There's a coach at the front door covered with white stuff – it's *snow*! Someone is getting out of the coach. Quick, I think it's Father Christmas!'

The four children were in the schoolroom, where they had been wrapping up their Christmas gifts to put under the tree that evening. Robert barely glanced up from his impatient struggle to make a nice bow with the ribbon he had purloined from Nanny to tie up his presents. The ribbon was wide and shiny and the bows kept coming undone, as a result of which he was not in a good mood. Now thirteen, he expected to be able to accomplish any undertaking he chose to do without female intervention. Venting his irritation on Leila, he said, 'Don't be such a ninny! Girls your age don't believe in Father Christmas, for goodness' sake!'

Leila blushed but tugged nevertheless at Victoria's arm, her gaze still on the drive below the window.

'I know it's not really him and it's someone pretending, but Joseph is out there helping the man with a huge sack full of presents – at least that's what I think they are!'

Victoria put down the dressing-table mat she had been embroidering for her mother and joined Leila at the window. Suddenly, she grabbed Leila's arm and started trembling.

'What is it? What's the matter?' Leila asked anxiously, Victoria's fear communicating itself to her. Victoria pointed to the red-robed figure who was pushing the white-fur-edged scarlet hood off his head, and now stood staring up at them, his fair head tilted as he waved.

Victoria was now gasping, struggling, Leila realized, to speak. At first, only two words escaped her throat. 'Papa! Ghost!'

Robert had now joined them at the window and he, too, looked almost as shocked as Victoria.

'He does look like the pater! But it isn't his ghost, Vicky, you chump! It's George. Good-oh, George is back in time for Christmas! Gosh, Vaughan, he's grown much taller. He looks frightfully grown up. Come and look!'

'Whoopee!' Vaughan shouted after a quick glance out of the window. 'I'm going down to see him.'

As the two boys rushed out of the room, Victoria sank to her knees sobbing uncontrollably. Leila meanwhile, with a last anxious look at Victoria, hurried off in search of Aunt Angela who she knew to be in their guest room with M. Castel wrapping their presents. Half-crying, half-excitedly, she said in a breathless voice:

'She spoke, Aunt Angela. She said two words. Victoria did – honestly! She thought like me he was a pretend Father Christmas when she went to the window but when she looked out, he'd pushed back his hood and then she thought it was Sir Aubrey, I mean her father. I mean, she thought it was his ghost, only it wasn't, it was George who looks just like him, and Robert and Vaughan think so too and Robert said it was because he'd become a man whilst he was abroad and because of his fair hair, that's why . . .'

It was Pierre who stepped forward and put a restraining hand on Leila's arm.

'Are you saying young George has arrived? That Victoria mistook him for her father?'

'Yes, Monsieur Castel, she did. She thought it must be his ghost so she's very frightened. That's when she spoke, so you see, she can speak even although Mummy told me Lady Beauford's doctor said he doubted she ever would.' She paused very briefly to draw breath before looking at Angela. 'Mummy said Vicky's mother thinks Victoria could speak perfectly well and is just being difficult – to draw attention to herself. But I knew that wasn't true.'

Angela was not in the least surprised to hear the note of disagreement in the girl's voice. Frances' attitude to Victoria since they had arrived back from France was one of barely concealed irritation. Several times a day she could be heard to remark: 'Do pull yourself together, Victoria. You're not a baby any more!' At least she had not referred publicly to the fact that Nanny had told her Victoria wet the bed nearly every night.

Angela looked now at Leila's concerned young face and thought, by no means for the first time, what an affectionate and caring child she was. She was endlessly patient with Victoria, sometimes answering for her when people not familiar with her muteness were present, so it would be less obvious to them that her friend for whatever reason simply could not talk. Were those two words she had just spoken the key to her silence? Her fear of her father's ghost? Would she now start talking again? It was interesting, she thought, how the two girls' status had changed since the accident. Where Victoria had once been the dominant one, the leader, seemingly the elder, now it was Leila who acted almost like a mother to her, deciding what to do, where to go, what to buy when they shopped for Christmas.

Aware that both Leila and Pierre were waiting for her to act, she took Leila's hand and told her to go back to Victoria whilst she and her husband went downstairs to greet George. Frances was in London where she had gone ostensibly to buy Christmas fare from Harrods. In her absence, Angela felt responsible for the household.

'I'll bring George up to see Victoria when I have had time to explain things to him,' she said.

As Leila left the room to return to the schoolroom, Angela hesitated.

'If everything Leila says is true, what will be Victoria's reaction when she comes face to face with the brother she thought was her dead father?' she asked Pierre.

'Were father and son truly so alike?' he enquired. 'In any event it would be best for Victoria to see George on his own after you have had time to bring him up to date with the events since his father's death.'

In the hall, Robert and Vaughan were pumping George's hand and telling him what a splendid fellow he was getting home in time for Christmas. Several of the servants, alerted by Joseph of George's arrival, stood at the green-baize door leading to the kitchen quarters, smiling and whispering to each other how large Master George had grown – and how like he was to poor Sir Aubrey, might he rest in peace. Seeing them, George went over to shake their hands and kiss the tearful Nanny's cheeks.

'I've only been away three years!' he said. 'I can't have changed all that much!'

But he had. The boyish look had gone and there was a maturity about him now, even in the timbre of his voice as he told Sally they would all have tea in the drawing room and would Cook please make his favourite drop scones and plenty of them and send up a pot of his favourite greengage jam.

Telling his two young brothers to carry the sack of presents into the drawing room and place them under the tree which he knew by tradition would be there, George allowed Crawford to help him remove his Father Christmas garb whilst turning to apologize to Pierre for not greeting him sooner. Giving Angela, 'my very favourite aunt', a hug, he congratulated them both on their marriage and said they would both always be welcome at Farlington Hall whenever they came to England.

When Robert and Vaughan went on ahead into the drawing room with the sack of presents, Angela took the opportunity to tell George about Victoria; how worried they all were by her seeming inability to speak; how shocked she had been to come upon their father's body in hospital and how, just a short while ago, she had mistaken him for their father.

'Joseph made the same mistake when he fetched me from the station waiting room,' George said. 'I'd planned it all, you see, bought the Santa Claus outfit in London after we docked at Tilbury. I put it on at the station whilst I was waiting for the lad to cycle up here and tell Joseph I wanted him to bring the old coach rather than the car to meet me – surprise the youngsters. Seeing me gave him "quite a turn", to use his phrase, so I'm not too surprised at Victoria's reaction. She was closer to Father than any of us boys. She must miss him terribly. I'm not surprised she thought she'd seen a ghost, poor kid! The last thing I meant to do was frighten her. Mother didn't tell me any details in her letter – only that Father had been killed in a car accident in France. You'll have to fill me in later, Aunt Angela. Shall I go up and see Vicky, do you think? I don't want to frighten her again.'

'No, she knows it was you, George, so yes, that would be

kind of you,' Angela replied, 'but I think I'll go up ahead of you and warn her you are coming.'

As Angela entered the schoolroom, she saw Victoria in the window seat, dry-eyed but with a look of utter desolation on her face which all but brought tears to her own eyes.

'Darling!' she said gently. 'George has come up to see you. Give him a big hug, won't you, because you haven't seen your big brother for three whole years!'

As George followed Angela into the room, she slid past him and made her way downstairs, knowing instinctively that they would be better on their own.

Looking up at the tall, broad-shouldered man approaching her, Victoria now saw why she had mistaken him for her father. They were quite extraordinarily alike – the way the fair hair grew in a slight quiff over their forehead; the shape of the nose; and as he stared down at her, the intense sky blue of his eyes. This was her brother not her father, but he was the nearest possible thing to him. Jumping up, she ran across the room and flung herself into his open arms.

'George! George!' she gasped as tears streamed down her cheeks. 'Oh, George, he's dead! Papa's dead and I killed him. It was all my fault and I wish I was dead!'

It was a minute or two before George spoke. When he did so, it was in his old teasing voice.

'I always said girls were sillier than boys! I never heard anything so silly in my life. Of course it wasn't your fault, you ninny. The accident wasn't your fault. The Mater wrote and told me all about it and there was no doubt whatever that the French *char-à-bancs* was responsible. So you see, old thing, you've been blaming yourself for no reason at all. As for wishing yourself dead, how unkind is that? What would I have felt coming home for Christmas and having to attend your funeral? And I thought you loved me!'

'Oh, I do, I really do!' Victoria whispered huskily. 'I'm so glad you're home, George. It's so awful without Papa, even with Leila and the boys here, and Mother gets cross because I don't speak.' She paused, her voice almost inaudible as she added in a low painful tone: 'It was so awful seeing Papa in that hospital bed . . . when I turned the sheet back and . . . and he was dead, George. I wanted to scream but nothing came out and then . . . then I found I couldn't talk either and—'

'And you're making up for it now, young lady!' George interrupted gently, and saw the first glimmer of a smile. He took out his handkerchief and wiping her cheeks, he said: 'Now I'll give you something to smile about. I've brought you a present from Ceylon, and,' he added, his eyes twinkling as he waited for her response to his mimicry of her exclamations in the past, 'I think you are really, really, really going to like it.'

When her reply came, he knew that everything was going to be all right now.

'Really, really, *really*?' she said smiling and sniffing at the same time.

'Really, really, *really*,' he repeated.

It was only then, as George put his arm round her and led her slowly downstairs, that Victoria realized the lump in her throat had gone.

Twenty-Seven

1924

'Good afternoon, Sir George!' As he opened the door of Lady Mary's Park Lane house, the butler's welcome was as warm as the February winds blowing down the street were bitter.

George placed a friendly hand on the old servant's shoulder and said, grinning: 'Come off it, Johnson. You've known me since I was knee high to a grasshopper. Master George will do well enough! You're looking remarkably well and not a shade older than when I last saw you, three years ago.'

The butler was smiling as he shut the door behind George and helped him out of his caped Ulster. He laid his trilby hat and the fur-lined pigskin gloves on the hall table.

'I have to say you've changed quite a bit since then, Master George. I reckon you've grown all of two inches, up and out. You make a fine figure if I may so, sir.'

'Grown up a bit, too, I dare say!' George said, the smile leaving his handsome young face as he added: 'My father's death was quite a shock to say the least and of course out there in Ceylon, I had no chance to say goodbye to him. I expect it was a dreadful shock for my grandmother, too.'

Johnson nodded, his expression sad as he replied: 'We were all very distressed. I was only one of Lady Mary's young footmen when your father was born – doted on him, your grandmother did, the servants, too. But you know her ladyship – never one to show her feelings, and I reckon as how you won't find her much changed, Master George!'

Johnson was right, George thought, crossing the drawing room to the fireside. His grandmother showed no emotion as she leant forward in her chair to receive his kiss on her cheek. Her voice was remarkably strong and clear as she instructed him to be seated and to tell her why, especially, he had asked if he could come to see her.

'I take it this is not a grandson's duty visit to his grand-parent!' she said caustically. 'Your letter said you had something important to discuss with me.'

'That's quite right, Grandmother!' George acknowledged, wondering how the mere presence of his elderly relative, looking as she did so like Her Majesty the Queen, could always make him feel the same trepidation as overcame him when he'd been summoned to the headmaster's study at Eton. Lady Mary was an imposing figure despite her age, stiff-backed, tightly corseted and her white hair immaculately coiffed. Pulling his thoughts together, George lent forward and addressed her.

'I have been discussing with my mother the unfortunate mix-up concerning the two girls. My mother tells me you are determined that Leila Varney will become a Beauford and that if necessary Victoria is to live with the Varneys by way of exchange.'

The old lady's mouth tightened. 'That's perfectly correct, George. I'm sure your mother has told you I have taken the very best legal advice on the matter and should the Varneys continue to obstruct my wishes, I will have to go to court. That is something I have been hoping to avoid because of the inevitable publicity such a case would arouse.'

George drew in his breath and straightened his back in readiness for the dispute which was to come. He had been fully apprised by his mother that his grandmother considered her wishes as sacrosanct. People simply did not argue with her; no one ever had since his grandfather died thirty years ago. Now it was he, her grandson, who had the temerity to do so.

'Mother admitted to me that Father had been opposed to the idea of an exchange; that he was quite unwilling to part with Victoria even if she was not his daughter; and that as far as he was aware, young Leila was perfectly happy living the life she did with the parents she considers are hers.'

Lady Mary lifted her chin and her eyes narrowed. 'I respected your father very much, George, but with no dis-respect to my son's memory, I was always in agreement with your grandfather, who considered Aubrey to be weak – upright, patriotic, fair-minded, honest, yes, but weak. Whatever he might have said to your mother about the girls, he would ultimately have agreed to act according to my wishes.'

Her words were no more than George had expected and yet he was nevertheless a little shocked to hear her speak of his father in such a way, of the son she had so newly lost. His resolve hardened.

'I have no wish to distress you, Grandmother, but in this instance, I agree with my father that the girls should not be exchanged unless they wish it. Moreover, I consider it is high time they were advised of their true origins, as at the present time, we have no knowledge of their feelings.'

For the first time in his life, George saw the implacable expression on his grandmother's face change as she lent forward in her chair, her eyes flashing as she said angrily: 'Their feelings – as you put it, George – are of no consequence. They are far too young to know what is best for them, as indeed, are you, young man.' Her back stiffened as she gazed disapprovingly at him. 'Do I understand you to say you are objecting to my intention that Leila be given her rightful place in the Beauford family? That you are prepared to let your father's child, your sister, remain in that lowly status – a commoner?'

The word itself, expressed so demeaningly, merely increased George's resolve to remain in control of the situation.

'With the greatest respect, I would remind you, Grandmother, that I came of age last year, and suitable or not as you may think, I am now the head of our family. I have no wish to become involved in a dispute with you but I think I should remind you that ultimately it is now my prerogative to make any final decisions concerning the family however misguided you might consider them bearing in mind my age.' Disregarding the look of shock on the old lady's face, he added quietly: 'I have come here today to advise you that I am determined there shall be no court case and that whatever the final outcome, the two innocent children shall be content with it.'

Her face pale, her mouth now a thin, tight line, Lady Mary stood up and shook her finger in George's face.

'You will not gainsay me, young man. Head of the family you may be but it is I who hold the purse strings. Did your mother not tell you that you will be unable to pay the death duties? That your father left a number of debts? Believe me, George, without my financial help, you cannot hope to maintain your London house, let alone Farlington Hall. I dare say your mother has already advised you that her inheritance from her father has long since been depleted, so unless you are prepared to vacate your family home, you will have to depend upon my generosity.' With a satisfied smile on her face, she added: 'I strongly suggest, young man, that you pay a visit to your bank manager and see for yourself that I am the piper who calls the tune, not you. You disappoint me, George. When you were younger, I thought you a very agreeable little boy who would go far in life. Clearly, your sojourn with your godfather in Ceylon has distorted your character.'

She paused briefly to cross the room and pull the bell rope.

'Johnson will call a taxi for you. You may call on me again when you have ascertained your financial position and come to your senses. Good day!'

George took his leave without kissing his grandmother goodbye and not sure whether to be angry or to laugh he told the butler he would walk home to Eaton Terrace; that he needed both the exercise and the fresh air.

What his grandmother did not know, and deliberately he had not told her, was that he had already seen his bank manager; that he had been shocked to discover how large were the death duties and how large the size of his father's overdraft. He was also advised of the monthly allowance which had been paid into his father's bank account by his grandmother. As a result of that disturbing visit, he had spent several days with his estate manager, who informed him that the estate could not possibly be run without those funds.

Glad that Aunt Angela and her delightful husband had decided to spend a few days in London following their honeymoon in Paris, George, having divested himself of his outdoor clothes, found Pierre alone in the drawing room immersed in the *Times*. Angela was upstairs changing her attire as they were going to Covent Garden to see *The Magic Flute*. Frances was at a friend's house playing bridge. The boys, of course, were back at Eton and Victoria and Leila were at their new boarding school in Bexhill.

Pierre looked up from his chair by the fireside, and seeing

the look of concern on George's face, he asked if there was anything he could do to lighten the load Angela's young nephew was clearly carrying.

'It cannot be easy for you coming home to so many new responsibilities, *mon ami!*' he said as George seated himself opposite him. 'Angelique has told me some of your concerns about *les enfants, non*? Do you wish to share your worries with me?'

George nodded, a half smile on his face as he said: 'We have a proverb, "a trouble shared is a trouble halved". So thanks for the offer.' He proceeded to relate his interview with his grandmother.

'It isn't just the girls' futures that worry me!' he added, relieved to be able to offload his concerns on to Pierre, an older man with a far wider experience of the world than himself. 'It's my dictatorial grandmother. She has always held the purse strings and my father . . . he took the easy way, I think, and allowed her to make the decisions for our family . . .'

'But you are not willing, is that so?'

George nodded. 'Absolutely not! Frankly, I'd like to tell her to go and jump in a lake and leave me to make my own mistakes, if such they may be. But you saw a lot of young Leila out in France, didn't you? You know how deeply she cares for her mother and father. How can we simply take her away with the announcement: "You don't belong to your parents any more! And by the way, your mother isn't your mother"?'

'I agree, and I have to say, George, I found Mrs Varney a very charming lady – devoted, I should add, not only to her own daughter but to Victoria, too. She is a natural mother, I think. But now, with her husband so – how do you say – rendered incapable, Angelique and I have asked each other what is to become of her and the nice husband, let alone the child.'

'I know!' George said. 'The new headmaster is kindly putting up at the Fox and Vixen temporarily, but at the end of the month, the Varneys have to vacate Foxhole Cottage. Mr Varney is very far from well enough yet to go to Roehampton Hospital to have his wooden leg fitted, and it could be another year before he leaves Brighton Hospital.

Poor Mrs Varney, who visits him every other day, has to take the stopping train to Brighton, the fares further eating into the last vestiges of their savings, so Aunt Angela tells me.'

He paused whilst one of the maids came into the room to replenish the fire. As the door closed behind her, he continued with a helpless shrug: 'If Mr Varney had been a war veteran things might have been easier financially for them, but even if the school board permitted Mr Varney to continue living in the schoolmaster's cottage, he could not afford to do so with no salary. Aunt Angela told me Mrs Varney is trying to find a part-time job that will still allow her to visit her husband. I understand he is very depressed and is only cheered by her visits. Mrs Varney is considering renting an unfurnished room in Brighton or Hove. She has not told the girls yet as she knows they would be horrified to think they will no longer be living close to each other.'

He gave Pierre an apologetic smile. 'In a minute you will be wishing you had not invited my confidences, Monsieur Castel, as I also have financial problems.'

Pierre lent forward and placed a comforting hand on George's knee.

'*Eh, bien, mon vieux!* I have nothing better to do, so please do continue.'

George sighed, his forehead creasing once more with concern as he said: 'At least Mother was able to persuade Grandmother to pay Leila's new boarding-school fees.'

Despite the gravity of the discussion, Pierre laughed. 'Your mama is a lady we French would call *formidable*. Nevertheless, I have sympathy with her. It cannot have been easy for her those years ago to wave goodbye to you, her young son who had always obeyed her discipline, only to have him return three years later and take charge of her family's future. I applaud your courage, George.'

George grinned sheepishly. 'I am not feeling very courageous. I have serious financial concerns which I shall tell you about shortly if you continue be so patient with me. Although I told my grandmother I considered the girls must be told about their respective parentage, I am far from sure if it won't upset them too much. Vicky in particular may lose the ability to speak again. As for Leila, I dread to picture her running to her father in his Brighton hospital crying that she does not wish to leave him. He is downhearted enough as it is worrying about the future.'

He leaned forward, his hands clasping his knees. 'Monsieur Castel, you and my aunt were so good to the Varneys in France as well as to the girls. Victoria told me how patient you both were with her. As for my grandmother – she is not considering the feelings of the children or their parents. Her only concern is that her granddaughter, Leila, should be reared as a Beauford. I can assure you, she is determined upon it and will not change her mind, or her intention to have her own way.'

Pierre took a cigarette case from the pocket of his dinner jacket and having ascertained that George would not object to him smoking, he lit one of his pungent French cigarettes before saying, 'As you know, George, when Angelique and I return to France we shall be going to live on my estate in Bordeaux. Angelique has said she would permit the Varneys to live freely in her villa in Nice, but of course she fears they would not wish to be so far from their daughter's new school in this Bexhill town you speak of by the sea, *hein*?'

George laughed. It was for the first time that day, he realized.

'It's a perfectly proper boarding school for young ladies!' he told Pierre. 'And judging by the girls' letters, they are both very happy there. They have made several friends already and are learning how to play lacrosse!'

He drew a deep sigh as he added: 'The alternative to boarding school was to employ a governess, but they need the companionship of other children. Robert and Vaughan are away at Eton and with Mother so often away here in London, I thought they would soon become excessively bored living at home. Victoria in particular needs stimulation. I was talking to Mr Varney about her when I visited him in Brighton and he endorsed my views and recommended the girls' boarding school in Bexhill. According to him, it was best for Victoria to be fully occupied, whereas at home she would have too much time for her very vivid imagination to run free without direction, and that would allow too many thoughts about the death of our dearly loved father and a return of her depression. It seems he was right, as her nightmares have stopped, according to the school matron.'

Pierre looked at the young man who was having to shoulder so many responsibilities when he should have been out and about enjoying himself. According to Angela, George had his father's caring nature combined with his grandmother's strong will.

'You are very fond of your young sister, *n'est pas*? Even now when you know she is not related to you?' he asked curiously.

George hesitated. 'Frankly, Monsieur Castel, I find it very difficult to believe she is Varney's child. My father adored her, you know. That's one of the reasons why I am so anxious about her future. I think my father would turn in his grave if the Varneys simply disappeared out of our lives, taking Victoria with them, and we had no idea what had become of her. No, Monsieur Castel, there must be some other resolution for the problems.' He gave another deep sigh before saying: 'I wish this was my only concern. May I talk to you about our family finances?'

They were deep in conversation when Angela joined them. Papers and accounts books lay strewn across the sofa table and both men were so preoccupied they did not at first hear her approaching them.

'I see you are both extremely busy!' she said with a smile as she sat down beside Pierre on the sofa.

George returned her smile before adding a request for Angela to permit them to continue their talk a little longer as they were reaching a decisive point in their deliberations. According now to Pierre, who fortuitously had made a study of economics, there was a way the death duties and debts could be paid without George having to surrender Farlington Hall. It involved Frances. He explained his suggestions to George, who put the proposition to his aunt.

'You are my mother's sister, Aunt Angela, so you must be a reliable judge of her reactions to Monsieur Castel's suggestion that I sell this house. As he has just pointed out, now that the war is well and truly over and fear of Zeppelins is long past, people are returning to the cities, and large London houses like ours are in demand – not as a family home now servants are so hard to find, but to convert to apartments.'

He pointed to the ledgers and files on the table. 'Monsieur

Castel has looked at all these and he thinks we should be able to raise a large sum of money, a small proportion of which could be used to find a *pied-à-terre* for Mother, somewhere like Whitehall Court where well-known people like George Bernard Shaw have an apartment. We would not only have the proceeds from the sale of the house but no longer have to incur the cost of running two establishments.'

Angela tried not to look too shocked. 'I suppose this house *could* be sold!' she said. 'I don't think your mother would be very happy about it, George, but if it's the only way to pay the debts . . .'

'Not the only way, *chérie*,' Pierre broke in. 'Before we left France I spoke to our lawyer and he gave me to understand that the *char-á-bancs* company will be paying George's mother a very large sum by way of compensation as they have been obliged to take full responsibility for the accident. That should take care of the more immediate debts.' He looked across at George, adding: 'I have suggested that George sells some of the land and farms. It is the same in France. So many of the young men who would have been working on the land have died and the old farmers are finding it hard to manage without their sons' labour. On my estate, several of my tenant farmers have asked if they can terminate their leases because they are too old and incapacitated to attend to the vineyards any longer.'

'I suppose that is a possibility, George,' Angela said thought-fully. 'I'm not too sure what your father would have said to the idea, but if it takes these measures to retain Farlington Hall, which he so dearly loved, he would understand if there is no better alternative. Had you thought about the Dower House, George? It is such a charming dwelling I have never understood why your grandmother never chose to live in it. I don't imagine Frances wishes to live there either. It is still empty, I suppose?'

When George nodded, she added: 'Is there any reason why you cannot sell that too? With its pretty garden and lovely Georgian architecture, I think it would be much in demand.'

George drew a deep breath and then, with an apologetic smile at his aunt, he said, 'I dare say you will consider I am about to behave most irresponsibly but I have been thinking a great deal about it and although I know it would bring in much-needed funds were I to sell it, I thought it could solve

many of our present problems regarding the girls were I to
offer it to the Varneys – rent free, I mean.'

'The Varneys?' both Angela and Pierre echoed. 'But—'

'There are no buts,' George interrupted. 'I can find none –
only advantages. Don't you see, if the Varneys were living so
close to us, the two girls could share both homes. I know
Vicky cares very much for Mrs Varney, who, I understand, is
far more motherly to her than Mama. I'm sure you will agree,
Aunt Angela, that your sister is a dutiful parent but not a very
maternal one.' He smiled apologetically at Angela before
continuing, 'As for Leila, she so much enjoyed the company
of Vaughan and Robert during the Christmas holiday, I don't
think she really misses her parents too much at all.'

Angela's face had brightened and she was now beaming.
'George, my dear boy, I think that is the most splendid idea.'
She turned to Pierre. 'Don't you see, my love, the girls will
be sharing homes and, in a way, sharing parents. With such
an arrangement, I can't see them worrying at all about which
family they are related to. And George,' she added as she
turned back to look at him, 'such a gesture would make a
world of difference to the Varneys, who have no home and
no money and no foreseeable hope for the future. When I
last saw Copper – Mrs Varney – she was distraught at the
prospect of having to give their beloved only child to our
family. I do believe that if you could implement your plan,
they might even be agreeable to your adopting Leila legally
so that she became a true Beauford and thereby satisfy your
grandmother, too.'

George rose from his chair and crossed the room and gave
his aunt a big hug.

'You can't know how much your approval means to me,'
he said. 'These last few days I have been telling myself that
everyone would think my idea crazy, ridiculous, bizarre, and
I suppose it is all those things, bearing in mind how strapped
we are for money! But solving my financial concerns is of
secondary importance to solving the girls' futures; and now
your husband, to whom I am immensely thankful, has shown
me a way by which I can deal with the financial demands
without having to part with Farlington, I feel greatly indebted
to you both.'

The entrance of Crawford with a tray carrying a cocktail

shaker and glasses relieved the emotional atmosphere of the moment. George, who had had to become at least ten years older when he'd returned home from Ceylon to his new responsibilities, now looked as if he was ten years younger as he nodded approvingly at the butler.

'I am beginning to like these newfangled drinks. What's it this time, Crawford?'

'Martini, sir, I hope they are to your taste. As Monsieur and Madame are going to the opera I took the liberty of serving them a little earlier than usual.'

'Quite right, Crawford!' He turned to Pierre and his aunt and said with a grin: 'Come on you two, cocktail time!'

Holding hands, Angela and Pierre sat close together on the sofa and smiled happily at one another as the family's elderly butler handed them their glasses.

Twenty-Eight

Crawford stood in the doorway of the large dining room at Farlington Hall waiting for the family to finish eating the succulent roast lamb, so that he could bring in the pudding – traditionally a large blackberry and apple tart, the blackberries bottled by Mrs Mount the previous autumn and the apples picked and stored on their racks in the cellar. It was the first time that the whole family had gathered for a festive celebration since Sir Aubrey's untimely death. His chair at the head of the long dining table had remained empty last Christmas. Now, by unspoken agreement, George was occupying it.

Time, thought Crawford as he regarded the occupants of the room, was at last beginning to fulfil its promise of being a healer. It was a family tradition to celebrate 23rd April, St George's Day – a custom which had seldom been broken since a George de Beauford had fought in the Crusades and been knighted by his king. The flag with its red cross was traditionally flying on this day from the flagpole on the roof of the house, just as it had done even during times of war. Also by tradition, the name of George had always been given to the eldest Beauford son, after their long-distant ancestor.

The noise of their laughter and conversation gave him an unexpected but welcome wave of pleasure. For the past months, ever since his dear master had died, it seemed as if the old happy days had gone for ever and that the family's misfortunes would never be resolved. Not the least of these was the ongoing problem of the two little girls. Like all the servants, he was aware of the fact that they had been exchanged at birth. When the rumours had first started, he had called all the staff together and forbidden them ever to mention outside the family one suspicion let alone fact. Loyalty to their employer was an essential requisite for servants in houses such as this one, he said, and he would personally see a taleteller dismissed without references if he heard they had been gossiping outside the Hall.

Of them all, Nanny had been the most distressed to think that Miss Victoria, who she had nursed since babyhood, might be taken away from the family and given to the schoolmaster and his wife. Not that she – or indeed, any of the staff – had anything against Miss Victoria's little friend, Miss Leila, who was a dear little girl, always polite and smiling and, Crawford had thought privately, she *did* resemble Sir Aubrey both in looks and character. She was particularly animated this day because her father – the gentleman she still thought of as her father – had been allowed out of hospital for the occasion. Joseph had driven down to Brighton to fetch him in Lady Mary's Daimler the previous day. The little girl was sitting next to him and when she was not holding her cutlery, she was clinging to his arm.

Crawford's gaze moved beyond her to the head of the table where his young master was sitting, smiling as he spoke to Mrs Varney who, too, was smiling. The poor lady had had a very distressing and worrying time since the accident in France, especially since her husband had lost not only a leg and part of his memory, but his position as headmaster, and with it their home. They had even had to face the fact that they might lose their only child.

Crawford felt his heart fill with pride as his eyes turned once more to George. How proud his father would have been of his eldest son had he known how skilfully he had solved everyone's problems. He gave a contented sigh as he thought how the house had become home to Mrs and Mrs Varney. Ever since Sir Aubrey's marriage, when Lady Mary had flatly refused to take up residence there and had gone to live in London, it had been occupied only intermittently, although it was a delightful house.

In a way, it was now home to both little girls, and to Master Robert and Master Vaughan on occasions. They were all in and out of each other's houses as if both were their homes, which, of course, had been George's plan. According to Nanny, he'd had the idea of giving the Dower House to the Varneys from the children's story about a boy called Fauntleroy which he had read in his nursery days.

The arrangement solved other problems, too. Lady Beauford spent more and more time in London in her new Whitehall Court flat and when she was away during the Easter holiday, Mrs Varney came up to the Hall to act as the children's governess, not that the sixteen-year-old Master Vaughan and fourteen-year-old Master Robert really required supervision other than to ensure they had clean clothes, were tidy for meals, had their hair washed and suchlike!

Crawford's gaze moved further round the table. Seated either side of Miss Victoria, the two boys were taking it in turns to tease her about coming top of her form three times in succession. They were calling her a 'bluestocking', much to her disgust judging by the expression on her pretty little face.

At the opposite end of the table, Lady Beauford was listening attentively to M. Castel, who it would seem had managed to change her customary critical expression to one Mrs Mount would have called coy. It was a week ago that the French gentleman had arrived with his new wife, who Crawford had known best in her twenties when Miss Angela had come to stay at Farlington Hall when her sister became engaged to marry Sir Aubrey. M. Castel had been overly attentive to the mistress. On the whole, Crawford mistrusted Frenchmen, who he thought of as being vastly inferior to English gentlemen, but M. Castel had so far proved himself the exception. He had certainly captivated her ladyship!

It was time, Crawford realized, to call in Sally to collect the dinner plates whilst he set aside the decanter of the excellent claret Monsieur Castel had brought with him from his vineyards in Bordeaux, and filled the grown-ups' glasses from a bottle of Sauternes he had brought up from the cellar knowing that it would go nicely with the pudding.

Quite unexpectedly, this had turned out to be a happy St George's Day celebration, he told himself as he stood aside to allow Sally to come into the room. It could not be entirely so, of course, without dear Sir Aubrey there. But being a religious man, Crawford had no doubt that his late master was looking down on the family scene and delighting in the way his eldest son was now managing what had been the family's troubled affairs so satisfactorily.

Angela, too, was thinking the same thing as she glanced at

her nephew. A few weeks ago George had had his twenty-second birthday, yet despite his extreme youth, he had found the perfect – perhaps the only – way to resolve the threatening disastrous mismanagement of the girls' confused identities. As it was now, Copper and her husband had raised no objection to Leila's surname being changed from Varney to Beauford since to all intents and purposes they were continuing as her mother and father. Leila herself was quite happy to think she and Victoria would nominally be sisters. As for Victoria, with her mother spending more and more time in London at her new flat, she was growing ever closer to Copper, who she now frequently called 'Mummy' because Leila did so. Both girls spent a great deal of time in and out of each other's houses, sometimes staying overnight, which they were permitted to do provided they had permission from Nanny or Copper.

Leaning back as Sally took away her empty plate, Angela's glance went to Harold Varney. No wonder the man, and, indeed, his wife, looked so happy. When she and Pierre had arrived in England, Pierre had brought with him a banker's draft made out after a long delay to Harold from the French *char-à-bancs* company. Although the sum they were now paying him was not astronomical, it was nevertheless large enough, Harold had told her, to provide a small income for life if he invested it wisely.

Understandably, he had lost a great deal of weight since the accident, which was nearly six months ago now. His dark hair was peppered with grey and his cheeks were gaunt; but she had been to see him in hospital with Copper and spoken to Matron, who had informed them his occasional lapses of memory were a thing of the past. As a result, he had begun to jot down things he suddenly remembered, not least the beautiful stained-glass window in Elmsfield church, which he had so much admired every Sunday. Stained glass was a subject which, he had told Angela, had always been of interest to him but which he'd never had time to pursue. When he'd had so little to do to occupy him whilst he was recovering from the septicaemia that had attacked his amputation wound, he had asked Copper if she could find him books on the subject.

So far Copper had found four nineteenth-century scholarly

tomes, by Winston, Warrington, Miller and Westlake, and he had become so engrossed he'd resolved to write his own book in a suitable manner for schoolchildren. With a return of his former enthusiasm, he explained that the children could attempt designs in their art classes and develop their religious knowledge from the stories the stained-glass windows told. Not only was this giving him a new mental occupation, but one of the senior consultants who had a literary agent brother had passed on his brother's comment that such a book might well be produced by an educational publisher. This had led to Harold's consideration that he might write other books of an educational nature befitting young children rather than adults. If he could establish himself as an author, he would once more be able to put money in his depleted bank account.

It was good to see him looking so cheerful, Angela thought. As for dear, long-suffering Copper, she had put back the weight she had lost and was once more her old contented self.

As Crawford assisted Sally to hand round the pudding, Angela's glance went now to Pierre, the wonderful husband she had grown to love with all her heart. She knew she was going to love her home in Bordeaux and her life there with him, but equally, she was happy to be back here at Farlington Hall celebrating the occasion with Frances' children, children her sister had never really wanted but had conceived for Aubrey's benefit. How proud Aubrey would have been of his eldest son, who they had all thought would become a dilettante, but was proving himself a worthy successor. His sympathetic imagination, unusual in so young a man, had enabled him to find the perfect solution for the two innocent little girls.

Victoria was calling to her across the table, her cheeks pink with the excitement of the day. 'Look, Aunt Angela!' she called. 'Look what Leila and me got in our crackers!'

From the end of the table, Frances' voice could be heard above the chatter. 'Leila and I, if you please, Victoria. How many times do I have to tell you?'

So she hasn't given up her maternal authority! Angela thought with a smile. I wonder how she will react when I tell her my news – news she had not yet told her darling husband – namely that the miracle had happened and despite her advanced age, she was going to give him a child. And the dictatorial Lady Mary – how would she react to the news that the black sheep of Frances' family was going to produce a half-French cousin for the Beauford children! Perhaps they would take it in their stride as both had quite remarkably ceded their former authority to the youthful George. Under his persuasion, his grandmother had accepted the compromise he had suggested, that nothing more need be done to ensure Leila's future than to change her surname legally to Beauford.

Taking her lead as always from her mother-in-law, Frances had also acceded to the plan. She was inclined to treat Copper as if she were a paid governess, but Copper took it in her stride, so happy was she to have her beloved Harold returning to life mentally now as well as physically. Her love for Leila, she had told Angela, had in no way lessened because the child had grown so attached to Victoria, who, she explained, needed mothering so much more than the quiet, capable Leila. As for Harry's feelings, she'd said, Leila would always be his much-loved daughter but he felt a special kinship with Victoria because her mind seemed to work exactly as his own.

As Sally put a plate of blackberry and apple tart in front of her, Angela looked up and saw Victoria smiling at her and holding up a tiny silver bell.

'Look, Aunt Angela! Isn't it sweet? I found it near the post office but Mrs Quick says no one has claimed it. It's for a baby, of course – only we haven't got one.' She turned to Frances. 'Couldn't we have a baby, Mother? I'd really, really, really like one. Leila would, too, wouldn't you Leila? We'd look after it, wouldn't we, Leila?'

Leila nodded her agreement. If there was a very slight, momentary hesitation, it was because she had learned when they ran away from the convent that Victoria's good ideas didn't always work out. But she could never override her wishes. Victoria was not only her very best friend, but they were now sisters – well, almost sisters. Her parents had told her that she and Victoria had been exchanged by mistake when they were born; that she was a Beauford and Victoria was her mummy and daddy's daughter.

It was all a bit confusing and when she and Victoria had discussed it, they had agreed that they would never feel differently about their parents – the ones they had always thought were their real ones. As Victoria said, it simply didn't matter.

George and her two younger brothers still loved her and she loved Leila's mother and father. It had been a little difficult for her, Leila, to say she loved Lady Beauford but she, too, loved George and Victoria had reminded her how once, donkey's years ago at her sixth birthday party, Leila had said she was going to marry George one day. Well, that wasn't possible now but it gave her a warm feeling to know that the handsome young man was actually her brother. All the same, it was a bit of a muddle at times.

Victoria repeated impatiently, 'You'd like a baby, too, wouldn't you, Leila?' And beamed happily at Leila when she nodded her agreement.

She would never be truly, truly, *truly* happy again without Papa, Victoria thought, but she couldn't remember him all the time and she knew he wouldn't expect her to. He'd be really pleased at the clever way George worked everything out so even Mr and Mrs Varney could enjoy life again. Somehow she didn't think he would mind that on occasions she called Mrs Varney 'Mummy', and as for Mr Varney, before the accident he and Papa had become friends, so Papa would be pleased for her to have a daddy now that he wasn't there to watch over her.

With a sigh of near contentment, she renewed her plea to her mother to provide a new baby which, she added persuasively, she and Leila would share.

'Most certainly not!' Frances said looking more embarrassed than disapproving. And as Victoria opened her mouth to protest, she added: 'For one thing, who do you suppose would look after it when you're at school?'

'Well, Nanny, of course. She'd know how to give it milk and things.'

'Babies are not like pet rabbits, Vicky!' Robert said importantly. 'My friend Jack at school has got one and he says it's disgusting – a baby, I mean, not a rabbit. It cries at night and once it was sick all over him and—'

'That's quite enough, Robert!' Frances broke in sharply. 'I don't want to hear another word about babies. Now eat your pudding properly or I shall tell Sally to take it away.'

Pierre, however, was not quite ready to change the subject. He turned to Frances and in a teasing voice, he said: 'We can't always know when a baby will arrive though, can we, *chère madame*? Jesus, for example, was a surprise to everyone, was he not? Not to the three kings, of course, and his mother!'

To Angela's surprise, Frances was smiling as Pierre put a hand gently on her arm in a gesture that was almost intimate. Her voice, normally quite strident, was softer as she became aware that Angela's handsome French husband was teasing if not actually flirting with her.

'Now, you know perfectly well there's a time and a place for everything, Monsieur Castel, and the last thing in the world I would want is an addition to our family,' she told him.

'Of course, madame!' Pierre said. 'I do understand. But there are others who would, as Victoria says, really, really, really want a child.' To the children's delight, he had rolled all his r's exaggeratedly. 'I for one am childless and would love a large family like yours.'

As all the children started talking at once, Angela saw that Pierre was no longer looking at Frances; he was staring at her, a look she did not recognize in his eyes.

I will tell him about the baby tonight, when we are alone, she thought, and then, as Pierre suddenly smiled, she realized that somehow, intuitively, he already knew.

At the end of the table, George suddenly rose to his feet.

'A toast,' he said, 'a toast to all those who did not return from the war; to absent friends and to the memory of our dear father who is always in our thoughts; and last, but not least, to our King and Queen, and St George.'

As Frances stood up, her glass raised, she realized with a sudden twinge of emotion, that George's toast was almost identical to the one his father had always made. So maybe, she told herself, she had not been able to love Aubrey as a wife should, but at least she had given him a son and heir to be proud of.

As she looked round the table at her large family, her gaze lingering momentarily on the two little girls, unexpectedly there were tears in her eyes.

Author's Note

There have been occasions in busy hospitals in past years when mothers have been given the wrong babies. Home births were mostly the norm in those days so happily such incidents could not occur. When the two children in *Truth to Tell* were born in the 1920s, there was no such thing as DNA (Deoxyribonucleic Acid) testing to provide proof of identity, as this was not used until the mid-1980s.

    C.L. (2008)